Praise for *Deep White Cover*

"In the real world, undercover work is a nasty, blood-covered place. Barrows gets it right."
—Jay Dobyns, *New York Times* bestselling author and ATF Special Agent (Ret.)

DEEP WHITE COVER

JOEL W. BARROWS

DEEP WHITE COVER

A Novel Based on Real Events

Down & Out Books
3959 Van Dyke Road, Suite 265
Lutz, FL 33558
DownAndOutBooks.com

The characters and events in this book are fictitious. Any similarity to real persons, living or dead, is coincidental and not intended by the author.

Cover design by Zach McCain

ISBN: 1-948235-81-1
ISBN-13: 978-1-948235-81-5

Author's Note

The views expressed in this novel are those of
Joel W. Barrows alone and do not reflect
those of the Iowa Judicial Branch.

For David Barrows,
the greatest storyteller I've ever known

CAST OF CHARACTERS

Eric Brandt, the leader of the vigilante group that kills the illegal immigrants in the opening scene.

Jason Richter, ATF Special Agent, Houston Field Division

John "Jack" Olin, Assistant Special Agent in Charge

C. (Clarence) Murray Winborn, Assistant Special Agent in Charge

Lucas "Big Luke" McCutcheon, Special Agent in Charge

Roy Davis, Richter's group supervisor

Joseph Slater (alias Ralph "Rogue Beast" Baker), undercover agent who has infiltrated *The Reaper's Army*

Carl Meade (alias, Carl Reese), *The Rat*, the member of *The Nation* who flips

Royce Lundgren, the leader of *The Nation*

Bill Lehman, ATF Special Agent involved in the May 11th and May 16th drugs for guns swaps, also a member of Ward's back-up team along with Richter

Troy Pierce and **Willard Simmons,** members of *The Nation* taken down in May 16th drugs for guns swap

Samuel T. Buckley, President of the United States

Amanda Peterson, Secretary of Commerce

Frank Butler, Secretary of Labor

Michael Cooper, Chief of Staff

Donald Page, Secretary of Homeland Security

Brent Dixon, National Security Advisor

William Bradford, Attorney General

David Ward (alias Edward Maddox), the ATF undercover agent

Bobby Roy Thompson, the confidential informant who introduces Ward to *The Nation*

Ben Sullivan and **Kyle Mueller**, members of The Nation who Ward meets at the initial introduction at *Bubba's Big league Bar & Grill*

Pete Willis, Deputy U.S. Marshal, Meade's (Reese's) handler in Des Moines/Ankeny

Randy Kroeger, Meade's (Reese's) foreman at *Global Harvester*

Daniel Goldman, Meade's (Reese's) history professor at Ankeny Community College

Erin Larson, the young coed that Meade (Reese) falls for

Charlie Kirklin, *The Nation's* accountant and treasurer, and **Jim Byrd**, *The Nation's* head of security, the men who screen Ed Maddox at the trailer

Rick Burke, ATF special agent and pilot

Klein, the leader of the assault on the *Angels of the Border*

Warren Graves, *The Nation's* public relations director

Harold Doyle, Lundgren's cousin and second-in-command

Ron Flagg, *The Nation's* private investigator

Elise "Ellie" Drake, White House Press Secretary

Jose Morales-Alvarez, the man who buys Meade/Reese a cola and ends up befriending him

Abraham "Abe" Steele, the Assistant United States Attorney assigned to the Pierce and Simmons case

Kent Payne, Pierce's attorney and mouthpiece for *The Nation*

Willie Hammond, the member of *The Nation* who threatens Meade while he is testifying

Joe Collins, the *friend* Meade contacts to start his heroic quest

Wesley Lindell, the corrupt congressman from Arizona

Jesse Carlson, Secret Service Special Agent , head of the Presidential Protective Detail

Thad Kolb, the assassin

CHAPTER 1

3:27 a.m., Monday, May 4th, along the Texas/Mexico border, southeast of Laredo.

It had been a long, grueling journey to get this far. And now, the harsh terrain of the South Texas desert lay before them. Still, Enrique Reynado-Pinales had to turn to his sister, Isabel, and smile. They had reached the Promised Land. They had reached *El Norte*.

The journey from Punta Arenas in Mexico's southernmost state of Chiapas had drained them, financially as well as physically. But the grinding poverty of that place had left them no choice. Enrique knew that it was wrong to enter the United States illegally, but the wait to obtain a visa, if you even could, was simply impossible. He was desperate. His wife and young children needed help now. The money he could make in the United States and send back to them could give them a better life. Maybe his children would then be able to obtain something beyond the third-grade education that he had received.

Enrique and Isabel had worked and saved for years to earn the five thousand dollars each that it had cost to have the *coyote* smuggle them across the border. It was an enormous fee, but many had told him a guide was essential, that crossing had become much more difficult. There was a cheaper way, of course— cocaine. If one agreed to mule a few kilos, a cartel would arrange passage over the section of the border that it controlled, forgiving

1

the usual transit fee. Many had agreed to this devilish bargain only to end up spending their youth in one of America's prisons. Enrique wouldn't risk that. He wouldn't let his sister risk that. Besides, he hated drugs. He hated what they had done to his country, the corruption, the violence. He thanked God that they had been allowed a choice. Many were not. The bodies of those that had refused could be found in the secret graveyards that lay scattered along the border. Enrique wondered how many had vanished without a trace, their families never to know their fate. At the thought, a chill crept up his spine.

The group of fifteen moved forward into Texas, into the United States. They were now illegal aliens. Despite his exhilaration at having made it this far, Enrique could feel this status descend upon him. He had never been an illegal anything, never broken the law in any significant way. This newfound sense of unease would stay with him, always. Wherever he went in this country, it would be there.

As for where he would go, a cousin who had already crossed over assured Enrique that he and Isabel could find work in the meatpacking plants of Nebraska. It was backbreaking, dangerous work, but the pay amounted to a fortune compared to what he could make in Chiapas, or anywhere else in Mexico. Enrique thought of his children. He could see their faces, hear their sweet laughter. His heart ached. He drew the back of his hand across his eyes, wiping away the tears. This was about them, about their future. He vowed that they would have the opportunities he never had.

As the small group moved ahead, the stars, undimmed by the ambient light of any city, illuminated the ground, helping guide their passage. Enrique stared up at the twinkling jewel box above them. The night sky suddenly seemed more brilliant than it had in years. He smiled at the sight, gesturing to his sister to look up. Isabel glanced skyward. Sensing her brother's emotions at that moment, she reached for his hand.

* * *

"There they are, just as we were told." The man lowered his light-gathering binoculars and turned toward the others. They were all dressed in black, almost invisible against the backdrop of the early morning desert.

"Let's go," the man ordered. He led the group forward. They pulled down their ski masks as they moved ahead. Their actions were quick, silent. This was not their first mission.

When they were within range, the leader, Brandt, held up his hand, stopping their advance. They were all heavily armed, but one of them had special skill. Brandt waved him over, nodding at the high-powered rifle slung over the man's shoulder. "On my order, take out the *coyote*," he whispered. He gave the rest of the men the signal to disperse and surround the group.

Brandt knew that the *coyote* was the only one likely to have a gun, the only one who might put up a fight. The rest of the illegals would be meek, like sheep. He looked at his watch. The rest of his team should be in place. Brandt turned toward his sniper, gave one quick nod and mouthed his order, *now*.

The rifle shot was muffled by a silencer, but the impact was immediate and devastating. The smuggler slumped to the ground. The immigrants froze in place, not sure what had happened. They didn't know whether to scatter or help the man.

Brandt smiled at the scene. "Helluva shot. Another win for the Americans." Brandt drew his handgun as they approached. The rest of his group converged from all sides.

The immigrants were lined up, side by side. He marched back and forth in front of them, studying their faces, chuckling. "Welcome to the United States. Welcome to *El Norte*." Brandt laughed at his own cruel humor.

Enrique Reynado clutched his sister's hand. Fear was like a rattlesnake coiled in his gut. He looked at Isabel. Tears streamed down her face. He could not show fear. He had to be strong for her. Enrique thought of his family, his young ones, wondering if

3

he would ever see them again.

"Do it!" Brandt ordered. He stepped back as the first shot exploded, point-blank, striking its victim at the base of the skull. A handsome young man at the far left of the line fell forward as the executioner moved to the left, behind his next victim.

Enrique struggled to remain stoic. Isabel sobbed. She sank to the ground. Enrique held her up, vainly wiping away his sister's tears. Could they make a run for it? They were badly outnumbered and unarmed. They didn't know the terrain. It was impossible.

A second shot rang out, claiming a fifty-two-year-old grandfather of nine. The immigrants had all watched him struggle through the arduous journey, desperate to provide some hope for his family's youngest generation. Enrique heard the cries of mortal fear from the grown men on either side of him.

The crack of the next shot seemed much closer. Isabel went limp. Enrique could barely keep her upright. There were now only two men remaining before they got to his sister. Enrique switched places with her. He would go first. The chivalrous move did not go unnoticed.

Brandt raised his hand to momentarily stop the executioner. "We'll go out of order," he announced. There was a perverse smirk on his face. "I'll do this one myself."

Brandt approached Enrique. "Very noble. That surprises me." Brandt placed the barrel of the gun against Enrique's forehead. "So be it. You shall have your wish."

Isabel dropped to her knees. "Holy Mother, please help us!"

"Shut up, bitch!" Brandt screamed. He drew his leg back to kick her.

The blow caught Brandt completely by surprise. Enrique Reynado had once been a promising middleweight, known for his power. Brandt's nose exploded in an eruption of blood. He howled in pain as he fell to the ground, grabbing at his face.

Several of Brandt's group moved quickly toward Enrique, guns drawn.

"No!" Brandt growled. "This *spic* is mine!" He climbed to his feet and smashed his gun against Enrique's head. Enrique staggered. One knee gave out, but he did not go down. Shaking off the powerful blow, he rose to his feet, adrenaline coursing through his veins. Enrique stood tall, proud, his stare defiant.

Brandt, still clutching his damaged nose with one hand, raised the gun to Enrique's forehead. A burning hatred of the illegals, especially this one, raged in his dark eyes. As Enrique lunged, Brandt pulled the trigger.

The mournful cry from Isabel was haunting. No wounded animal had ever delivered a more distressing call, no banshee had ever wailed with more unearthly pain.

Brandt didn't want to hear it. He shot her in the head.

One by one, the rest of the immigrants were exterminated. Some fought. Some didn't. They all died. In the end, only one smallish twelve-year-old boy was left, nestled against his father's lifeless body.

Brandt raised his weapon, emotionless as he pulled the trigger.

CHAPTER 2

7:38 p.m., Tuesday, May 5th, The Snake Pit roadhouse, some-where outside Yoakum, Texas.

The Snake Pit was the kind of place where tough men were tested, where desperate plans were hatched by desperate people, and where the word *trust* was seldom used and never meant. The locals avoided the old roadhouse, its dirt parking lot populated by motorcycles and little else.

ATF Special Agent Joe Slater eyed his surroundings. To call the place lacking interior decorating would be one hell of an understatement, unless your idea of décor went to stuffed arma-dillos, beat-up road signs, and, for comic effect, the occasional wanted poster. Tonight, The Reaper's Army made up almost three-quarters of the customers. They were the most vicious and racist lot that Slater had infiltrated in his seven-plus years of undercover work. To them, he was known as Ralph "Rogue Beast" Baker, a carefully prepared false identity that would bear out if anyone attempted to verify it. And these people would attempt to verify it. Slater was sure of that.

Slater sipped on a beer, nursing it. Being one of the few who was relatively sober had saved his ass more than once. He needed to stay on top of his game to do the deal. Meade would be here any moment. Slater would start the ball rolling. He had his orders, and this time they came from the top.

As he waited, Slater thought back on his years working undercover. His wife, Amy, understandably hated it. She could live with the shaved head and goatee, even the tattoos, given that the swastika was a temporary. It was the danger, of course, that bothered her. At least twice Slater had almost bought it. Almost three years ago a biker with two known kills had put a gun to his head. It was right before a deal that would result in the man's arrest. It took a while to get over that one. Amy had asked him to quit. He'd thought about it.

Slater's reminiscing was interrupted by the man who slid onto the neighboring bar stool.

"What's up, Beast?"

Slater turned his head toward the voice. It was Jacob Meade. Slater took a drag from his cigarette, then slowly exhaled. "Jake," he said.

"Buy you a beer?" Meade asked, as he ordered one for himself.

"I'm good." Slater eyed the young member of The Nation. He'd concluded early on that Meade was a punk, all show and no go. Slater wondered if Meade could really produce the goods if they did agree on a deal. It seemed doubtful.

Meade gestured toward the crowd as he raised his beer in a toast. "All white, all right," he offered. It was his favorite saying.

Slater gave Meade as much of a smile as he could conjure up in return. He wasn't in the mood to listen to any of Meade's racist bullshit tonight.

After limited chitchat, only as much as Slater felt necessary, they got down to business.

"You give any more thought to what we talked about?" Slater asked.

"Yeah, man," Meade replied, trying to sound cool. "What can we get for six ounces of meth?"

"Depends on whether it's good shit."

"Ice, bro. Pure crystal meth. The best."

Slater grunted. "The best, huh?" He paused. "Well, if it *is* good shit you can get a lot for six ounces."

"Can we get .45's?" Meade was desperate to do a deal that

would impress his superiors.

"I can arrange that," Slater responded.

After limited haggling, they agreed on an assortment of handguns. Meade's inexperience showed. It was a good deal for Slater. A time and place was set for the exchange.

"They need to be clean," Meade noted, as if he'd done this a hundred times before. "No serial numbers."

Slater gave Meade a withering look. He was tempted to smack the stupid fuck.

"Yeah, I know how it works," Slater replied, trying to not sound utterly dismissive.

Meade realized that he'd fucked up. He tried to make up for it the only way he knew how. "White power, bro," he said, extending his hand.

Slater flashed back to some of the more tasteless things that he'd been forced to do in his line of work. As any good undercover agent knew, sometimes you just had to swallow hard and do your damn job. He needed to end on a good note with this idiot. Slater gripped Meade's hand and looked him square in the eye.

"Damn right, man," he said with practiced enthusiasm. "White power."

Overall, it was a convincing performance.

CHAPTER 3

7:51 p.m., Tuesday, May 5th, Lolo, Montana, just south of Missoula.

David Ward stood on his back deck, staring out over the Bitterroot River. He was lost in thought, playing back the events of a few weeks ago. The ending to his last operation had been a bit bloodier than he would have liked. California's most violent motorcycle gang, The Henchmen, had been the subject of his latest undercover effort. In the end Ward had been forced to kill the group's leader in order to save another man's life. The ensuing firefight had been one of the most dangerous episodes in his long career, and one from which he barely escaped alive. The same could not be said for several of the gang's members, their bodies strewn throughout the clubhouse by the time Ward made his escape.

Ward took a swig of his beer and drew in a lungful of the clean Montana air. It was good to be back in Lolo, his sanctuary. Very few of his neighbors had any idea what he did for a living. A handful had heard only that it was some sort of government job, and that he was damned secretive about it. That's the way it had to be.

Two men who did know Ward's occupation, at least in general terms, were setting up in the basement. Tommy Stafford and Jim McNeal were retired Missoula cops. Ward felt that he could trust them with the knowledge that he worked for ATF. But even with these two close friends, he rarely shared operational details.

"Hey, Dave!" Stafford yelled from the sliding glass door. "We gonna play or not?"

Ward smiled. "I'll be right in."

The not-so-regular jam session of their so-called band was about to begin. Ward and McNeal played guitar, while Stafford played bass. They needed help...a lot of help. A drummer would be good, Ward thought, not to mention someone with a decent voice. One thing they were, however, was enthusiastic. Stafford, in fact, was convinced that they could play in public. His comments urging this were usually met with McNeal's observation that Stafford had clearly breathed in too much passive dope smoke during his days as an undercover drug cop. But good or not, Ward enjoyed the get-togethers with these two kindred spirits as much as anything he could think of. They always played when he returned from an operation. It helped him come down and return to something resembling normal. Neither man ever asked him about the details. It was understood that he would share if he needed to get something off his chest, depressurize. In their own way, both Stafford and McNeal had been there. They understood.

Ward came in from the deck, locking the sliding door behind him. He checked it twice, then slid in a wooden dowel to block the door from moving on its track. On his way through the living room he caught a glimpse of the one remaining photo of his ex-wife, Maria. Ward let out a soft sigh. It had all been too much for her. She'd left him last year, just before Christmas. She had given him the ultimatum more than once...*quit or we're through*. He always ignored it, unable to give up the work, his calling. He told himself that she didn't really mean it. Finally, though, she did. He came back from an operation to find her gone. It still broke his heart. She had been his one true love. Now, Ward wished that he hadn't been so blind to how deeply his work affected her. Still, he couldn't say for certain that he'd have done much differently. There was real evil in world, truly bad people who needed to be dealt with. And he had the skills, and the desire, to do something about them.

Ward was snapped from his depressed reminiscence by the sound of his friends tuning their instruments. Their presence, the anticipation of the evening ahead, made him smile.

"You guys ready to play or what?" Ward asked, as if *he* had been the one left waiting.

"Holy shit!" Stafford exclaimed. "It's about fuckin' time. I swear, if you didn't supply the meeting place, the booze, the food *and* the groupies, you'd be out of the band. No commitment. No commitment, whatsoever."

"We have groupies?" McNeal asked.

Ward grinned. He pulled up a chair and began to tune his guitar. "What's it gonna be tonight, boys?" he asked. "What are you in the mood for?"

"Let's see," Stafford replied, "out of our vast repertoire, what should we play? Maybe, I don't know, one of the same fifteen songs that we play every time?"

"You're an asshole," Ward chuckled.

"Wait a minute!" McNeal insisted. "Tell me about these groupies."

The three men shared a laugh. Soon, they broke into one of the classic rock tunes at which they were barely adept.

CHAPTER 4

9:35 a.m., Wednesday, May 6th, Bureau of Alcohol, Tobacco, Firearms and Explosives, Houston Field Division, Houston, Texas.

Special Agent Jason Richter plowed through the monotonous paperwork. Compliance checks on federally licensed firearms dealers were not exactly why he had joined the ATF. Eight years with the St. Louis Metropolitan Police Department—there had been some action in those days. The arrests, the raids, they all came back to him.

Richter glanced up at the Officer of the Year plaque. He remembered the rescue as if it were yesterday. First on the scene, he saw the vehicle start to slide below the muddy, swirling current of the Mississippi. Two small children were in the back seat. Their tiny, pleading hands pressed up against glass as the deadly river pulled them under, cries for *Mommy* barely audible through the closed windows. It was a vision he would never forget.

Richter reacted. He knew that even if the doors were unlocked the water pressure would soon prevent them from opening. His patrol unit was equipped with a hammer-type device designed to break out the windows of a submerged vehicle. He grabbed it and hurtled toward the sinking car. The struggle to free the children had almost taken his life. His lungs burned as he made one dive, and then another, knowing that the river had already staked its claim. On the last dive he freed them, one under each arm, straining for the surface as he began to inhale water. He had little left as he pulled them onto the bank, one conscious, one not. Richter started mouth-to-mouth resuscitation, reviving the precious little boy.

Thunk. Richter was startled back to reality. Another stack of paperwork had been deposited on his desk, this time delivered by Jenny, one of the office secretaries.

"Sorry, Jason," she said with an apologetic smile.

Richter's head slumped. He sighed. "Not your fault, Jen. I won't kill the messenger." "Well," she said hesitantly, "you haven't heard all the messages."

"What is it?" Richter asked. "You can tell me."

Jenny inhaled. "The SAC wants to see you...now."

Richter's mind raced. What did I do...or not do? It was rare for an agent to be summoned by the special agent in charge, and usually meant bad news.

"Again, sorry," Jenny offered.

Richter looked at her and smiled. "Thanks, Jen," he said. "I'll be all right."

Richter made his way to the SAC's office. He felt increasingly uneasy with each step. By the time he reached the SAC's personal secretary, he was uncharacteristically nervous.

"Hi, Colleen," Richter said, doing his best to sound upbeat.

Colleen Simpson looked up from her desk. Concern swept over her face. "Hon, you don't look happy," she noted with a soft Texas drawl.

"I suppose I don't," Richter conceded. "I guess *he* wants to see me."

"Sweetie, *they* want to see you."

Richter's brow furrowed. This could be even more serious that he thought. He stared at the door.

"Go on in, then," Colleen said. "No use in waitin'."

"I suppose you're right," Richter agreed. He took a deep breath, then stepped forward and raised his hand to knock.

The SAC's door swung open just as Richter's knuckles were about to make contact. Richter was caught off guard, not quite stumbling into the room, but less than graceful.

"Nice entrance, Jason," the man opening the door whispered.

It was Assistant Special Agent in Charge John "Jack" Olin. He was one of the good guys, a rare supervisory agent who hadn't achieved his position solely by seeing how much ass he could kiss. ASAC Olin had made it on competence, a factor not yet completely banned in federal promotional decisions.

"Yeah, thanks, Jack," Richter muttered. Quickly scanning the other men in the room, he noticed that his group supervisor, Roy Davis, was not in attendance. Unfortunately, another not-so-welcome participant was.

"Special Agent." The terse greeting came from the man standing to the left of the SAC's desk.

Richter tried not to cringe. The hope had been that maybe, just maybe, the worthless bastard wouldn't be here. Assistant Special Agent in Charge C. Murray Winborn, the other ASAC for the Houston Field Division, was the antithesis of Olin. Winborn was dangerous. In Richter's estimation, a more pompous, self-serving, backstabbing son of a bitch had never walked the earth. Winborn was quick to claim credit for any of his subordinates' good work. At the same time, he was a master of plausible deniability whenever the shit hit the fan. In short, the man was a scumbag.

"Jason, thanks for coming." A giant of a man rose from behind his desk and extended his hand. Special Agent in Charge Lucas "Big Luke" McCutcheon was a legend in federal law enforcement. At six feet six inches tall, and two hundred eighty pounds, little of it fat, McCutcheon was an imposing figure. It was said that his mere arrival at the scene of an interrogation often yielded a confession from an otherwise intransigent suspect. While McCutcheon could be political, he also knew how to get the job done.

Richter reached out to shake the SAC's hand. Even though

pretty solid in his own right, he braced himself, knowing that the squeeze of McCutcheon's giant paw could be painful. It was. Richter resisted the temptation to shake the blood back into his hand.

"Have a seat." McCutcheon pointed to one of the chairs in front of his desk.

Richter sat. Olin took the chair next to Richter's. Winborn continued to stand, hovering over Richter and adding to the young agent's already considerable uneasiness.

"I understand that you're working a case that might result in a drugs-for-guns trade with members of The Nation," the SAC began.

"We've read the reports," Winborn chirped, trying to show that he was on top of things.

Unable to restrain himself, Richter shot Winborn a look, then turned back to McCutcheon. "It looks that way," he told the SAC. "I've been watching that group for a couple of years now. Several of my informants have mentioned hearing that members of The Nation were trying to acquire untraceable weapons, even machine guns."

"What's that all about?" Olin asked.

"Don't know," Richter answered. "They're white supremacists and pretty hard-core on the illegal immigration thing. Arming for the revolution, I suppose. You know how that goes."

Olin grunted. As everyone in the room was aware, ASAC Olin had worked several cases involving similar organizations. He was the division expert on fringe groups.

"Anyway," Richter continued, "we have an undercover agent who has infiltrated a skinhead biker gang, The Reaper's Army."

"That would be Special Agent Joseph Slater," Winborn interjected. "We tried to get him here for the meeting, Luke. He was...*unavailable.*"

"He's deep undercover," Olin said. "Slater doesn't need to risk exposing himself by coming in for something like this. Use your head, Murray."

"That's enough, ladies," McCutcheon ordered. "Let the man finish his story."

Richter suppressed a chuckle, then picked up where he'd left off. "As I was saying, we're into The Reaper's Army. They frequent a roadhouse called The Snake Pit over in DeWitt County. The Nation has a compound nearby, and some of the group's members hang out at The Pit. I guess they like the clientele. Anyhow, Joe Slater is in there one night and strikes up a conversation with one of these guys. Joe's heard the rumors about The Nation and guns, so he sees how far he can take it. He tells this guy that he did a stint in the mid-nineties for dealin' meth and sometime up in Colorado for possession of a fully automatic machine gun. Well, the bait's been cast. After half a dozen beers, and damn near two hours of listening to this yahoo explain the group's crazy ideology, the conversation swung around to maybe doin' a deal sometime. They had another meeting last night. Slater thinks he can make it happen. It would be dope or cash, our choice, for guns. Obviously, they want them clean, no serial numbers, and, if possible, machine guns. Joe never got around to asking this guy what they intended to do with all the firepower."

"What's this member's name?" McCutcheon asked.

Richter thought for a moment, trying to recall. He could feel everyone in the room staring at him, waiting. Finally, it came to him. "Jacob Meade."

"Jacob Meade," McCutcheon repeated. "You intend to flip this guy?"

Richter nodded. "Slater says this guy was talkin' about a one-on-one deal between the two of them. Thought we'd do a small transaction with Meade, explain the facts of life to him, then try to sign him up, get him working for us. If that works out, we'll set up a bigger deal and target upper management."

"You don't sound very confident," McCutcheon noted.

The SAC was right. Richter didn't feel very confident. Slater had pointedly expressed his doubts about whether the *punk wannabe* Meade had the balls to pull it off. "My understanding is that The Nation has a strict code of silence," he said. "Word is they'll take out a cooperator."

"I've heard that," McCutcheon noted. "In fact, I've done a little research on this group."

Richter wasn't surprised. He should have seen this coming. The SAC always knew more than he initially let on.

"Several civil rights groups have become alarmed by the rhetoric they're hearing from the organization's leadership," McCutcheon continued, "especially their main guy, Royce Lundgren. He's become increasingly strident in his views, especially regarding illegal immigration. It appears that he may be inciting his members to take direct action."

"Meaning what, exactly?" Olin asked, having a pretty good idea of the answer.

"Vigilante border patrols...maybe worse," McCutcheon replied. "So far, no one's been able to confirm that. But the feeling is, if it hasn't happened yet, it will. It's just a matter of time. There has been a rise in violence against Mexican immigrants. The Nation may be behind some of it."

"Now that I think of it, I have seen this Lundgren guy on some local news broadcast," Winborn said, unable to stand the fact that more than a few minutes had gone by without his input. "He's a loon. Reminds me a little of Jim Jones, maybe even David..." Winborn caught himself.

Richter didn't know whether to wince or smile. Winborn had almost said the name, David Koresh. Just mentioning Koresh or the Branch Davidians was extreme taboo. McCutcheon had been at Waco. It was the only blot on an otherwise distinguished career.

McCutcheon delivered a penetrating stare that seemed to cause Winborn to physically shrink. "In any event," McCutcheon said, still staring at Winborn, "The Nation is a worthy target." McCutcheon turned back toward Richter. "Jason, you'll have whatever resources and manpower you need. ASAC Olin will supervise the investigation."

Richter breathed a sigh of relief, thankful that Winborn would be left out of the direct chain of command. As excited as he was by this assignment, it was made that much better by the fact that he would be answering to Olin. Still, he couldn't understand why Roy Davis wasn't here. After all, Davis was his direct supervisor.

"I'll keep Roy in the loop," Olin said to Richter, sensing his concern. Olin gave him a quick wink.

"I'll expect regular status reports," McCutcheon added, directing the comment to Olin.

Olin nodded. "No problem, Luke." After Winborn's magnificent Waco blunder, Olin couldn't resist continuing to display his superior relationship with the boss. "So, civil rights groups have been complaining," he began.

McCutcheon held up his hand to stop it before it started, nipping Olin's little dig in the bud. "Asshole," he said with a grin. "You know better than that. Fact is, the FBI's been sniffin' around this. I don't want those glory hogs stealin' our case."

Olin chuckled, amused more by the envious look on Winborn's face than he was by the exchange with McCutcheon.

The SAC gave Olin a knowing look then returned his focus to Richter. "Jason, I'll be paying close attention to this one. You know that, right?"

"Yes, sir," Richter replied. He got the point.

"Okay then," McCutcheon said. "You're excused."

Richter stood and quickly removed himself from the room. When he was back out in the hall he paused at Colleen's desk, collecting his thoughts.

"You okay, hon?" Colleen asked.

A grin spread across Special Agent Jason Richter's face. "Never better," he said. "Never better."

CHAPTER 5

7:23 p.m., Monday, May 11th, the Lamp Post Motor Lodge, just off of Texas State Highway 111, southeast of Yoakum.

The Lamp Post Motor Lodge had seen better days. To call it rundown would be generous. Slater had picked it for that very reason. There would be few, if any, fellow guests present to cause complications. Acting as Ralph "Rogue Beast" Baker, Slater made it clear to Meade: come alone or the deal's off. Meade promised that he would.

Room number five was fully wired, sound and video. Every aspect of the deal would be captured for posterity. A connecting door led to room six. There, four members of the eight-man ATF tactical team would monitor the transaction, waiting for Slater's takedown signal. Included among them was Jason Richter, the case agent. He would be the face of the ATF in dealing with Meade. The plan called for Slater to be arrested as if he were the target of the investigation, thereby avoiding disclosure of his true identity, at least for the time being. The other four members of the tactical team were situated around the motel grounds. All of them were in communication via walkie-talkies, ready to swarm the room when summoned. Two deputies from the DeWitt County Sheriff's Office were also nearby for any needed support.

Meade was scheduled to arrive at seven-thirty. Slater looked at his watch. It was getting close, and Meade was supposed to call first. Slater wondered if something had spooked him. He clenched his teeth. *If one of those deputies had done something to screw this up...*He was always nervous about involving the locals, but it often couldn't be avoided. After all, it was their turf.

A few minutes later, Slater's cell phone went off. It was Meade.

"Yeah," Slater answered, sounding annoyed.

"Beast, it's Jake. I got hung up."

"I noticed," Slater growled. He turned toward the fiber-optic video feed and gave the tactical team a thumbs-up. "Where are you?"

"I'm about five minutes out." Meade sounded nervous.

"You alone?"

"Yeah, man."

"Hurry up."

Slater terminated the call. He smiled. This was the part he loved, the anticipation before the takedown. It made other men nervous. But for Slater, this was what gave him the juice to keep going. He checked his weapon and walked to the window and pulled the curtain aside. It wasn't long before a battered red Chevy pick-up turned into the dusty gravel lot. Jacob Meade stepped out, a small backpack clutched in his left hand.

Meade looked around, clearly uneasy. Apparently satisfied that no one was watching, he moved quickly toward room five. Slater could see that the punk was tense, but also excited by the chance to prove himself. When Meade reached the door, he stopped, hesitated. "C'mon, kid," Slater muttered. He watched as Meade sucked in a deep breath, then another, and knocked.

Slater opened the door. "Get in here," he said gruffly, intending to take charge from the outset.

Meade hustled into the room.

"You got the stuff?" Slater asked, shutting the door behind Meade.

"Yeah, man. I got it right here." Meade hefted the backpack.

"Let's see it."

Meade laid the backpack on the bed and opened it. He reached inside and pulled out a small package wrapped with gray duct tape.

Slater examined the package, weighing it in his hand. He pulled out a pocketknife and sliced a small opening through the tape. The blade passed through a layer of grease and then cellophane before hitting powder. The multiple layers were designed to prevent detection, primarily by drug-sniffing dogs. It was unusual to see this type of packaging for a mere six ounces. Typically, such measures were reserved for pound or kilo quantities. Slater retrieved a black bag from under the bed. He opened it and removed a test kit and digital scale, noticing the look on Meade's face as he did so.

"Not that I don't trust you," he said with a smirk.

The test showed positive. Slater set the scale on a small table. He placed the package on top of it. The weight came in at well over six ounces. The extra was not generosity on Meade's part, but the added weight of the packaging.

"Very good." Slater nodded in approval.

"I wouldn't screw with you, Beast," Meade said, fear in his voice.

Slater grunted.

"You got the guns?" Meade asked. His voice quavered. Sweat beaded on his temples.

"Yeah...I got the guns," Slater answered. He reached into the black bag and pulled out the weapons, one by one. A .45 caliber semi-automatic was tossed onto the bed, then another. There were eight in all, various makes and models. Four 9-millimeter handguns and a pair of .40 caliber Glocks followed. "All clean, as requested," he added.

Meade let out a sigh of relief.

"We good?" Slater asked.

"We're good," Meade replied.

"White power," Slater said with a smile. That was the signal. The room erupted before Meade could reply. Both doors were kicked in by heavily armed men in black S.W.A.T. gear, masks covering their faces. "On the ground!" they screamed. Meade was stunned, momentarily paralyzed. A blur of weapons, helmets and shields swirled around him.

"On the ground, asshole!" one of the men yelled as he pushed Meade to the floor. Meade's arms were yanked behind his back, the handcuffs clicked on in one fluid motion. Two men hoisted him to his feet and sat him on the edge of the bed. The drugs and handguns that had been there seconds earlier were already gone.

Ralph "Rogue Beast" Baker was also pinned to the floor, facedown, handcuffed, a knee pressed into the small of his back. The man on top of Baker announced that he was a special agent with the Bureau of Alcohol, Tobacco, Firearms and Explosives and that Baker was under arrest.

Slater glanced over at Meade. Meade looked like he was about ready to pass out or throw up, or both.

"Holy shit," Meade said to no one in particular. His head dropped.

One of the ATF agents, dressed in black, said, "Jacob Meade?"

"Yes," Meade replied.

Slater knew that Richter didn't want to arrest Meade, at least not yet. An arrest came with certain rights, a timeline. They couldn't start the clock until they knew whether Meade would play ball, and to what degree. If Meade told them to pound sand, so be it. He would be arrested that very evening. On the other hand, if he chose to cooperate, he would be charged later, or, if he were damn lucky, not at all.

"I'm Special Agent Jason Richter, ATF," Richter told Meade. "You're not under arrest, at least, not at this point."

Slater saw Meade's brow furrow. He was confused. So far so good. It was then that Slater felt two fellow agents roughly grab his arms. Ralph "Rogue Beast" Baker was hoisted to his feet and hustled out the door.

"We'd like to talk to you," Richter said, "if you're willing. But first, I need to read you your rights. You have the right to remain silent," Richter began. "If you give up that right, anything you say can, and will, be used against you in a court of law. You have the right to an attorney, and to have an attorney present during any questioning. If you cannot afford an attorney, one will be appointed for you. Do you understand these rights?"

Meade nodded his head to show that he understood.

"I need you to answer out loud," Richter insisted.

"I understand," Meade said.

"Good."

Richter pulled up a chair and sat facing Meade. A second agent stood nearby as a witness. What was about to happen was commonly referred to as the *Come to Jesus Speech*. Richter would explain the facts of life. Meade would then make a decision, cooperate or take his chances.

"You're in a world of hurt, Jacob," Richter said. He turned to the other agent, Bill Lehman. "What's he lookin' at, Bill?"

"Whew, a good ten years on the drug charges," Lehman answered, "plus five for the guns. Fifteen years, mandatory minimum."

"And that's federal time," Richter added. "There's no parole in the federal system, Jacob. You do the time."

Meade's head dropped. His eyes closed.

Richter studied Meade for a moment. The change in approach was subtle. "Can I call you Jake?"

"Sure," Meade said softly, without looking up.

Richter leaned forward, his body language becoming more relaxed. "Jake, as I see it, you got a choice here. And you need to know, this is not a choice that we give everybody. You can help yourself by helping us...*or*...you go to trial and see what happens. It's up to you. Now, I can't make you any promises, it's ultimately up to the prosecutor and the judge, but the guys that cooperate with us, they usually get a pretty good sentence reduction. Isn't that right, Bill?"

"That's right."

Meade shook his head as if bees were swarming inside his skull. "Cooperate against who?" he finally asked. "Are you talkin' about The Reaper's Army?"

Richter and Lehman laughed.

"We don't need your help with them. We've had Baker under surveillance for a long time," Richter lied, keeping Slater's cover in place. "You just kinda showed up in the wrong place at the wrong time."

Meade shook his head. "So, what do you want me to do?"

"For starters, you can talk to us; tell us what you know about The Nation."

Meade groaned. Sweat dripped down his neck. He struggled to breathe.

"Maybe set up a deal," Richter continued.

Meade looked like he was going to be sick. Richter had seen this reaction before. A lot of them started out like this. He looked at Lehman and nodded toward a trashcan. Lehman grabbed the can and set it in front of Meade, just in case.

"You don't understand," Meade began, "these people will kill me. I'll end up shot in the head, stuffed in a car trunk, or buried somewhere in the desert."

"We can protect you, Jake," Richter assured him. "We do it all the time. We're good at it."

"You mean like the Witness Protection Program, something like that?" Meade asked.

Richter glanced at Lehman as he mulled over how best to respond. The truth was, it was tough to get someone into WITSEC.

"That might be a possibility," Richter said. "But you need to understand, that's not my call. And you would probably have to do some time even if you did get in. WITSEC isn't exactly like it is on television, you know."

Meade nodded his understanding.

"In any event," Richter continued, "we have lots of ways to protect you."

"That's right," Lehman agreed.

"So, you wanna talk to us?" Richter asked. "Maybe help yourself out?"

"I don't know," Meade said.

"Suit yourself," Richter said, as if he couldn't care less. "You think about it for a minute. We're gonna talk to your cohort."

Richter and Lehman left the room, ostensibly to see if Ralph "Rogue Beast" Baker would cooperate. Naturally, Slater's undercover persona would choose to do so. They would give it some time with Meade, let it sink in. He would come around. Most did.

Slater was seated in the back of an ATF vehicle. To all outside observers he was in custody. Richter climbed in the driver's seat. Lehman jumped in on the passenger side.

"How long you gonna give him?" Slater asked.

"Fifteen, twenty minutes," Richter replied. "That should be enough."

They spent the next fifteen minutes talking about sports, women and whatever else came to mind.

Richter looked at his watch. "That should do it," he said. "Let's go."

They re-entered the room, looking grim.

"The Rogue Beast is on board, Jake. Baker wants to cooperate. How 'bout you?" Richter asked.

Meade nodded, never taking his eyes off the floor.

"Good man. You're doin' the right thing," Richter assured him.

Lehman removed Meade's handcuffs.

Richter handed Meade a Miranda rights waiver form. Meade looked it over and signed off.

"We'll save the full debriefing for later," Richter began. "Right now, let's talk about how things are gonna play out with this deal, and about the one that you and Baker are gonna set up. What we have in mind is—"

"If I don't come back with those guns," Meade interrupted, "people are gonna be upset...*real* upset."

"I understand that," Richter said. "You'll need a cover story."

"I at least have to go back with the drugs," Meade said, a note of panic in his voice. "I'll just tell them that the deal didn't go through."

"Calm down, Jake," Richter said in his most soothing tone. "We do this all the time."

Meade took a deep breath, then another. "Okay," he said. "I'm okay."

Richter sat in the chair facing Meade and leaned in. "Here's the story. Baker had to unload the guns in a hurry. He peddled them to another customer. You with me so far?"

Meade nodded.

"As a goodwill gesture, Baker paid you a premium for the dope, fifteen hundred dollars per ounce. That's a pretty fair price for this part of Texas."

Meade acknowledged that it was.

"Baker has some more guns coming in," Richter continued. "He can do another handgun deal, if that's all you want, but he can get you sawed-off shotguns and a fully auto machine gun. Naturally, we want some higher-ups in your organization involved."

"How much higher up?" Meade asked nervously.

"As high as you can get," Richter replied.

CHAPTER 6

4:17 p.m., Saturday, May 16th, on a remote county road somewhere in DeWitt County, Texas.

Slater looked at his watch. They had agreed to meet at four o'clock. He was getting nervous. This was a major operation, one he desperately wanted to go well.

A dozen agents were hidden at various locations around the meeting place, a secluded bit of pasture just off of an old, seldom traveled, red-clay road. There was some tree cover, but not as much as the agents would have liked. The spot was chosen, insisted upon really, by Troy Pierce and Willard Simmons, members of The Nation, the same two members that Slater had been forced to negotiate with during an earlier meeting. They were hard bargainers. The deal was a pound of meth for a dozen assorted pistols, three sawed-off shotguns and a fully automatic machine gun. It was a good arrangement for them, one that Slater would not have been too proud of were he really in the business.

Richter and Lehman monitored the transaction from an ATF vehicle that was hidden nearby. Slater was wired up. It was dangerous practice for an agent to wear a microphone, but Slater had insisted, adamant to do whatever it took to make the case. At trial, there was no better evidence than the words of the accused.

"This little bastard had better come through," Slater said into his body mike. A cooperator getting cold feet was always a concern. Meade might have decided to tip off the targets. If so, they could probably still make a conspiracy case against Pierce and Simmons. But that route was made considerably more difficult when the earlier negotiations couldn't be recorded due to technical difficulties. It wasn't the first time that good evidence had been lost to faulty equipment.

The other possibility, Slater knew, was that the Rogue Beast had been made. Pierce and Simmons had insisted on *this* spot. They knew the terrain. It was possible that they, or someone with them, had spotted something.

At twenty-five after four, Slater started to think about how long he would stick around. "I'll give it ten more minutes," he said into the microphone, knowing that Richter and the boys were getting impatient. Slater walked toward the back of his quad cab pickup. He opened the rear door on the truck's cap, pulled down the tailgate and took a seat. Moments later, he heard the sound of an approaching vehicle. Soon, a familiar white truck appeared over a rise in the road. It was followed by a cloud of red dust.

"It's showtime," Slater announced. He hopped down, slammed the tailgate shut and closed the cap door. The white truck slowed and pulled in behind him. The driver, Pierce, gestured for Slater to approach.

Slater was on high alert. He didn't want to get too close to the vehicle. There was no telling what to expect. So far, however, the hairs on the back of his neck lay flat.

Pierce sensed the hesitation. "Relax, Baker," he said. "I need you to open the gate." Pierce tossed out a set of keys. "It's the small gold one."

Always careful to appear cool, Slater acknowledged the instruction with a nonchalant jerk of his head. He unlocked the gate and swung it open, motioning for Pierce to come ahead.

"You first," Pierce yelled out the window.

Slater didn't like this development. He was reluctant to risk having an avenue of escape cut off. Slater climbed into his pickup and drove through the gate, carefully watching the white truck in his rearview mirror.

Slater drove thirty yards into the pasture and swung his pickup around so that it faced the gate. Pierce followed, parking within twenty feet of Slater's vehicle, but foolishly left the white truck pointed in the opposite direction, away from the gate. Slater allowed himself a smile.

Pierce, Simmons and Meade piled out of the white truck. Meade looked nervous, Slater noted, too nervous. "Don't screw this up, Jake," Slater muttered as he reached for the door handle.

As he stepped out, Slater noticed that Simmons carried a small blue bag.

"That for me?" Slater asked, looking at the bag.

"Depends on what's in the truck," Pierce said.

"Fair enough." Slater could see that Pierce would do all the talking.

Slater opened up the back of his truck and pulled out an olive drab crate. He then reached in and retrieved a large cooler.

"Nice of you to bring drinks," Pierce quipped.

Simmons chuckled. Meade's laugh was forced; at least it seemed that way to Slater, who barely smiled at the joke.

"Nothin' too refreshing in here," Slater said as he opened the cooler and tilted it toward the men, displaying the contents. Inside was an assortment of handguns.

"Nice," Pierce said.

Slater closed the cooler. He retrieved a small key from one of his pockets and opened the padlock that secured the crate.

"Take a look," Slater said as he lifted the lid.

The men stepped forward. Inside were three sawed-off shotguns and the machine gun. They gave each other approving looks.

Slater wanted to have them on record discussing the fully automatic nature of the machine gun. A nice taped discussion would eliminate certain issues at trial. If Pierce and Simmons chose not to cooperate, which was entirely possible, there would almost certainly be a trial. The machine gun alone would yield thirty years stacked on top of the sentence for the dope charge.

"All of the weapons are clean," Slater said. "Machine gun's fully auto, as agreed."

"I'll check it, just to be sure," Pierce said coolly.

Bingo, Slater thought. He handed the weapon to Pierce.

Pierce confirmed the gun's fully automatic action. Satisfied, he placed it back in the crate.

"Very good," Pierce said. He motioned for Simmons to hand over the dope.

Simmons gave the bag to Slater. Inside was one large brick-sized package wrapped in gray duct tape. Slater cut through the tape and tested the product. It was good.

"Gentlemen, we have a deal," Slater said. That was the signal.

The takedown was swift. ATF agents emerged from all sides. Pierce and Simmons had no time to react. Within seconds, they, along with Meade and the man they knew as Baker, were face down on the ground, their hands cuffed tightly behind their backs.

Before the men could be separated, Pierce turned to Meade. Through clenched teeth he spat a warning that only the two of them could hear. "If you set us up...you're *dead*. If you cooperate, we'll find you. He'll see to it."

"It wasn't me, Troy!" Meade lied. "I promise you. I had nothing..."

Meade's denial was interrupted as he was hoisted to his feet and hustled away by two burly agents. The last thing he saw as he was loaded into one of the ATF vehicles was the hateful glare of Troy Pierce.

CHAPTER 7

9:20 a.m., Sunday, May 17th, ATF's San Antonio Field Office, San Antonio, Texas.

Things hadn't gone well at the U.S. Marshals Service holding facility. Pierce and Simmons refused to cooperate. Richter wasn't surprised that both men lawyered-up only minutes into the attempted interviews. Of course, Richter also knew that, given some time, they *might* come around. Many did. In this case, however, he wasn't so sure. The Nation's code of silence was strictly enforced, and it was clear that Pierce and Simmons took that code seriously. The ATF was damn lucky to have Meade on board. As for Meade, it was time for a more thorough debriefing.

Richter and Lehman walked into the small interview room. Meade was already there, sitting at a table, nervously sipping a Dr Pepper.

"Jake, nice job out there yesterday," Richter offered.

Meade nodded. "Yeah...thanks. Hope it doesn't get me killed." He told them about the threat from Pierce.

"We'll talk about all of that," Richter promised. "Right now, we want to ask you some questions about the organization."

"What do you want to know?" Meade asked. "You guys already interviewed me once."

Lehman tapped his pen on the notepad. "That was just a warm-up, partner. This time we need details...lots of details."

Meade cradled his forehead in his hands and rubbed his face. "Okay," he said. "It's not like I have much choice."

"That's the wrong attitude, Jake. You're doing the right thing here," Richter assured him.

"Easy for you to say," Meade replied. "You're not the one who'll end up takin' a bullet."

"Like I said, we'll talk about that." Richter made some notes. "The important thing right now is for you to tell us the truth. If you don't, you're worthless as a witness."

"You mean I might have to testify?" Meade asked, now panic-stricken.

"I've told you that," Richter said, staring Meade in the eye. Meade was sweating again.

"Yeah, but I didn't think—"

"You didn't think what?" Richter asked. "These guys don't want to cooperate. *You* told *us* that they probably wouldn't. What makes you think that they're just gonna plead guilty and go away?"

"Holy shit!" Meade said, once again cradling his head. "I'm a fuckin' dead man."

"Look, Jake, we *can* protect you. We *will* protect you. We're good at it. Right, Bill?"

Lehman nodded. "For now," he said, "we'll put you up in a hotel, someplace nobody can find you. We'll talk to the U.S. Attorney's Office tomorrow about how all of this is gonna shake out, and what else we can do for you. That's the best we can do at the moment. Is that cool?"

"Yeah," Meade sighed, "that's cool, I guess."

"All right then," Richer said, rolling his eyes so that only Lehman would catch it, "let's get down to business."

"Where did the dope come from for yesterday's deal?" Richter asked.

"I don't know."

Richter looked up from his notepad, trying to read his subject. "You don't know?" he asked.

"They didn't tell me."

"Do you have an idea?"

"Not really."

Richter rested his right hand on the table. He tapped his pen for what seemed like several minutes, eyeing Meade the entire time. "Okay," he finally said, as he jotted something in his notepad.

Meade began to get fidgety, constantly readjusting himself in his chair.

"Where did you get the dope for the May 11th deal, the one at The Lamp Post?"

Meade stared at the floor, mouth pressed into a hard-white line.

"Jake?" Richter asked.

"Pierce gave it to me," Meade finally responded.

"And where did Pierce get it?"

"I don't know."

Richter sat back in his chair and folded his arms. A concerned look appeared on his face.

"We're not getting off to a good start here, Jake," Richter said.

"Fuck this," Lehman said, tossing his notepad on the table. "He's just blowin' smoke up our asses. I've got better things to do."

Richter looked at Meade expectantly. It seemed that the man was about to cry.

"I'm telling the truth!" Meade insisted. He appeared defeated, eyes welling up, his complexion as white as bone. "Look...I'm a *nobody* to these people. That's why I was trying to do the deal with Baker...trying to prove myself. Don't you get that? They don't tell me shit."

Richter glanced over at Lehman. They exchanged a subtle knowing look. Both men felt that Meade was probably being straight with them.

"Fair enough, Jake," Richter said, his tone now soothing.

"Let's talk about what you do know."

For the next two-plus hours Meade told the agents what he knew about The Nation and its leader, Royce Lundgren. ATF had encountered many such hate groups over the years. In this case the organization's rabid racism combined with its unusually strident views regarding illegal aliens gave added cause for concern. This was something new and frightening. The agents knew there were a number of radical groups in Arizona and Texas with similar views on illegal immigration issues, but it sounded as if members of The Nation were ready to take matters into their own hands.

"So, you're saying that they're arming themselves to defend the border?" Richter asked.

"That's right," Meade answered, "and for the revolution that will happen if we can't defend the border."

"The revolution?" Lehman asked, sounding incredulous.

"That's what Royce says," Meade answered.

"Is that what you believe?" Richter asked.

"Kinda, yeah," Meade said sheepishly.

Richter shook his head. "And so, what's their plan for defending the border?" he asked. "Are they just gonna start shootin' people?" Richter almost meant the question as a joke.

Meade didn't answer.

The realization hit both agents at the same time.

"Jesus," Richter muttered. "That's it, isn't it?"

"It may have already started happening," Meade said. "I've heard rumors."

"Rumors?" Richter asked.

"I've heard that some illegals were killed. I couldn't tell you who did it, when, where...any of that. I don't even know if it's true. A lot of these people can talk a big game, but they're really just full of shit."

Richter and Lehman nodded their agreement.

"I also heard that they're takin' dope off some of them," Meade continued. "That's where they're gettin' most of the stuff they're usin' to trade for guns."

Richter thought Meade was starting to like sharing his information with the agents, watching their reaction. It made him feel empowered, like he was becoming a part of their team.

"There's one other thing that I should tell you," Meade said.

"What's that?" Lehman asked.

"I overheard somethin', a conversation between two of the members. One of them was a guy named Brandt, Eric Brandt. He's been around since the beginning, as hardcore as they come. The other fella, I didn't know him. I'm assumin' he was a member." Meade paused for effect. "I only caught a little bit of what they were sayin', but he, the other guy, said somethin' about killin' somebody. I heard him mention a sniper. All I know is this wasn't anything I was supposed to be hearin'. I got the impression, you know, from the way they were talkin', that this was somethin' big...*real* big, and somethin' that was gonna happen soon."

Richter's brow furrowed. He shot Lehman a quizzical look, and then turned back to Meade.

"Special Agent Lehman and I need to talk about something. We'll be back in a minute."

Richter and Lehman left the interview room. They moved down the hall until they were out of earshot.

"What do you think of all this?" Richter asked.

"I don't know," Lehman replied. "His stuff is gettin' pretty dramatic and pretty vague. Usually not a good sign."

"Yeah, I agree. Good chance he's starting to exaggerate, trying to get in good with us, get a better deal."

"Maybe he just sees himself as being on our team now," Lehman pointed out. "He doesn't strike me as the hardcore true-believer type. The real hatemongers, you can see it in their eyes."

Richter thought for a moment. "You know, he's been asking about witness protection since the first time we talked to him. Could be he's just trying to make all of this seem more dangerous, hoping to increase his chances of getting in."

"I suppose that's possible. I can't blame the guy for being nervous. That threat from Pierce would get a man's attention."

"If it actually happened," Richter said. He paused. "Well, one way to find out if he's telling the truth."

Lehman had read his mind. "Let's hook him up to the polygraph."

CHAPTER 8

2:40 p.m., Tuesday, May 19th, ATF's Houston Field Division, Houston, Texas.

"So, you're telling me that this Meade character passed his polygraph with flying colors? Have I got that right?" Assistant Special Agent in Charge Jack Olin was more than a little surprised by the outcome.

"That's what I'm telling you," Richter said.

"And they covered this assassination business?" Olin asked.

"Yep."

Olin turned his gaze to Bill Lehman. Lehman shrugged his shoulders as if to say, *surprised the shit out of me, too.*

"Well, we sure as hell need to get somebody into this organization," Olin said, "somebody damn good."

"No question about that," Richter agreed.

"And as soon as possible," Lehman added.

"I'll talk to the SAC this afternoon," Olin promised. "In the meantime, what do you want to do with this Meade guy?"

"I don't know, Jack," Richter replied. "Maybe we should consider WITSEC." Richter was hesitant to make the suggestion, knowing the rigid criteria for acceptance into the program.

"Tough to get in," Olin said. "That's up to the Department of Justice."

"Understood."

"Anyway, are you talking about prison, or do you wanna

give this guy a walk and let the Marshals Service take care of him?" Olin asked.

Richter had been around long enough to know that the call on whether to charge Meade would be left to the U.S. Attorney's Office. Still, he would have some input on the decision.

"The guy really put his ass on the line, Jack. I think the threat from Pierce was legit. They'll come after him, especially if they think he's gonna testify. They've done it before."

"I agree," Lehman added. "These guys are serious."

"I suppose," Olin said. "On the other hand, the guy did do a drugs-for-guns trade. He gets charged, he's still gonna get a helluva reduction for cooperation. The Bureau of Prisons can protect him on the inside."

"That's what they say," Lehman said.

"This is one thing that they're pretty good at, boys," Olin assured them. "I've never heard of a successful infiltration."

"I think he's probably earned a pass, Jack," Richter said. "And we need to keep him safe to testify."

Olin nodded. "All right, gentlemen. I'll talk to the U.S. Attorney's Office tomorrow morning."

CHAPTER 9

7:44 p.m., Tuesday, May 19th, Lolo, Montana.

The phone rang, shattering the evening calm. Not now, Ward thought. He was in a good place, relaxed, a mellow three-beer buzz settling over him as he watched the Bitterroot flow by from his back deck. He ignored the call.

A second ring, a third, someone was determined to spoil his evening. Then a thought occurred, last weekend, the bar in Missoula, that attractive brunette. They had exchanged numbers. You just never knew.

Ward relented. He rose from his chair to grab the phone.

Ward recognized the voice immediately. It was Jack Olin. The two of them went back a long ways. They took a moment to chitchat before Olin got to the point.

"How'd you like to do somethin' for me?" Olin asked.

Ward could sense what was coming. "Whatever you need, buddy."

Olin breathed in, hesitating before he spoke. "Dave, we could really use your help."

CHAPTER 10

2:14 a.m., Wednesday, May 20th, along the Texas/Mexico border, south of Eagle Pass, Texas.

Emilio Aguelar-Pescado knew it had been a mistake to accept the drugs. The *narcos* had promised him: *carry it over the border and your trip will be free of troubles.* They had lied.

Emilio was no drug dealer, but that wouldn't matter to the men in black. They searched the first body until they found what they were looking for, a small brick-shaped package. Emilio knew what was inside, methamphetamine, the same methamphetamine that he was now carrying. Had the *narcos* simply double-crossed him, he wondered? Were they stealing back their own drugs now that he had carried them across?

A shot rang out. Another body slumped to the ground. Emilio's stomach churned. Why hadn't he simply said no? At the time the choice had seemed simple. The chances of being caught seemed so remote. All he wanted to do was go to *El Norte* and work, escape the poverty of his village, send money back to his family. Now, he would never again lay eyes on his beloved Eliana. Instead, she would never know his fate, believing that he had abandoned her for someone in *los Estados Unidos.*

Ten of them had crossed together. Four now lay dead. Two of them had carried drugs, two had not. It was becoming clear they would all die. The men in black were masked. They couldn't be identified. Why wouldn't they simply take the drugs and any money the men carried, and leave the small group to find their way in the desert? Emilio couldn't help but notice that they seemed to enjoy the killing. Tears began to well up in his eyes. At seventeen, he was far too young to die.

He resolved to show courage. Just then, one of the black-clad figures, their leader, approached him.

"A young one," the man said. He turned toward a confederate. "It's good to take them out. The horny bastards will impregnate our women. And you know what I always say, there's nothing worse than a half-*spic*...except a whole one." He chuckled at his own joke as he pulled a .45 caliber handgun from his waistband.

The other men laughed as they voiced their agreement.

As the menacing figure stepped closer, Emilio's knees grew weak. He felt himself start to shake as the gun rose from the man's side. Terrified, the young boy struggled to meet his killer's gaze. The shot erupted just as Emilio Aguelar-Pescado started to mouth a silent prayer.

CHAPTER 11

9:23 a.m., Wednesday, May 20th, the White House, Washington, D.C.

President Samuel T. Buckley stared out the window, his back momentarily turned to the collection of powerful men and women assembled in the Oval Office. This morning's subject was immigration policy. As usual, the debate had already become heated. Even within the party, views on the subject varied widely, from those of the so-called *economic realists* to the hardliners who favored strict enforcement of the nation's immigration laws. Buckley was well known as a member of the latter group. To his way of thinking, it was the right position, one favored by the majority of the American people. And *majority* was one of the President's favorite words.

The President turned back toward the assembled group. Secretary of Commerce Amanda Peterson spoke up.

"Mr. President, I think that we should seriously consider a guest worker program. It's a realistic approach to our labor needs. Of course, it would be limited to jobs that no American wants, and there would need to be a certification to that effect by the employer. Also, this would not be a route to citizenship, or even a green card. We would make that very clear. Simply put, our economy needs these workers."

Buckley shook his head. "The American people don't want it, Amanda. I think that was made clear in the last election."

"Business needs it, Mr. President. I think we can make the public understand that. They certainly understand that having illegal aliens live underground is a tremendous burden to school districts and law enforcement, not to mention the healthcare system. Look at the overuse of emergency rooms for routine care. That comes at a tremendous cost."

"There is also the humanitarian aspect of all of this," Peterson continued. "Most of these undocumented workers are here out of desperation. When they arrive here they are easily exploited. These immigrants have no rights. They have no legal recourse. Human trafficking and modern-day slavery are the result."

There were murmurs of agreement from some in the room.

"I know all of that, Amanda," the President said. "It's all been discussed a thousand times before. It doesn't matter because the electorate simply won't stand for it. They see a guest worker program as something that takes American jobs. Besides, there are security issues with that type of program that make it almost impossible to implement. Realistically, how would we track those workers? Could we produce an identification card that couldn't be counterfeited? I doubt it. It's just another route in for terrorists."

Secretary of Labor Frank Butler edged forward on his chair like a schoolboy anxious to add something useful in class. "Actually, Mr. President, if the cards stored biometric data..." he began.

Buckley cut him off. "We're a long ways from introducing that technology, Frank...at least at the scale necessary for a guest worker program."

Butler slid back in his chair, feeling rebuked.

"The fact is," the President continued, "the public wants to see the border secured before we even talk about anything like this. They want to see better enforcement of our immigration laws. Right or wrong, they tend to equate a guest worker program with amnesty."

"I still think we should talk about *some* form of amnesty," said Chief of Staff Michael Cooper.

The response to the comment from those present was just short of a collective gasp. Cooper was the only person in the room who could dare broach such a proposal. He was the President's right-hand man.

The President knew what was coming. Cooper was constantly banging this drum. "No amnesty, Mike," he said, trying to nip it in the bud. "People view that as rewarding illegal behavior, and they're right. Besides, it simply encourages more illegal immigration. That's one of the lessons from the 1986 amnesty."

Cooper was undeterred. "Right now, there are millions of people living in the shadows. I'd rather have those folks paying taxes and, generally speaking, more accountable for their actions. It also wouldn't hurt us with the Hispanic electorate."

The President waved his hand dismissively. "One hundred percent of the Hispanic vote wouldn't cover the backlash. In terms of voters, we would lose more than we would gain."

"I'm not convinced of that," Cooper continued. "We could limit amnesty to those who have been here for a certain number of years, be it five, ten…whatever. Another requirement could be that they were working some or most of that time."

The President chuckled at his friend's persistence. "No amnesty, Mike," he repeated.

"We would call it something other than amnesty," Cooper said. "I would also remind you, Mr. President, that Mexico's been putting a lot of pressure on us for changes in our immigration policy. They do have a lot of oil. Is it enough to displace Arab oil? Maybe."

"One thing that could resolve this whole situation is a better Mexican economy," Buckley shot back. "God knows they could do a better job of using their oil money to help create more opportunity for their own citizens."

With a nod of his head Cooper conceded that the boss had a point.

"Amnesty is a nonstarter," the President said. "The country doesn't want it. I don't want it. What I do want is what any sane person wants, a secure border." Buckley turned toward his Secretary of Homeland Security, Donald Page. "What are we doing to beef up enforcement, Don?"

Don Page had been a United States Attorney, Deputy Attorney General and a federal judge before being tapped by Buckley to head Homeland Security. He also knew something about terrorist attacks. Page had been a mere ten blocks from the World Trade Center on September 11th, 2001.

"Mr. President, there have been a number of steps taken to enhance border enforcement," Page said. "We are employing more pilotless drones equipped with infrared sensors, more seismic motion sensors, more Border Patrol agents, better computer systems. Border crossings are down. Enforcement has improved immensely."

National Security Advisor Brent Dixon ran his hand over his face in frustration. He sometimes wondered if Page was simply in a state of denial on this issue.

"C'mon, Judge," Dixon blurted, using Page's preferred title. "You sound like a campaign ad. *If* border crossings are down it's because of the economy. We had to scrap the virtual border fence. And you know damn well that we've hired a fraction of the Border Patrol agents that we need to really do the job. Hell, to get the increased numbers that we actually have in place we've had to lower hiring standards. That, combined with the fact that we pay these people peanuts, creates a security risk, not an improvement."

"I dispute that, Brent. These are good people that we've put in those positions," Page shot back, clearly agitated.

The President couldn't suppress a grin. He enjoyed it when these two went at each other.

"I don't doubt that most of them are good people," Dixon responded, "but when you lower the standards and pay them that little it presents a fertile breeding ground for corruption. As for the other improvements that you mentioned, those things are not rolling out at anywhere near the pace we were promised.

And haven't there been problems with some of our contractors?"

"A few," Page admitted. "But I still think…"

"The border's a sieve, *Don*," Dixon interrupted.

Page grew red in the face. His eyes narrowed. "I've been the Secretary of Homeland Security for less than four months. I will see to it that this nation's borders are secured."

"Well, do it quickly," Dixon said. "Terrorists are coming in on a daily basis."

"Look, you son of a—"

"That's enough," the President commanded. He had let it go a little too far. "We all bear some responsibility in this area," he said, eyeing Dixon. "I campaigned on a platform that promised the citizens of this country that we would secure the border. I aim to keep that promise. If we don't, the people might start to take matters into their own hands."

"I'm afraid that's already happening." Attorney General William Bradford had been silent up to this point. Bradford was a venerable Beltway institution, long regarded as the personification of seasoned judgment.

"How's that, Bill?" the President asked.

"There have been increasing reports of vigilante activity along the southern border…some of it violent, I'm sorry to say. Various civil rights groups have reported an upsurge in hate crimes aimed at Mexican immigrants. And as you're aware, a number of states have already adopted their own immigration measures. Arizona, you'll recall, enacted a law allowing for suspension and eventual revocation of an employer's business license if it knowingly hires an undocumented worker. That law was upheld by the Supreme Court. Many more states are considering legislation aimed at an immigration problem that they think the federal government can't, or won't, handle."

Buckley nodded. Momentarily lost in thought, he returned to the window where he stood when the discussion began. Gazing out over the Rose Garden, the President was almost certain that he could hear the faint rumblings of a looming storm.

CHAPTER 12

10:35 a.m., Sunday, May 24th, in the airspace somewhere over Colorado.

Ward rested his head against the airliner window, the majesty of the Rockies spread out below him. He remembered the trip to Aspen, one of the few vacations that he and Maria had been able to enjoy together. What was it now, eight years ago? The memory drifted to their first night at the lodge. His feelings became a strange combination of arousal and depression. God, he missed her.

"Can I get you something to drink, sir?" a flight attendant asked.

The question startled Ward. He hadn't seen the woman approach. Usually, he was more observant. "No, thank you," he replied. "I'm fine."

He wasn't fine. The memory of Maria haunted him today. It wasn't like this every day, just most of them. Ward turned back toward the window.

Ward did what he always did at times like this; he focused his attention on the job at hand. Olin had shared very little over the phone, preferring to wait until the full briefing tomorrow. A few hours on the Internet, including a visit to The Nation's own rudimentary website, gave him some basics. From what he could gather, the group appeared to espouse some combination of the ideologies embraced by the anti-illegal immigration extremists and the white supremacists. Ward knew that the hardcore rhetoric came out at the meetings, and, to an even greater extent, in private correspondence.

This would not be the first hate group that Ward had infiltrated. Over the years, he had played pool with members of the Klan, bought drinks for neo-Nazi skinheads, even visited the headquarters of the Aryan Nations at Hayden Lake, Idaho. He knew the lingo, knew how to fit in. He could maintain his composure in the face of the most virulent and repulsive racism. He did it by keeping his eyes on the prize, the eradication of these groups.

If they only knew, he mused, thinking back on some of miscreants he had shared a beer with. A few did. He had testified at their trials. They wanted him dead. Ward was sure that some of those men, many of them, devoted hours each day to fantasizing about inventive and painful ways to kill him.

CHAPTER 13

9:25 a.m., Monday, May 25th, ATF's Houston Field Division, Houston, Texas.

As soon as Ward entered the office of ASAC Jack Olin, a broad grin appeared on his face. He walked directly to his old friend.

"Damn, it's good to see you, Jack," Ward said. A firm, friendly handshake was followed by a swat to Olin's shoulder. "You old warhorse, how the hell have you been?"

"Better, now that you're here," Olin replied. He turned to introduce the other men in the room. "Dave Ward meet Special Agents Jason Richter and Bill Lehman. They'll be your primary backup team. Jason is the case agent."

"Nice to meet you, guys," Ward said, sizing up the two men as he shook hands.

"Dave and I have a lotta history together," Olin noted. The amused look on his face said that their exploits had been both on and off duty.

"Sounds like we need to milk you for some information," Richter joked.

"Don't bother," Olin said. "With Ward and I, it's mutually assured destruction. I've got just as much on him as he has on me."

"True," Ward said with a laugh, "very true."

"Well, you and I can catch up later. Right now, I need to get you up to speed on what we've got here." Olin motioned toward a chair.

Richter launched into a description of ATF's available intelligence on The Nation, including a summary of what they had learned from Jacob Meade.

"Where's this Meade now?" Ward asked after Richter had finished.

"WITSEC," Richter replied.

"No shit," Ward said. "You guys are serious."

"He passed a polygraph with *no* signs of deception," Richter added.

Ward looked at each of the men around him. "Gentlemen," he said, "I'm full in."

Olin grinned. "Glad to hear that...as I've already cleared it with your supervisors."

"Of course, you have." Ward shook his head. He laughed. "Son of a bitch."

"Bill here is gonna help you put together your new identity," Olin said, gesturing toward Lehman. "He's a native of that part of the state. That should help. You know the drill on getting the new driver's license and any other ID. That's already in the works."

"You were pretty confident I was gonna go for this, weren't you?" Ward asked.

"I thought I could probably talk you into it, yeah. Well, men, let's get started," Olin said as he stood up. All of a sudden, he eyed Ward as if seeing him for the first time.

"What?" Ward asked.

"You know, you might want to hit the barber shop," Olin said. "That biker look probably isn't gonna help you with these people. As perverse as it sounds, a lot of 'em consider themselves to be upstanding citizens. You know, kinda like the Klan does. They view this as a family organization."

"Picnics and preachin' hate to the kids. I know the type," Ward said. "I had already planned to get cleaned up."

Olin raised his hands. "Sorry, Dave. I should have known."

"Don't worry about it. Part of me will miss it, though." Ward stroked his goatee. "I think I look good in a ponytail."

CHAPTER 14

9:35 a.m., Wednesday, May 27th, at an undisclosed safe site operated by the United States Marshals Service.

Jacob Meade waited and waited for even *more* orientation. Special Agent Richter had first described the Witness Security Program for him not long after the polygraph. Then there was the preliminary interview with the United States Marshals Service and an even more detailed explanation. Following that, and a psychological assessment designed to see if he would be a danger to his new community, the Department of Justice gave the go-ahead for his entry into WITSEC. Meade then signed a detailed memorandum of understanding that outlined everything expected of him as a participant. There were a few key rules. A violation of any one of them would get you kicked out of the program, immediately. The big one was no contact, and they meant *no* contact. You could *not* communicate with any of your old associates, or even with members of your own family, unless, of course, the particular family member was also in WITSEC. That wasn't an issue for Meade. He wasn't married. There was no one to bring along. The other chief no-no was returning to your old town. Meade had little desire to do so. He didn't care if he ever saw Yoakum, Texas again as long as he lived.

Meade looked around. He could see out the window, but the view was nothing except nondescript woods. These people took their secrecy seriously. They had assured him that no one who followed the rules had ever been hurt while in WITSEC. He thought back on the threat from Pierce. *If you set us up...you're dead. If you cooperate, we'll find you. He'll see to it.* It was not an empty threat.

A tall, intense-looking man walked into the room. He strode over to Meade, shook his hand, and introduced himself as a Deputy U.S. Marshal. No name was offered.

"Jacob, I assume that by now you understand the basics?" the deputy asked.

"I do."

"Good. One thing that may not have been explained to you is that the no contact rule even includes the case agent. Let's see, that was Special Agent..." the deputy shuffled through some papers.

"Richter," Meade said.

"Right, Richter. Not even him. Understood?"

"Understood," Meade assured him. He was sorry to hear that Richter was off-limits. He had grown to like Richter and considered the ATF agent to be his last real connection with his past life.

"Even Richter won't know where you're at." The deputy studied Meade for a moment. "Contacting *anyone* is one of the best ways to get killed, Jacob," the deputy promised. "Nobody wants that to happen."

"Well, not quite *nobody*," Meade replied. "Otherwise, I wouldn't be here."

"Point taken," the deputy replied with a smirk, looking back down at his notes. "So, you've been given the name Carl Ramsey, Carl William Ramsey." He lifted his head, studying the reaction.

Meade felt disoriented, not sure what to say. He opened his mouth, but no words came.

The deputy grabbed a small packet and held it out. "Here's your documentation."

Meade stared at the packet for a moment before reaching to accept it. The magnitude of what he was about to do hit him hardest at that moment.

"My middle name is...*was* Wallace," Meade said. "Folks used to call me J.W." He lowered his head. He would miss his brothers and sisters. His old man was gone, good riddance, and his mom was in the ground.

The deputy had seen this sort of reaction many times. "Having second thoughts?" he asked. He needed to make sure that *Carl Ramsey* was ready to assume his new identity.

"No. I'm ready."

"You're sure?"

Meade paused briefly, then spoke. "I *am* Carl Ramsey," he said.

The deputy nodded. "All right, Mr. Ramsey. Let's talk about what happens next. As you know, we will supply housing, medical care, employment and some subsistence funding for the basics, at least until you're on your feet. I'm sure you've been told that we can't move any of your personal belongings, household items, anything like that."

"One carry-on bag is what I was told." Meade gestured toward the corner of the room. "It's over there," he said, eyeing the black bag that contained all the worldly possessions he would be allowed to bring with him.

"Very good," the deputy said. He looked down and began thumbing through his papers. "Here it is," he announced. "Your new home will be Des Moines, Iowa. Ever been there?"

"Can't say that I have," Meade replied, heart sinking. Iowa?

"It's a nice town. You'll like it," the deputy assured him.

"If you say so," Meade responded, his lack of enthusiasm apparent. "Doesn't it snow there a lot?"

CHAPTER 15

11:50 a.m., Thursday, May 28th, on the streets of Des Moines, Iowa.

The flight into Des Moines International Airport had been relatively uneventful. Meade studied Des Moines as the Deputy U.S. Marshal drove him through the city. One thing he noticed right off, the place was clean. As they approached the downtown area, Meade was surprised to note that it sported some appreciable skyscrapers. That surprised him.

"How many people live here?" Meade asked, turning toward the deputy.

"Metro area, six hundred thousand plus."

Meade nodded. He returned his gaze out the window, now surveying a picturesque park off to their right. The park surrounded a small lake. He wondered if there were any bass in the lake. Did people up here even fish for bass, he wondered? Being a southern boy, he wasn't too excited about the notion of living in a *Yankee* city.

But Des Moines it was. Meade had no say in the matter. Besides, he thought, it might not be that bad. The Marshals Service had been decent enough to let him do a little research before leaving for Iowa. A couple of hours on the Internet yielded some interesting facts. One thing that really caught his eye was a description of the city, and the state, as lily-white. That was a relief, a huge relief. He might like it here after all.

"So, what's your name," Meade asked the deputy. "You guys don't seem to like to introduce yourselves."

The deputy smirked. "Deputy Willis," he replied, never taking his eyes off the road.

"That's it? Deputy Willis?"

The deputy turned toward Meade. "Yeah, that's it. Deputy Willis."

"Okay. Deputy Willis it is," Meade said.

They moved through downtown and crossed a bridge over the Des Moines River. The city's eastside, and the gold dome of the state capitol, lay before them.

"You eat lunch yet?" Willis asked.

"No. I'm pretty hungry, now that you mention it."

"I know a place. You'll like it," Willis said, a mischievous smile creeping onto one corner of his face.

Within a few minutes, they were in the parking lot of a Mexican restaurant, a half block east of the capitol grounds.

"You gotta be kiddin' me," Meade said.

Deputy United States Marshal Pete Willis jumped out of the car and walked around to the passenger side. He opened the door. "What's the problem, Mr. Ramsey? Your new life starts today."

Moments later, they were seated. Willis flipped open a menu. "I'd recommend the enchiladas," he said, needling Meade.

Meade looked at the menu. "Can I get a cheeseburger here?" he asked, disgusted.

"A cheeseburger?" Willis asked. "Seriously?"

Soon, a waitress arrived with tortilla chips and salsa. Willis greeted her in Spanish. After some light banter, she took his order. The waitress then turned, smiling, toward Meade. He did not return the smile. A puzzled look flashed across her face as Meade requested his cheeseburger. She stole a glance at Willis.

"You don't know what you're missing," Willis said.

"I like American food."

Willis shook his head.

As they waited for their order to arrive, Willis munched on the chips and salsa.

"Want some?" he asked, pushing the basket toward Meade.

"No thanks."

"Suit yourself," Willis said.

Nothing was said for several minutes. "You gotta admit," Meade said, looking around, "these people don't do much other than work in Mexican restaurants, pick fruit and sell drugs."

"And do all the jobs that Americans don't wanna to do," Willis shot back. The deputy's eyes narrowed. He looked away, frowning, then turned to lock eyes with Meade. "Look, I can't change your way of thinking, ignorant as it is. But I'll tell you what—this economy couldn't survive without *these people*, as you call them."

"Whatever," Meade said.

Just then, their food arrived.

"Gracias," Willis said to the waitress as she put the plates on the table. He waited for the woman to leave.

"You ever been to a meatpacking plant?" he asked, nodding toward Meade's cheeseburger.

"Can't say that I have," Meade replied, his tone defiant.

Willis's nostrils flared. "Well, it's a nasty but necessary business. And it's not John Smith and Bob Jones workin' at that plant, it's Manuel Rodriguez and Jose Gonzalez. Smith and Jones don't want that job. They think it's beneath them, or they just don't want to work that hard. Rodriguez, Gonzalez and a million other immigrants are damned grateful for the work. They're grateful even though the company will use them until their bodies are broken. *These people*, as you call them, will cut meat until their hands are useless from carpal tunnel syndrome. They will haul carcasses until their backs give out. You know what happens to them then? They're thrown away, discarded. Hell, the industry is happy to hire the illegals. When one of them can't work anymore, you just get another. And the best part is...you don't have to worry about benefits, or lawsuits.

They don't have any rights."

Meade was unmoved. He smirked. The Nation had taught him well.

Nothing more was said during lunch. Willis barely touched his food, apparently having lost his appetite. When the check arrived, he quickly paid it, leaving the waitress a generous tip.

"Let's go," Willis said brusquely as he rose from his chair. "I can't wait to drop you off."

Willis exited onto the freeway and headed north, away from downtown Des Moines. Soon, they were leaving the city limits.

"Where are we headed?" Meade asked. "I thought I was supposed to be living in Des Moines?"

"Ankeny," Willis replied.

Meade could see that he was now getting the silent treatment. "You mind fillin' me in on some of the details?"

Willis shot Meade an annoyed look. "Ankeny is a few miles up the road. Population's around forty thousand. We got you an apartment up there, and a job."

This was the first Meade had heard of any of this. "What kind of job?" he asked.

"I understand you're a welder," Willis said, skepticism dripping from his words.

"That's right."

"You've got a job with a farm implement manufacturer, Global Harvester. Ever heard of 'em?"

"Sure, everybody's heard of Global," Meade replied. "Didn't know they had a plant here."

"A big one, over four hundred fifty acres. You'll be workin' the line as a welder. We have an arrangement with the management."

"An arrangement, huh?"

"That's right, an arrangement," Willis said. He paused for a moment, then turned toward Meade, looking him square in the eye. "And I'd appreciate it if you don't fuck it up."

"C'mon, man," Meade said. "Take it easy. I'm just happy to be here. I'm not gonna fuck it up." He decided to make it right with Willis. He might need the guy. "Hey, I'm sorry about those Mexican comments."

"Those *Mexican* comments?" Willis asked. He shook his head. "Whatever, man."

"I'm just sayin'…"

"Why don't you stop talkin' for a minute," Willis said.

"Fine," Meade replied. *What was this asshole's problem, anyway?* He stared out the passenger window.

Willis exited off Interstate 35 onto First Street, headed west. Minutes later, he pulled up in front of an apartment complex.

"Here's your key," Willis said. He pointed to one of the buildings. "You're over there, apartment five."

"Just like that?" Meade asked.

"Just like that." Willis looked more than ready to go. Meade supposed he should be glad the deputy at least stopped the car before booting him out the door.

Meade took a deep breath. He felt lost. "Okay," he finally said.

Willis sighed, hunched his shoulders, then relaxed and turned back to Meade. "The apartment's furnished. Everything you need is there. Rent's paid for the next six months."

Meade nodded.

"Look…I'll come up tomorrow and show you around, okay?"

"I'd appreciate that," Meade said.

"The plant's just a few blocks south of here," Willis added. "You start on Monday."

"Fair enough."

Meade got out of the car. He was truly about to begin his life as Carl Ramsey.

As Meade walked away, something occurred to Willis. "Hey, Ramsey!" he yelled out.

"Yeah?"

"I almost forgot. We bought you a car."

Meade brightened up a bit. "What kind?" he asked.

"Nothin' fancy, a used *Impala*. It's in good shape, though. Low miles, real clean."

"Sounds nice," Meade said. With that, Carl Ramsey turned and walked toward his new apartment, and his new life.

CHAPTER 16

8:50 a.m., Friday, May 29th, ATF's Houston Field Division, Houston, Texas.

Ward yawned. He reached for his coffee. It had been a restless night, but that was due as much to a desire to get on with it as anything else. There was the usual apprehension about the whole thing. If that weren't the case, he would be certifiable—only crazy people looked forward to going undercover in a den of snakes.

A small conference room had been set up as their command post. Every operation needed a war room and a name. This one had been dubbed *Operation Tex-Mex*, in large part because they came up with the idea after too many margaritas at one of Houston's better Mexican restaurants.

Ward flipped through case files that dealt with the infiltration of several well-known white supremacist groups. He was always looking for new ideas, new tricks to add to his arsenal. The names were familiar, those of both the hatemongers and the agents who had taken them on. Some of the reports he was reading were still classified. If the information contained in them was ever made public…he shuddered to think. Many good men and women would die, quickly, violently. Their families would never find a trace. Ward knew, as ignorant as these racists were, they were adept at killing, and doing so in a way that left few clues.

Ward took another sip from his coffee. Suddenly, a packet

landed in the middle of the files that were spread out on the conference table. Lost in thought, Ward was momentarily startled.

"There it is," Bill Lehman announced proudly.

"The new me, I presume," Ward said as he opened the package.

"Driver's license, birth certificate, passport...the works."

"Outstanding." Ward flipped through the contents. He held up the passport. "*Edward Michael Maddox...Ed Maddox*," he said approvingly. "I like it. Yeah...that'll work." Ward examined the new, more wholesome version of himself that appeared on the Texas driver's license. "Old Ed's not a bad-lookin' guy."

"You clean up pretty good," Lehman agreed.

"Cuero, Texas?" Ward asked, looking at the address on the driver's license.

"It's about twenty miles southwest of Yoakum. We've already got a place set up for you there."

"Oh, just southwest of Yoakum," Ward said, as if that actually helped.

Lehman laughed. He flipped through some papers. "I understand that you have some background in geology."

"Minored in it, University of Montana."

"Perfect. You work in the oil industry and recently moved here from Alaska. Your job requires quite a bit of travel. We've got your cover in place, you know, in case inquiries are made."

Ward nodded. He was quite familiar with the process. Still, the oil business would not have been his first choice.

"Your military experience has also been incorporated as part of your background," Lehman added.

"Understood."

"We'll start on the particulars this afternoon. I've arranged for you to get a thorough primer from a friend of ours in the industry. Can't be too careful. Folks in Texas know the oil business." Lehman paused, looking apologetic. "Sorry, guess I don't need to tell you that."

"Hey, I'm all for careful," Ward replied. He had learned long ago that the small details could save your life.

CHAPTER 17

3:15 p.m., Monday, June 1st, Global Harvester's Des Moines Works, Ankeny, Iowa.

As Meade waited to speak with one of Global's human resources officers, it occurred to him that this was the best job of his life. The plant produced cotton pickers, tillage equipment and sprayers. It stayed consistently busy throughout the year. The wages were good. He would have health insurance and a retirement plan, both new to him. He would start on second shift. Not his first choice, but it beat nights.

It was a helluva lot better than his old gig. Building cattle pens was sporadic work, the pay low, and there were no benefits to speak of. The conditions were often miserable, brutally hot most of the year, hotter still if you were welding. His new apartment was also much nicer than the dump he had called home in Yoakum. The furnishings were, to put it mildly, a huge improvement over the hand-me-down crap in his old place. Then there was the Impala. Deputy Willis had dropped it off on Friday. Meade had to admit, it beat the shit out of his old pickup.

"Carl Ramsey!" a voice called out.

Meade didn't immediately react.

"Is there a Carl Ramsey here?"

Meade looked up to see a heavyset woman holding a clipboard. He guessed her to be somewhere in her mid-forties. She appeared to be annoyed.

"I'm Carl Ramsey," Meade said as he rose from his chair.

"Let's go, Mr. Ramsey. I haven't got all day."

Meade tried not to roll his eyes. He reminded himself to keep his temper in check. The woman gestured for him to follow her. They proceeded to a cubicle where she pointed to a chair.

"Have a seat," she said. "I'm Connie Watkins."

"Nice to meet—"

"We need to confirm your employment eligibility," Watkins interrupted. She had no time for niceties.

"My employment eligibility?" Meade asked. With his last job he simply showed up and started working.

Watkins looked at him like he was an idiot. "We have to verify that you can legally work in the United States," she said slowly, as if speaking to a dull child.

"What do you mean?" Meade asked, concealing his agitation. "Do I look like I'm from Mexico?" *Nobody* had ever asked him to prove that he was an American.

"Everybody has to do this," Watkins said.

Meade took a breath, trying to stay cool. "I've got a driver's license," he said, reaching for his wallet.

It turned out that he didn't have the necessary documents with him. They were back at the apartment. Watkins, clearly annoyed, spent the next fifteen minutes covering the basics, showing little inclination to give anything more than rudimentary answers to the few questions posed by Carl Ramsey. Finally, at the point when neither of them could stand each other for one minute more, she excused Ramsey to retrieve his documents.

As Meade stood up to leave, Watkins stopped him. "One last thing, Mr. Ramsey."

"*Yes,*" Meade said, now making no effort to hide his feelings.

"Global sponsors a welding program at the local community college. It includes a number of courses that might be of benefit in an effort to improve your skills." Watkins smirked as she slid a brochure across the desk. "I suggest you take advantage of the program."

Meade couldn't help it. Just for effect, he gave her a smile that hinted at bad things to come. "Maybe I'll do that," he said.

Watkins was not remotely intimidated. "Then you better get on it," she snapped. "Classes are about to start."

Meade's new foreman, Randy Kroeger, walked him through the facility. At over two point eight million square feet, and with close to fourteen hundred employees, it was an impressive place. Everything was state of the art.

Kroeger seemed like a decent guy. Every question Meade asked was answered enthusiastically, almost too enthusiastically, as if Kroeger was the company's public relations guy. Still, as they toured the plant, the young foreman seemed to exchange pleasantries, or share a joke, with almost everyone they encountered. And the job responsibilities that were described certainly seemed manageable. Meade was confident that the welding wasn't anything he couldn't handle. He'd always had a knack with the torch.

"Any questions?" Kroeger asked, as he had repeatedly throughout their tour.

"Not really," Meade answered. Then, without giving it much thought, he asked, "What percent of the folks workin' here are white?"

Kroeger's brow furrowed. "I don't know," he answered. "Most of 'em, I suppose. Why would you ask that?"

Meade realized that he had made a major miscalculation. Workin' with *Yankees* was gonna take some gettin' used to.

"I didn't mean anything by it," Meade lied. "I just noticed that a lot of the workers are white."

"Are you saying we're not diverse enough?" Kroeger asked. "Because, if you are, I can assure you that we employ a cross-section of the community, and of the nation. Our hiring practices are a model of—"

"It was just an observation," Meade said. "I promise, I really didn't mean anything by it."

"Okay," Kroeger said, "but I want you to know that we do employ a significant percentage of African-Americans and Hispanics here at the Des Moines Works, especially Hispanics."

Meade gave a nod. That's too bad, he thought. He hoped they were mostly on the other shifts.

Kroeger looked at his watch. "It's almost time for lunch...or dinner. I still call it lunch, even at this hour. Did you bring yours?" he asked.

"I did."

"There's a lunchroom right there," Kroeger noted, gesturing toward a set of double doors just twenty yards away. "I'd join you, but I have to meet some people to discuss a production issue."

"No problem."

"I'll catch up with you afterwards. Wait for me there. I'll come find you."

"Sounds good."

As Kroeger walked off, Meade headed the other direction to retrieve his lunchbox.

Soon, Meade had returned to the lunchroom. He walked in, not knowing what to expect. It was a huge facility, capable of seating several hundred people. Meade bought a drink from one of the many vending machines that lined the wall and looked for a place to sit. As he did, he noticed a scattering of minorities. Not many, but too many for his taste. Some of the white workers made eye contact and nodded in greeting. Meade wasn't looking to make friends, not yet. He found a spot well off from the crowd.

It wasn't long before the seats around Meade began to fill up. He said hello to those who spoke, but otherwise made no attempt to engage anyone.

When he was halfway through his lunch, Meade noticed a group of Hispanic men heading his direction. They took the table next to his. There were five of them.

Great, Meade thought. That's just fuckin' great. These people are everywhere. He remembered the description of Iowa as lily-white. What the fuck happened to that, he wondered. He threw his sandwich into the lunchbox in disgust.

"Can I borrow this chair?"

Meade looked up, startled. One of the young men from the next table stood before him. Meade gestured for him to take it, saying nothing.

"Manuel Sanchez," the man said, extending his hand. "Don't think I've seen you here before."

"Yeah, I'm new," Meade replied coolly. He didn't want to shake hands with a *spic* but was afraid to create an incident this early into witness protection. He shook the man's hand, breaking away far too quickly to be polite.

Sanchez seemed unruffled by the obviously dismissive gesture. He continued to smile. One of the other men, the oldest of the group, took note of the exchange.

"I didn't catch your name," Sanchez said, his tone now less friendly, but not quite threatening.

"Carl Ramsey," Meade said as he wiped his hand on his pants. He knew he should have waited until Sanchez stepped away, but he just couldn't.

Sanchez noticed. His nostrils flared, but he said nothing, biting his tongue...at least for now. His mother had taught him to ignore such ignorance. He took the chair and shoved it toward his table. But before he sat, he turned back to Meade.

"Gracias...*amigo*," Sanchez said pointedly.

Meade snorted. He eyed the table next to him, giving them the once-over.

The older man stared at Meade, defiantly. The years of discrimination had not left him resigned, they had steeled his resolve.

"Yes, we're here legally...*amigo*," the older man said.

"Name's Ramsey," Meade shot back. "And I'm not your *amigo*." He assumed that these men, all of them, were working on forged green cards.

One of the other men rose from his chair. There was fire in

his eyes. The older man placed a hand on the young one's fore-arm, causing him to immediately return to his seat.

Meade scoffed. He closed his lunchbox, stood and walked away, determined to find the nearest restroom so he could wash his hands.

CHAPTER 18

3:15 p.m., Monday, June 1st, Global Harvester's Des Moines Works, Ankeny, Iowa.

As Meade waited to speak with one of Global's human resources officers, it occurred to him that this was the best job of his life. The plant produced cotton pickers, tillage equipment and sprayers. It stayed consistently busy throughout the year. The wages were good. He would have health insurance and a retirement plan, both new to him. He would start on second shift. Not his first choice, but it beat nights.

It was a helluva lot better than his old gig. Building cattle pens was sporadic work, the pay low, and there were no benefits to speak of. The conditions were often miserable, brutally hot most of the year, hotter still if you were welding. His new apartment was also much nicer than the dump he had called home in Yoakum. The furnishings were, to put it mildly, a huge improvement over the hand-me-down crap in his old place. Then there was the Impala. Deputy Willis had dropped it off on Friday. Meade had to admit, it beat the shit out of his old pickup.

"Carl Ramsey!" a voice called out.

Meade didn't immediately react.

"Is there a Carl Ramsey here?"

Meade looked up to see a heavyset woman holding a clipboard. He guessed her to be somewhere in her mid-forties. She appeared to be annoyed.

"I'm Carl Ramsey," Meade said as he rose from his chair.

"Let's go, Mr. Ramsey. I haven't got all day."

Meade tried not to roll his eyes. He reminded himself to keep his temper in check. The woman gestured for him to follow her. They proceeded to a cubicle where she pointed to a chair.

"Have a seat," she said. "I'm Connie Watkins."

"Nice to meet—"

"We need to confirm your employment eligibility," Watkins interrupted. She had no time for niceties.

"My employment eligibility?" Meade asked. With his last job he simply showed up and started working.

Watkins looked at him like he was an idiot. "We have to verify that you can legally work in the United States," she said slowly, as if speaking to a dull child.

"What do you mean?" Meade asked, concealing his agitation. "Do I look like I'm from Mexico?" *Nobody* had ever asked him to prove that he was an American.

"Everybody has to do this," Watkins said.

Meade took a breath, trying to stay cool. "I've got a driver's license," he said, reaching for his wallet.

It turned out that he didn't have the necessary documents with him. They were back at the apartment. Watkins, clearly annoyed, spent the next fifteen minutes covering the basics, showing little inclination to give anything more than rudimentary answers to the few questions posed by Carl Ramsey. Finally, at the point when neither of them could stand each other for one minute more, she excused Ramsey to retrieve his documents.

As Meade stood up to leave, Watkins stopped him. "One last thing, Mr. Ramsey."

"*Yes*," Meade said, now making no effort to hide his feelings.

"Global sponsors a welding program at the local community college. It includes a number of courses that might be of benefit in an effort to improve your skills." Watkins smirked as she slid a brochure across the desk. "I suggest you take advantage of the program."

Meade couldn't help it. Just for effect, he gave her a smile that hinted at bad things to come. "Maybe I'll do that," he said.

Watkins was not remotely intimidated. "Then you better get on it," she snapped. "Classes are about to start."

Meade's new foreman, Randy Kroeger, walked him through the facility. At over two point eight million square feet, and with close to fourteen hundred employees, it was an impressive place. Everything was state of the art.

Kroeger seemed like a decent guy. Every question Meade asked was answered enthusiastically, almost too enthusiastically, as if Kroeger was the company's public relations guy. Still, as they toured the plant, the young foreman seemed to exchange pleasantries, or share a joke, with almost everyone they encountered. And the job responsibilities that were described certainly seemed manageable. Meade was confident that the welding wasn't anything he couldn't handle. He'd always had a knack with the torch.

"Any questions?" Kroeger asked, as he had repeatedly throughout their tour.

"Not really," Meade answered. Then, without giving it much thought, he asked, "What percent of the folks workin' here are white?"

Kroeger's brow furrowed. "I don't know," he answered. "Most of 'em, I suppose. Why would you ask that?"

Meade realized that he had made a major miscalculation. Workin' with *Yankees* was gonna take some gettin' used to.

"I didn't mean anything by it," Meade lied. "I just noticed that a lot of the workers are white."

"Are you saying we're not diverse enough?" Kroeger asked. "Because, if you are, I can assure you that we employ a cross-section of the community, and of the nation. Our hiring practices are a model of—"

"It was just an observation," Meade said. "I promise, I really didn't mean anything by it."

"Okay," Kroeger said, "but I want you to know that we do employ a significant percentage of African-Americans and Hispanics here at the Des Moines Works, especially Hispanics."

Meade gave a nod. That's too bad, he thought. He hoped they were mostly on the other shifts.

Kroeger looked at his watch. "It's almost time for lunch...or dinner. I still call it lunch, even at this hour. Did you bring yours?" he asked.

"I did."

"There's a lunchroom right there," Kroeger noted, gesturing toward a set of double doors just twenty yards away. "I'd join you, but I have to meet some people to discuss a production issue."

"No problem."

"I'll catch up with you afterwards. Wait for me there. I'll come find you."

"Sounds good."

As Kroeger walked off, Meade headed the other direction to retrieve his lunchbox.

Soon, Meade had returned to the lunchroom. He walked in, not knowing what to expect. It was a huge facility, capable of seating several hundred people. Meade bought a drink from one of the many vending machines that lined the wall and looked for a place to sit. As he did, he noticed a scattering of minorities. Not many, but too many for his taste. Some of the white workers made eye contact and nodded in greeting. Meade wasn't looking to make friends, not yet. He found a spot well off from the crowd.

It wasn't long before the seats around Meade began to fill up. He said hello to those who spoke, but otherwise made no attempt to engage anyone.

When he was halfway through his lunch, Meade noticed a group of Hispanic men heading his direction. They took the table next to his. There were five of them.

Great, Meade thought. That's just fuckin' great. These people are everywhere. He remembered the description of Iowa as lily-white. What the fuck happened to that, he wondered. He threw his sandwich into the lunchbox in disgust.

"Can I borrow this chair?"

Meade looked up, startled. One of the young men from the next table stood before him. Meade gestured for him to take it, saying nothing.

"Manuel Sanchez," the man said, extending his hand. "Don't think I've seen you here before."

"Yeah, I'm new," Meade replied coolly. He didn't want to shake hands with a *spic* but was afraid to create an incident this early into witness protection. He shook the man's hand, breaking away far too quickly to be polite.

Sanchez seemed unruffled by the obviously dismissive gesture. He continued to smile. One of the other men, the oldest of the group, took note of the exchange.

"I didn't catch your name," Sanchez said, his tone now less friendly, but not quite threatening.

"Carl Ramsey," Meade said as he wiped his hand on his pants. He knew he should have waited until Sanchez stepped away, but he just couldn't.

Sanchez noticed. His nostrils flared, but he said nothing, biting his tongue...at least for now. His mother had taught him to ignore such ignorance. He took the chair and shoved it toward his table. But before he sat, he turned back to Meade.

"Gracias...*amigo*," Sanchez said pointedly.

Meade snorted. He eyed the table next to him, giving them the once-over.

The older man stared at Meade, defiantly. The years of discrimination had not left him resigned, they had steeled his resolve.

"Yes, we're here legally...*amigo*," the older man said.

"Name's Ramsey," Meade shot back. "And I'm not your *amigo*." He assumed that these men, all of them, were working on forged green cards.

One of the other men rose from his chair. There was fire in his eyes. The older man placed a hand on the young one's forearm, causing him to immediately return to his seat.

Meade scoffed. He closed his lunchbox, stood and walked away, determined to find the nearest restroom so he could wash his hands.

CHAPTER 19

11:00 a.m., Friday, June 5th, Ankeny Community College, Ankeny, Iowa.

When Connie Watson, the human resources officer, had suggested that he take welding courses at the community college, Meade had been less than enthused. He was confident that there was precious little some college instructor could teach him about welding. However, when his new foreman, Randy Kroeger, also suggested that he enroll, Meade decided that he'd better give it a shot. Kroeger had made it clear that the advanced training would improve his pay and promotion potential. To Meade's surprise, the program sponsored by Global was actually pretty good. The first two classes had gone well. Meade decided that he might even pursue a welding diploma.

When he called Deputy Willis to see if it would be possible to sign up, Meade expected to hear something like *it can't be done.* Instead, Willis told him that it shouldn't be a problem. Within two days, *Carl Ramsey* had a Texas high school transcript and was enrolled.

Besides job promotion and better pay, the other reason for taking courses was that Meade needed something to do during the day. There didn't seem to be much going on in town, and he could only watch so much television. He enrolled in *History of the United States since 1877.* Normally, a student was expected to first complete *History of the United States up to 1877,* but it wasn't a strict prerequisite. Besides, Meade thought, Royce Lundgren and The Nation had already taught him pretty much everything he needed to know about the American Revolution and the Civil War.

Meade flipped open his history textbook, then glanced at his watch. The first class was about to begin, but the professor still hadn't arrived. He looked around the room. Most of the students were younger than him, in their late teens. A few were older, one or two even appeared to be of retirement age. But other than the senior citizens, it reminded him of a high school classroom.

As he continued to survey his surroundings, Meade made eye contact with the young man seated to his right. The fellow student's smile said that he wanted to talk.

"Hey, man. How's it goin'?" the classmate asked.

"Fine," Meade replied, now stuck.

"I'm Andy."

"Carl Ramsey," Meade replied.

"Are you just startin' here?" Andy asked.

"Yeah."

"Me, too. Took a year off after high school to work," Andy said, trying to impress the obviously older Ramsey.

A slight smirk appeared on Meade's face. Clearly, Andy was a man of the world, not like the others in the class.

"That so?" Meade asked, making a half-assed attempt to hide his amusement. "What did you do?"

Andy's head dropped slightly, his hopes to impress about to suffer a significant setback. "I, uh, sold cell phones out at the mall," he replied.

Meade nodded, managing not to roll his eyes.

"So, where ya from, Carl?" Andy asked, now eager to change the subject. "You sound like you have an accent."

Meade didn't immediately reply, considering how best to answer. He didn't want to share any more details than necessary, even if they were from his false identity.

The delay caused Andy's face to go ashen, afraid that he

might have asked some sort of offensive question. "I didn't mean anything by—"

Meade smiled, as if to say, *don't worry about it, kid.* "I'm from down south," he said.

Just then, the professor entered the room, saving both of them from further conversation.

"Good morning. I'm Daniel Goldman. I'll be your instructor this summer." Goldman placed his briefcase on the desk, opened it and fished around until he found the student roster. "I know you'll all hate me for this," he said, "but humor me. I want to take roll. As I do, please stand up and tell us where you're from, why you took the course, and anything else you want to share with the class."

You gotta be kiddin' me, Meade thought.

Meade listened as the students rose to share their mini bios with the class. Most of them were painfully self-conscious. Then there were those who had clearly received far too much positive reinforcement from their parents.

"Carl Ramsey?" Professor Goldman called out, moving down the list.

Meade stood up. "Here," he said.

"Tell us about yourself, Carl," Goldman urged.

"Well," Meade began, "I just moved here, started a job at Global. Thought I'd take this class to, uh, broaden my horizons." There, that should make him happy, Meade thought.

"Where did you move from, Carl?" Goldman asked.

"Texas," Meade said, not planning to provide any more specifics.

"Where at in Texas?" Goldman pressed.

"Dallas," Meade lied. The Marshals Service had been good enough to let him keep Texas as his birthplace, but not Houston as his hometown.

"I have a sister in Dallas," Goldman offered cheerily. "I've been there many times."

Great, Meade thought. I suppose he'll want to compare notes

or something.

"We'll have to compare notes," Goldman continued. "What did you do in Dallas?"

Unbelievable, Meade thought. Somebody stop this guy. "Welder," he replied curtly, trying to end the inquisition.

"An excellent profession," Goldman said, eager to display his affinity with the working man. He looked back down at his list. "Jennifer Sanders?"

Thank God, Meade thought as he dropped into his chair.

CHAPTER 20

8:45 p.m., Friday, June 5th, Bubba's Big-League Bar & Grill, Victoria, Texas.

Bobby Roy Thompson's pickup pulled into the parking lot at Bubba's Big-League Bar & Grill at eight forty-five, right on time. Ward was relieved. You could never be sure with one of these guys. Still, it remained to be seen whether Thompson could hold it together during the introduction. Many an undercover operation had ended abruptly because an informant overacted at this stage. If the target was an outlaw motorcycle gang or a violent neo-Nazi organization, an overplayed performance during the intro could get you killed. For Ward, this was always one of the tensest moments in an investigation. Richter and Lehman were nearby as backup, just in case.

Bubba's was located in Victoria, Texas, about thirty-five miles south of Yoakum. According to Thompson, Bubba's had the best collection of high-definition big-screen TVs in three counties. He promised that, tonight, every one of them would be tuned to the Astros game. More importantly, he said that two members of The Nation would be there to watch, as they were most nights during baseball season.

As Thompson approached his SUV, Ward hopped out.

"How you doin', Bobby Roy?" Ward asked.

"I'm fine, thank you," Bobby Roy said quickly. He looked around to see if anyone was watching.

Ward noticed that the drawl was not quite as drawn out as before. For such a tough-lookin' hombre, Bobby Roy seemed awfully nervous.

"You gonna be able to pull this off?" Ward asked.

"Yessir. I'm good to go."

"All right," Ward said. "Let's do it."

They entered the bar. The game was in full swing, coming at them from every angle as a dozen or more TVs stared down at the patrons. Thompson looked around.

"There they are," he said, nodding toward the far corner of the bar.

"Just how well do you know these guys?" Ward asked.

Thompson thought for a second. "Too well," he said. "Let's just say we've done business."

"I got ya."

They moved toward the targets. One of them spotted Thompson and waived him over.

"How y'all doin'?" Thompson asked.

"Good, Bobby Roy," the older of the two answered.

"Bobby Roy," the other said.

"Get you boys a beer?" Thompson asked.

"Hell yes," the younger man replied. "Your money's good here."

Thompson laughed, a little too enthusiastically for Ward's taste, and then ordered a round.

"Say, this here is Ed Maddox," Thompson said. "Ed just transferred in from Alaska."

"Nice to meet you," Ward offered, now fully in character as Ed Maddox.

Both men gave Ward a nod as they eyed him warily.

"Ed, this here is Ben Sullivan," Thompson said, introducing the more senior of the two first.

Ward shook Sullivan's hand. He took stock of the man. Sullivan was hard and lean, with the weathered features of a rancher. A permanent squint was worn in around his fierce blue eyes.

"And Kyle Mueller," Thompson added.

Mueller tilted his beer bottle at Ward, not bothering to get off his bar stool and shake hands.

"Alaska, huh?" Sullivan asked. "What'd you do up there?"

"Oil," Ward answered, not wanting to offer more than he had to.

"What company?" Sullivan asked.

"Odessa Oil," Ward replied, hoping that further questioning about the business would come to a quick halt. He had been well briefed but was still not entirely comfortable with the choice of professions.

"Kyle here is an oil man," Sullivan said.

Shit, Ward thought. It usually took longer than this to get in a jam. Stay calm, he reminded himself.

"What's your line of work with Odessa?" Mueller asked.

"Geologist," Ward answered.

Mueller shrugged, as if to say, *Oh, one of them fancy employees*. He seemed to lose interest in pursuing the matter, turning his attention back to his beer and the game. Ward tried not to show his relief.

Soon, their beers arrived. Thompson slid a twenty to the bartender and told him to keep them coming. He and Sullivan spent the next twenty minutes swapping stories about mutual acquaintances, taking the heat off Ward. When it was time for the next round, Ward offered to buy.

"Appreciate it, Ed," Sullivan said when the beers showed up.

"Thank ya," Mueller added, a bit friendlier now that Ward was buying the drinks.

"So, how they doin' this year?" Ward asked, nodding toward the ballgame.

"Pitchin' staff needs some help," Sullivan offered, "middle relief in particular."

"I've read that," Ward said.

"In my opinion, they could use a few less *spics* on the team," Mueller chimed in, clearly pleased with his observation.

Sullivan nodded his agreement. "Could use less of them in general," he said.

Ed Maddox saw his chance. "I hear that," Ward threw in, as if it were a given.

Sullivan looked up, now seeing this Maddox fella in a new light. "They're fuckin' ruinin' this country."

"You won't get no argument from me," Ward said, expertly masking his disgust. This performance was old hat for him. "I'd ship every fuckin' one of 'em back, whether here legal or not." He reminded himself that this was for the greater good.

Sullivan raised his beer in a toast. "I like the way you think, mister," he said, clinking his bottle against Ward's.

CHAPTER 21

10:55 a.m., Monday, June 8th, Ankeny Community College, Ankeny, Iowa.

Meade settled into his seat and turned his attention to the other students. They slowly wandered in. As the students waited for Goldman to appear, most of them used the school's wireless network to access one social networking site or another. Meade was sure that it had been an unthinkable amount of time since they last checked in, that being the amount of time it had taken for them to walk from their dorm rooms to class.

Meade observed the scene as one would observe an exhibit at the zoo. Still, it caused him to look down at his spiral bound notebook and feel somewhat out of place, wondering if he should have just stuck to the welding courses. His momentary self-doubt was interrupted by the arrival of a student, one that he had not seen before. Meade concluded that she must have registered late; there was *no* way that he would have failed to notice *her*.

The luxurious dark hair framed a face that was friendly, yet sultry. Hazel eyes glimmered with the spark of life. The radiant smile that she flashed when greeting a fellow student appeared as natural to her as breathing might to the ordinary mortal. She was graceful, almost athletic, but still feminine. Hers was not the beauty of the runway model, but everything about her came together in a way that, for Meade, was vastly more captivating.

To look at her was to know, immediately, that this was someone special.

There was an empty desk in the row to Meade's right, just ahead of him. He prayed that she would take that seat. Meade looked around to see if there were any empty chairs behind him. There were two. He glanced to his right. His new *friend*, Andy, had, by now, noticed the same woman, and was clearly willing her to take the spot in front of him. Andy's interest was a non-issue. In Meade's estimation, Andy, nice guy that he was, presented little competition.

She took the chair. As she sat her backpack on the floor, she turned to her left and smiled at Meade. He thought his heart would stop. Some small part of him understood that the smile was probably just a mere pleasantry toward a fellow student. Still, Meade chose to read it as something else. The fact that she continued her turn back toward Andy, saying hi, thereby momentarily paralyzing the hapless idiot, did little to dissuade Meade. She was obviously just being polite to that goofball.

Meade briefly contemplated saying something to her, but Professor Goldman entered the room, saving him from what would have been a plainly overeager effort.

Goldman rummaged through his briefcase and brought out what once again appeared to be the student roster.

"We have two additions to the class," Goldman said, "Sara Montgomery and Erin Larson. Sorry ladies, but everybody had to do this. Please stand and tell us why you signed up for the class, where you're from, and anything else that you would care to share with us. Ms. Montgomery, why don't you go first?"

Sara Montgomery stood and began. Meade heard little of her speech, some blather about her plans to attend law school. He chose instead to focus his attention on *her*, the woman he now knew to be Erin Larson.

"Thank you, Ms. Montgomery," Goldman said. "Ms. Larson?"

Erin Larson rose to her feet. Meade noticed that every male in the class was paying attention with an intensity that they hadn't shown for poor Sara.

"Hi," she said cutely, a slight drawl to her voice. "I'm Erin. I'm originally from Atlanta."

A southern girl, Meade thought. She was simply too good to be true.

"My family moved to Des Moines when I was fourteen," Erin continued. "I graduated from high school in 2007 and spent two years in AmeriCorps."

"Oh, wonderful!" Goldman said. "Which program were you with?"

"It was the Habitat for Humanity Disaster Response," Erin replied. "We helped people who had been displaced by Hurricane Katrina."

Goldman nodded. There were murmurs of approval throughout the classroom.

Meade was normally wary of do-gooders, figuring that they all had an agenda. He also had his opinions about New Orleans, and what happened there. His hometown, Houston, had provided tremendous assistance to the victims of Katrina, as much, in fact, as any other American city. Royce Lundgren said that all Houston got in return was a higher crime rate. He was likely right, Meade thought. Still, it was pretty bad, what happened to those people.

"And why this class?" Goldman asked.

"Well," Erin said, pausing to think, "I guess that to understand who we are as a people, and as a nation, you have to understand how we got here. You do that by studying history."

"Good answer," Goldman said. "Thank you, Ms. Larson."

The students all turned their attention back to the front of the classroom, all of them, that is, except Meade. He couldn't take his eyes off of Erin Larson.

CHAPTER 22

6:50 p.m., Tuesday, June 9th, Bubba's Big-League Bar & Grill, Victoria, Texas.

Ward's SUV sat parked a block from Bubba's, as it had each of the last three nights. There was a clear view of the bar's parking lot. Ward had been careful to note the trucks driven by Sullivan and Mueller after they all left the place together the previous Friday night. He even memorized the license plate numbers so that he could jot them down when he got back to his own vehicle.

Making a chance encounter seem like just that, a *chance* encounter, was one of the most important tricks of the trade. Ward had already seen Sullivan and Mueller return to the bar once since his introduction. But he couldn't rush it. Saturday night would have been too soon, too unlikely. Better to give it a few days. There was a game tonight. This would be just about the right amount of time.

Ward looked at his watch, six fifty-five. C'mon boys, he thought, any time now. Less than a minute later, Sullivan's beat-up old Ford pickup pulled into the lot. Ward watched the lanky Texan amble into the bar. Five minutes after Sullivan's arrival, Mueller's blue Dodge skidded into the lot. Ward kept his binoculars trained on the truck as Mueller slid off the driver's seat and landed heavily on the ground. He was a big man, but soft, the kind of doughboy who, if it proved necessary, could be one-punched into submission. Ward guessed him to be in his late twenties. There was one thing he knew for certain after spending just a single evening with Mueller—the kid was mouthy. Ward didn't like Mueller, and not just because he was a racist punk. He had a generally bad and suspicious attitude, assuming the worst of everyone. Ward knew the type. This was the kind of guy who could cause a problem.

At ten after seven, Ward decided that he had given them enough time to get settled. He jumped out of the SUV and headed for the bar. It was a hot, humid night, the air so thick it almost pushed you to the ground. A half hour in this, Ward thought, and it would sap your will to live. He envisioned Montana, the crispness that would still be in the air there, even in June. The return to Lolo would be sweeter than usual after this operation.

As Ward entered Bubba's, the humidity was replaced by air-conditioned cigarette smoke. Looking around the bar, he quickly spotted Sullivan and Mueller in what was apparently their regular spot. Ward headed toward the two men. There was a stool open next to Sullivan. Ward thanked his luck.

"You fellas mind if I join ya?" Ward asked.

"Hey, Ed. Pull up a chair," Sullivan offered. "How ya been?"

"Good," Ward replied. "Better now than I was Saturday mornin'. Had a bit of a hangover after drinkin' with you boys."

Sullivan laughed. "Don't worry none. We'll get ya in shape. Ain't that right, Kyle?"

"I guess," Mueller replied, not taking his eyes off the TV.

"How's it goin', Kyle?" Ward asked.

"Fine," Mueller answered, totally uninterested.

He didn't mean to, but Ward rolled his eyes, just slightly. Sullivan noticed.

"Don't mind him," Sullivan said. "He don't like *Yankees*...at least not 'til he gits to know 'em."

Ward fantasized about one *Yankee* taking a certain fat fuck outside and smackin' him upside the head.

"Well, maybe he'd like this *Yankee* a little better if I bought the next round," Ward offered.

"I don't know about him," Sullivan replied, "but I would."

Ward laughed. He noticed that Mueller even chuckled a bit.

When the drinks came, Mueller turned to Ward and tipped his bottle. "Ed," he said, "you ain't bad...for a *Yankee*."

Mueller smiled and nodded. Tonight, he would make some real progress with these two.

CHAPTER 23

4:10 p.m., Friday, June 12th, PayGo check cashing center, Killeen, Texas.

The members had learned that PayGo was the paycheck cashing center of choice for illegal aliens working in the area. That made PayGo, which was located at the end of a five-store strip mall, a perfect choice for The Nation's ongoing campaign of harassment.

Eric Morgan remembered his commandment and would gladly obey. Royce Lundgren had instructed his followers to make life difficult for *them*. The *Cinco de Mayo* speech put the exclamation point on that message. Morgan could still remember Lundgren's words, spoken so forcefully at the May Fifth rally. *America will be white again! She will be free again...free of the brown horde that plagues us! We must, and we will, do everything possible to remind them of their status! We must, and we will, do anything necessary to force their departure!*

During the planning stage, days earlier, Royce Lundgren had explained that maximum effectiveness would require organization and numbers. They were told to assemble quickly, leaving the authorities little time to intervene. They were also told to come in force, more people equaling greater confusion for law enforcement. They had done both. The members had arrived promptly at four o'clock and now numbered almost a hundred strong. He would be pleased.

Morgan smiled at Susan, his wife of twelve years. He put his arm around her as they looked at their young children, Matthew, age nine, and his little brother, Luke, a very boisterous seven. It was a family affair for them, as it was for most of the members of The Nation. The boys, like their parents, held placards demanding that the *Wetbacks Go Home* or that the illegals *Leave America to the Americans.* Royce Lundgren had taught them that it was never too early to teach their children about the natural supremacy of the white race. And he had explained that, as soon as possible, parents must begin to instruct their young on the need for national and racial purity.

Morgan and his wife had enthusiastically followed their leader's guidance. There was a lesson almost every day, and the boys had learned well. A teacher had complained that Matthew often told the Hispanic children to, *Go back to Mexico!* Even little Luke had called a classmate a *spic.* But the complaints from teachers and school administrators were growing tiresome. Morgan felt strongly that the boys should no longer be exposed to the liberal views of Killeen's public-school system. It was time to revisit the subject of home schooling, something Royce Lundgren encouraged.

When the first small group emerged from PayGo, they were met with a barrage of racial slurs and demands that they *go home.* The terror in their eyes was unmistakable. Several retreated back into the business. One young man began to protest that he was here legally but was silenced by an older member of the group. It didn't matter. By now, the crowd had worked itself into a frenzy. They surged forward, forcing the men to run back into the building. Inside, one of the company's employees called the police.

A pickup carrying two young Hispanic men and a small boy approached PayGo from the east. Their view of the unruly crowd was obscured as they entered at the opposite end of the parking lot. By the time they understood what was happening, it was too late. The members quickly surrounded the truck. They began to rock it back and forth until it was on verge of tipping, causing the small boy to cry for his mother.

"Pull 'em out of the truck!" yelled one member.

The doors were yanked open as the terrified men tried to fight off the crowd and protect the boy. A large rock smashed through the windshield. Punches were thrown. The men kicked at their assailants, trying to force them away from the truck. A fierce blow landed on the driver's jaw, momentarily stunning him, giving the attackers their opportunity. They grabbed his legs and yanked him violently from the pickup. His head cracked onto the pavement. Blood oozed from the wound. A crimson pool began to form. It made little difference to the members. They kicked and stomped the man, ignoring the frantic cries of *papa, papa* that came from the little boy inside the truck.

The passenger fared no better. He lay on the pavement, shielding himself from the blows that now came from both adults and children. Eric and Matthew Morgan were among them. Matthew imitated his father, kicking the man in the gut, screaming, "Go back to Mexico, *spic*!"

Luke Morgan tugged at his mother's dress. "Mommy why are they hurting that man?" he asked, his little hand pointing toward Miguel. "Why doesn't Daddy like him?"

Some maternal instinct deep inside Susan Morgan briefly overwhelmed the brainwashing of Royce Lundgren. Her hands went up, shielding Luke from the carnage before them.

In the distance, a siren wailed. Some realization of what had happened began to settle on the mob. Blood lust was replaced by panic. The flight instinct took over. Everyone was gone by the time the police arrived, everyone but the victims.

CHAPTER 24

6:58 p.m., Friday, June 12th, Bubba's Big-League Bar & Grill, Victoria, Texas.

Ward looked at his watch. The game was about to start. This time his meeting with Sullivan and Mueller was no chance encounter. From an investigatory standpoint, the Tuesday night outing with the boys had gone well. Probably, Ward thought, because Ed Maddox had purchased most of the drinks. In any event, it had been well worth it. They had all agreed to meet again tonight. Mueller was still a bit of a problem, but Ward and Sullivan had hit it off. According to Bobby Roy Thompson, Sullivan had sufficient rank in The Nation that he could vouch for a man and he was as good as in. To Ward, it was obvious that Mueller was nothing more than the typical weak-minded follower that this sort of organization sucked in as one of its foot soldiers. Despite their common ideology, it was difficult for Ward to understand why Sullivan associated with Mueller. He wondered if they were kin of some sort.

Bubba's was growing crowded. Ward hoped that the two men would arrive soon. So far, he had been able to fend off the patrons who had attempted to grab the bar stools he was saving for them. The last attempt, however, by a large, already drunk cowboy had nearly caused a fight. Getting hauled in on an assault charge would not be a good way to start the evening. When deep undercover, an encounter with the locals could be difficult and dangerous. Invoking professional courtesy as a fellow law enforcement officer didn't always work and it carried risks. You never knew who you could trust. It wasn't impossible that a local would have sympathies toward The Nation. If there was one thing Ward had learned over the years, it was that people liked to talk. Everybody thinks they can tell that one trusted friend. It adds up. Even cops wag their tongues. It only takes one comment to the wrong person and the entire operation is exposed. Worse yet, it could get you killed.

Moments later, the first pitch was thrown, but still no Sullivan and Mueller. Ward was getting nervous. Had he done something to spook them? He couldn't think of a thing. What about Bobby Roy? Even Richter wasn't sure about the guy. The militia types always made Ward nervous. Most of them were true believers, dedicated to their warped ideologies.

At ten after, they walked in. Both men appeared to be in good spirits. Ward wondered if they'd made a stop or two before hitting *Bubba's*. He raised his hand, catching Sullivan's eye.

"Been savin' you boys a seat," Ward said as the two men approached. "Bartender, get these fellas a beer, would ya?"

Several more beers were downed over the course of the next hour as the ballgame dragged on into the fifth inning. It was a dull game, with little offense...a pitcher's duel. Ward engaged the men in idle chitchat. He knew better than to push it. It had to just happen.

Four young Hispanic men wandered into the bar. Ward noticed them immediately. He also noticed that there were no other Latinos in the place. As the men searched for a place to sit, Ward began to get an uneasy feeling. Something told him this could get ugly.

Finding a table not far from the spot held by Ward and his companions, the four settled in to watch the rest of the game and enjoy their evening.

"When did this place start servin' *wetbacks*?" Mueller asked loudly.

Ward cringed inside, careful to hide his true reaction.

The four young men nervously glanced in Mueller's direction, then looked around the bar. One of them made a gesture as if they should leave. Another said no.

Ward studied the young men. He could see the pain, the disappointment...the anger. He felt terrible for them. But there was a job to be done, a part to be played.

"Fuckin *spics*," Ward said. "I say we ship every last one of 'em back to Mexico."

"Damn straight, Ed," Sullivan agreed, rising from his stool. He took a few steps toward the table. "Why don't y'all go find a *wetback* bar to drink yer *cervezas*?"

There were murmurs of approval from some in the bar. Others just hung their heads, ashamed, but did nothing.

Ward knew that the next few seconds could be a turning point in the investigation, good or bad. He did *not* want to get involved in a fight with these young men. But if he avoided participating in any violence, as operational protocol required, he would jeopardize the operation. Sullivan and Mueller would be unlikely to trust him. If he participated in a show of force, however, that might be enough. Ward made his decision.

"You heard him," Ward said, taking the position to Sullivan's left. He gestured toward the door with a jerk of his head, praying that the men would comply.

Several others in the bar stood and joined Sullivan and Ward. The young Hispanics were now badly outnumbered. The bouncer, an enormous tattooed behemoth, approached from his post at the door. He folded massive arms across his chest and glared menacingly at the young men.

Just then, Mueller appeared on Sullivan's right. "Hit the road."

Ward wasn't surprised that Mueller was the last to step up, even though he had started the whole damn thing.

The young men spoke to each other in Spanish. Ward knew enough to catch the gist of it. One seemed determined to stand and fight, his fists clenched, his body rigid. The others beseeched him to be realistic about the odds, leave it for another day. Ultimately, thankfully, the one who would fight relented. They stood to leave.

Before he turned for the door, the would-be fighter locked eyes with Ward. The look was one of pride, a wounded, anguished pride, but pride nonetheless. That look would stay with Ward for all his days.

After the young men left and things settled down, Sullivan turned to Ed Maddox and placed a hand on his new friend's shoulder. "Ed," Sullivan began, "there's some folks I'd like you to meet."

It was the breakthrough Ward had been waiting for. He wondered if it came at some cost to his soul.

CHAPTER 25

1:50 p.m., Monday, June 15th, Ankeny Community College, Ankeny, Iowa.

Meade made it to his car just as the first spatters of rain started to fall. He watched the storm sweep in across the Iowa plains. A deep purple bank of thunderclouds lined the horizon, strikes of lightning crackling out of their darkness. He sat transfixed, fascinated by the storm. It had been this way since he was a boy, always hypnotized by Mother Nature's fury.

The wind hit suddenly, lightly rocking Meade's Impala. A wall of rain followed. This would be a strong storm. It reminded him of those that swept in off the Gulf of Mexico, inundating the Texas coast. For a moment he was homesick. It was a hard thing to walk away from your life, even if that life hadn't been all that great.

Meade started the car. It was then that he saw her. Erin Larson struggled against the sheets of rain that whipped into her as she trekked across the parking lot. She clutched her books, trying to protect them from the deluge. The light jacket she was wearing did little to fend off the weather.

Meade quickly glanced at his watch. There was plenty of time before he had to be at work. He grabbed his umbrella and jumped out of the car, heading for Erin on a dead sprint. He caught up with her just as a fierce gust almost knocked her off her feet.

"Please, let me help!" Meade yelled over the storm. He held the umbrella over Erin, leaving himself exposed to the weather.

"Thank you!" she said, her eyes displaying a sincere gratitude.

They battled toward the library entrance. Once there, Meade yanked open the door as Erin dove through. Meade plunged in after her, the wind slamming the door behind him as it sealed them inside.

"Wow, that came up fast," Erin said. She shook the rain from her hair.

As he watched her, Meade was momentarily spellbound, realizing almost too late that he should actually respond.

"Seems like it came out of nowhere," he finally said. "The heavens just opened up." It occurred to him that the latter comment could just as well refer to her.

Erin smiled sweetly. "Thank you so much," she said. "That was very kind. And look, now you're soaked because you held the umbrella for me."

"I couldn't very well leave you to struggle through that when I was sitting right there with the means to help," Meade said.

Erin noticed the slight drawl for the first time. "You're a southern boy, I take it?"

"Yes, ma'am. Texas born and bred," Meade said, a grin creeping onto his face.

"You look familiar," she said. "Professor Goldman's history class...right?"

"That's right." Meade was ecstatic that she had noticed him enough to remember.

"I'm Erin Larson," she said, extending her hand.

Meade felt a jolt as her hand touched his. The long fingers were soft but strong, her grip gentle yet firm. He felt his pulse quicken.

"And you are..."

"Carl," Meade replied. He paused. "Carl Ramsey." It pained him to lie to her, necessary as it was.

"Nice to meet you...Carl Ramsey."

Meade thought he could see a sparkle in her eyes as she said the words. Was he deluding himself? This woman was really too much to hope for, especially for someone like him.

"Nice to meet you...Erin Larson." Meade was sure that his statement was accompanied by a ridiculously sheepish grin.

An awkward silence followed as Meade struggled for something clever.

"Well, I should get going," Erin said. "I guess I'll see you in class."

Rally, you idiot, Meade said to himself. Think of something.

"I don't suppose I could buy you a cup of coffee?" Meade asked, relieved that he had been able to think of anything. "Might help warm you up. You know...after the rain and all." Oh my God, he thought to himself. That was impressive. He was now certain that she would reject him.

"I'm sorry," she said apologetically. "I'm going to be late for class." She looked at her watch. "Scratch that. I'm already late for class."

"Maybe some other time," Meade said hopefully.

Erin smiled. She looked out at the storm. "I guess I'll have to take a rain check," she said, gesturing outside. Erin turned and started to walk away. "See you later, Carl Ramsey," she called back over her shoulder.

"See you later," Meade replied. He was now utterly, hopelessly, smitten.

CHAPTER 26

6:30 p.m., Monday, June 15th, somewhere north of Victoria, Texas.

These were the rides that worried Ward the most, out in the middle of nowhere, headed to an unknown destination with an unknown entity at the helm. He'd been in this position before. There was no getting used to it. Ward eyed Sullivan carefully, looking for a sign of deception, a sign that something bad was coming. There was no hint that this was anything other than what had been promised, a meeting with some friends. Ward took that to mean members of The Nation. It couldn't mean anything else.

Sullivan's old Ford pickup raced up U.S. Highway 77. At this point, Ward had no idea where they were, other than north of Victoria. Richter and Lehman were in the backup vehicle, probably a good half-mile behind. That was great, but Ward knew that these situations could turn deadly in an instant, particularly when you weren't wearing a wire.

Ward had offered to drive, offered more than once. Sullivan wouldn't hear of it. That could be a bad sign. Ward scanned the interior of the truck for places that could hide a weapon. There were several. He tried to steal a glance under the driver's seat when Sullivan was distracted by something off to the left but couldn't get a good look. There was a rifle in the gun rack, a .30-06. Ward wasn't worried about that, figuring there was no way

Sullivan could get the drop on him with a weapon that large. No, it was the hidden handgun that always worried him the most.

Sullivan seemed completely at ease, even happy. He offered Ward a smoke. Ward declined. Sullivan then lit one for himself and took a long draw. Something about it caused Ward to relax. Most professional hit men wouldn't be this cool, he told himself. The ol' boy's insistence on taking his truck probably just meant that he thought it impolite to do otherwise. That's probably all it was. Ward decided that he was being paranoid. Then again, a little paranoia had saved the life of many an undercover agent.

They hit a long flat patch of highway. Ward checked the side mirror. If Richter and Lehman were back there, they were too far back to be seen. His eyes returned to the road in time to see the truck zoom past the turnoff for Texas Highway 111, the road to Yoakum. Ward was surprised, having expected to head in that direction.

"Just where are we goin'?" Ward asked, expertly disguising his concern.

Sullivan laughed. "We're headed up to Sweet Home, Texas. Like I was sayin' before, I got me a couple a good boys up there that's real anxious to meet ya. Told 'em some 'bout what happened in the bar the other night. Said you sounded like a good man."

"Sweet Home it is, then," Ward agreed.

Sullivan turned left onto 531, an old ranch road. Within minutes, he spotted their destination.

"There it is," Sullivan said. He pointed to a mobile home that sat back a good hundred yards off the road.

It was exactly the sort of scenario that Ward had feared. If anyone in or around that place was watching, there was no way that his backup team could get close without being spotted.

"This is Sweet Home?" Ward asked.

"Well...sorta," Sullivan said. "It's just up around the bend there. Sweet Home's the mailin' address."

Ward nodded.

Sullivan pulled off the road and up to a rusty old ranch gate that guarded the path to the trailer. He started to climb out of the truck.

"I can get it," Ward said, trying to be helpful. He grabbed the door handle.

Sullivan put a hand on Ward's arm before he could exit the truck.

"You best let me, son," he said ominously.

Ward removed his hand from the door. He watched as Sullivan slid out of the truck and raised his arm, gesturing toward the trailer in a way that appeared to be some sort of signal. Sullivan waited a moment, pulled a set of keys from his pocket, then unlocked the creaky old gate. He climbed back into the pickup and drove ahead.

After they had passed through the entrance, Sullivan put the truck in park. He jumped out and locked the gate behind them. Ward didn't like that. If things went to shit, there would be no way that Richter and Lehman could get there in time, that is, if they even realized that there was a problem. Sometimes that's how it worked; you were just out there alone.

Sullivan got back in and drove up the dirt path leading to the mobile home. As they drew close, Ward could see the front end of a car that was parked behind the trailer. There were no other vehicles. He was surprised that, despite the inherent dangerousness of the situation, the hair on the back of his neck had yet to rise. That was good, real good. He had learned to trust such indicators.

Sullivan also parked around back. He turned to Ward and gave him a smile. To Ward's immense relief, it was not a smile that said, *this is the end of the road*, but one that said something more along the lines of, *welcome to the faith*.

"You ready, pardner?" Sullivan asked.

"I guess," Ward replied.

"Nothin' to be nervous about," Sullivan said, sensing some apprehension. "Like I told ya, these here are just a couple a good ol' boys that wanna meet ya. After I told 'em about ya, well...let's just say that we all think you might fit in pretty good with our little, uh...group."

"From what you've told me, I suspect I will," Ward said.

"Atta boy," Sullivan said. He opened the door and stepped out.

Ward followed. He assessed the lay of the land. Nothing in particular caught his eye. So far, there was little that might cause his antennae to rise.

Sullivan knocked on the door. A short, balding man in what Ward guessed was his mid-forties answered.

"Ben, good to see ya," the man said as he shook Sullivan's hand.

"Charlie, how ya been?" Sullivan asked. "How's the family?"

"They're all fine, just fine, thanks." The man turned to Ward. "This here must be the fella you been tellin' us about."

"It is," Sullivan said with a hint of pride. "This here is Ed Maddox."

"Ed, it's good to meet ya," Charlie said, extending his hand. "Ben here says you're our kinda guy."

"I suspect he's right," Ward said.

Charlie laughed. "You boys come on in."

As they entered, Ward quickly scanned the sparsely decorated interior. It lacked the typical furnishings that would indicate someone might live there, instead giving the impression that it was used primarily as a meeting place. There was a conference table in what would have been the living room. It was surrounded by a dozen chairs, only one of which was occupied. Seated there was a hard-looking man, a man whose face held no hint of a smile. He slowly rose to greet them.

"Ben," the man said.

"Jim," Sullivan replied. There was one firm handshake, no more. No pleasantries were exchanged.

"Mr. Maddox," the man said with a nod. He did not offer his hand.

There was a brief, tense silence. Ward took note of the fact that neither man offered his last name. He wasn't surprised, given the circumstances, and he wasn't inclined to ask.

"Let's have a seat, get to know each other," Charlie said nervously.

Ward sensed that Sullivan and Jim had some history. He could see it mostly in Sullivan's eyes. He could also see that Jim was the one that he would need to get by. Ward could feel the man sizing him up.

"So, where do you work, Ed?" Charlie asked.

"Odessa Oil. I'm a geologist over there."

"An oil man, huh? That's good."

"Ed just moved here from Alaska," Sullivan offered.

Charlie nodded approvingly. "Always wanted to go there," he said.

"You should. There's nothin' like it." Ward could already see that Charlie would be an easy yes vote.

"Ben says you boys met down in Victoria. That where you're livin' now?" Charlie asked.

"No, I've got a place over in Cuero."

Charlie nodded. "We know a few folks over in Cuero. Ain't that right, Jim?"

"Yep."

Ward met Jim's gaze. The man was expressionless, nearly impossible to read. Ward wondered if he played poker.

Sullivan jumped in. "Let me tell you boys the rest of the story from the other night." As Ward listened to the slightly embellished tale, he kept envisioning the look in the eyes of the young man who wanted to stand and fight. That look haunted him.

"Ed stepped up when it mattered," Sullivan explained. "He was ready to personally escort those *spics* back to Mexico."

"Good man," Charlie acknowledged.

Ward looked at Jim. He wasn't sure, but he thought he saw a glimmer of something that looked like respect.

"What did you do before you joined Odessa Oil?" Jim asked,

finally breaking his silence.

Ward wondered if Jim suspected an infiltrator. He just couldn't tell. The guy was nearly inscrutable.

"I spent some time in the military," Ward said, being purposefully vague.

"What branch?" Jim asked.

"Army."

"What was your MOS?" Jim pressed.

Ward smiled. An MOS, or military occupational specialty, was Army jargon for a soldier's job classification. If this was some sort of test, it was one that no decent undercover agent would ever fail.

"Let's just say that I was Special Forces," Ward replied.

Charlie and Jim exchanged a look.

"Ed," Charlie began, "we're a group of concerned citizens who feel that our government has failed to protect us from an invasion, an invasion of immigrants, primarily those coming across our southern border. Our position is that if our government won't take care of the problem, we'll do it ourselves. We believe that this country is losing its cultural identity."

"I couldn't agree more," Ward said. He glanced at Jim, who, almost imperceptibly, nodded his head in approval.

CHAPTER 27

10:59 a.m., Wednesday, June 17th, Ankeny Community College, Ankeny, Iowa.

Meade arrived early, hoping for a chance to visit with Erin. No such luck. Class was about to begin, and she was nowhere to be seen. Meade prayed that she hadn't dropped the class.

Professor Goldman moved to the podium, about to start his lecture. Just then, Erin Larson slipped into the room. She gave Goldman an apologetic look.

"Sorry, Professor," she said as she hurried toward her seat.

"Not a problem, Ms. Larson," Goldman said. "We haven't begun."

Erin moved down the aisle. When she saw Meade, she smiled.

"Hi, Carl," she said softly.

"Hi, Erin," Meade replied, sure that his grin was so big he looked like he was about to bust.

In one deft movement, Erin pulled out her notebook, dropped her backpack to the floor and slid into her seat. Meade sat captivated, sure that no ballerina had ever moved more gracefully.

Goldman's lecture covered the Irish immigration that exploded with the Potato Blight of 1845 and continued strong throughout most of the Nineteenth Century. He described the squalid living conditions and employment discrimination that greeted Irish-Catholics in particular as they landed in the United States. He told the students about the Know Nothing Movement of the mid-1850s that attempted to drive Catholics from public office, the stereotypes of Irish as drunken brawlers and worse. He told of the rise of the Irish in professions such as law enforcement, their role in the labor movement and their eventual dominance of big city political machines and the boss system, not shying away from the corruption that often accompanied the latter.

Meade sat transfixed. Goldman's lecture was new ground for him. The professor repeatedly referred to the country as *a nation of immigrants*. History had never been one of Meade's better subjects. In fact, he'd taken nothing more than the required courses, and paid little attention in those. But as Goldman talked, Meade recalled how his mother had mentioned that her family came from Ireland before the Civil War. She said little else about it. Meade wondered how much she actually knew. He'd certainly never thought of his people as immigrants, let alone a group that had faced such discrimination. He found that it gave him a sense of pride, something that surprised him. Maybe he was just longing for a connection to his past...any connection.

Goldman wrapped up his lecture and gave the students their reading assignment for the next class. Meade looked over just as Erin Larson turned and met his gaze. Before he could ask, she beat him to the punch.

"I'd take that cup of coffee now," she said, "if you have time."

"Absolutely," Meade replied.

As he sat across the table from Erin Larson, sipping from his mug, Meade was absolutely certain that no cup of coffee had ever tasted as good, and no woman had ever been as beautiful. He hung on every word as she described her childhood in Atlanta, her teen years in Des Moines and the life-changing experience of working with AmeriCorps and Habitat for Humanity Disaster

Response. Meade was impressed by her sincerity and the compassion she felt for the people she had helped. He kept his opinions on New Orleans, and those of Royce Lundgren, to himself, letting Erin do the talking.

"Well," Erin said, "you've let me babble on about myself for almost half an hour now without sayin' much of anything. It's your turn. Tell me about yourself."

"Not much to tell, really," Meade replied. He wondered how he could ever get close to this woman with only a fabricated background to share.

"I don't buy that for a minute," Erin said. "I suspect there's a real interesting story to what makes up Carl Ramsey."

Meade began with his new job at Global and his transplantation from Texas. He talked about Dallas as if he'd actually grown up there. Fortunately, he knew the area well and Erin didn't. What details he couldn't make up, or weren't supplied by the Marshals Service, he borrowed from his actual childhood, changing the facts just enough to prevent identification, and to give a better impression.

As the story progressed, Meade was disturbed by how easily he lied, quickly inventing facts as needed. He wasn't raised to be a liar, and it pained him to be dishonest with this kindhearted woman. Would he ever be able to tell her the truth? Did he want to? While he certainly didn't regret all of the decisions that he'd made, Meade wished that his life had taken another course, and that his route to Erin Larson had been a more honorable one.

CHAPTER 28

10:45 a.m., Saturday, June 20th, in the air above Compound One, headquarters of The Nation, outside Yoakum, Texas.

The small, high-wing ATF surveillance plane banked right. Special Agent Jason Richter stared down at the Texas landscape. They should be close by now.

"There it is," the pilot yelled over the roar of the engines, "at two o'clock. That's their compound, the headquarters."

Richter was in the co-pilot's seat. He could see the facility below them, just ahead and to the right. A gravel drive led to a large main house that sat a good hundred yards back from the road. Two metal buildings, separated by what appeared to be a parking area, were another thirty yards further back. Behind them was a pasture that Richter estimated at forty acres. The rest of the land consisted of woods, interrupted by small meadows. A creek ran through the north end of the property. A few mobile homes were scattered about. For the headquarters of a rabid hate-group, it was a rather idyllic setting.

Special Agent Rick Burke was in the pilot's seat. Burke was assigned to the San Antonio Field Office and had come highly recommended, both as a field agent and as a pilot.

"How long have they been out here?" Richter asked Burke.

"About four years," Burke replied. "Before that, they had a meeting place over by Wrightsboro, about twenty miles west of here. They were pretty loosely organized back then. That was before Royce Lundgren took over. He moved 'em to Yoakum. That's when they really took off. Guy's a real Svengali, very charismatic. I've heard him speak. You feel like you're listenin' to Hitler."

"So, I've heard."

"A lotta people buy into his crap. Hell, for that matter, I've heard of half a dozen organizations like this one throughout the Southwest, all of 'em with a similar ideology."

Richter nodded. "Problem is, this one is becoming increasingly violent."

"That's what I hear," Burke noted. He started to snap pictures of the compound using a bubble-encased camera that was mounted on the underside of the plane. Satellite surveillance was useful, but it couldn't replace the detailed, high-resolution photos that could be produced by a flyover, even one at a height of four thousand feet. Burke wished that he could go lower, but to do so would risk suspicion. The group's members were paranoid as hell. One more pass and they would have to fly off, lay low for a while. There was a small airstrip nearby. It would be a good place to wait.

The pickup bounced along the old ranch road. Ward braced himself as the larger ruts threatened to toss them into the ditch. He looked over at Sullivan. The old rancher was unconcerned, conditioned by many years of driving the back roads of rural Texas. Sullivan's wife, Martha, sat between them. Ward remembered an old adage about how long-married couples grew to look like each other. It was certainly true in this case. Martha was the female version of Ben Sullivan, at least in appearance. A hardscrabble ranch life had left her weathered, tough. But while Ben Sullivan had maintained a sense a humor over the years, Martha had not. To Ward, she seemed a sour, bitter old woman.

"Keep your eyes on the road, you ol' fool!" Martha barked. "You're gonna kill us all!"

Sullivan ignored her.

"You're really gonna enjoy yerself," Sullivan told Ward. "These here are good people, *our* kinda people."

Ward nodded. "I'm lookin' forward to it, Ben. Be good to meet some like-minded folks."

"You'll sure enough do that," Sullivan promised.

Ward estimated that there were a hundred or more vehicles parked on both sides of the gravel drive. It led to a rambling ranch house, which he guessed to be a good thirty-five hundred square feet, probably more. As they neared the residence, Ward could see that many more cars and trucks were parked behind it in a small lot situated between two large metal barns.

As Ward jumped out of the truck, the unmistakable aroma of Texas barbecue swept over him. Several grills, including a large hog roaster, were fired up and blazing away in front of one of the barns. The men tending them were doing their best to ward off the heat with beer and lemonade.

In front of the other barn, a dozen tables sat laden with an assortment of picnic foods. Martha had baked a lemon cake for the occasion. She placed it on one of the several dessert tables, alongside fifty other cakes, pies and plates of brownies. Despite his reason for being there, Ward found himself getting hungry.

Directly behind the house, a wooden stage had been constructed. Ward saw a microphone. A small speaker sat off to one side. Playing ignorant, he asked Sullivan about it.

"Royce'll give us a talk after everybody's ate," Sullivan said.

Ward nodded. Sullivan had said little about Royce Lundgren so far, only describing him as the group's leader.

For the next forty minutes they mingled, Sullivan introducing Ed Maddox as a prospective member. Some greeted him like family and went out of their way to make him feel welcome. Others, suspicious of any newcomers, were more reserved, inclined to view any new blood as a possible infiltrator until proven otherwise. Ward took note of the latter individuals. Eventually, they ran into Charlie and Jim, the two-man screening committee from earlier in the week.

"Ed, glad you could make it!" Charlie said enthusiastically. He pumped Ward's hand.

"Happy to be here, Charlie," Ward replied. "You folks sure know how to do up a barbecue."

"That we do."

"Jim, good to see you, sir," Ward said to the other man.

Jim nodded his greeting, which was neither friendly nor unfriendly. It was more an acknowledgement than any sort of welcome. Ward thought that he could still detect some doubt in the squint of the man's eye.

"Food's ready!" came the call from a man standing by the hog roaster. Men, women and children grabbed their plates and lined up for roast pork, brisket and ribs, then made their way toward the side dishes that were heaped on until the plastic dinnerware was close to collapse. Ward joined them, happy to make his cover appear legitimate with a good meal.

Shortly after noon, Ward noticed that a man had exited the residence and was approaching the stage. A small entourage accompanied him. He climbed the steps leading to the platform and walked toward the microphone. He was tall, confident, his stride purposeful. A hush fell over the crowd. No introduction was needed. It was *him*. It was Royce Lundgren.

Ward looked to Sullivan, who met his gaze.

"Let's move up," Sullivan said. "I want you to hear every word."

Ward could tell from the look of admiration on Sullivan's face that Lundgren was much more to him than the mere leader of an anti-immigration group. Lundgren was something akin to a spiritual leader. Ward could see the same look on the faces of many others in the crowd. Parents whispered in their children's ears and pointed to Lundgren as if they were pointing to Washington or Lincoln. A familiar uneasiness swept over Ward.

"My friends, my family," Lundgren began, raising his arms as if to embrace the crowd, "welcome!"

Several in the crowd raised their arms in return. There were joyous smiles on their faces. The crowd chanted its approval as their leader began to speak. Even before Lundgren was fully underway, Ward could see tears on the cheeks of several nearby followers.

"We come here today to show allegiance to our sacred cause," Lundgren continued. "Our government has failed us! If Washington will not act…we will! It is *you* who will take back our country! It is *you* who will rid us of the brown horde! We must, and we will, return America to its white citizens! It is our mission! It is our duty! It is the commitment we have made for the sake of our blessed children, their children and their children's children!"

"God bless you, Royce," someone cried out. The crowd echoed the sentiment.

"God bless you!" Lundgren replied. "All of you!"

The crowd cheered.

"We will do what is necessary to remind *them* of their status!" Lundgren exclaimed. "And we *will* force *them* to leave!"

"Damn right!" a man yelled.

Ward looked at Sullivan. His right arm was raised in a salute as he shouted his agreement. There was a gleam in his eye that Ward had seen before.

"Take back your country!" Lundgren demanded. "It is your moral right to use any means necessary!"

Ward noticed that Lundgren fell just short of directly inciting specific acts of violence. He guessed that duty was probably left for his lieutenants.

"Go forth!" Lundgren commanded them. "Save our nation! Save The Nation!"

A roar erupted from the throng. Ward looked around. It was a near religious fervor. He was beginning to fear that The Nation was a more serious threat than he had realized.

Lundgren descended into the crowd. Members reached out to touch him, to embrace him.

"Do you want to meet him?"

Ward turned around. It was Charlie.

"Absolutely," Ward said, doing his best to appear thrilled. "It would be an honor." He gave Sullivan a grin.

They waited several minutes to allow some of the pack surrounding Lundgren to disperse. When it was clear that those who would leave had, they approached.

"Wait here," Charlie said, holding up a hand.

Charlie moved toward Lundgren. Ward watched as they embraced. Charlie whispered something in Lundgren's ear. Lundgren glanced at the new recruit. There was a nod and more whispered comments. Ward speculated that the discussion included a reference to his military background, something that had caused great interest during the earlier interview. Charlie waved them over. Ward glanced at his sponsor. Sullivan wore the expression of a proud father.

Charlie did the introduction. "Ed Maddox, I'd like you to meet Royce Lundgren, our leader."

"Pleased to meet you, sir," Ward said, feigning the requisite degree of awe. "It's my privilege."

"Charlie tells me good things about you," Lundgren said, assessing the man before him. "I trust we'll see you here again."

It was an assumption by a man not disposed to self-doubt.

"You will," Ward assured him.

"Very good," Lundgren said, extending his hand.

They shook. Ward's smile conveyed nothing other than *it's an honor*.

With that, Lundgren moved away. Ward felt as if he had just held the hand of the devil.

As his followers swarmed back around him, Royce Lundgren briefly closed his eyes and let himself be enveloped. Their adoration was worshipful, their touch stimulating in a way that transcended anything merely sexual. He was a god to them.

Lundgren knew that he was special, that he had been chosen to lead. Destiny commanded it. His mission was sacred. Only he could lead these people, this country, back to its rightful place at the pinnacle of the hierarchy of nations. He alone had the vision. Soon, his wisdom would become obvious to all who would truly listen. The rest would be crushed under the weight of his righteousness.

CHAPTER 29

6:23 p.m., Saturday, June 20th, Thomaston, Texas, ten minutes southeast of Cuero.

It had been a long afternoon, too damn long. The tension from maintaining his alias for an entire day in the face of what seemed like constant scrutiny had left Ward exhausted. Still, he wanted to brief Richter and Lehman on the day's festivities face to face. Thomaston, on U.S. Highway 87, about halfway between Cuero and Victoria, had been selected as their rendezvous point during the operation. A seldom-used dirt road just outside of the tiny unincorporated town is where they agreed to meet.

Ward took the usual evasive measures to avoid being followed as he left his undercover residence in Cuero. There was no sign that he'd been tailed. At this point in the game it was unlikely that anyone would try, but Ward knew better than to take chances.

Ward turned onto the dirt road. He wasn't surprised to see that Richter and Lehman were already there waiting for him. Ward pulled up behind their vehicle and got out. As he approached the driver's door, Richter exited.

"I'm thinkin' Ed Maddox had a pretty interesting day," Richter said.

"Yes, he did," Ward agreed. "Yes, he did."

Lehman came around from the other side of the vehicle to join them. "Looked like a pretty good turnout," he said. "How many you think were there?"

"Three, four hundred," Ward guessed.

Richter pulled out a notepad. "Tell me everything."

Ward took them through it, start to finish. As they listened, Richter and Lehman just shook their heads. Like Ward, they were beginning to understand that The Nation was something even more dangerous than they'd realized.

"The atmosphere was part Hayden Lake, part Jonestown," Ward observed.

Richter stopped writing. "So, what you're telling me is that we've got a white supremacist cult that's been whipped into a rabid anti-immigration fervor."

"That about sums it up," Ward said.

The three of them stood silent for a moment, mentally preparing for the battle ahead.

CHAPTER 30

7:40 p.m., Saturday, June 20th, just north of the United States/Mexico border, somewhere in the southwestern corner of New Mexico.

Jorge Mendez deposited the food and water in a spot where he knew it would be found. Five years of experience had created a patchwork of locations that were now known to many of the immigrants who would pass through this rugged corner of New Mexico and to those who would guide them. The work was more than rewarding; it was a blessing, and a way to remember those who had failed to successfully complete the crossing. There had been too many, their bones scattered along the nineteen hundred-plus miles of the southern border. Jorge's brother, Pepito, had been one of those, leaving for *El Norte* eight long years ago, never to be heard from again. Jorge still thought of him daily.

The memory of his brother had prompted Jorge to found Angels of the Border, an ecumenical Christian organization dedicated to helping those who found themselves in trouble as they made the crossing. The group was often misperceived as one that aided or encouraged illegal immigration. Jorge didn't see it that way. To his way of thinking they were a rescue team. And after a rocky start, many members of the U.S. Border patrol had come to see them that way as well. Now, the two organizations frequently worked hand in hand.

Their mission was every bit as critical here as it was in the terrain that most people associated with illegal immigration, the desert. This section of the border was different. Unlike most of the border area found in the neighboring state of Texas, much of southern New Mexico was mountainous, with peaks ranging from five to ten thousand feet. But the increased altitude did nothing to lessen the danger. Many had starved or died of thirst in the mountains. Jorge too often found the bodies of those who had been unprepared, misled, or worse. It was common for the week's patrols to discover a dozen or more individuals who were lost and seriously weakened or badly injured.

Of course, water was most essential. It was dehydration that claimed the majority of the victims. As for the food, it had to be items that could last out in the open. Cookies and canned tuna were typical. Clothes were important as well. The mountains could become bitterly cold at night. Pants, shirts and sweaters were often left with the food and water. Shoes, when the group could get them, were also provided.

Jorge said a short prayer, asking God to protect the travelers. He crossed himself as he stood looking over the supplies that had been provided. Soon it would start to get dark. He called out to some of the group's members who were nearby. It was time to leave. He used his walkie-talkie to radio the others. They would rendezvous back at the small caravan of vehicles that had delivered them. Another day's work was done. Hopefully, many would be saved by what they had left behind.

Their leader lowered his binoculars. "They're coming. Let's move," he told the others. The men pulled down their ski masks and marched forward. All were similarly clad in black, head to toe, their hands gloved. Some sported blackjacks or brass knuckles. Each was armed with a pipe or baseball bat. There were also handguns, but those were not to be used, not this time. The point was to send a message, a strong message, that assistance to the illegals would not be tolerated.

The six-man team was led by Klein, the chief weapons and tactics-training officer for the New Mexico chapters. Lundgren had selected him to lead this mission. Klein's earlier efforts had greatly impressed the leadership, notably his ability to leave no evidence behind. That would be especially critical on this assignment. Normally no witnesses were left alive. This time, barring complications, they would all be left alive; left to share the story of what had happened to them.

"Remember," Klein told the others, "no fatalities." He checked his watch. They had synchronized earlier. "We'll converge in…two minutes." He signaled for them to disperse.

The six vigilantes slipped into place. They surrounded the three vehicles that had delivered the Angels of the Border. On this outing, The Angels were five men and three women. Most were middle-aged, in poor shape. None were armed. They would be no match for the six.

As the volunteers approached, Jorge Mendez thanked them again for accompanying him. Most of them were veterans, but it was the first rescue mission for two of his helpers, Paul and Maria, a young couple from Las Cruces. Jorge could see it in their eyes, the fulfillment that came from doing this good work. But he also knew the heartbreak they would feel when they found the first one who didn't make it.

Suddenly, men came out of nowhere. They were masked, dressed in black, weapons drawn. Moving quickly, they said nothing as blows fell heavily on the volunteers.

Jorge knew immediately what these men were about. They were no mere *desperados*. He had long feared that something like this might happen. Throwing himself in front of one of the women, he was rewarded with a crushing blow to the knee. Pain exploded in his leg. It dropped him to the ground. The second blow hit his side, fracturing several ribs. He doubled over, barely able to breathe.

Jorge struggled to get up but was unable to leave the ground. He saw Paul step in front of his wife, Maria, bravely trying to fend off the assault. A pipe cracked into Paul's forearm, smashing it to pieces. The young volunteer howled in pain, but struggled to stay on his feet, desperately trying to protect his wife. It was then that the brass knuckles smashed Paul's jaw. He collapsed to the ground. Jorge moaned in anguish as he saw the pipe swing toward Maria.

Then Jorge saw one of them, wading through the carnage, coming toward him. The man appeared to be their leader. Jorge tried to lie still, but the pain in his side felt like a dagger. He gave out a low moan.

"Roll him onto his back," the man growled.

Two of them grabbed Jorge, manhandling him. He screamed as the broken rib bones twisted inside him. Tears of pain filled his eyes.

The big man, the leader, squatted down beside Jorge and grabbed his face, making certain that their eyes made contact.

"Your assistance to this illegal filth will end," the man said. "And know this, if there's a next time, it won't end as well for you and your helpers."

The man smirked. He shoved Jorge's face aside and stood. Jorge heard him grunt with effort as the boot made contact. The searing pain, the animal-like howl, Jorge felt as if he were experiencing them from outside his own body. Seconds later, everything went black.

CHAPTER 31

8:00 p.m., Saturday, June 20th, outside Erin Larson's apartment, Des Moines, Iowa.

Meade looked at his watch. It was eight o'clock...finally. The last fifteen minutes had been spent driving around the neighborhood. It was a wonder no one called the police. As he climbed the steps to Erin's apartment, Meade thought back on the phone call in which he asked her to dinner. There had been a good half dozen rehearsals of what he would say even before picking up the phone. When he did, he immediately set it back down, too petrified to punch in the numbers. Three tries later, he let the call go through. Meade wasn't sure what language he was speaking during their conversation, it certainly wasn't English, but she said yes anyway when he finally asked. For some mysterious reason, she seemed to find him charming. He just wondered how long it would take for whatever charm he had to wear off.

Meade knocked on the door.

"Just a minute," Erin called from inside.

Seconds later, the door opened. Erin wore a sundress and sandals. A tan caused an already brilliant smile to rise to the level of dazzling. A necklace sparkled against her brown skin.

The vision before him left Meade feeling weak-kneed...and giddy. The *thud, thud, thud* of his heart was almost painful. He was sure that she could hear it. What was wrong with him? He had never reacted like this before. Was it...love, or just infatuation? Suddenly, Meade realized that he wasn't speaking. Talk, you idiot, he told himself.

"You look...wonderful," Meade finally managed to say.

"Thank you," Erin replied. There was a slight bounce as she said it. "C'mon in, I'm almost ready. I'll just grab my sweater." She disappeared into the bedroom.

Meade stepped inside, hoping it would be the first of many times. He looked around the small apartment. To him, it spoke of taste, but not wealth. Erin struck him as someone who made her own way and relished life as she did so. He couldn't be more impressed. Then, suddenly, the happiness was replaced by the crushing weight of reality, accompanied by a profound sense of guilt. What made him think that he could be with a woman like this? She deserved so much better. Meade felt wholly inadequate. Still, when he looked at her...

"I'll be there in a minute," Erin called from the other room.

"No problem," Meade replied. Maybe it was the sound of her voice that snapped him out of it. Didn't he deserve some happiness in life? There had been so little up until now.

"I'm ready if you are," Erin said cheerily as she reappeared before him.

"I couldn't be more ready," Meade replied.

The cool evening breeze blew through the open windows of the Impala as they drove the street leading to Erin's apartment. Meade looked at his date and smiled. It was amazing. She seemed even more beautiful and charming with each passing moment.

A co-worker had suggested Bistro 99, one of the city's more fashionable restaurants. The place had been suitably impressive. It should have been, given the cost. But, despite his limited means, Meade considered it a small price to pay. He would have gladly spent double, even triple the amount to impress her. And thankfully he'd somehow managed to overcome his earlier verbal paralysis and regain a reasonable amount of wit, or at least Erin thought so.

The lying still bothered Meade. In fact, as his feelings for Erin continued to grow, the lying bothered him more than ever. On top of the fact that it just felt wrong, Meade had to wonder, how could he even hope to remember all of the details, the fictional tidbits that Erin might someday recall? How could he keep his story straight?

They pulled up in front of Erin's apartment building.

"Here we are," Meade said. He was unsure what to do next. Should he try to kiss her? Should he walk her to the door? He was suddenly afraid that the slightest misstep could send the whole thing crashing to the ground. In fact, he was certain of it.

"I had a really nice time tonight," Erin offered. She sounded like she meant it.

There was an awkward silence.

"Carl, why don't you walk me to the door," she said knowingly.

"I'd love to," he said, immensely relieved.

When they stopped in front of Erin's apartment, she took his hand.

"I had a wonderful time tonight," Erin said.

Meade felt like he'd won the lottery. "Me, too," he said. "I hope we can..."

Before he could finish, Erin leaned in to kiss him. Their lips met, then pressed together, leaving no doubt as to whether there would be a second date. They gently embraced as the kiss lasted just long enough.

She turned and opened the door. As she entered the apartment, she looked back, a shy smile on her face. "Good night, Carl Ramsey. I'll see you in class."

CHAPTER 32

4:50 p.m., Monday, June 22nd, Global Harvester's Des Moines Works, Ankeny, Iowa.

Meade flipped up his welding hood and cut off the gas supply to his torch. He watched as the metal began to cool, the red glow fading away. He had drawn another expert bead.

"Not bad."

Meade looked up. It was his foreman, Randy Kroeger.

"You do nice work, Ramsey," Kroeger said with a nod of approval.

"Thanks."

"How are those welding classes workin' out?" Kroeger asked. "They teachin' you anything out there?"

"There's not much to teach me, boss," Meade replied. He grinned. "Just kiddin'. I've actually picked up a thing or two."

"Good. Glad to hear it," Kroeger said. "Keep up the good work."

The foreman moved down the line, stopping to inspect another man's work.

Meade flipped his hood down and went back at it.

Moments later, a horn sounded. It was break time. Meade yanked off his hood and removed his heavy welding gloves. He stood and stretched, twisting from side to side in an attempt to pop his spine into place. Welding could be tough on the back. It could also make you damn thirsty. He decided to head to the lunchroom for a can of soda.

Workers crowded around the vending machines in a hurry to grab a quick snack or something to drink. Breaks were short. There was no time to waste.

Looking over the selections, Meade decided on a cola. The sugar and caffeine jolt would help him make it to dinner. He fished around in his pockets for some change, retrieving a mere thirty-five cents. The wallet came next. There were two singles, both old and in rough shape. Meade did his best to iron out the wrinkles of the first bill by rubbing it back and forth on the edge of the vending machine. He slipped it into the dollar slot, not hopeful about the outcome. The machine kicked it back out. He tried again. Same result.

"Son of a bitch," Meade muttered. Looking back over his shoulder, he saw that a long line had already formed behind him He ironed out the second bill, which looked markedly worse than the first. He slipped it in the machine. Out it came. Meade suppressed a rising urge to smash his fist into the machine.

"What's the problem," a voice called from the back of the line. "We ain't got all day."

Meade could feel his face grow hot. He slid the bill in one more time. The machine spit it back at him, taunting him. Meade raised his fist, and then put it back down.

"Time's up," said the second in line.

Meade spun around, his jaw clenched. The man behind him was large, solid. He had the hardened look of an experienced barroom brawler. Meade noticed his hands. They were clenched into fists, fists that resembled sledgehammers.

The man at the next vending machine had watched the situation develop. A second bottle of cola clunked into the delivery chute. He grabbed it and tapped it against Meade's arm.

"It's on me," the man said.

Meade was startled by the coldness of the bottle. But he was even more surprised to see who was holding it.

"Name's Jose," the man said.

At first Meade said nothing, staring blankly at the man offering the cola...a Mexican. Meade didn't know what to do. He stared down at the drink and then back up at Jose.

"Go ahead...take it," Jose insisted.

"Yeah, take it," said the man with the sledgehammer fists.

Meade took the bottle and stepped away from the vending machine. Jose looked at him expectantly.

"Thanks," Meade said unenthusiastically, barely able to believe that the words were coming out of his mouth. He was actually thanking one of...*them.*

"Don't mention it," Jose replied, underwhelmed by the lackluster expression of gratitude.

Meade walked off, leaving Jose standing alone.

Randy Kroeger stood nearby, a puzzled look on his face. Meade wondered if Kroeger had witnessed the entire incident.

Meade went to the opposite end of the lunchroom. He stood with his back against the wall, staring at the unopened bottle of cola. He failed to notice Kroeger as he approached.

"You gonna open that?" Kroeger asked.

"Huh...what?"

Kroeger eyed Carl Ramsey suspiciously. "You got a problem with the Mexicans?"

"Who...me? No," Meade lied.

"Good," Kroeger said, unconvinced. "Keep it that way."

The foreman started to walk off but stopped. Turning back, he offered some advice.

"It wouldn't hurt you to be a little more open-minded," Kroeger suggested.

Meade lowered his head, saying nothing in response.

"You're a good hand, Ramsey," Kroeger offered. "Don't screw it up."

CHAPTER 33

5:55 p.m., Tuesday, June 23rd, just northeast of Yorktown, Texas.

It was Sullivan's idea. The call came late in the day, insisting that they meet at Bubba's around five. Beyond that, Sullivan had merely promised a good time. Ward had no clue what the man was up to, or where they were headed. That made him nervous. There was barely enough time to notify Richter and Lehman to get the tail vehicle in place.

Mueller had offered to drive. His truck was a club cab with front and back seating. Ward sat in the front passenger seat. Sullivan was in back, sitting next to several gun cases and a cooler of beer, an old ammunition box lodged between his feet. Ward had questioned Sullivan as to what was in the cases. *You'll see* was the answer. Ward suspected that the weapons were something along the lines of an AR-15, the semi-automatic version of the military's M16. Of course, Sullivan also might have got his hands on an AK-47. There were plenty of those around, especially the semi-autos. The chances were slim, however, that they were transporting anything that was fully automatic. Ward didn't doubt for a minute that The Nation possessed such weapons, but even if they would entrust them to this crew, it was way too early to expose them to the newcomer.

Ward did a quick check in the side mirror. Charlie and Jim were thirty yards back. There was no sign of Richter and Lehman.

Ward started to get anxious. Mueller was really hauling ass, at times flirting with ninety miles an hour. As stupid as that was, or seemed, given a truck full of booze and high-powered weapons, he might have actually lost the tail. Was it intentional?

All of a sudden, Mueller hit the brakes. Ward jerked forward.

"Damn! I almost missed it," Mueller said as he turned off Texas Highway 72 and onto a private dirt road.

"What the hell?" Sullivan asked from the back. "Sumbitch is gonna get us killed, Ed," he yelled up at Ward. Sullivan choked out a laugh that turned into a hacking cough. Forty-plus years of two packs a day had taken their toll.

"Well, they should mark the goddamn thing better," Mueller complained.

"Like with what," Sullivan asked, "a sign sayin' this way to The Nation's shooting range?" He hacked out another laugh. "Shit."

Ward ignored the two of them. He was far more concerned by the fact that they had turned off the highway so quickly and were hard to see from the main road. Things were made that much worse by a stand of trees that shielded them from view. Even if Richter and Lehman were close, they might drive right on by. Ward turned and looked at the weapons. He glanced back at the truck behind them. Jim was in the passenger seat, expressionless, staring straight ahead. They briefly made eye contact. Ward turned away, doing his best to appear nonchalant. Jim would have to be watched closely. If these guys had made him, if this was an ambush, Jim was a good bet for the trigger-man. There was little doubt that he could whack a suspected infiltrator without losing any sleep. Then again, Ward thought, they might all open up on him. He resolved to get his hands on one of the weapons as soon as possible and keep all four of them in front of him at all times.

Mueller's truck bounced to a stop in front of a gate. It was new and padlocked. The barbed-wire fence on either side appeared to be well tended. Ward could see two *No Trespassing* signs prominently displayed. Whoever owned this land did not want people poking around.

Ward decided to give it a shot. "Whose place is this?"

"A friend's," Sullivan replied. The tone suggested that no more questions should be asked.

"Fair enough," Ward said.

Sullivan got out and opened the gate. He stood to the side as both vehicles passed through. Ward noticed that when Sullivan locked the gate behind them he checked twice to make sure it was secure. Not a good sign.

The range itself was another three-quarters of a mile in. When they pulled up, Ward let out a low whistle. It was a first-class facility, complete with numerous shooting stands and a variety of target holders. There was also an area for trap and skeet. Whoever put it together knew what they were doing. He had to admit, he was impressed.

As the three men exited Mueller's pickup, Charlie and Jim were already unloading their arsenal.

Ward checked the ground. There were few casings to be seen. "Must not get used much," he observed. "Don't see a lot of brass."

Sullivan smirked. "It gets used plenty," he said. "We just pick up the casings."

Within a few minutes, an assortment of semi-automatic rifles and handguns were laid out before them. Mueller walked out and set up various targets, everything from the basic bull's-eye to a series of human silhouettes.

Charlie and Jim went first. Charlie was an okay shot at best. Jim, on the other hand, was deadly. In Ward's estimation, Jim approached expert marksman status with both pistol and rifle.

Sullivan walked up to Ward and offered him a beer, then opened one for himself. "Not bad, huh?" he asked, referring to Jim's shooting display.

"Not bad at all," Ward agreed. He took a drink of the beer. It tasted damn good in the Texas heat.

"Jim's got some military background himself," Sullivan noted.
"It shows."

They were interrupted by Mueller. "You ready?" he asked
Sullivan.

"Yep," Sullivan replied. He took a hit from his beer and
grabbed an AR-15. Mueller was sporting a .40 caliber Glock.
They walked up to the firing line and took their positions.

Ward watched with amusement as Mueller failed to hit much
of anything. He cussed and made excuses enough for three men.
Sullivan, on the other hand, was a solid shot. The old rancher
clearly had a good eye. After ten minutes or so, they took a
break.

"You ready to give 'er a try?" Sullivan asked. He was eager
to see what Ed Maddox could do.

Ward looked around. Jim and Charlie were fifteen yards
back of the firing line, selecting different weapons. Jim had
picked up an AK-47 and was cradling it like a baby. Ward
would have them at his back if he shot from Sullivan's location.
There was only one thing to do.

"That's a little close for me," Ward said boldly. "How 'bout
I give it a try from back here?" He knew it was cocky, and argu-
ably insulting, but there was no other way.

Jim and Charlie suddenly stopped what they were doing.
They exchanged a look. Things were about to get interesting.

"Suit yerself," Sullivan said, mildly annoyed. He marched
back toward Ward and handed him the AR-15.

"It's just that I was trained to shoot from a distance," Ward
offered, by way of excuse.

"That' fine," Sullivan said. "Let's see what you got."

When Mueller was safely to one side, Ward assumed his
shooting stance. The weapon had no scope, only iron sights.
That was fine with Ward. He lined up and fired.

It was quickly apparent to everyone present that Ed Maddox
knew his shit. Five out of six shots hit the bull's-eye. On the
human silhouette, four of six hit the heart, with the remaining

two landing right between the eyes.

"What'd you say you did in the Special Forces?" Sullivan asked.

An evasive smile appeared on Ward's face. "I didn't," he said.

"C'mon, Ed? You're among friends." Sullivan was dying to know.

"Classified," Ward responded.

"Classified by a government that's lost touch with its people," Charlie interjected as he walked toward them.

The four men gathered around Ward. He didn't sense a threat, but could see that he would have to tell them something.

"Let's just say that I've seen my share of counter-terrorism and unconventional warfare," Ward offered. "That includes a stint along the Afghanistan-Pakistan border."

The men nodded their approval. Attempts to probe for more details proved futile.

An hour and a half later the festivities ended. The weapons were loaded into the trucks and the men departed. Charlie and Jim took a different route home. Along the way, their conversation turned to Ed Maddox.

"Can you imagine what that sumbitch could do with a machine gun down at the border?" Charlie asked jokingly. "He could put a good dent in the Mexican problem by himself."

Jim grunted. "All I know is it's too damn early for Maddox to be seein' any machine guns. We don't know shit about this guy."

"Hell, it was just a joke," Charlie replied. "Besides, he seems okay to me. You get a little paranoid."

"I'm just careful," Jim said. "We can't be too careful."

CHAPTER 34

*7:35 p.m., Wednesday, June 24th, Bubba's Big-League Bar &
Grill, Victoria, Texas.*

Ward looked at his watch. He was late. Sullivan and Mueller
would already be seated at the bar, watching a ballgame that
was well underway. They would also be at least three beers into
it by now. Ward had to give it to 'em, these men could drink.
He patted his belly. If he didn't watch it, he was going to end up
looking like Mueller by the time this was over.

Ward walked in. The crowd was light. He immediately spotted
Sullivan in his usual spot. Mueller was missing. In his place was
Charlie. Ward wondered if tonight was to be a continuation of
the vetting of Ed Maddox. That was fine with him. It was obvious
that Charlie had the ear of Royce Lundgren. Charlie could be
the key to entering the inner circle.

"Gentlemen, how y'all been?" Ward asked as he approached.
"Charlie, good to see you, sir." Ward reached over to shake
hands.

"Kyle decided to take the night off," Sullivan announced.
"Some nonsense about needin' to do laundry. Can you imagine?
What the hell do you suppose that's all about? Never heard of
such a thing. Anyway, Charlie here was good enough to come
along."

"Glad he did," Ward noted. He ordered a drink. "Get you
boys one?" he asked.

Sullivan slammed the remnants of his beer. "Absolutely," he said.

Charlie checked the level in bottle. "Sure, I'm about ready. Thanks, Ed."

"How we doin' tonight?" Ward asked, nodding toward the television.

"Not worth a shit," Sullivan replied. "Bottom of the second and we're already down three to nothin'."

"It's not good," Charlie agreed, "not good at all."

They talked baseball and watched the game for a few minutes. Eventually, Charlie turned the conversation to the events of the night before.

"That was a helluva shooting display last night, Ed. Never seen nothin' like it."

"Thanks, Charlie. But I gotta tell ya, fact is, everybody in my unit could shoot like that. If you couldn't, you were probably gonna die. That's a pretty good motivator for honing your skills."

"Damned impressive, nonetheless," Charlie emphasized. He was silent for a moment. Ward thought the man had something on his mind. He wondered what was coming next. He could see that Charlie's wheels were turning.

"Ed, I gotta ask ya," Charlie began, "a guy like you, why are you interested in *us*?"

Ward knew instinctively that this was the watershed moment. He would have to summon all of his skills to give this man a satisfactory answer, an answer that, hopefully, would open the door for him. If he failed, the investigation could be over.

"I can understand why you would ask that," Ward began. "Let me tell you. I think Lundgren's right. Our government has failed us...in many ways. It has certainly lost control of the border and shows no signs of doing the job right anytime soon. I've been in countries where there's no control of the border. Afghanistan and Pakistan are both prime examples, but there are countless others. A breakdown in border security leads to economic and political destabilization, not to mention terrorism. Eventually, the country will fail. In fact, Mexico has almost no control over *its* southern border. Immigrants and drugs flow in easily. That has contributed to the country's economic problems, and to its ongoing war with the narco-traffickers. This is not a problem that we can ignore. If the politicians in Washington can't get the job done…well…we need to take matters into our own hands, take our country back. The Founding Fathers would expect it of us."

"Here, here," said Sullivan, raising his beer in a toast."

"Amen to that," Charlie agreed.

"For me, though, it's more than that," Ward continued. He put his head down and took a breath, as if he were becoming choked up. "I've been there when the politicians abandoned the fight, lost what little will they once had because the polls had changed. I've seen funding cut in the middle of important missions, supplies cut off, soldiers effectively abandoned in the field. I've seen the people in other countries who, at enormous personal risk, helped the United States, only to have the politicians abandon them in the end, leaving them to a grisly fate."

Ward was silent for a moment. He put his hand over his eyes. Finally, he took a deep breath and continued. "I had a translator, a brave and decent man. He risked his life for us. I tried everything to get him into this country. But the bureaucrats, they wouldn't budge. He was targeted as a collaborator." Ward paused again. A tear formed in the corner of his right eye. After a few seconds, it rolled down his cheek. "His severed head was left on the doorstep for his wife and children to find."

"Jesus," Sullivan exclaimed.

"Gentlemen," Ward said, "I love my country. But I owe this government no allegiance. If this nation is going to be strong again…it's up to us."

Ward thought it possibly his most masterful performance. There was no doubt it had the desired effect. Sullivan put his hand on Ward's shoulder and nodded his head, a gesture meant to show that they were kindred spirits. Charlie also showed his respect.

"Bartender," Charlie said, "please bring my friend here anything he wants." He turned to Ward. "Ed, you're a helluva man. I'm proud to know ya. You ever need anything up in Yoakum, you just ask ol' Charlie Kirklin. I'll take care of ya."

"Thanks, Charlie." Ward made a mental note to have Richter check out ol' Charlie Kirklin.

It was almost ten o'clock as Ward approached Cuero. He managed to limit the drinking to a beer an inning, an accomplishment when you were teamed up with Sullivan. After any number of their evenings together, Ward had feared that he might have to talk his way out of a drunk-driving charge, a problem he didn't need. Still, there was one thing he'd learned after many years of undercover work, drinking with a man was the way to make a bond.

Just as he hit the city limits, Ward's cell phone went off.

"Yeah," he answered.

"It's Richter. I ran your guy. No criminal history for a Charles or Charlie Kirklin out of Yoakum."

"Any intelligence on him?"

"Nope. But I did notice that he's an accountant. Has his own firm in Yoakum."

"So maybe he's their money guy, huh?"

"Could be."

"I can tell you one thing," Ward said. "He has Lundgren's ear."

"Sounds like a man to stay close to."

"Indeed, it does."

CHAPTER 35

9:05 a.m., Thursday, June 25th, Meade's apartment, Ankeny, Iowa.

Meade was somewhere in that netherworld between sleep and awake, on the tail end of a dream about Erin. He could see her now, unimaginably beautiful, standing outside his apartment, knocking at the door...knocking, knocking. But was it a dream? Meade felt sure that he was awake. He could hear her. There it was again, a banging at the door. He had to get to her. He had to let her in. Then his eyes flicked opened. There was nothing, not a sound. He looked at his alarm clock. It was just after nine. It was a dream after all.

Suddenly, the sound came again. *Bang, Bang, Bang!* Now it was an insistent knock, as if to say, *get your ass out of bed!* A heavy sleeper, Meade rubbed his eyes in an attempt to clear the grogginess.

Bang, Bang, Bang! Meade grabbed a frying pan from the kitchen. It would have to do. He put his back up against the wall and quietly slid toward the apartment door. Would they come for him like this? Probably not, he realized as his thoughts began to clear. They were more likely to whack him when he least suspected it, in the parking lot at school, stopped at a traffic light, something like that. Still, under the circumstances, he couldn't be too careful. Meade held his breath and carefully, silently, moved his eye to the peephole.

It was Deputy Willis. Meade muttered several expletives. He composed himself and then pulled the door open.

"You might have called first," Meade said.

"Nice to see you, too," Willis shot back.

Meade didn't respond.

"Can I come in?" Willis asked.

"I suppose. You guys paid for the place."

Willis walked in and looked around. He acted surprised to see that Meade had kept the place relatively clean and orderly.

"You can put that down," Willis said, pointing at the frying pan still clutched in Meade's hand.

"Sorry," Meade said. He placed the pan on the kitchen counter. "Something I can do for you? Or are you just here to check up on me?"

"A little of both," Willis replied.

"Have a seat," Meade offered, gesturing toward a chair. He decided to cut Willis some slack. After all, the deputy had helped get him admitted to college, and that was what led him to Erin. Besides, Willis didn't really strike him as bad guy. He was just doing his job.

Meade sat on the couch. "So, what's this about?"

"Thought I'd give you some friendly advice."

From the deputy's expression, Meade wasn't sure that the advice would be all that friendly. "And what would that be?" he asked.

"I don't want to see you get yourself in trouble," Willis began.

"Ooookay," Meade said slowly. He wondered where this was going.

"Let's not have any racial incidents. You've got a good job. Don't screw it up."

Meade got agitated. His face started to turn red. "You've got somebody spyin' on me?"

Willis didn't respond.

"It's a simple question," Meade snapped. "Do...you...have...somebody...spying...on...me?" He assumed that his foreman,

Randy Kroeger, was the source. Who else could it be? Did Kroeger know that he was in witness protection? That wasn't supposed to happen.

"You're in no position to cop an attitude with me," Willis calmly reminded him. "I've got sources. Let's leave it at that. Besides, it's for your own good."

Meade sat silent, jaw muscles flexing. It frustrated the hell out of him, but Willis was right. He was in no position to cop an attitude. He had no bargaining power, none at all.

"Fine," Meade said. "Message received." There was no point in drawing this out.

Willis hesitated, his expression doubtful at first, then determined. What now, Meade wondered.

"You need to be careful about what you tell the girl," Willis cautioned him.

Meade's eyes narrowed. His nostrils flared. "Her name's Erin," he said through clenched teeth. "And that's none of your goddamned business."

Willis leaned forward. "Well, in fact, it is my goddamned business," he said, "because my goddamned business is to keep your stupid ass alive."

"At least until you use me as a witness," Meade spat back.

"That's not the case, Jacob, and you know it." Willis opened his hands in a calming gesture. "Look, we've dealt with this type of thing before. You want to make a connection with this woman. I understand that. It's tough. What do you tell her when she asks about your family, where you grew up? If you make it all up, it gets hard to keep your story straight. The temptation is to fill in little details here and there from your real past. Then, when there are no consequences for those disclosures, you feel safe. You figure, what the hell, I can tell her a little more."

Meade hung his head. Willis had it pegged. He had already started down this path with Erin.

Willis studied Meade for a moment. "Jacob, I understand

how badly you need some companionship right now. I really do. You just need to be careful."

Meade nodded. Willis was right to bring it up. Still, he doubted that the deputy had even the slightest idea just how desperately he needed someone, especially when that someone was Erin.

Willis got up to leave. As he reached the door, he turned back. "You know, Jake, you also need to ask yourself…is it fair to her? She seems like a nice girl."

As the door shut behind Deputy Willis, Meade pondered the question. Was it fair to her? Willis had no idea how many times Meade had asked himself that very thing.

CHAPTER 36

9:20 p.m., Friday, June 26th, Royce Lundgren's private residence, Compound One, outside Yoakum, Texas.

Royce Lundgren sat at the end of the conference table, eyes closed, hands held together as if in prayer. It wasn't a request for divine guidance, though he considered his mission sacred. Lundgren was simply concentrating, dissecting the advice of those assembled. They were the men that could be called the disciples, his most ardent followers.

To Lundgren's right sat The Nation's accountant and treasurer, Charlie Kirklin. His presentation showed that fundraising had exceeded expectations and that the organization's benefactors were growing more numerous by the day.

To Lundgren's left was Eric Brandt, the organization's chief assault team commander, a leader of what Lundgren liked to think of as his special forces. Brandt was as ruthless as he was devoted, a man glad to do whatever was required to further the mission. Brandt's team, and several others, had achieved spectacular successes in the war against the brown horde.

Next to Brandt was Warren Graves, the closest thing Lundgren had to a Joseph Goebbels. Graves was the public relations man. While Goebbels had been Reich Minister for Popular Enlightenment and Propaganda, and a man whose work Lundgren had studied carefully, it was unanimously agreed that Graves should carry the more American-sounding title of Public Relations

Director. Deserved or not, the term *propaganda* had a negative connotation. Their message was a gospel, and semantics could not be allowed to taint its purity. While Graves helped Lundgren spread the word, his primary responsibility was handling the press. In that, he was a master, always knowing just what to say and how to say it. More importantly, he knew what not to say, and there was a lot not to say.

At the far end of the table, attentive as always, was Lundgren's second-in-command, Harold Doyle. Doyle was Lundgren's first cousin and right-hand man, his only real confidant, the one man he truly trusted.

Rounding out the group of assembled advisors was Jim Byrd, and it was Byrd who now addressed them. Lundgren found Byrd to be humorless, cynical, and paranoid, characteristics that made him the perfect choice as head of security.

"As most of you know," Byrd began, "Troy Pierce and Willard Simmons were arrested on May 16th while trying to swap drugs for guns. The deal was supposed to be a pound of methamphetamine in exchange for some handguns, a few sawed-off shotguns and a machine gun."

"We never should have become involved in the narcotics business," Graves interrupted. It was an opinion he had expressed many times before.

Byrd shot him a sideways glance. "That ship has sailed, Warren. We need the weapons. It's a way to get them."

"I agree," Brandt said. "Why shouldn't I take the dope off these fuckin' spics? Why not use it against them? They're the ones bringin' it here. What's the point in throwing it away?"

"Gentlemen," Lundgren said calmly, "let's return to the topic at hand. Jim, please continue."

"Thank you, Royce." Byrd continued. "The only point I'm tryin' to make is that the arrest has caused some potential security issues."

"Such as?" Graves asked.

"If you'll let me finish," Byrd shot back, now agitated.

"Pierce says that they were set up by one of our members...correction, one of our *former* members, a Jacob Meade."

There were nods around the table. Most of them had already heard the same thing.

"Meade has disappeared," Byrd said, "which means that he could be in witness protection. Obviously, we have to assume that he's flipped, told them everything he knows. Thankfully, that isn't much."

"We *will* find Mr. Meade," Lundgren announced. "And we *will* send him, and all those who would betray us, a strong message."

Byrd nodded. They all knew what was meant.

"What about Pierce and Simmons?" Brandt asked Byrd. "Any chance they'll flip?"

"No," Lundgren replied before Byrd could answer.

The meeting continued for another twenty minutes before Charlie Kirklin turned the subject to Ed Maddox. Kirklin described the man's military background and the impressive shooting display at The Nation's firing range. He also related the sentiments expressed by Maddox at Bubba's two days earlier. It was a speech that had left Kirklin deeply moved, even inspired.

"Sounds like a man we could use at the border," Brandt said.

The others nodded their agreement, all except Byrd. "What do we really know about this guy?" he asked. "I saw him shoot. He's good, damn good, no doubt about it. But as for his military experience, that's just him sayin' so. We need to check him out."

"Have I met this man?" Lundgren asked.

"Yes, sir," Kirklin replied reluctantly. "I introduced him to you at last week's barbecue."

Lundgren thought for a moment. "Yes, I remember it now," he said. "I agree with Mr. Kirklin, this is a man who may be of some use to us."

Kirklin smiled, pleased with himself at having initiated the subject.

"But Mr. Byrd is also correct," Lundgren continued. "There needs to be a complete background check before we discuss the matter further. Mr. Byrd, you will see to it."

"Of course," Byrd replied.

CHAPTER 37

7:50 p.m., Saturday, June 27th, three blocks from Erin Larson's apartment.

As Meade drove toward Erin's apartment, the words of Deputy Willis still haunted him. *Is it fair to her*, he had asked? Meade knew the answer: Absolutely not. There was nothing fair about it. During their lunch date the day before, as he looked into Erin's eyes, listened to her hopes and dreams, shared her laughter, he couldn't shake the thought that she deserved someone truly special, someone other than him. It hadn't left his mind since then.

The smell of the flowers momentarily distracted him. The bouquet sat on the passenger seat, a collection of tulips and Gerber daisies. It spoke to his ambivalence. Why would a man buy flowers if he intended to break off the relationship? It didn't make sense. None of it made sense. But then, not much in his life did these days.

Meade rolled to a stop in front of the apartment building. He took a moment to make sure that he was safely in Carl Ramsey mode. Then, slowly, he walked toward Erin's apartment. It seemed as if guilt made each step more difficult. Even the flowers felt as if they weighed a hundred pounds. As he climbed the stairs, Meade felt leaden, crushed down by the weight of his own conscience. He reached her apartment and knocked on the door.

"I'll be right there," she called out from inside.

Meade had to smile at the sound of her cheery voice. It

brightened the heart. He was sure that everyone who walked away from a meeting with Erin did so with a better outlook, more bounce in their step. How could anyone not love her?

The door opened. She appeared. Meade felt his resolve evaporate. She was every bit as ravishing as she was the first time he laid eyes on her.

"You take my breath away," he said before he could catch himself.

"Oh, Carl." She reached out for his hand and gently took it.

Meade was amazed at the joy that came from this simple act. Their touch communicated in a way unlike anything he had ever experienced. The soft caress, the gentle, reassuring exploration of their fingers, spoke of a deep affection.

Erin smiled. "Do you have something for me?" she asked, looking at the hand hidden behind his back.

Meade grinned. "I almost forgot," he said, presenting the flowers. "I hope you like them."

"They're beautiful!" She pulled the bouquet to her face and inhaled the aroma. "I love them!"

Erin realized then that she might love more than the flowers. She moved close to Carl and went up on her toes to give him a kiss. It lasted long enough to let him know that it was much more than a mere *thanks for the flowers* kind of kiss.

They parked on one of the bridges that crossed the Des Moines River and joined the east and west sides of the city. From there, it was a short walk to the Simon Estes Riverfront Amphitheater, a beautiful spot overlooking the water and downtown Des Moines. The concert had been Erin's idea. She assured him that the band, Radical Departure, was a local favorite. The seating was, for the most part, bring your own. Erin spread out a blanket on the grass and sat down. She patted the spot next to her, signaling Carl to join her. He did, sitting not quite as close as he would have liked. Erin scooted closer.

As the night progressed, and a slight breeze came up, Erin appeared chilled. Carl put his arm around her. She leaned against him.

Meade didn't want to move, didn't want to take his arm off her shoulders. He wanted that night, that moment, to last forever. Their conversation flowed more naturally than it ever had before. She had always been able to keep the conversation going in a way that seemed effortless. But for Meade, on this night, it was his comfort level that allowed it to happen. He sensed her very real affection for him and felt more able to be himself. Some of his old wit, and whatever charm went with it, returned.

Meade listened with genuine interest as Erin told him of her career goals. She wanted to be a teacher. It was a choice that didn't surprise him. She was clearly someone who loved to help people. Her intelligence and patience, along with a warm, nurturing nature, would make her a natural.

"I'd also like to have a family," Erin said. Under his arm, Meade felt her tense up. "I mean, you know, someday."

Meade was immensely pleased that she had shared this with him and was tempted to read more into it than was probably there. "Me, too," was all he said. He gave her shoulder a soft squeeze as his thoughts briefly drifted to the brothers and sisters he would probably never see again. He missed them terribly.

As the concert came to a close, clouds gathered in the west.

"Looks like rain," Meade said.

"Maybe we should get going," Erin announced reluctantly.

They packed up and headed for the car. The rain began just as they made it safely inside. On the way back to Erin's apartment they held hands. Any thoughts Meade once had of ending it had now vanished.

By the time they got back to Erin's apartment it was a full-blown thunderstorm. Rain pounded against the window of the Impala as lightning lit up the night sky. Meade looked at his umbrella and then looked at her.

"I don't think this is gonna do us much good," he said.

"Let's make a run for it," Erin said gamely.

"No time like the present," Meade shot back. He jumped from the car and jogged around to her side. They ran up the front walkway, hand in hand, laughing hysterically. Gusts of rain blew sideways, blasting into them even as they climbed the steps to her apartment. When they reached her door, the covered entrance provided some relief from the downpour. Not that it mattered. They were both drenched.

Erin turned toward Carl. The laughter had stopped, but an adoring look had replaced it. She took both of his hands in her own and pulled him close.

The kiss was soft, tender, exhilarating. It told both of them what they longed to know, that this person wants *me* more than anyone or anything else. It seemed to go on forever, but also to end too soon. It was followed by another, and then another.

Erin pulled back, causing Meade to fear that he had somehow gone too far. But the look in her eyes told him something else.

"Would you like to come in?" Erin asked.

"I would love to," Meade answered softly, amazed at his good fortune.

When they entered the apartment, little was said. There was an embrace, another kiss. The kisses soon became more passionate. Erin took Carl's hand and led him to the bedroom. They began to undress each other, peeling off the rain-soaked clothing. Before Carl could try, Erin undid her bra, exposing firm, round breasts, beautifully proportioned to the rest of her body. Then, in one graceful move, she slid her panties down over her hips, letting them fall to the floor before stepping free.

The sight before him caused Meade to ache, both in his loins and in his heart. She was so lovely...so sexy. Even though he knew that he didn't deserve her, he had never wanted a woman more. Suddenly, he became anxious about his performance, wanting so badly to please her.

Erin moved toward him, kissing him as she slipped her fingers inside the waistband of his boxers and pulled them down.

The lovers fell gently onto the bed, never losing contact. There was little foreplay. Neither of them wanted it or needed it. They both desperately ached to be together. Erin gasped as Carl entered her. They were soon moving in a powerful, driving rhythm.

"I love you," Erin whispered in his ear between kisses.

"I wish I'd said it first," Meade replied. "I love you, too."

It ended better than either had dared hope. Afterwards, they lay in each other's arms, almost afraid to speak for fear of saying something that might lessen the magic of the moment. Meade felt selfish, but there was no regret. Part of him said to tell her the truth, but that voice was repressed. She had said the words, words he never thought he would hear, *I love you*. He could hardly believe it. He would tell her, though...someday, someday when it would no longer risk their relationship. In the meantime, he was determined to do one thing...make her proud.

CHAPTER 38

*7:45 p.m., Sunday, June 28th, aboard Air Force One, some-
where above central Arizona.*

As Air Force One winged its way to the east, President Samuel
T. Buckley gazed out the starboard window, lost in thought. The
sun was beginning to set behind him, giving the sky a lavender
hue. The clouds were a mix of orange, coral pink and purple.

Buckley's view encompassed much of southern Arizona and
on into Mexico. Whenever he flew this route, questions of
immigration policy forced their way into his thoughts. It was a
problem that plagued him, plagued his party, and plagued the
country. It was one of the most contentious issues of modern
times, and one for which no proposed solution would ever be
good enough to please everyone.

"They're out there right now," Buckley said, turning to the
man seated across from him. "They're coming in by the hun-
dreds...by the thousands."

"Who's that, Mr. President?" Attorney General William
Bradford asked.

Buckley smiled. Bradford knew damn well who he was referring to. "That would be the illegal immigrants, Bill."

"Of course, Mr. President," Bradford replied. "Yes, they are
out there right now, coming in by at least the thousands."

"And it's not just workers is it? It's Al-Qaeda and a dozen
other varieties of terrorist," the President continued.

"More than a dozen, I'm afraid," Bradford added.

"What's the status of our technological enforcement?" Buckley asked. "I'm afraid that my Secretary of Homeland Security can't bring himself to tell me anything other than what he thinks I want to hear. I know you'll give it to me straight, Bill."

A half-smile crept onto Bradford's face. "To be frank, Mr. President," Bradford said, "the news is not good. As you know, we've tried to continue using some elements of the virtual border fence program. I'm afraid there are still a variety of software problems. The radar systems and cameras that are mounted on the towers still don't synchronize properly. In some locations there have been issues with radar simply failing to identify objects because of the terrain. Then there's the vandalism. As you might imagine, there are a number of people who aren't too interested in having us see who, or what, is crossing the border."

"Drug dealers?" Buckley asked.

"That's correct, sir," Bradford replied. "Now, to be fair, I should note that there have certainly been instances in which the technology has produced very real results, but we are a long way from where we should be at this point."

"Believe me, I've heard the rumblings from Congress," the President noted. "As usual, there's a lot of complaining up on the Hill, but nobody at the other end of Pennsylvania Avenue seems to be able to offer any solutions." Buckley paused for a moment. "Of course, that would take some guts," he added. "Enough said."

"Nobody wants to touch this right now," Bradford noted. "It's just too complicated. Sure, there are members who are happy to demagogue the issue one way or the other, depending on their constituency, but nobody wants to do the heavy lifting to come up with a real solution."

"How are we coming with the physical fence?" the President asked. He had a pretty good idea as to the answer.

"Still way behind schedule," Bradford replied. "There's a host of logistical and legal impediments. You'll recall the lawsuit brought by Texas landowners contending that Homeland Security didn't negotiate fairly for access to their property."

"Damn it, Bill. We have got to secure this border." The President shook his head, disgusted. "I am not gonna have another 9/11 on my watch!" he said, stabbing at the air with his finger.

"Maybe it's time to ratchet up the pressure on Congress," Bradford suggested, "give a major policy speech on immigration, put the ball in the opposition's court. The timing is good. The violence of the drug cartels is to the point where it is threatening to destabilize Mexico, which could drive even more people across the border."

The President nodded. He stared out the window, a far-off but contemplative look in his eyes. After a few moments he spoke.

"I like it," Buckley said. "For emphasis, let's do it somewhere on the border...really put an exclamation point on it."

"I think that's a good idea, sir," Bradford agreed.

The President called for the White House Press Secretary to join them. Elise "Ellie" Drake had been in the position for less than two months. The young Deputy Press Secretary had stepped in to fill the void left by her predecessor until a permanent replacement could be found. Her performance had proved so exemplary that the President had decided to leave her in place. It was a lofty position for any thirty-five-year-old.

"Ellie, I want to give a speech on immigration policy," Buckley announced. He filled her in on some of the background. "Let's get the speechwriters working on it."

"Yes, sir, Mr. President!" Drake replied, a bit more enthusiastically than was warranted, especially given the subject matter.

"And let's start thinking about location," the President said. "Give it some thought. I'd like your input."

"Yes, sir! I'll do that." Ellie Drake couldn't suppress a grin as she floated back to her seat.

CHAPTER 39

8:05 p.m., Sunday, June 28th, somewhere along Arizona/Mexico border.

It had been a long and arduous journey to get to this point. Abdullah had sustained himself with thoughts of the death and destruction he would bring to the infidels. Now, it would not be long. He would wait in their country, patiently, until the instruction came, until it was time to fulfill his holy mission and wage *Jihad*.

As he set foot on American soil, Abdullah was both repulsed and thrilled, repulsed by everything that this corrupt and immoral land stood for, but thrilled at the thought of spilling the blood of its citizens. There were many like him, *mujahedeen* who would bring the United States to its knees. They entered with ease, laughing at what these fools called border security.

Abdullah stared out at the land before him, a land that would soon be conquered, conquered in the name of *Allah*.

CHAPTER 40

9:10 a.m., Monday, June 29th, the offices of Ron Flagg, Private Investigator, Houston, Texas.

Ron Flagg poured himself a cup of coffee, strong coffee. It had been another late night on another cheating spouse detail. He didn't hate the work. It paid the bills. And God knows there were enough cheaters in Houston, Texas to keep an army of private investigators in business. But it was nice, once and a while, to break up the monotony with a simple background check, a missing person investigation...something. It had been a long time since he'd seen the more lucrative jobs, insurance fraud, workers' comp, internal theft.

Flagg inhaled the aroma of the coffee and took a sip. It started to bring him back to life. At fifty-five, he was too goddamn old to be sitting surveillance every night. Ten years ago, even five, it wasn't a problem. A short power nap in the afternoon and he was good to go. Maybe it was all just starting to catch up with him. Twenty-seven years as a private investigator was a long time.

"Ron, you've got a call. It's that Jim Byrd."

"Give me just a second, Shelly," Flagg yelled out to his receptionist. He knew that Shelly didn't like Byrd. He made her nervous. He made a lot of people nervous, Flagg concluded.

It had been almost a year since he'd received a call from Byrd, and it could only mean one thing, The Nation once again needed his services. While not a member, Flagg had to admit he shared some of their views. But the methods he suspected them of using gave him pause. He never tried to confirm his suspicions. He didn't really want to know. It had gotten to the point where a paying client was a paying client.

Flagg settled in behind his desk and took another sip of coffee, as much to fortify himself as to wake up. "Okay, Shelly," he said.

The call was transferred.

"Jim, how are you?" Flagg asked. "It's been a while."

"I'm fine. We've got a job for you," Byrd said, straight to the point.

Personable as always, Flagg thought. "What can I do for you?" he asked.

"Need a background check," Byrd said. "Got a new member who might be...useful. Let's leave it at that."

"Fair enough," Flagg said. "What's his name?"

"Far as I know, Edward Maddox."

"And what do we know about Mr. Maddox?"

"Not a helluva lot," Byrd answered. "Claims to work for Odessa Oil, supposed to be some sort of geologist."

Flagg grabbed a pad of paper and began to jot down some notes. "That's easy enough to check out," he said. "What else?"

"Says he transferred in from Alaska."

"Okay."

"He has a place over in Cuero, for what that's worth."

"Anything else?"

"Claims to have some sort of Special Forces background," Byrd noted, "including a stint in Afghanistan."

"Interesting. Don't suppose he provided any details?" Flagg asked.

Byrd snorted. "Whenever you press him on that he just says classified or changes the subject."

"That could be legit," Flagg noted. "If true, he wouldn't really be able to talk about it."

"I suppose," Byrd acknowledged. "I've seen him shoot. He got some training somewhere."

Flagg thought for a moment. "I'm sure you don't have a date of birth, Social Security number, anything like that?"

"If I had all that I might not need you," Byrd shot back.

Flagg ignored the comment. "Anybody been able to get a look at his driver's license, get the number?"

"No, but we might be able to get that accomplished."

Flagg contemplated his plan of attack. He would check the standard databases. That was simple enough. And it would be easy to come up with some sort of ruse to contact the employer. The military records might be tricky, that is, if this Maddox had actually been a Green Beret. Surveillance would be essential. He smiled as the fee began to add up.

"Cost a factor?" Flagg asked.

"Not on this one."

Flagg was pleased. It was rare to get a blank check. Mr. Maddox would receive a *thorough* background investigation.

"How soon do you need the results?" Flagg asked.

"The sooner the better," Byrd replied, "but I'm not gonna put a deadline on it. I want no stone left unturned."

"Understood."

"If this guy's not who he says he is," Byrd continued, "there'll be a weak spot in his cover story. Nobody's that good."

CHAPTER 41

9:30 a.m., Monday, June 29th, Bureau of Alcohol, Tobacco, Firearms and Explosives, Houston Field Division, Houston, Texas.

Jason Richter walked the hallway leading to the office of Special Agent in Charge Lucas "Big Luke" McCutcheon. While there was progress to report, his sense of dread increased with every step. These meetings were never wholly positive. It simply was not the nature of the beast.

Colleen Simpson, the SAC's personal secretary, saw him coming. She waved for him to hurry up.

"They're already in there, hon," she said. "Y'all better scoot."

"Dammit!" Richter looked at his watch. "What gives? I'm right on time."

"Don't know," Colleen replied. "Maybe it's just the pre-briefing briefing. You know, the management stuff, the stuff y'all aren't supposed to hear."

Richter rolled his eyes. He did know. Boy, did he know. "Who's in there?"

"Aside from the boss, there's ASAC Olin and Roy Davis. They just arrived, maybe five minutes ago."

Richter nodded.

"And," Colleen continued, her face pinched into a grimace, "ASAC Winborn has been in there since nine o'clock."

Richter let out a sigh. "Of course, he is."

"Sorry," Colleen said.

155

Richter wasn't surprised. He knew that the little weasel wouldn't miss an opportunity like this. So be it. Let the second-guessing begin. He knocked on the SAC's door.

"Good luck, hon," Colleen said.

Richter turned and gave her a wink. As he did, the door swung open. It was Olin.

"Jason, thanks for comin' in," Olin said. He gave his young agent a quick pat on the back to bolster him.

Richter entered the room. "Hey, Roy," he said, nodding his head at his group supervisor. He liked Davis, even if he did have a tendency to claim an exaggerated share of the glory from his agents' exploits. In Richter's estimation, Davis shared that trait with every other supervisory agent in the federal government.

"Jason, how's it goin?" Davis asked.

"Good."

"Special Agent." It was the standard greeting from ASAC Winborn, always one to remind others of their relative rank.

"Assistant Special Agent in Charge," Richter said with a hint of regal pomposity. The gesture was not lost on the others in the room. Olin chuckled. Even McCutcheon had to cover his mouth.

Winborn's face reddened. He would not tolerate such insubordination. Richter would be asked some tough questions about the slow progress of his case.

Richter sensed Winborn's enhanced resolve to make things difficult. As much as he'd enjoyed getting in a dig at the little prick, he realized that it might have been a mistake. Richter looked to Olin for assurance.

Olin, catching the concerned look, responded with a smile and dismissive wave of his hand, as if to say, *don't worry about him*. Olin knew the limits of Winborn's influence on the SAC better than anyone in the room, including Winborn.

McCutcheon was secretly enjoying the group's dynamics, but decided it was time to get down to business. "Jason," he said, "have a seat and bring us up to speed on what's happening with

The Nation."

Richter had no more than planted his ass in the chair before Winborn started in.

"Why isn't Special Agent Ward here?" Winborn asked. "How are we supposed to really understand what's happening without talking to him?"

Richter could not suppress an exasperated sigh. "We didn't want to risk having him followed here," Richter said.

"Well, I think he should have been here," Winborn said, undaunted.

"If I recall correctly," Olin noted, "you're not in the chain of command on this one, Clarence."

Winborn's eyes narrowed. Olin knew damn well how he felt about the use of that name.

Davis snorted. Richter turned his head so that Winborn couldn't see the look of sheer delight on his face.

As badly as McCutcheon wanted to laugh, he knew better than to encourage this behavior.

"Okay, let's move this along," McCutcheon said. "Jason, go ahead."

Richter started to brief them, sparing few details. But after a few minutes, Winborn was right back at it.

"I don't hear much for results," Winborn said. "Seems like a lot of resources being expended on something that isn't likely to amount to much. How long do you plan to leave this guy in?" he asked Olin. "Will another month do it, another six, maybe a year?"

Olin ignored the question.

"Well, I wouldn't give this much longer," Winborn continued. "Maybe another month, then get out, cut our losses."

Olin couldn't take it any longer. "Have you ever heard of RICO, racketeering charges, anything like that?" he asked, once again astonished by Winborn's ignorance. "We're trying to take down an organization. These cases take time."

"Apparently," Winborn shot back.

Richter could feel his blood pressure start to rise. What the hell did Winborn want? The man was a fucking idiot. Ward was doing an expert job of laying the groundwork to infiltrate a truly dangerous organization. Richter started to protest, but McCutcheon intervened.

"I don't see any reason to pull the plug on this," McCutcheon announced. He leaned forward, resting his powerful forearms on his desk. McCutcheon looked around the room to make sure that *everyone* was paying close attention. "It's still early, gentlemen...and this *is* a worthy target." McCutcheon turned to Richter. "Jason, why don't you finish what you were trying to tell us." The SAC leaned back in his chair, then added, "We'll try to limit the interruptions." He shot Winborn a stern look.

Richter continued, encouraged by the SAC's support. He emphasized the potential dangerousness of The Nation, mentioning every single thing he could think of that they were, or might be, involved in. Twenty minutes later, he was finished.

McCutcheon nodded his approval. He rose from behind his desk and came around to where Richter sat. The SAC extended his hand as Richter stood to take it. "Keep up the good work, Jason," McCutcheon said. "Let's bring this one to a successful conclusion. And convey my best wishes to Special Agent Ward. Man's got some balls."

"I'll do that, sir," Richter promised. "Thank you."

Olin stood. "Luke, if we're done here, I'd like to walk Jason out."

"Why don't you do that," McCutcheon said. He turned to Davis. "Roy, you can go ahead and take off. Murray and I have some things to discuss."

Richter thought he knew what that meant. The SAC intended to give C. Murray Winborn the benefit of one of his motivational speeches. He hoped so and would pay a thousand bucks to be a fly on the wall to hear it. Olin hustled Richter out of the room. Davis was close behind. When they were out in the hall, Olin gave Richter some friendly advice.

"Don't misunderstand what just happened in there," Olin warned. "McCutcheon is pissed off at Winborn, but he also expects to see some results, the sooner the better. He's getting' some real pressure on this one…and it's comin' from the top."

"And Winborn doesn't get that?" Richter asked.

"Winborn doesn't know about it. And neither do you."

"Understood," Richter noted. He thanked Olin and Davis for their support and left.

As Jason Richter walked out of division headquarters, he felt a pressing sense of urgency.

CHAPTER 42

12:45 a.m., Tuesday, June 30th, Meade's apartment, Ankeny, Iowa.

Neither of them had been able to wait another day. The looks exchanged in class that morning, the flirtations over lunch, while mostly loving in nature, had, at other times, bordered on obscene. Meade had barely been able to force himself to leave for work. But he recalled the warning from Deputy Willis, and the encounter with his foreman, Kroeger. He needed the job at Global and didn't need to compound the situation there with absenteeism. They had promised to meet after work and meet they did.

"Oh God!" Erin gasped. She collapsed on top of Meade, kissing him passionately, repeatedly. "Oh, Carl," she exclaimed between kisses. After a few seconds, she regained enough composure to check on his...status. There was no need to worry.

A few moments later, Meade was once again able to speak. "Wow," he said. It was all he could say. He swallowed hard.

"Are you all right?" Erin giggled.

"I'm more than all right," Meade assured her. "I'm fantastic, although possibly paralyzed."

"We'll see about that later," Erin purred. She slid off him and curled up alongside, gently stroking her fingers down his stomach.

Meade laughed. "You know, I'm already regaining some feeling."

"It's a miracle," Erin whispered as she nibbled at his earlobe. For the next few minutes, little was said. Words weren't needed. They simply held each other, enjoying the moment. Finally, Erin spoke.

"I'm really happy," she said. "I just want you to know that."

For Meade, sweeter words were never spoken.

"Me, too," he replied, wishing that he could find some profound way to express his feelings. He turned and kissed her forehead.

Erin sighed, snuggling in even closer. She closed her eyes.

He stroked her hair. She stirred.

"I'm sorry. I didn't mean to wake you," Meade apologized.

"I wasn't asleep, just lost in thought."

"Oh? I've got a penny around her someplace."

"That's okay. You've earned a freebie." She paused. "That didn't sound very good, did it?"

Meade laughed. "Actually, it sounded pretty good to me."

Erin giggled. "I was just thinking about us, allowing myself a little daydream." She looked at the clock. "If you can use that term at one o'clock in the morning."

"You can use any term you want any time you want," Meade replied.

Erin gave him a squeeze.

"Do you want to tell me about your daydream?" he asked.

She looked up and smiled. "Not right now," she said.

"Okay." He thought he understood.

"It was a nice daydream," she offered.

Meade smiled. He was surprised to find himself wanting to know everything about her. No women had ever made him feel this way.

"Tell me more about your family. What does your father do?" Meade asked.

"Daddy's a plant biologist. He works on new seed strains, that sort of thing."

"Sounds complicated."

"It is. He came in pretty handy when I needed help with my biology homework."

"I'll bet," Meade said. He thought about his own father, who was certainly no help with any homework. Even on those rare occasions when he was around, he was too damn drunk to help with anything.

"And what about Mom?" Meade asked.

"She's a teacher."

"Teacher, huh? Did she inspire your career choice?"

"Absolutely, her and some of my own teachers. Mom loves her job, and the kids love her."

"What does she teach?"

"Social studies...to seventh graders."

"That's a tough age group."

"You'd think so, but she likes it. She has a real knack for communicating with those kids."

"So, I guess she also sparked the interest in history?"

"She did. Well, her and the fact that our family has such a fascinating history in its own right."

"How so?"

"Dad's grandfather emigrated from Denmark. He eventually made his way to Atlanta. That's where he found my great-grandmother. They had eight children. The youngest, my grandfather, had his own bakery."

"Did he teach you to bake?"

"He sure did. I'll prove it to you sometime soon."

"What about your mom's side?"

"Mom's father, my Grandpa Ed, was a Mexican immigrant."

The comment hit Meade like a shot to the gut. There was an involuntary jerk. His body tensed up.

"Are you okay?" Erin asked.

"Yeah, I'm fine. Just had a little spasm in my back," he said, thinking quickly.

"Do you need to get up, stretch?"

"No, no. I'm alright," Meade lied. "You were saying something about your Grandpa Ed?"

"Eduardo, actually," Erin clarified. "Grandpa liked to use the Americanized version. You know, trying to fit in and all. He came here with nothing, worked in the fields, taught himself English. He had almost no formal education but read everything he could get his hands on. He was an amazing man. Grandma certainly saw something special in him. She was a blonde-haired, blue-eyed Texas girl. You can just about imagine how well received it was when folks found out she'd taken up with grandpa."

Meade could imagine. He could imagine very well. "Did your grandpa come here...legally?" he asked.

Erin thought it an odd question. "I think so," she said. "Now that you mention it, I don't recall that it was discussed much."

Meade stared at the ceiling. His head was spinning. He could never have anticipated anything like this. A raging sea of conflicting emotions battled inside him. The teachings of Royce Lundgren swept over him in a wave. Lundgren's powerful words still made sense to him. Now, to learn that *this* woman, a woman he loved so dearly, a woman more special to him than any other, *she* was part Hispanic, part...*spic.* He couldn't believe it. Part of him wanted to recoil from her, throw her out, shower off the filth. But most of him wanted her to stay. Meade suddenly felt that he was drowning, battling for the surface, struggling for air.

"Are you sure you're okay, Carl?" Erin asked, appearing concerned.

He turned to her and tried to force a smile. "I'm fine," he lied.

CHAPTER 43

9:15 p.m., Wednesday, July 1st, headed northwest on U.S. Highway 87, through the outskirts of Victoria, Texas.

Ward headed out of town and back toward Cuero. It had been another night at Bubba's, another ballgame, and another beer-an-inning drinking session with Sullivan and Mueller. Ward reached down and grabbed the roll of fat that was beginning to form at his midsection. Tomorrow morning, he vowed, there would be a six-mile run.

The evening had produced minimal useful intelligence on The Nation. Sullivan was too caught up in the game. As for Mueller, Ward had concluded early on that the younger man was trusted with nothing of importance. Mueller was the type who would be prone to let things slip, dropping some tidbit into a conversation to puff himself up. He had already shown himself to be all talk. Ward was confident that the organization would assign Mueller only the simplest of tasks, such as the clumsy attempts to get a look at Ed Maddox's driver's license every time Ward opened his wallet to pay for a round of beers. It wasn't a surprise. Some vetting had been expected.

Ward finally decided to make it easy for Mueller, leaving the wallet flopped open as he reached forward to pay the bartender. Still, Mueller managed to make it painfully obvious. In reality, very few people would stare out of the corner of their eye for almost ten full seconds while holding a beer bottle to their lips the entire time. It was all Ward could do not to laugh. And, of course, it didn't matter. Any check with the Driver License Division of the Texas Department of Public Safety would show a valid license issued to Edward Michael Maddox of Cuero, Texas. Truth was, it was good to know that they were checking him out. Ward had confidence in his cover story, and the more of it they verified the better off he was.

Ward yawned. It was a steamy night. He cranked the air conditioning and aimed the vents straight at his face. After too may beers and too much sweltering Texas heat, the frigid air brought him back to life. It was a welcome, necessary relief. The last thing he needed was to be stopped for drunk driving or, worse yet, to fall asleep at the wheel. He checked the rearview for any sign of the city police or Texas Highway Patrol. There was nothing, just a dark-colored vehicle. It was too far back to be sure of the make, maybe a Toyota. In any event, it wasn't a patrol unit. He would need to keep a watchful eye for law enforcement. One reality of undercover work was drinking, and that drinking was often accompanied by driving. It was hard to avoid. While he could probably take care of the situation if stopped, it was better not to go there. Management didn't want to hear about it, even if they sometimes understood the need for it.

Despite the late hour, Ward was set to meet Richter and Lehman at their Thomaston rendezvous point. It had been a while since the last debriefing. There was much to discuss, and Richter wanted to fill them in on his meeting at headquarters. Apparently, Olin's counterpart, some asshole named Winborn, had been stirring the pot, complaining about a lack of progress. Ward wasn't concerned. There was always some prick who didn't believe in long-term undercover cops, the stat guy. He was the one who just wanted to gin up the numbers and make Washington happy. Management was full of them. Ward had a different philosophy. In his view, federal agents should be willing to do the heavy lifting or find another job. The real criminal organizations were brought down with patience and fearlessness. He had no time for the bean counters.

Richter had suggested they meet at nine-thirty. Ward looked at his watch, nine-twenty. He should be right on time. He checked the rearview again. There was little traffic. It appeared that the same dark-colored vehicle was still behind him but had dropped back. He decided to keep an eye on it, just in case. The driver's-license incident, joke that it was, had reminded him to be more vigilant.

Minutes later, with Thomaston a few miles ahead, Ward began to slow down, glancing in the mirror as he did. The car was still there. It had closed on him but remained a good hundred yards back. Ward noticed that as his speed dropped the other vehicle appeared to slow down at about the same rate. Maybe it was just too many years doing undercover work, but something didn't seem right. He decided to force the issue. Ward pressed on the brakes. His speed quickly fell to fifty miles an hour, a snail's pace for any highway in the Lone Star State, let alone a divided U.S. Highway.

The car came up fast, its driver apparently surprised by Ward's abrupt deceleration. Ward could see now that it was a Toyota, a sedan. It refused to pass, braking hard to stay twenty yards back. Ward sped up. He grabbed his cell phone and called Richter.

"You almost here?" Richter asked.

"Meeting's off," Ward replied. "Not sure, but I think I'm being followed."

"We're outta here," Richter said. "Call me when you get to Cuero."

"Will do."

Ward checked the rearview as he pulled away. He saw the Toyota's turn signal come on just before it turned off Highway 87 onto a ranch road. Was it a false alarm? Was this guy simply slowing down to make a turn? Ward took a deep breath and tried to relax, but reminded himself, once again, that paranoia was the undercover agent's friend.

* * *

"Damn it," Flagg said out loud. He realized that Maddox might have sensed he was being tailed and hit the brakes as a test. The right move would have been to slide into the left lane and pass as quickly as possible. Who was this guy, Flagg wondered? Did he learn that trick in the Special Forces? Or was it law enforcement training? Was it something else? Hell, maybe he was just braking for an armadillo.

Flagg turned around and headed back toward Highway 87. He would have to be more careful. Wherever this Maddox guy got his training, he was not the typical surveillance target. Horny business executives were the norm these days, and they were not particularly observant. A steady diet of tracking them could cause a man's skills to rust. This was different. He would have to be on his game with his guy.

Flagg turned onto Highway 87 and headed back toward Victoria and his hotel room. The clock on the Toyota's dash said nine-forty. That was early by Flagg's standards. He hoped to get a decent night's sleep for a change. He needed it. Unlike most people, a hotel bed didn't bother him. In his line of work, he'd seen plenty of 'em.

Flagg yawned. Tomorrow he would hit the trail hard. At this point, his preliminary work hadn't yielded much. There was nothing indicating that Edward Maddox was anyone other than who he said he was. A phone call to Odessa Oil, using a simple ruse, confirmed that they did have an Edward Maddox on the payroll. A few minutes of friendly banter with the very helpful Cindy also established that Ed had recently transferred in from Alaska. So far, Maddox's story checked out. But then again, it was still early.

CHAPTER 44

8:45 p.m., Thursday, July 2nd, Global Harvester's Des Moines Works, Ankeny, Iowa.

The sparks stopped. Meade lifted his welding hood, leaned back and turned off the gas to his torch. A quick inspection showed that it was another good bead. It needed to be. The foreman, Kroeger, had been keeping a close eye on him for the last week and a half. Kroeger walked by constantly, studying every weld. To Meade, it seemed that the foreman's once pleasant demeanor had now been replaced with something approaching hostility. There were no smiles, no acknowledgment of a job well done. The look was always critical. It was as if Kroeger were waiting for something to go wrong. Meade knew that it wasn't just his imagination. He remembered the warning from Deputy Willis. He was under heightened scrutiny.

Meade flipped his hood down, turned on the gas flow and ignited his torch. All he could do was what he had been doing all along, a good job. If that wasn't enough, if Kroeger was determined to get rid of him, so be it. In the meantime, Meade wasn't going to give him a legitimate excuse.

As he worked, Meade thought about Royce Lundgren, and about what Lundgren would say if he knew Meade were dating a woman who was part Hispanic. To Lundgren, if they were part *spic*, they were all *spic*. Meade was feeling less comfortable with the term, but he still embraced Lundgren's ideology. The speeches came back to him, powerful, compelling. He could hear the man's voice, feel the emotion, the response from the listeners. Lundgren played on the fears and prejudices of his followers, that was true. But no one could doubt the man's sincerity. Lundgren was filled with a real passion, and a real hate. He was extraordinarily dangerous—at least that's what the ATF would call him—precisely because his charisma and ability to manipulate were combined with a strong belief in his own words. Lundgren could also spot the followers of the world a mile away. They were drawn to him because he gave them a sense of identity, an ideology, a cause to cling to that gave their lives some meaning. Of course, not all of The Nation's members fell into that category. Many were true believers, hardcore racists. They shared Lundgren's beliefs wholeheartedly and came to him with many of those beliefs already in place. Lundgren provided the leadership. Meade sometimes wondered which category he fell into, believer or follower.

The sound of the break horn startled Meade back to reality. He flipped up his hood and checked his work. It appeared that his distracted train of thought had not affected the quality of the weld. Meade quickly stowed his gear and headed for the lunchroom. The July heat had found its way into the plant. Combined with the always-hot job of welding, it left him incredibly thirsty. When he entered the break room, he was happy to see that he'd beaten most of the crowd. The lines at the vending machines were still short. Meade dropped in his change and hit the button for a cola. The bottle clunked its way down the chute and appeared before him. Meade grabbed it and held it to his forehead. Between the welding hood and the heat in the plant, his head felt like it was two hundred degrees. The coolness of the container provided some relief. He unscrewed the cap and took a drink. Meade could feel the cold liquid as it traveled through his overheated core. He let out a sigh.

As he turned away from the vending machine, Meade noticed Jose, the man who had bought him a soda the week before, and possibly saved him from a fight. Jose was seated by himself. He appeared to be reading a paperback of some sort. Meade decided that he would make a gesture, as much due to the fact that Kroeger might be watching as anything else. Maybe the foreman would get off his back. Meade slipped a few coins into the machine and hit the button for another cola. He picked up the drink and headed toward Jose's table.

"How's it goin'?" Meade asked, mostly indifferent.

Jose looked up. He was startled to see who was doing the asking.

"Okay, I guess," he replied.

"Thought I'd return the favor," Meade said, offering the cola.

Jose shook his head. "You don't owe me anything." Recalling the man's reaction from the week before, Jose was unsure whether to say thanks or be offended. Was this guy being sincere, or was it simply a matter of not wanting to be in debt to a Hispanic?

Meade sensed the reason for the attitude. He persisted.

"Just take it. Look, I'm sorry about last week and, you know, not being more...grateful. I just wanted to return the gesture." Meade couldn't believe the words were coming out of his mouth. He looked around to see if Kroeger was in the room, wanting to make sure that he got some credit for this.

Jose stared at him for a moment, and then nodded. He took the drink. "Have a seat," he said, gesturing toward a chair.

Meade sat, reluctantly. He didn't want to take this too far. "Name's Carl Ramsey," he said.

"Jose Morales, actually Morales-Alvarez," Jose offered.

"What are you reading?" Meade asked.

Morales chuckled. "*Don Quixote*. Odd choice, huh?"

"Haven't read it," Meade admitted. "All I know is something about tilting at windmills."

"Yeah, that's right." Morales studied the man seated across from him for a moment. "So, you just started here, what, a few weeks ago?" he asked.

"June first," Meade replied, a quizzical look on his face.

"We keep track of the new guys," Morales said, noticing the look. "No offense."

"I suppose I get that," Meade replied. He understood quite well.

"Where you from, Carl?"

"Dallas," Meade lied. He wouldn't offer much more, afraid that he might not keep his story straight. Besides, he didn't want a friend.

"Grow up there?" Morales asked.

"Yep," Meade lied again. He provided a few more details from his fictional background, more as a way to fend off further inquiry than anything else.

"How 'bout you?" Meade asked, eager to change the subject. "Where ya from?"

Morales knew he shouldn't but couldn't resist. "What, I don't look like a native Iowan?"

Meade couldn't help it, he smirked.

"Sorry, couldn't help myself," Morales said.

Meade had to admit, it was an effective icebreaker. This Morales was a bit of a character.

"My family came from Mexico," Morales said. "My parents worked in the vineyards, picking grapes. I was born in California. I didn't want to end up in the fields, so I learned a trade. Eventually, I ended up in L.A., got married, had kids."

"How'd you end up in Iowa?"

"I didn't want my kids to grow up around the gangs of East L.A. I saw one of Global's ads looking for welders and applied."

"Quite a change from L.A., I suppose?"

"It is. Been here five years now. We like it."

Meade nodded, wondering if he might ever learn to like it here.

CHAPTER 45

3:45 p.m., Friday, July 3rd, Wichita, Kansas.

At seventeen, Colin Thomas was already filled with a rabid hate. It was homegrown, learned from his father. Harold Thomas had introduced his son to the great man's teachings, directed him to the group's website. The older man had become fed up with the wetbacks. They were ruining the city, stealing white jobs, overwhelming the schools and hospital emergency rooms. He couldn't stand the sight of them.

The words of Royce Lundgren had shown them the light, the way to national salvation. Harold Thomas had shared Lundgren's teachings with Colin. It had been a source of bonding for the two. Colin ached for his father's approval. In the past, any sign of it had been rare. But Colin now felt that it was within reach. Their shared hatred of the brown horde had brought them together. Colin was certain that what was about to happen would make his father truly proud. He was sure of it.

Colin was the leader of the small band. The others were Evan Boyd, seventeen, and Travis Reynolds, sixteen. Colin wasn't sure about Travis, whether he had the stomach for it. He said the right things, but Colin suspected that Travis was just trying to fit in and didn't think that they'd really go through with it. He was about to learn otherwise.

Miguel Sanchez appeared at the other end of the seldom-used alley. It was his usual route home from school. The boys had tracked his movements for days. He always walked by himself, always followed the same path...an easy target. Now, the time had come. He would pay for his actions.

Travis and Evan crouched behind the Dumpster, waiting for the right moment to attack. Colin was hidden at the opposite end of the alley. He would block that avenue of escape, and then join in the beating. Colin saw himself as the leader of a military squadron. He had ordered his soldiers to deliver a message that Sanchez would remember for the rest of his life, a message that he could take back to the rest of *them*.

Colin saw Evan move, too soon. Travis was supposed to hold him back until Sanchez was even with the Dumpster. Those were their orders. But it was no use. Colin knew that Evan seethed with hatred for this *spic*. The *beaner* had stolen his girlfriend. Evan wanted blood and was determined to get it.

"Yo, *spic*!" Evan said as he stepped from behind the Dumpster. "Nobody takes my bitch and gets away with it." He slapped the Louisville Slugger into the palm of his hand as he moved toward Sanchez.

Miguel dropped his backpack and turned to run. He saw Colin blocking his way, carrying a piece of lead pipe. There was no way out. "Holy Mother," he said, crossing himself.

"That's right, say your prayers, *spic*," Evan growled as he swung the bat, not waiting for Miguel to turn and face him.

The blow landed with a sickening thud in the middle of Miguel's back. He dropped to his knees, arms clenched to his sides in a spasm of pain, unable to protect himself from the onslaught to follow.

Colin moved quickly. He swung the pipe with frightening accuracy, catching Miguel under the chin. The blow shattered Miguel's jaw. The boy fell to his side, spitting blood, bone fragments and bits of teeth from what remained of his mouth. His eyes drooped closed.

As Miguel lay motionless, Evan and Colin began kicking him. It was relentless, never-ending. They had worn their cowboy boots today for this very purpose. Ribs cracked as the boots made contact, but it was stomps to the head that brought on the final darkness. There was a visible shudder, a final gasp for air, then a long exhalation as Miguel let out his final breath. It was as if his soul had escaped its tortured confines.

Colin watched Travis. He had joined the others, aiming some halfhearted kicks in the direction of Miguel's legs. But now he seemed panicked. He pushed the others away and dropped down beside Miguel's lifeless body. Travis felt for a pulse. There was none. He began to cry.

"He's dead!" Travis shrieked. "Oh my God, he's dead!"

Colin stepped back, catching his breath, the magnitude of what they had done now sobering him as the homicidal craze began to dissipate.

"Holy shit!" Colin exclaimed, becoming frightened. He had never meant for this to happen. He looked at Evan, who met his stare.

"I didn't…" Evan began. "I mean, I only wanted to…"

"We need to get out of here…now!" Colin said.

"What about the body?" Travis asked.

"Leave it," Colin ordered. He pulled Travis to his feet. "It's too late for him. Let's go."

Colin pushed Travis ahead of him. The boys ran for blocks before stopping in a culvert that they often used as a meeting place. When they did, Colin grabbed Travis by the arm and yanked him around. He could see it in the younger boy's eyes—Travis was considering calling the police. Colin knew what Travis would tell them, that the fatal blows had come from the other two, and that he really didn't want to take part. A change came over Colin. It was the animal's impulse for self-preservation taking control. An icy coldness swept across his steely blue eyes. He glared at the sixteen-year-old tagalong.

"I should have known better than to let you come with us," he said.

Travis began to back away, only to bump into Evan who had

moved up behind him.

"If you breathe a word of this to anyone," Colin said menacingly, "you're dead."

"Why take the chance?" Evan asked.

Travis could feel Evan's hot breath on the back of his neck. "Please don't," he begged. He began to whimper, and then cry.

Colin stared at the sniveling specimen before him. Travis was a very weak link. He and Evan still had their weapons, already stained with the blood of Miguel Sanchez. What would a little more blood matter at this point?

Travis fell to his knees. "I won't tell anyone. I promise," he sobbed. "Please don't kill me." He clutched at Colin's leg.

Colin kicked the arm aside. Using the heel of his boot, he shoved Travis backward into a filthy puddle. At that point, it could have easily gone either way. But the sight of the pathetic punk, wallowing in the muck, begging for his life, rekindled some element of humanity. Colin made his choice.

"He won't talk," Colin said, more to himself than to Evan.

Evan shook his head. "I hope you're right," he said doubtfully. "I hope you're right."

CHAPTER 46

10:15 a.m., Saturday, July 4th, Compound One, headquarters of The Nation, outside Yoakum, Texas.

Ward and Ben Sullivan walked into one the metal barns that sat behind Lundgren's residence. Sullivan had insisted that they come early. He didn't explain why, saying only that it would be clear when they got there. On the drive over, he'd explained that Independence Day held special significance for members of The Nation. They saw themselves as Americans who were truly faithful to the vision of the Founding Fathers, a vision that no longer mattered to the country's so-called leaders. Sullivan promised that the barbecue that afternoon would dwarf the one they had attended two weeks earlier, and that the fireworks that followed would be as good as any Ed Maddox had ever seen. Ward didn't mention that he'd twice seen the Fourth of July fireworks display at the National Mall in D.C., and strongly suspected that Royce Lundgren's production wouldn't compare.

As they entered, Ward looked around; he estimated there were fifty to sixty men already seated, with another thirty or so milling about.

"What is this?" he asked Sullivan.

"A little pre-barbecue business meeting," Sullivan replied. "Not everybody gets invited to this. You should consider yerself fortunate. This here's the group's leaders, present and future."

"So, why am I here?"

"I asked 'em if I could bring you along," Sullivan replied.

"Pretty much everybody thought it was a good idea."

"*Pretty much* everybody?" Ward inquired.

Sullivan smiled and tilted his head. "Mighta been one or two what thought it was a bit early," he said. "But I took care of that."

"Should I ask?"

"Nope."

As Ward pondered the identity of the *one or two*, Charlie Kirklin approached. Two men accompanied him.

"How you boys doin'?" Kirklin asked.

"Just fine," Sullivan replied.

"Wanted to introduce a couple a fellers to Ed, here," Kirklin said. "Ed Maddox, this here's Eric Brandt."

The men shook. Ward felt Brandt's vice-like grip, which lasted a bit too long. It was clear that Brandt was one of those men who viewed shaking hands as some sort of contest of wills.

"And this is Warren Graves," Kirklin continued.

Graves extended his hand.

"Ed's the fella I was tellin' you about," Kirklin said, as proud as if he were introducing a favored son. "A real patriot, this one," he added, giving Maddox a quick pat on the back. "Not to mention, a helluva good shot."

Ward smiled modestly and briefly lowered his head, both to feign submissiveness and to help avoid questions.

"Eric is our—" Kirklin began.

Brandt shot him a look of warning.

"—our...*training* coordinator," Kirklin finished.

Ward noted the exchange. He studied Brandt, a hard-looking man with a certain military bearing. Ward guessed him a probable leader of the group's rumored vigilante efforts.

"Charlie tells us you've got a Special Forces background," Brandt noted.

"True statement," Ward replied, without elaboration.

"I'd like to hear more about that sometime," Brandt said.

"To the extent I can talk about it, sure," Ward offered. "Be happy to."

"And Warren here is our public relations guy," Kirklin continued. "Damn good at it, too. He's gonna address the group this morning. Isn't that right, Warren?"

"That's correct," Graves answered. "I have a few things that I'd like to cover. Glad you could join us, Mr. Maddox. I hope you enjoy yourself."

"I'm sure I will," Ward said. He could see that Graves worked to project an academic image. It was a joke. As if any serious scholar would embrace the views of these racists. He imagined that the PR man was salivating over the propaganda value of having a former Green Beret in the organization. The problem with that was if it got any real publicity, someone, somewhere, might contact them and say, *Green Beret my ass.*

"Warren, you about ready?" asked a round-faced man who approached the group.

"Yes, Harold. Whenever you are," Graves replied.

Ward picked up on a note of annoyance in Graves' voice.

"Who's this?" the round-faced man asked, nodding at Ward.

Kirklin spoke up. "This is Ed Maddox, Harold. You remember, I mentioned him to you a while back."

"Oh, right, right," Harold said, showing no sign of recollection.

"Ed, this is Harold Doyle," Kirklin offered, continuing the introduction. "Harold's our...second-in-command," he added, as if struggling for the right term.

Ward noticed what appeared to be a brief flash of disgust sweep across Brandt's face. Kirklin, on the other hand, simply appeared submissive in Doyle's presence.

"Nice to meet you," Ward said, extending his hand.

Doyle shook hands quickly.

"Harold is Royce's cousin," Graves added gratuitously.

Ward got the point, although he was not certain that Doyle did.

For a moment, no one said anything.

"Well then, let's get started," Doyle insisted.

Graves moved toward a small podium as the men found seats among the hundred or so folding chairs that had been set up for the occasion. As he sat, Ward noticed Jim eyeing him from across the room. Ward nodded his greeting. Jim did the same, slowly, deliberately.

Graves began. He was good. But in Ward's estimation, he was not a speaker of Lundgren's caliber. It didn't matter. These men didn't need to hear any propaganda. They were already highly motivated. What they wanted were specific ideas on how to better carry out the mission. Graves was happy to oblige. He provided the particulars, and the direct incitement to action that never seemed to come from Lundgren's mouth.

"There are a number of things our people can do," Graves announced. "We can harass the illegals at places they are known to frequent, such as check cashing and money transfer establishments. We can take measures that will make it difficult for their children to attend school. For example, we can, and should, train our children to harass and intimidate them. This should occur not just at our schools, but also at other public facilities such as public parks and municipal swimming pools."

As much as these ideas horrified Ward, now they were getting somewhere. Evidence of this type of organizational planning would help build the government's case against The Nation.

Graves continued. "I also encourage you, if you haven't done so recently, to visit our website. It has been updated and greatly improved. After seeing it, I think you will agree that it can be a tremendous educational tool. Please encourage as many people as possible to view our site, particularly the young and others who have not yet seen the light."

Ward made a mental note to check out the group's webpage as soon as he got home.

Ten minutes later, Graves' speech was over. It was followed by updates from the local chapter leaders on various events in their respective areas, including measures taken to implement what was obviously an already well-established campaign of harassment. Ward hoped that he could remember it all until his planned debriefing with Richter and Lehman. It would clearly be too risky to try to jot down some notes.

When the speeches were over, Sullivan, Kirklin and Ward walked over to where Graves was discussing the website with Doyle. From what he overheard, it was obvious to Ward that Doyle fancied himself as tech-savvy.

"Great speech, Warren," Sullivan said, shaking Graves' hand.

"Absolutely," Kirklin agreed. "What did you think, Ed?"

"I thought you had some fantastic ideas," Ward said. He thought for a moment, and then decided to take a chance. "About the website, I was wondering..."

"Yes?" Graves asked.

"I mean, not having seen it, I was just wondering if you were linked in with other...like-minded groups, you know, as a way to possibly increase membership, and get the message out."

There was a brief silence. Ward wondered if he had gone too far.

Graves appeared contemplative as he stood quiet, running his hand over his mouth. After a moment, he began to nod his head. "We haven't done that, but I think it's an idea with some merit."

Sullivan and Kirklin beamed, thrilled with their protégé's contribution to the cause.

"I think it's a damn good idea," Doyle threw in. "Don't know why we haven't already done it."

Ward breathed a sigh of relief. His gamble had paid off. He realized that this could create a real opening, particularly with Doyle.

"We'll come up with a list of contacts," Graves said to Doyle. "I'll start working on it tomorrow."

"Good idea," Doyle said. "I'll mention it to Royce."

Ward wondered if most of Doyle's comments didn't end with those same words. Judging from the reaction of the others, that was likely the case. The beginnings of a plan began to hatch in

Ward's mind. He decided to push his luck.

"I could help with setting up the links," Ward offered. "I have some experience with website construction." Fortunately, it was one of his areas of expertise.

"I'm sure that Warren would appreciate your help," Doyle announced.

"Of course," Graves agreed, realizing that he had little choice.

By now, Sullivan and Kirklin were so proud that they could bust, convinced that Ed Maddox was the single greatest recruit in The Nation's history.

As the day progressed, Ward had several opportunities to visit with members of The Nation's leadership. Most important among them was Doyle, who he had greatly impressed. Ward assessed Doyle as a weak link, insecure, and highly susceptible to flattery. By the end of the afternoon, he had secured an invitation to sit with Doyle and Lundgren during the fireworks display. Ed Maddox gladly accepted.

Ward was right. The fireworks were not nearly as impressive as those he had seen at the National Mall. But, he had to admit, they were pretty damn good. Of course, the quality of the fireworks display was of no concern. What was important was that he had now gained an opening to the inner circle. Seated to his left was Harold Doyle, The Nation's second-in-command. To Doyle's left was Royce Lundgren, the leader. So far, there had been little opportunity to speak with Lundgren, other than a brief exchange of pleasantries, but that would come. Doyle was his ticket. Ward had listened with great interest as Doyle told Lundgren of the plan for the webpage links, describing the idea as if it were his own, with Ed Maddox merely providing the technical know-how. That was fine, if that's how Doyle wanted to play it. Ward didn't need any credit. What he did need was to make himself indispensable to Doyle, and indispensable to The Nation.

CHAPTER 47

12:15 a.m., Sunday, July 5th, Erin Larson's apartment, Des Moines, Iowa.

For Meade, it had been the most enjoyable Fourth of July of his life, even better than any at Lundgren's compound. After catching a ballgame and the fireworks that followed, they had come back to Erin's apartment to make love. As he held the now sleeping Erin in his arms, stroking her hair, Meade was still astonished that this beautiful creature loved *him*. It defied reason. But then, he thought, that's what love does. It defies reason.

Meade stared at his sleeping beauty. Despite her heritage, he still found himself fantasizing about a future with her, the children they might have. He couldn't help it. Besides, she was *mostly* white…three-quarters, anyway. He dreamed of their family, and lives filled with love and happiness, something he had never experienced as a boy. Meade thought of his brothers and sisters. What were they doing now? Were they okay? It made his heart ache to know that he would never be able to speak with them. Did they have any idea what had happened to him? Were they able to piece it together? If any one of them could, it would be his oldest sister, Gretchen. She was savvy beyond her years, streetwise, tougher than a nineteen-year-old should ever have to be. Meade flirted with the notion of trying to get a message to her but decided against it. The Nation would be watching her, watching them, anticipating such a move. Any attempt at contact could put them all at risk. It was all too painful to think about. He returned his thoughts to Erin.

As he held her, breathed in her scent, felt the warmth of her skin on his, Meade felt blessed. But he also felt cursed. He longed for something real, something wholesome on which to build a future, their future. It troubled him greatly that their relationship was founded on a lie. How could it last? Maybe Deputy Willis was right. It wasn't fair to her. He was just being selfish. Besides, there would be questions, questions he wouldn't be able to answer. What if they did get married? What if she wanted a big wedding? How could he explain no guests on the groom's side? For that matter, how could he explain never meeting his family, not one of them? It was impossible. Love had simply blinded him to the reality of it all. He would have to tell her and live with the consequences.

Just then, Erin began to stir. Her eyes fluttered open. She smiled up at him.

"Hi there," she said.

"Have a nice nap?" Meade asked as he kissed her forehead.

"I guess the experience was so intense that I passed out," she cooed.

Meade laughed. "Whatever." He stared at her for a moment, saying nothing. His look grew solemn.

"Is there something wrong?" Erin asked, looking concerned.

Meade took a deep breath. It was killing him, but he was resolved to do this. He *had* to do this. The best way was to just begin.

"There is something that we need to talk about," he began.

Erin propped herself up on one elbow. She looked scared.

"It's about us," Meade said. He looked away from her.

"Oh my God, are you breaking up with me?" Erin asked plaintively. Her eyes welled. A tear rolled down her cheek.

"Oh, no," Meade replied, surprised by her reaction. He reached out for her. "Oh, honey. That's the last thing I would ever want." They embraced. Meade felt guilty at the reassurance, even pleasure, he drew from her emotional response.

Relieved, Erin once again propped herself up. "So, what was it you wanted to talk about?" she asked, stroking his chest.

Meade rolled over to face her. "It's just that…" He paused. "It's just that…I'm not who I seem to be."

"What do you mean?" Erin asked, looking perplexed.

Meade let out an audible breath. He felt sick. His heart was pounding. "Erin, my name is not Carl Ramsey."

"What the hell are you talking about?" she asked, now sitting upright, the bed sheet wrapped around her.

"My name is Jacob Meade." There, he'd said it. Now, he could tell her the truth.

"You better explain yourself," Erin said, backing away just slightly.

"I'm in the Witness Protection Program," Meade began.

"You're in the what? What do you mean you're in the Witness Protection Program?" She backed up even further, her look one of disbelief. "Maybe you should leave."

"Please," Meade begged her, "let me explain."

Erin looked down at the bed, unable to meet his gaze. "Go ahead," she finally said.

Meade told her everything, starting with his childhood in Houston, his abusive father and depressed mother, their alcoholism. He told her about his brothers and sisters, his love for them, how much he missed them. Then, he told her about Royce Lundgren and The Nation. As difficult as it was, he explained their beliefs, and how he had shared those beliefs. He made it sound as if they were a thing of the past, though he knew those beliefs still lingered. Finally, he told her of his arrest and his agreement to cooperate. Throughout it all, Meade emphasized again and again that his love for her had been, and still was, very real.

Erin's eyes filled with tears. He tried to hold her, but she twisted away, tucking herself into a ball. She shook her head almost wildly, like a child refusing to hear what was said.

Meade could see that he was losing her. He began to choke up. "You...you saved me," he said. "I want you to know that. And, whatever happens, I'll always love you." He lowered his head and began to cry.

Erin looked up, her expression now tight, angry. "I think you should leave," she said. Her eyes dropped to the bed where they had just made love.

"Please, Erin," he pleaded. "I love you more than I've ever loved anyone."

"Please, Carl...or Jacob...whatever your name is. Just go."

Not another word was spoken. Meade stood and gathered his clothes. He felt so weak that it was a struggle to get dressed. Walking toward the door, he stopped, and then looked back. She hadn't moved, her gaze still fixed on the bed, her expression one of bitter disappointment. Meade opened his mouth to speak but caught himself. There was nothing to say, not now. He turned back toward the door, the image of her seared into his memory.

As he pulled the apartment door closed behind him and descended the stairs, Carl Meade vowed that someday, somehow, he would win her back.

CHAPTER 48

6:50 a.m., Tuesday, July 7th, Cuero, Texas.

Ron Flagg sat patiently, eyeing the residence of Edward Maddox in his rearview mirror. It was better to be pointed away from the house. It drew less attention. Besides, from his vantage point, he could easily see Maddox back out of the driveway and head for work, work that may or may not be at Odessa Oil.

A check with his source in the Driver License Division of the Texas Department of Public Safety confirmed what Flagg had expected; the license number did come back to an Edward Michael Maddox of Cuero, Texas. No surprise there. He wouldn't expect Maddox to be that sloppy. The license had been issued in May. According to records, Maddox had relinquished an Alaska driver's license at the time. Flagg had to admit, if the guy was laying a cover, he was damn good at it.

The address noted on the driver's license was a small house, a brick ranch with two bedrooms and an unattached garage. A quick check of property records gave Flagg the layout. The owner was listed as a Paul Menke. With a few phone calls, Flagg was able to learn that Menke was a local landlord with several properties. Flagg made a mental note to check with the company, Menke Rentals, to confirm that the lease was held by Maddox or Odessa Oil, and that the payments came from one or the other. A different source would raise a red flag. But how to approach the rental company? Flagg pondered the question for a moment. An idea occurred to him. He would claim to be a state tax official. It had worked before. If he got too many questions, he would ask about the income reporting practices of Menke Rentals. Yeah, that should do it, he thought.

Flagg wondered if Maddox had chosen a house over an apartment to improve his cover. It made sense. Tenants in an apartment building could see things, hear things, things that couldn't be heard from a neighboring house. He had received some of his best information from nosey neighbors in nearby apartments.

Flagg looked at his watch. It was almost seven. He had already been there for over half an hour, the assumption being that an oil man, if that's what Maddox was, would get to work early. A light was on in one of the bedrooms when Flagg arrived. The kitchen light joined it fifteen minutes later. It wouldn't be long, and they would be on their way.

The neighborhood was stirring. Flagg could see signs of life in the other homes, parents getting ready for work, children preparing for school. He hoped that Maddox would hit the road soon, before the neighbors started to wonder about the unfamiliar Dodge Charger. The man slunk down in the driver's seat. He wanted to talk to some of them later, try to find out what, if anything, they knew about Ed Maddox. Where was he from? How long had he been living in Cuero? Did he keep regular hours? It was always difficult to do without word getting back to the target. It took a clever ruse, and a certain type of nonchalance. He suspected that, in this case, the neighbors would know nothing. Perhaps a few had said hello, maybe talked about what type of work they did, possibly the weather. But if Maddox was not the man he claimed to be, there would be few shared details.

The Charger was a rental. Flagg liked the ride. It had muscle. A car with serious horsepower was always useful during a tail. After the close call of the other night, changing vehicles was a given, as was waiting a few days before attempting to follow Maddox again. Flagg was still pissed off at himself over the screw-up.

Just then, a flicker of movement caught Flagg's eye. He

stared into the rearview. Maddox was moving, walking toward the garage. Flagg slid further down in his seat. He had set up the right-side mirror so that he could see the garage from that position. He grabbed a newspaper and pretended to read. It wasn't the best means of deflecting attention, but at least it would cover his face in case Maddox was inclined to look.

Within minutes, an SUV backed out of the driveway and headed up the street. Flagg glanced at the vehicle out of the corner of his eye as it slowly drove past his position. It didn't appear that Maddox had noticed him. If he did, he didn't show it.

When the SUV was almost a hundred yards ahead, Flagg started his car and put it in gear. They moved quickly through the small town of Cuero and onto Highway 87, heading southeast, toward Victoria. Traffic was light, but adequate to provide cover. Flagg stayed well back, determined to remain unseen, keeping at least two, preferably three, vehicles between himself and Maddox at all times. The target was moving fast, weaving in and out of the traffic in the two southbound lanes. Flagg pushed to keep up, glad that he had opted for the added horsepower of the Charger.

About twenty minutes later they were in Victoria. The traffic became much heavier. Flagg had little trouble concealing his vehicle. They drove south along the western edge of the city until Highway 87 intersected Highway 59. There, Maddox turned, taking 59 across town. Flagg was familiar with the route. Highway 59 headed northeast, all the way to Houston.

On the east side of town, close to the airport, Maddox turned into a gated facility. A chain-link fence lined the perimeter of the approximately ten-acre site. As Flagg slowly approached, he could see two large metal buildings and a smaller office structure. There were various pieces of heavy machinery scattered about. As he drew closer, Flagg recognized much of the equipment as associated with the oil business. A sign on the gate said, Odessa Oil, Victoria Branch Office.

"Well, son of a bitch," Flagg muttered.

* * *

Ward sat for a moment, leaving the SUV running. It was standard operating procedure for him to drive to work as part of his cover, usually at a high rate of speed and with some evasive maneuvers. It wasn't so much to avoid being followed as it was to see if he was being followed. When he had to leave his supposed workplace, at least for anything related to his real job, he sometimes used a different SUV, one stored on-site. There was such a vehicle parked in the building directly in front of him.

Ward looked in the rearview mirror. He reached for his cell phone. The number he punched in had long since been committed to memory.

"Richter," answered the voice on the other end.

"I was followed again," Ward said. "Take down this tag number, would ya?"

"Let me get a pen."

Ward could hear rummaging through a drawer.

"Okay, shoot."

Ward provided the license plate number, as well as the make and model of the vehicle.

"Think it's a rental?" Richter asked.

"Probably," Ward replied. "But, who knows, maybe the guy was dumb enough to use his real name on the application."

Richter didn't hesitate. "Not if he's any good."

CHAPTER 49

9:30 a.m., Tuesday, July 7th, The United States Attorney's Office, Southern District of Texas, Victoria Branch Office.

Assistant United States Attorney Abraham "Abe" Steele poured himself a cup of bad coffee and headed for the conference room. Once again, it was trial prep time for the veteran prosecutor. And this was a big one, the United States of America versus Troy Pierce and Willard Simmons, two significant members of The Nation. Steele had been watching this organization for years and now had his first solid shot at a couple of its members. Both men faced a combination of gun and dope charges that, if convicted, would effectively yield life in prison. In fact, Pierce had a prior felony drug conviction that made his situation that much worse. But despite Steele's repeated efforts to flip them, and the almost certain sentencing reduction that would follow, neither man would cooperate against The Nation or its leader, Royce Lundgren. It wasn't simply fear of retaliation, which Steele knew was warranted. It was more than that. These men were true believers, refusing to give up the faith even while staring down the barrel of a possible lifetime in federal prison. With all the evidence confronting them, neither man would even help himself out by pleading guilty. It was true that a reduction for acceptance of responsibility wouldn't do either one of them a helluva lot of good, not with their respective starting points on the sentencing grid, but it would help.

Steele walked into the conference room. His troops were waiting, special agents Jason Richter, Bill Lehman and a particularly gnarly undercover operative by the name of Joe Slater. Steele had worked with Richter and Lehman before. They were both good men. Slater, he knew only by reputation, a reputation approaching the status of legend.

"Jason, good to see ya," Steele said as he walked toward the young agent.

"You, too, Abe," Richter replied. He shook the prosecutor's hand firmly, and with respect. Abe Steele was highly regarded by the ATF. He was one of the good ones, a prosecutor who backed up his agents. Steele was a man who wouldn't let you down.

"Bill, thanks for comin'," Steel continued. "It's been a while."

"Yes it has," Lehman agreed, jumping to his feet to shake Steele's hand.

"And you must be the legendary Joe Slater," Steele said with a grin. "Pleasure to meet you, Joe. I've heard a lot about you."

"And it's still a pleasure?" Lehman joked.

They shared a laugh.

"Can I get you boys some coffee?" Steele asked. He always tried to be a good host to the agents, at least those he liked.

"I'm good," Slater replied.

"Me, too," Lehman added.

Richter raised a to-go cup. "Brought my own...the good stuff. No offense, Abe. I've had your brew before."

"None taken," Steele said. He took a sip from his cup. He grimaced. There was no disagreeing with Richter's logic.

Steele placed the Pierce/Simmons case file on the conference table, took a seat and pulled out a yellow legal pad. A dozen pages were already filled with his scribbled notes and calculations.

"Before we get started, Jason, what's the latest with your undercover op into The Nation?"

"Things are goin' well," Richter answered. "We recently had a major break, what looks to be an opening into the inner circle." Richter described the events of July Fourth and the undercover agents befriending of Harold Doyle.

Steele nodded. "Sounds promising."

"Our man thinks Doyle is a good route in," Richter empha-sized, "very insecure, susceptible to flattery."

"That's the guy you want," Slater agreed.

"Why won't Pierce or Simmons cooperate?" Lehman asked. "Is it just the retaliation thing or what? I mean, these guys are lookin' at a lotta time."

Steele shook his head. "These guys are as hard to crack as anybody I've encountered in my eighteen years of doin' this. I'm sure they figure they'll get whacked if they talk. But it also sounds like they really buy into this shit." Steele was disappointed. They all were. Everyone had hoped that the two defendants would cooperate. It would have been a huge step forward in disman-tling the organization.

"That's fucked up," Lehman said.

"What are their attorneys tellin' you?" Richter asked.

Steele grunted. "Simmons has Herb Stone. He's been around forever. Stone can read the writing on the wall as well as anybody. He knows he's gonna lose, and he wants his guy to cooperate, but Simmons won't budge. Stone has no client control. So, there's no way he's gonna get his guy over the hump."

Richter groaned. Steele caught it. He understood the frustra-tion. Usually, these mopes would come around in the end. But on this one, it wasn't gonna happen. Full-scale trial prep often meant dropping everything else, and they were all spread pretty thin. But it was part of the deal when you signed on, prosecutor or agent, and everybody knew it. Now it was go time. The oppo-sition would see only strength from their camp. That's the way it had to be.

"What about Pierce?" Richter asked hopefully. "Any chance he might fold, agree to testify against Simmons? That might do it."

Steele shook his head. "Sorry, man. If anything, Pierce is a harder case than Simmons. Pierce has an attorney by the name of Kent Payne. I've never heard of the guy, so I asked around. Apparently, he's represented some of The Nation's members in the past. It's been mostly minor stuff, misdemeanors, but it looks like he might be the group's mouthpiece...or the closest thing to it. There is no way in hell that Pierce is gonna come around."

"Shit," Lehman muttered.

Slater chuckled. "Well, boys, looks like it's full speed ahead."

"So be it," Lehman said.

"Game on," Richter threw in. "If we're gonna go, we're gonna go. No more fuckin' around with these two assholes."

"That's the spirit," Steele said. "Hell, this is a great case. There is no freakin' way these two walk. We've got Joe's eyewitness testimony, recordings, not to mention guns and dope in hand. It's a lot more evidence than I usually have."

"About those recordings," Richter said hesitantly. "Have you listened to the tapes, Abe?"

Steele's eyes closed. He had been down this road before. "What's the problem?" he asked as calmly as he could.

"Quality's not too good," Richter answered sheepishly.

Steele rubbed his hand over his face. "How does this keep happening?" he asked, annoyed. "Why can't ATF invest in some halfway decent fucking..." Steele stopped himself. "How bad is it?" he asked

"You can make it out," Richter said, "sort of."

"Okay, we'll make do." Steele said. It would take something more than subpar recordings to save Pierce and Simmons.

"What about Meade?" Slater asked. "You bringin' him back?"

"I've already contacted the Marshals Service," Steele said. "You've gotta give them some considerable heads up, especially when your witness is in WITSEC. What I haven't decided," he added, "is whether I'll put him on the stand. We would have to disclose to defense counsel everything that we've done for him... minus the specifics of the program, of course. Testifying would increase the threat to him. But that was the deal he made."

"That's right," Lehman agreed.

"If there's a problem with the tapes," Steele continued, thinking out loud, "I might want to use him. I don't know." He paused. "Joe, from the reports, it looks like he heard some admissions from Pierce and Simmons that you can't testify to."

"That's right," Slater agreed.

"And, of course, he's the one who made the introductions, knows the background," Steele added. He thought for a moment. "Why risk it? Let's use him."

"If Pierce and Simmons know that Meade will testify, do you think that maybe they'll…" Richter started to ask.

Steele cut him off. "No way. This one's a go."

CHAPTER 50

8:25 p.m., Friday, July 10th, Bubba's Big-League Bar & Grill, Victoria, Texas.

It was another Friday night, another ballgame, and another beer at Bubba's. Ward felt his growing paunch and recalled something about a promised six-mile run. Once again, it would have to wait. These opportunities to bond could not be ignored, and Ward was hopeful that this night might yield something more than the usual barroom banter. Surprisingly, he and Sullivan had been joined by Jim Byrd. Ward wondered at the reason for Byrd's presence. It was not camaraderie. A fourth man also joined them. Willie Hammond had been introduced as a friend of Byrd's.

Sullivan tilted his bottle toward Ed Maddox. "Warren was mighty impressed with your work on that website," he said. The comment was mostly for Byrd's benefit. Sullivan was eager for the man to accept Ed as one of them.

Ward thought he heard a snort from Byrd. He ignored it. "Thanks, Ben," he replied. "It was no big deal...really. And there's still a lot of work to be done with linking in the other groups."

"That's what I hear," Byrd added, gratuitously.

Ward felt a wry smile start to creep onto his face, before he stopped it. The truth was, not only had he helped set up links to a handful of like-minded organizations, he had greatly improved the readability of the site and the means to navigate it. The PR guy, Warren Graves, had been duly impressed, as had Harold Doyle. Wouldn't they be surprised when, after the arrests started, the government pulled the plug?

"Well, I hear Royce looked 'er over and was real pleased," Sullivan noted, eyeing Byrd.

Sullivan grabbed a cup from the bar that he'd set aside for the purpose and spat tobacco juice into it. It was a statement as much as anything else.

Ward appreciated the effort. Part of him was fond of the old rancher. It happened with every undercover op. There was always one or two of them that, despite their racist beliefs, despite their terrible crimes, you somehow grew to like. Sullivan was bigoted and pretty damned ignorant. There was little doubt about that. But in other respects, he was good-hearted, the kind of guy who would give you the shirt off his back. Ward was always puzzled by this moral dichotomy. He wondered what made Sullivan think the way he did. Upbringing, he guessed.

"Well, enough of this," Byrd said. He gestured up at the television screen. "Damn game's over," he said. "It's the top of the seventh and we're already down nine to fuckin' three." He waved his hand dismissively. "Hell, with it. Let's get outta here, get some barbecue. I know a place. It's about eight, ten blocks."

"Sounds good to me," Hammond threw in.

"Sure, why not," Ward said. "Okay with you, Ben?"

Sullivan glanced at Byrd. "I suppose," he said reluctantly. "I've had a few tonight. Guess I could use somethin' to soak up the alcohol. Don't need another goddamned DWI. That's for sure."

Ward wondered how many drunk-driving convictions the three men had collected between them. If they all drank like Sullivan, as appeared to be the case, he suspected it was quite a few. He decided not to ask.

As they left the bar, Ward, listening carefully, overheard Byrd's quiet comments to Hammond.

"Pierce and Simmons are goin' to trial Monday," Byrd whispered. "Trial's gonna be here in Victoria."

"That's what I hear," Hammond replied.

"They're good boys," Byrd continued, "kept their mouths shut."

Hammond nodded.

"We'll take care of the families if it don't turn out good," Byrd noted.

"Of course," Hammond agreed.

"Be interesting to see who shows up on the witness stand," Byrd grunted.

"Maybe we should arrange a welcoming committee…just in case," Hammond whispered ominously.

Byrd didn't respond.

The four of them climbed in Byrd's truck, a Silverado crew cab. They pulled out of the parking lot and headed for the barbecue joint. After traveling about three blocks, they approached a liquor store, Victoria Spirits. There were three young Hispanic men standing out front. A fourth was exiting, carrying a brown paper bag.

"This place serves a lotta Mexicans," Byrd said with disgust.

Hammond grunted. "The only thing worse than a *spic* is a drunk *spic*," he said.

"You got that right," Byrd agreed.

Sullivan laughed.

Ward studied Hammond. He didn't like the look in his eyes.

"Let's follow this one, see where he goes," Hammond said, pointing toward the man leaving the store. "Maybe we'll get a chance to…*welcome* him to America."

"Or send him back to Mexico," Byrd said as he slowed the truck.

Byrd pulled off to the side of the road to let the Mexican get a half block ahead of them. Then, they would follow him, waiting for the opportunity to corner him in a secluded area.

Ward was growing uneasy. It was obvious that the others

were serious, and that they had done this before. He began to finger the cell phone in his pocket. He had trained himself to be able to send a distress signal to Richter and Lehman without looking. The phone was also equipped with a GPS device that would let them locate his exact position, give or take a few yards. Hopefully, it wouldn't come to that. The whole operation could be compromised. The other option was to send a 911 call. The GPS device allowed the police to locate the caller, or at least the phone. Normally, they would respond even if the caller was unable to speak to the dispatcher.

As Byrd pulled away from the curb, Ward could see the young Hispanic man look back over his shoulder. At first, he seemed unconcerned, but after a few minutes he seemed to sense that there might be a problem. Ward prayed that the young man would walk into one of the houses that lined his route. Instead, he crossed the street and started across an empty parking lot.

Shit, Ward thought. He's gonna leave himself wide open.

Byrd drove down the street and took a left. He started toward the opposite end of the lot, planning to cut him off.

"Let me out here," Hammond said. "I'll make sure the fuckin' cockroach doesn't get away."

Byrd complied.

Ward nervously ran his thumb over the face of the cell phone.

When he reached the other side of the parking lot, Byrd stopped. The young man was now no more than twenty yards away. Byrd jumped out of the truck. Sullivan was right behind him.

"Hey, boy," Byrd yelled. "Let's have us a little talk."

The young man looked confused, scared.

"Run," Ward said under his breath. "Run." He punched in 911 but did not hit send.

Byrd looked back at Ed Maddox. "Ed, you comin' or what?" he asked.

"Damn right!" Ward yelled enthusiastically. He now realized that this had become a test. He wondered if Byrd hadn't intended it as such from the beginning.

Hammond approached from behind the young man, who did not see him coming.

"Let's teach this *spic* a lesson," Hammond said.

The young man turned around, a look of terror in his eyes as the full realization of what was happening hit him. He dropped the brown paper bag onto the concrete as he prepared to defend himself. The bottles shattered, the strong smell of the tequila wafting upwards, filling his nostrils.

Ward stepped from the truck. He knew this would not end well if he didn't do something. He hit send. The 911 call went out. Please hurry, he prayed.

"Time to go home, *wetback*," Byrd said as he approached. He shoved the young Hispanic, sending him tumbling backwards. Byrd eyed Ed Maddox to gauge his enthusiasm.

Ward knew that this would have to be the performance of a lifetime. He could not take part in a crime of violence. As an undercover agent, one who was trying to infiltrate a dangerous criminal organization and bring it down, he had to appear to take part. In fact, he had to appear to enjoy it. But as a sworn law enforcement officer, he was obligated to help this man. Not just because it was his duty, but because it was the right thing to do.

Hammond moved in. He delivered a swift kick to the man's side, and then drew his leg back to give him another. It would not make contact.

The young man rolled to his side and jumped to his feet. He would not go down without a fight.

"Well, the *spic's* got some fight in him," Hammond laughed. "This'll be fun."

They began to circle. Ward took his place among them, sickened by what he was forced to do, knowing that if it got too bad he would have to intervene, no matter the risk to himself or the operation.

Byrd took swing. The young man ducked it, but as he did he

got too close to Sullivan. The old rancher landed a solid blow to the head, letting out a whoop of delight as he did so.

For Ward, it was a reality check, a good reminder of why he was there. He was disappointed in Sullivan, not that he should have expected anything different, but he had grown to like the man. Now, as far as he was concerned, Sullivan could go down with the rest of them.

Stunned by the blow from Sullivan, he was an easy target. Byrd landed the next shot. Still, the young man stayed on his feet. Byrd eyed Ed Maddox with expectation, as if to ask, *what are you waiting for?*

Ward would have to act. What the hell was taking the police so long? He drew back to throw a punch, telegraphing it to such a degree that he knew almost anyone could avoid the impact. He swung, catching nothing but air.

"Fuckin' *spic*," Ward growled convincingly.

"Get him, Ed!" Sullivan yelled.

Ward moved forward, praying for the police to arrive. Then he had an idea. He lunged and took the young man to the ground. The others cheered as Ed Maddox straddled his target and began to pummel him. What they didn't know was that Ward was expertly pulling his punches, dramatically lessening the impact. They didn't know, but the young man on the ground did.

When he met Ward's stare, there was a fleeting look of sympathy in his attacker's eyes, a look that said *I'm on your side.* The young man didn't understand what was happening, but something told him that, whatever it was, he had better go along with it. He began to yelp with pain as Ward's blows made contact.

Between them, it was a beautiful, and convincing, performance.

Just as Hammond moved in for his turn, the wail of a siren could be heard in the distance.

"We need to get outta here!" Sullivan said.

"Let's move!" Byrd ordered.

The men ran for the truck. Before leaving, Hammond took the time to kick the Mexican and spit on him.

As they pulled away, Ward suggested an escape route. While part of him wanted them to get caught, he knew better. They had to avoid the police. He had to avoid explaining his way out of this with the locals. Anything else risked scuttling the operation. That possibility was not acceptable.

Once they had safely fled the area, Byrd spoke up. "Well, boys," he said, "let's go get us that barbecue. I done worked up an appetite."

Hammond and Sullivan echoed the sentiment.

Ward was disgusted. Now, more than ever, he wanted to dismantle The Nation and lock up its members, all of them. Nonetheless, he managed to continue the performance.

"Sounds good," he agreed. "I'm hungry."

Nothing could have been further from the truth.

CHAPTER 51

8:50 a.m., Saturday, July 11th, Meade's apartment, Ankeny, Iowa.

Meade started the coffee. He was exhausted. It had been another sleepless night, full of self-torment, thoughts of Erin haunting him as he lie awake. The week since the break-up had done nothing to ease the pain. He longed for her touch, her laugh, the smell of her hair…everything.

Meade reached for a loaf of bread and went to the refrigerator for some butter. Lack of sleep made him hungry. A little toast might tide him over until he could get something more substantial. He was no cook. His barren cupboards proved that. Most meals were at local fast food joints, several of which already considered him a regular.

As the toast popped up, there was a knock at the door. A flicker of hope passed through Meade's heart. Could it be Erin? Was she having second thoughts? After all, she never really said that it was over. Meade hurried to the door. He swung it open, a smile on his face. The smile quickly faded, turning to a frown. He felt crushed all over again.

"Oh, it's you," Meade said.

Deputy Willis looked almost put off.

"Nice to see you, too," he said.

Meade shrugged. "Sorry."

Willis waited for an invitation. None came.

"Mind if I come in?" he asked.

Meade swung the door open, saying nothing.

"I'll take that as a yes," Willis said.

The Deputy U.S. Marshal entered the apartment and looked around. The place was a mess. It started to dawn on him, what must have happened.

"The girl, Erin…it's over?" Willis asked sympathetically.

Meade nodded.

"Sorry, man."

"Want some coffee?" Meade asked.

"Sure," Willis replied.

Meade managed to find two clean mugs. He poured the coffee and slid one of the cups toward Willis. As he did, Meade took in a deep breath. The aroma helped to clear his head. The first sip started to bring him back to life.

"So, what brings you here?" Meade asked. "I assume this isn't a social call."

Willis chuckled. "You'd be right about that."

Willis reached into his coat and pulled out a small manila envelope. He handed it to Meade.

"Go ahead. Open it," Willis said, nodding at the packet.

Meade tore open the envelope and emptied the contents onto the counter. There was cash and a plane ticket for Carl Ramsey. He looked up, confused.

"It's time, Carl," Willis said.

A flash of understanding crossed Meade's face. "You mean…"

Willis nodded. "It's time to testify."

Meade said nothing for a moment. He stared at the counter, the ticket. Part of him had hoped this day would never come, even blocked out the possibility, hoping Pierce and Simmons would simply plead guilty and go away. Of course, that was unrealistic. He knew them better than that.

"You okay?" Willis asked.

"Yeah, I'm fine," Meade replied. In truth, he *was* fine. Despite the risk to himself, he now wanted to do this. Meade found that he wanted to do some damage to The Nation. He felt they had cost him a normal life, a happy life, a life with Erin. Maybe, by doing this, he could somehow prove himself to her. Meade examined the ticket. It was a circuitous route, with many stops, ending in Corpus Christi. He noticed that there wasn't a change of flight in Houston.

"Where's the trial?" Meade asked.

"Victoria."

"Corpus Christi is over an hour's drive from there," Meade noted. "Why not…"

"That's the way it works," Willis replied.

Meade nodded. He understood.

"Of course, we can't let you go through Houston," Willis added. "It's for your own good. We've found that the temptation is just too great. Protectees think they can make a call, have a quick meeting at the airport before their connecting flight leaves. It's too risky."

Meade was disappointed, but that very disappointment told him that Willis was probably right. He might very well take the chance on just such a meeting, especially now. He was so lonely.

"What about work, school?" Meade asked.

"It's been taken care of."

Meade didn't ask. He wasn't terribly concerned about missing work, not as long as it had been *taken care of*. But he was concerned about missing class and missing the opportunity to see Erin. She wouldn't speak to him, not at any length, but she would acknowledge his greeting. Even if it was only a quick, emotionless hello, it was all he had. He clung to it. Willis interrupted his thought.

"You leave tomorrow morning," Willis said.

Meade picked up the ticket. "I see that," he noted, "and pretty damned early."

"I'll make sure you're up," Willis promised, "and I'll get you to the airport."

Meade looked up at the deputy. "I'm sure you will."

*　*　*

As the plane winged its way south on the last leg of his flight, Meade stared out the window, watching Texas pass below. He wondered what his brothers and sisters were doing, what had happened in their lives, how often they talked about him, thought about him.

"Sir, would you please put your seat in an upright position?" a young flight attendant asked. "We'll be landing shortly."

"Oh, sorry," Meade replied, startled by the request. He did as asked.

"Thank you," the flight attendant said. She moved on to the next transgressor.

Meade looked back out the window. Willis had warned him, they had seen the witness list. The Nation knew that he was coming. They would be waiting.

CHAPTER 52

8:45 a.m., Monday, July 13th, northbound on Highway 77, between Corpus Christi and Victoria.

The black Suburban roared up Highway 77. Dark tinted windows kept the world from looking in but didn't keep Jacob Meade from looking out. He stared at the Texas countryside as it passed by, growing homesick for a home that had never really existed.

For Meade, it had been a sleepless night in a Corpus Christi hotel room. His nerves were starting to get the better of him. The destination was Victoria, Texas, and the trial of Troy Pierce and Willard Simmons. Meade imagined their icy stares as he took the stand. He prayed that he would be able to keep his composure. He had to do this. He wanted to do it. Along with the day that he decided to cooperate and enter witness protection, this was possibly the most important moment in his life.

Meade focused on what the Assistant U.S. Attorney, Steele, told him at their witness prep meeting the night before. "Stay calm," he said, "take your time, and, most important of all, answer only the question that was asked." It sounded simple enough, but doing it was another thing altogether. Steele had warned him about how defense counsel would try to rattle him, challenge his motives, attack his character. Meade felt that he was ready for that, at least as ready as he could be. What he was more concerned about was the threat from observers in the courtroom, and their colleagues, the ones who might be waiting outside. Steele assured him that there was ample protection. He described the extraordinary measures that had been taken. It would have been enough to calm the fears of most people, but Meade knew the determination of the enemy. The Nation would not tolerate a traitor to their cause. And if that traitor cooperated, he would be dealt with in a way that would send a clear message to anyone who might consider a similar course of action. Meade knew that these people would hound him to the ends of the earth.

Meade looked at the Deputy U.S. Marshals seated around him. They were businesslike, rugged-looking men, who exuded an air of confidence. He prayed that they knew their job and knew it well.

"Mr. Steele call your next witness," The Honorable Terence P. Morehouse thundered from the bench.

Morehouse, possessed of an arrogance that could suck the oxygen out of a room, was aware that the local bar consistently, and less than affectionately, referred to him as Terence the Terrible. Many an attorney had been dressed down by the judge, some so thoroughly, it was rumored, that they had been left standing in a puddle of their own making. There was no real proof of the latter, there being few lawyers who would admit to such, but the legend was enough to serve the purpose. No one would purposely incur the wrath of Judge Morehouse.

Assistant United States Attorney Abraham Steele rose from his chair. "Your Honor, the United States calls Jacob Meade to the stand." Steele turned to Richter, who signaled the Marshals Service to bring in Meade.

Meade was waiting outside the double doors that led into the courtroom. A foursome of tough-looking Deputy U.S. Marshals surrounded him. When the signal came, two of them opened the courtroom doors and he walked in. The packed courtroom turned to look at Meade and study him. For one, it was more than a mere curiosity. There was evil intent.

Meade slowly walked the aisle leading to the front of the courtroom and the witness stand. His legs felt weak. His guts rumbled as all bowel control threatened to desert him. The full reality of what he was about to do was now staring Meade in the face.

As he passed the Assistant United States Attorney, Meade looked to him for some sort of guidance, maybe reassurance. Steele remained expressionless. Meade felt more alone than at any point in his life.

The court attendant had Meade stop before reaching the witness stand, raise his right hand and take the oath. Meade's heart was pounding, he felt lightheaded. Nonetheless, he managed to spit out the words, swearing to tell *the truth, the whole truth, and nothing but the truth, so help me God*. He had every intention of doing just that. As he climbed into the witness box and took his seat, Carl Meade prepared himself to write the final chapter in his previous life.

"Good afternoon, Mr. Meade," Steele began.

"Good afternoon."

Meade made eye contact first with Pierce, then with Simmons. The unrelenting stare of each man said the same thing: *you are as good as dead*. Meade had prepared himself, but the impact was still there. His blood ran cold.

"Would you state your name for the record and spell it?" Steele asked.

"Jacob Wallace Meade," Meade answered. He spelled it out for the court reporter.

"Mr. Meade, how do you know the defendants?"

The question brought an objection from Pierce's attorney, Kent Payne. It annoyed Steele. There was nothing inappropriate about the question. This was subject matter that had been addressed by the court before trial, with both sides well aware of the limits on this line of questioning. The Nation was not under indictment and Judge Morehouse would not let the trial become about them. Steele knew very well what he was allowed to ask. Jacob Meade had been carefully instructed as to what he was allowed to say, and, more importantly, what he was not allowed to say. He could not name the organization or discuss its beliefs. He could only say that he knew the men through membership in an organization. Steele wasn't sure what Payne hoped to achieve with this stunt.

"Counsel, sidebar!" Judge Morehouse said angrily.

As the attorneys approached the bench, Meade looked through the crowd. There were several familiar faces, faces he did not want to see. One of them, in particular, caught Meade's eye. It was Willie Hammond, a devoted follower and notorious thug. Hammond had a bad temper and a thirst for blood. Meade tried to avoid locking eyes with the man but couldn't help himself. A wicked grin appeared on Hammond's face. When he was sure Meade was looking, he used his index finger to draw a line across his throat. Meade looked away, struggling to avoid giving in to the nausea that suddenly threatened to overwhelm him.

The lawyers returned to their seats, the issue seemingly resolved. Meade noticed a smirk on Payne's face as he sat down. It was clear to Meade that Payne planned to make this a memorable experience for him.

The questioning resumed. Meade explained, to the extent allowed, how he knew Pierce and Simmons. He described his own arrest and how he had been set up by a man he knew as Ralph "Rogue Beast" Baker, a man he now knew to be Special Agent Joseph Slater. Meade told the jury that he decided to cooperate. He then explained how he set up a drugs-for-guns swap between Baker and the defendants, and what happened when the exchange took place.

"Let me ask you about that decision to cooperate," Steele said. He knew that he had to get out front on this issue. He had to be the one who asked the questions about what the witness hoped to gain, or did gain, by cooperating. If not, if defense counsel brought it up first, it heightened the possibility that the jury might view the cooperating witness's testimony as bought and paid for.

"What benefit, or benefits, did you get by agreeing to cooperate for the government?" Steele asked.

"Basically, I wasn't prosecuted," Meade answered. "And I was put into the Witness Protection Program…if you can call that a benefit."

The few jurors who weren't already paying close attention now moved to the edge of their seats.

Steele avoided further questions related to the Witness Protection Program. It was also an area that had been addressed before trial, the judge allowing the attorneys to establish Meade's participation and that's it. Defense counsel had been caught in a tough spot on this one. They wanted to challenge Meade's credibility with what he had received from the government, but also understood the speculation that would arise from nothing more than a reference to witness protection. Steele glanced at the jury. He surmised that the damage had been done.

"As part of your deal with the government, what are your obligations?" Steele asked.

"I have to testify when requested to do so," Meade replied. "And I have to tell the truth."

"What happens if you don't tell the truth?"

"Then, the deal's revoked. I can be prosecuted."

"Thank you, Mr. Meade," Steele said, concluding his direct examination. "I have nothing further for this witness, Your Honor."

"Mr. Payne, you may begin your cross-examination," Judge Morehouse announced.

"Thank you, Your Honor," Payne said. "Good afternoon, Mr. Meade."

"Good afternoon," Meade said warily. He was prepared for the worst…or thought he was. Payne had a smug look on his face.

"Mr. Meade, do you currently go by any other name?" Payne asked.

"Objection!" Steele erupted, summoning all the righteous indignation he could muster. "The government requests a side-bar, Your Honor."

"Approach," Judge Morehouse commanded. He was not happy.

The lawyers came forward. Morehouse turned off his microphone and gestured for the attorneys to come to the side of the bench away from the jury.

Steele didn't wait for an invitation to speak. He was hot. "Your Honor, counsel is merely trying to intimidate this witness. Either that or he wants the members of The Nation to be able to find Mr. Meade." Steele turned to Payne. "Which is it, Kent?"

Judge Morehouse said nothing, interested to hear how Payne might respond.

"Your Honor, I was simply trying to further establish the benefits that Mr. Meade received from the government, benefits that might shade his testimony," Payne answered lamely.

"Uh huh," Morehouse grunted. "Objection sustained. Mr. Payne, I've already ruled on what is permissible in this area. One more question like that and I'll hold you in contempt. Do we understand each other?"

"Yes, Your Honor."

The attorneys returned to their counsel tables. Payne resumed his cross-examination. Despite Payne's best efforts to rattle him, Meade remained consistent.

As his flight took off from Corpus Christi, Meade was surprised to find that he was experiencing something akin to pride. It was an unusual feeling for him. He liked it.

After receiving the case late Wednesday morning, the jury had deliberated for less than two hours, and that included their lunch break. Steele told him afterwards that his testimony had clearly helped put Pierce and Simmons away. And from what the federal prosecutor said, they would be going away for a long, long time.

Though pleased with himself, Meade knew that the threat to his existence would now be greater than ever. The Nation would exhaust all means in an attempt to find him. If they did, he shuddered to think what might happen. Merely killing him would not be enough. A chill swept through Meade as he envisioned Hammond, his evil grin, the gesture he made in the courtroom. Meade knew that now, more than ever before, he could never return home.

CHAPTER 53

7:40 p.m., Wednesday, July 15th, the offices of Ron Flagg, Private Investigator, Houston, Texas.

Ron Flagg was growing frustrated. Everything about this Maddox guy checked out. But there was still something, a certain awareness on the part of his target that told Flagg this man was not who he seemed to be.

A check with the rental company showed that the house in Cuero was, in fact, leased to Edward Maddox. The man clearly either worked for Odessa Oil or it was a brilliant cover. His driver's license had already checked out. And today, Flagg finally received a response from the National Personnel Records Center in St. Louis. Edward Michael Maddox had served in the United States Army. Beyond that, little information was available. Even Flagg's normally reliable source there couldn't provide much. The records were classified, lending credibility to Maddox's claim to have been in Special Forces. If this guy was someone other than Edward Maddox, he had truly covered his bases.

A tumbler of Scotch sat on the desk. Flagg leaned forward, wrapping both hands around the glass to keep it steady. He raised it to his lips and took a drink, letting the warm liquid slide down his throat. It was like an old friend…supportive, reliable, always there. Another sip quickly followed.

Flagg lowered his head. He had done better with the drinking, hadn't he? It sure as hell wasn't like the old days. Back then, he could go off on a real bender. No, now he could quit whenever he wanted to. It was really no big deal. Besides, there was nothing wrong with a little drink to get fortified before making a call like this, was there?

"Goddamn buttons are too small on this thing," Flagg cursed as he slowly punched in the numbers. "There," he said as he hit the last one. He raised the receiver to his ear. The phone rang once, twice. Flagg secretly hoped that there would be no answer. No such luck. On the fourth ring a man answered, his voice gruff.

"Hello."

"Jim, it's Ron Flagg."

"You got somethin' for me?"

Flagg wasn't surprised by the lack of pleasantries. It was business as usual with Jim Byrd.

"Not much," Flagg said. "So far our boy checks out."

Byrd grunted. "That so?"

Flagg related the details of his investigation.

"I assume your efforts aren't completed?" Byrd asked, irritation in his voice.

Flagg took a deep breath. "No, of course not," he said, already exasperated. "I just wanted to let you know where I'm at."

"You've done that."

Flagg started to count to ten. He needed this client.

"You still there?" Byrd asked.

"Yeah…I'm still here," Flagg said between gritted teeth.

"What's your next step?" Byrd asked.

Flagg thought for a moment. "Has anybody asked Maddox about his hometown?"

There was a disgusted snort on the other end of the line. "You seriously think I hadn't thought of that?" Byrd asked. "It was one of the first things we asked him."

"So, what'd he tell you?"

"All he says is that he was an Army brat," Byrd replied, "says he moved around a lot. When we pressed him, he mentioned several good-sized cities, some of them overseas. It was nothin' useful. Don't you think I would have mentioned it if we knew his hometown?"

"Sorry…just asking." Flagg eyed the scotch on his desk. It beckoned. He was growing very tired of Jim Byrd.

"So, again, what's your next step?" Byrd asked.

"I'll run his credit history," Flagg answered. "That usually turns up something. See what you can find out about where he went to school. That's always a good source of information."

"I'll make sure we do that," Byrd said.

"If need be, I'll go to Alaska," Flagg added. "See what I can find out. If I can't fill in some of the blanks up there…then we've got a definite problem."

"Pleased to hear that you have a plan," Byrd noted. "I'll expect to hear from you soon."

There was a click on the other end of the line, then a dial tone. Flagg held the phone out in front of him, staring at it, fuming at the man's rudeness. He shook his head and hung up.

Flagg slumped back in his chair, as exhausted by the conversation as he was angered by it. He again eyed the scotch. Leaning forward, he wrapped his hand around the tumbler, took a drink, and then held the glass up to his temple. It was fair to say that life had not turned out the way he'd planned. Money was always short, his wife had left him years ago, and his only child, Theresa, barely spoke to him. Then there were the clients, angry, bitter spouses and assholes like Jim Byrd. It was great, just great…one kick in the balls after another. He laughed a bitter laugh. There was little else he could do.

CHAPTER 54

6:20 p.m., Friday, July 17th, on a ranch road, a mile and a half from Compound One.

Ward held tight to the steering wheel. The ruts in the old ranch road violently jerked his SUV toward one ditch, then the other. He didn't understand it. From what he'd seen, Royce Lundgren had to have the connections to get somebody from the county out to grade the road. It was a good thing that there was just over a mile to go.

The invitation had come directly from Doyle, the second-in-command. Ward was pleased. His efforts with Doyle had started to pay off. Lundgren's cousin was one of the easier marks he had encountered in his days as an operative. Ward wondered at Doyle's place in the organization. Did Lundgren feel that he could truly trust only family? Surely, he must be aware of Doyle's limitations? Ward shook his head. Whatever the reason, it had all worked to his advantage.

Ward came over a rise in the road. He was close now. A pickup, coming from the other direction, turned off the road a quarter mile ahead. Slowly, the truck made its way up the gravel drive toward Lundgren's residence. It was another one of his men. Doyle had described the meeting as upper management, an even more elite group than that present at the Fourth of July barbecue. It would be a who's who of The Nation, and, Ward knew, a spectacular opportunity to gather intelligence. He only hoped that he could remember the names long enough to get the information to Richter. There was no question about it, a good memory was critical for an undercover cop. Without it you could lose a lot of information, and maybe your life.

Ward turned up the gravel drive leading to the residence. He followed it around back and parked between the two large metal barns that sat behind Lundgren's ranch house. As he stepped out of the truck, he spotted Charlie Kirklin in the backyard. Kirklin was talking with two men. Ward didn't recognize either of them. It was an animated conversation with much gesturing. Ward made his way toward the group.

Kirklin spotted Ward as he approached. Excusing himself from the others, he made a beeline in Ward's direction, as if to intercept him. Ward took note. He also noticed the confused look on Kirklin's face.

"Ed how are ya?" Kirklin asked, sounding anxious. "I didn't expect to see you here tonight."

"Doyle invited me," Ward said. "In fact, he kind of insisted on it." Ward could see that Kirklin was truly nervous. Clearly this was a meeting of some importance, a meeting at which organizational strategy would probably be discussed.

"Is there a problem with my being here?" Ward asked.

"Oh, no," Kirklin insisted. "No problem at all. You're quite welcome. It's just a surprise, that's all." He patted Maddox on the back and directed him toward the house.

Ward grew edgy. Kirklin's nervousness bothered him. Was this some sort of set-up? If so, the others had probably warned Kirklin to keep his mouth shut. Ward tried to read the man. He just couldn't tell. Maybe it was time to come up with an excuse, get the hell out of there. No, Ward thought, too obvious. A stunt like that would auger in the whole operation. He took a breath, steadied himself, and headed for the door.

* * *

Forty-five minutes into the meeting, Ward almost wished that he'd worn a wire. It was simply too much information to process. The thirty-plus men present were clearly the organizational backbone of The Nation. Ward did his best to memorize every name, as well as the town each of them called home. It was obvious that these were what he would call the regional commanders, for lack of a better term. They were the men to keep an eye on to track what the group was up to, and to gauge its strength. It was an intelligence gold mine.

Ward was surprised by the fact that there seemed to be little formal structure to the meeting. He wondered if that would come later. So far, it was as much a social gathering as an operational strategy session. He took advantage of the situation, doing his best to meet everyone in the room. For most of the evening he was accompanied by Doyle, who was clearly proud of his new protégé. At times Doyle essentially introduced him as such. Ward could not have hoped for a better entrée to the inner circle.

Most of the men were drinking; some, like Doyle, heavily. The talk was not loose, but it was also not guarded. These were colleagues, kindred spirits, men who could be trusted. Still, specific details were sometimes avoided. To Ward, that seemed to be the standard *modus operandi*. It wasn't the first time that he had encountered such a thing. Even among co-conspirators, there was often a need to protect oneself.

Doyle pulled Ward toward Lundgren, who was holding court on one side of the main room. Out of the corner of his eye Ward noticed that this, like his other movements that night, had not gone unnoticed. Jim Byrd watched his every move.

Byrd was seething. Even a half-wit like Doyle should understand the need for caution with newcomers. What the hell was he thinking, inviting Maddox? The men at this meeting had proven track records of adherence to The Nation's principles. They had been subjected to thorough background checks. Most had the blood of a dozen or more *spics* on their hands. They had earned the right to be here. In Byrd's estimation, the presence of Maddox was an affront to the organization.

Byrd watched as Maddox engaged Lundgren. It was maddening. Lundgren actually appeared to be listening to the man. Doyle stood with them, nodding in agreement like some sort of bobble head doll. After a few minutes, it was more than Byrd could take. He determined to put a stop to it.

Byrd approached. Maddox was discussing techniques used by the Special Forces to win over tribesmen in Afghanistan. Switching to The Nation's mission, he then suggested some methods that might be employed to win over various locals to their cause, particularly those in the border areas. Lundgren was paying close attention.

Byrd waited for a brief pause in the conversation, and then interjected himself. He planned to make a point and wanted to do it in front of Lundgren.

"Ed didn't know you'd be here tonight," Byrd said, intending to get right to it.

"I invited him," Doyle announced proudly.

Lundgren looked interested, but didn't speak, watching closely.

Byrd shot Doyle a look, and then went back to Maddox. "You know, Ed...you and I really haven't gotten to know each other. To tell you the truth, I really don't know much about you at all."

Doyle looked to Lundgren, who remained impassive.

Ed Maddox cocked his head and smiled. So damned smooth, thought Byrd. Too smooth.

"Tell me again, where was it that you grew up?" Byrd asked.

Ward smiled. "I thought I mentioned that I was an Army brat." He turned to Lundgren. "We moved around a lot. I didn't really have what you would call a hometown. The Army was our home. That's how I ended up in Special Forces, I guess." He paused, looking thoughtful. "The disenchantment came later."

Byrd grunted. "Where did you graduate from high school? I'm just curious."

"I did my last semester in Columbia, South Carolina. Dad was stationed at Fort Jackson."

Byrd pressed. "Which high school?"

"East High," Maddox shot back. Byrd thought Maddox might be getting a little rattled by the questions. That was good. He wanted him on the defensive.

"So, how 'bout after that?" Byrd quizzed him. "Where'd you go to college?"

"University of Georgia," Maddox said proudly.

"Sounds like Ed here has some good Southern roots," Doyle interrupted, intending to end the inquisition. He stared at Byrd, challenging him to continue. He didn't like having his judgment questioned like this, particularly in front of Royce. There would be a discussion later.

Byrd let out a snort. He decided to back off, at least for the time being. Further inquiries would be made. He was now more determined than ever to find out the truth about Edward Michael Maddox.

As soon as he was safely away from Compound One, Ward punched in Richter's number and hit send. He needed some reassurance. Byrd was making him nervous, damned nervous.

"What's up, partner?" Richter answered. "How was the meeting?"

"Better than I could've reasonably hoped for," Ward replied. He did his best to outline everything that he'd seen and heard over the course of the preceding three hours. As he talked, Richter responded with a series of low whistling noises.

"Hell, I can't even remember it all," Ward said after concluding his summary. "I'll start on the report tonight."

"Man, I'd like to see that little prick Winborn try to shut us down now," Richter declared.

"He couldn't do it," Ward agreed. "McCutcheon is gonna smell blood. This is the kind of stuff that SACs live for." Ward thought about his old buddy, Jack Olin, and how happy this would make him. "Olin will love this," Ward added.

"I can't wait to call him," Richter said, almost gleefully. "He is gonna rub Winborn's face in it."

Ward chuckled, but then grew silent. There was still the matter of Byrd's interrogation to discuss.

"Sorry to say it's not all good news to report," Ward announced.

"How's that?"

"I got a lot of attention from Jim Byrd tonight." Ward described the third degree he endured regarding where he grew up, his educational background.

"Not good," Richter noted. He paused, hesitant to say what had to come next. "You know, if you wanna pull the plug, you just say the word. It ain't worth gettin' killed over."

"No way," Ward shot back. "I know the rules. If I think he's gettin' close, you'll be the first to know."

"All right, all right" Richter agreed.

"Just do me a favor," Ward added.

"Name it."

"Make sure *everything* is in place with the schools and all, would ya?"

"You can count on it, partner," Richter assured him. "You can count on it."

CHAPTER 55

3:30 p.m., Tuesday, July 21st, Columbia East High School, Columbia, South Carolina.

Ron Flagg strode through the front entrance at Columbia East High School. He had done some preliminary homework. In a city of just over one hundred twenty-five thousand and a metro area almost six times that size, Columbia East was easily the largest of the local high schools. At this time of day, on a sweltering July afternoon, the main building was almost empty. Flagg could hear his footsteps echo down the hall as he made his way toward the principal's office.

Flagg had acted quickly to follow up on Jim Byrd's information, not that there had been much choice. The Nation's Head of Security had been insistent, *get down to Columbia and check this guy out.* Flagg would do just that. The first step would be to get a copy of Ed Maddox's high school transcripts. The rest should be easy.

The ruse would be one that had worked well many times in the past. Flagg pulled out his credentials, admiring the craftsmanship of the bogus identification. His smiling picture was laminated onto a card that identified him as Sylvester Harding, United States Office of Personnel Management. The story would be that he was conducting a federal background check. Mr. Maddox had applied for a position in the federal government that required a high-level security clearance. Of course, Sylvester Harding would not be at liberty to identify the agency, or the job. If pressed, he would give a conspiratorial wink and whisper something along the lines of, *let's just say it's in the intelligence field, and leave it at that.*

Flagg had never known this approach to fail. He had been concerned when OPM took over background investigation duties from the FBI. People didn't question FBI agents. But his fears were unwarranted. The level of cooperation was still one hundred percent. And on those occasions when he did encounter someone who was a bit of a stickler, Flagg would simply produce a waiver form, complete with a nicely forged signature of the individual under investigation. In this case, that individual was one Edward M. Maddox. The form, naturally, allowed the government to access any relevant records as part of its review. As a final touch, it would be explained that it was all very hush-hush, and not to be shared any more than was absolutely necessary. Flagg understood that people loved to be part of something secret. It was human nature. And if they felt compelled to share it with someone after he was gone, as many of them did…well, it was after he was gone…long gone.

The top half of the door to the Office of the Principal was an old-fashioned frosted glass pane. It was similar to the one that Flagg had walked through many times at his own high school. He had a brief, unpleasant flashback to a troubled youth. Flagg had been well acquainted with his high school principal, Mr. Simpson. Their relationship had been one of something less than mutual admiration and had included several suspensions. In Flagg's estimation, some of them had been warranted, others not. Childish as it was, he had to admit, he found a certain perverse satisfaction in scamming a principal's office.

Flagg opened the door into a small waiting area. There was a long counter to his right. Behind it sat several desks. Past them he could see another door, presumably leading to the actual principal's office. A heavyset woman sat at one of the desks, the only person present. She looked up.

"Can I help you, sir?" she asked politely, the heavy drawl of the Old South weighing down her words.

"I hope so," Flagg replied. He gave the woman a smile and looked around. "Pretty slim pickins in here today. You holdin' down the fort all by yourself?"

"Oh, you got that right, hon," she said. "You won't find too many of 'em around this time a year, especially on a day like this. I'll tell you, this ol' building gets hot, now. Whew!" She fanned herself and gave a laugh, happy to have someone to talk to.

Flagg laughed with her.

"I'm Betty, by the way," the woman said.

"Nice to meet you, Betty," Flagg offered. "I'm Sylvester Harding."

"What can I do for you, Mr. Harding?"

"Well, I'm with the U.S. Office of Personnel Management," Flagg lied. He pulled out his credentials and flashed them. "I'm here as part of a background check on..." Flagg held out his clipboard, examining it as if he had forgotten the name, "Edward Michael Maddox. His questionnaire says he went to high school here."

"Background check?" Betty asked. Intrigued, she rose from her desk and headed for the counter.

"He applied for a job with the government," Flagg explained.

"What kind of job?" Betty asked.

"I can't really say," Flagg whispered. He looked side to side, as if checking to see if anyone was listening, and then leaned in. "Let's just say it's in the intelligence field, and leave it at that." He gave her a wink.

"Ohhhhh," Betty replied. She also glanced side to side. "What can we do to help?" she asked, eager to be cooperative.

"We need a copy of his high school transcripts," Flagg said. He was always amazed that it never seemed to occur to anyone that a real job applicant would submit a certified copy of their transcripts along with their application.

Betty looked troubled. "Transcripts, huh?"

Flagg knew what was coming. "Is there a problem?"

"It's just that...we're not really supposed to give those out, not without a request from the student."

Flagg pulled out the waiver. "That's why we get these from the applicant," he said.

Betty examined the form. She smiled, satisfied that it would do. "This looks fine," she said.

To assist Betty's efforts, Flagg supplied all of the information that he had on Maddox.

"It'll take a few minutes," Betty told him.

"Take as long as you need," Flagg said agreeably.

Betty trundled off to retrieve the transcripts. She returned ten minutes later.

"Here they are," she said, handing over the documents.

Flagg examined them. The coursework reflected only one semester, which was in accord with Byrd's information. "They don't seem to say what school he transferred in from," Flagg noted.

A puzzled look appeared on Betty's face. "That's odd," she said. She took the transcripts and studied them. "Sure enough," she agreed. "Let me see if there's anything else in the file."

A few minutes later she walked back into the office, rubbing her chin.

"I don't see anything else in there. I don't know what to make of that."

"How unusual is it for those transfer records to be missing," Flagg asked. His antennae were beginning to rise.

"Oh, it's unusual," Betty said. "Not unprecedented, but unusual. We get a lot of students who have parents in the military. Sometimes the records don't get to us the way they should."

That *might* explain it, Flagg thought. "What part of town is this?" he inquired, pointing to the home address noted in the records. "I thought I might try to visit with some of the old neighbors, see what they can tell me."

"Goodness, you folks are thorough," Betty exclaimed. She glanced at the address, and then shook her head.

"What is it?" Flagg asked.

"I don't think that's gonna help you much, hon. That address is military housing out at Fort Jackson."

Of course, it is, Flagg thought. He was either damned unlucky or this guy was damned clever. Flagg pondered the transcripts a moment longer.

"I'd like to talk to some of his teachers, if any of them are around."

"Not too many of 'em around today." Betty looked at the list of classes.

"Oh, wait a minute," she said. "You might be in luck. This class, *The Civil War*, has been taught by Mr. Bagley for as long as I can remember. I saw him maybe a half hour ago, just before you got here. If you hurry, you might be able to catch him."

"That would be great," Flagg said enthusiastically. He got directions to Bagley's classroom and rushed out the door.

Flagg found Bagley's classroom. He was in luck. The veteran teacher was still there, bent over his desk. Flagg knocked on the door. Bagley looked up from the text he was studying. Peering over the top of his reading glasses, he studied the man standing in the doorway. After a moment, he rose to approach him.

"Can I help you?" Bagley asked.

"Mr. Bagley, my name is Sylvester Harding. I'm with the U.S. Office of Personnel Management." Flagg flashed his bogus credentials.

Bagley eyed the credentials. Satisfied, he nodded. "What can I do for you, Mr. Harding?"

"Betty, in the principal's office, said I might be able to find you here. I'm doing a background check on one of your former students, an Edward Maddox. He applied for a position that requires a security clearance."

"Edward Maddox, huh?" Bagley thought for a moment. "I'm sorry. Frankly, I don't recall him."

Flagg handed Bagley the transcripts. "Does this help?" he asked.

Bagley reviewed the records. "No, I'm afraid not," he replied. "Even though it's a big school, I'm usually pretty good about remembering my students. Of course, the memory's not what it used to be...and this was some time ago." He returned the transcripts.

"Yes, it has been a few years," Flagg agreed. "As you can imagine, this is a problem we often run into when the student in question has been gone for a while."

"I'm sure it is."

"In any event, I thank you for your time."

"Sorry I couldn't be of more help," Bagley said apologetically.

As soon as he exited the building Flagg pulled out his cell phone and punched in Byrd's number.

"What'd you find out?" Byrd asked.

"Not much," Flagg replied. "So far, this little excursion has been more noteworthy for the lack of information I've been able to dig up." Flagg relayed what he had.

"Too suspicious for my taste," Byrd noted.

"The transcripts do exist," Flagg admitted. "I'll give him that. But they raise a lot of questions."

"Yes, they do," Byrd agreed. He was silent for a moment. "I assume you're headed to Athens next," he finally said. The tone was that of someone instructing a rather dull eighth-grader.

Flagg bristled at the condescension but forced himself to let it go. "The University of Georgia is my next stop," he said through gritted teeth.

"Call me as soon as you know something."

Byrd ended the call abruptly, as he usually did.

Flagg pulled the phone away from his ear and stared at it, shaking his head. He allowed himself a brief fantasy, one that did not end well for Jim Byrd.

CHAPTER 56

6:15 p.m., Tuesday, July 21st, Harold Doyle's ranch, just outside Yoakum, Texas.

Doyle downed his beer and tossed the can to the side. He raised the .45 caliber Smith & Wesson revolver and aimed it at an old plastic milk jug that sat atop a wooden fence post less than thirty feet away. The shot wasn't much of a challenge, not as far as Ward was concerned. Any competent marksman would hit the target eight out of ten times from that distance. Of course, Ward had no intention of letting Doyle know that.

No hearing protection had been offered and none was requested. Still, preferring not to contribute to whatever deafness he had already suffered because of his years in law enforcement, Ward stepped back and covered his ears. The fact that Doyle was already mildly intoxicated just increased the need to get behind him.

The Smith & Wesson exploded like a small cannon. Ward watched as the recoil caused Doyle's wrist to snap back. He was afraid that the drunken fool might topple over backwards as the kick of the gun caused him to stumble. Amazingly, Doyle managed to hit the target. The water-filled milk container blew apart as the .45 slug ripped through it. Doyle righted himself and turned toward the man he knew as Ed Maddox, a huge grin plastered on his face.

"How 'bout that?" Doyle asked proudly, eager to impress

his new friend.

"Helluva shot, Harold!" Ward said, feigning as much enthusiasm as he could muster. "Helluva shot!"

Doyle beamed with pride. He walked to his pickup and grabbed another beer from the cooler that sat on the tailgate.

"You ready for another?" Doyle asked.

"No, I'm good," Ward replied.

Doyle cracked open his beer. "You better pick it up, pardner. You're fallin' behind."

Ward smiled. He raised his drink, draining the last ounce from the can, then flipped the empty into the back of Doyle's truck.

"If you say so," Ward fired back. He motioned for Doyle to throw him another.

"Attaboy!" Doyle exclaimed as he tossed the replacement.

Doyle pulled two more-gallon jugs from the back of the truck. He walked them over to the fence, placing each on top of a separate post.

"Let's move 'er back a little," Doyle said as he returned to the firing line.

"Sounds good," Ward agreed.

Doyle stepped off another ten feet. "Your turn, Ed," he announced as he handed the .45 to Maddox.

Ward hefted the gun to get a feel for it, testing its weight, its balance. It had been a while since he'd fired the big Smith & Wesson. But marksmanship wasn't his concern. The real question was, did he show this guy up or let him think he was a better shot. Ward quickly decided that the better approach was to keep him in awe. It had worked well so far, and anything else risked being seen as patronizing.

Ward raised the gun. He cracked off two shots in quick succession, obliterating both targets.

"Holy shit!" Doyle blurted. He laughed. "Damn! Ain't you somethin'."

A wry smile crept onto Ward's face. He could see that he had played it exactly right.

There were a dozen remaining plastic jugs in Doyle's truck. He grabbed two of them. "How far back can you go?" Doyle asked.

Ward stepped off another thirty feet.

"No way," Doyle insisted.

Ward said nothing. He simply nodded toward the posts.

"Okay," Doyle said. He marched over to the fence, placed the jugs in position, and then hustled back to the truck.

Ward left the gun at his side. He took a deep breath. Then, in one fluid motion, he quickly raised the .45 and fired off two shots, annihilating both targets. He lowered the weapon as smoke drifted up from its barrel. A satisfied look swept across his face.

"Son...of...a...*bitch*!" Doyle exclaimed, shaking his head in disbelief. "I've seen enough," he laughed, throwing his hands up. "C'mon, I'll give you a tour of the rest of the ranch."

They climbed into the pickup and headed down an old dirt road that ran through the property, Doyle occasionally stopping to point out various landmarks to his friend, Ed Maddox. Ward feigned great interest, asking questions that allowed Doyle to answer with a landowner's pride.

The ranch, consisting of sixty-five acres, included a creek that had been partially damned to form a small pond. A spillway allowed water to flow through, thus preventing any lawsuits regarding the neighbor's water rights. Doyle pointed out that he and his father had stocked the pond with bass years earlier, and that it was now routine to catch one weighing in at over eight pounds.

"Next time you're out we'll have to do some fishin'," Doyle suggested.

"I'd like that," Ward replied. Fishing allowed plenty of time for talking, and he wanted to keep Doyle talking.

The road curved around a line of trees. On the other side was a small pasture. There, a dozen cattle grazed contentedly, bothered only by the flies that they swatted away with their tales.

"There's the herd," Doyle announced. He eyed Maddox,

waiting for a reaction.

Ward silently counted the cattle. He was perplexed, expecting to see maybe a couple hundred head. That was his idea of a ranch.

Doyle laughed. "Not much of a herd is it?"

Ward was at a bit of a loss.

Doyle let him off the hook. "I'm like a lot of folks in this area," he said. "We keep a few cattle on the land, so we can get the property tax break that goes with operating this here, um, *ranch*."

"I get ya," Ward said. "Hey, I got no problem with avoidin' taxes."

"You got that right," Doyle said, raising his beer in toast.

Ward returned the gesture. Another point scored, he thought.

As the tour continued and the beer flowed, Ward slowly moved the conversation toward a discussion of The Nation. Talk turned to the group's personalities, who had the real influence, who had Royce Lundgren's ear. It was Doyle who took it there, wanting to confide in his new friend.

"Graves has some influence," Doyle noted. "So, does Charlie Kirklin. But the truth is, Royce marches to the beat of his own drummer. He *is* the real driving force."

Ward nodded. "What about Jim Byrd?" he asked.

"Byrd," Doyle scoffed. "Yeah, I guess he's got some influence." Nothing else was said.

"You don't seem too fond of the guy," Ward observed.

"You could say that."

"I'm beginning to understand why," Ward said. He saw this as an area where he might make a real connection with Doyle.

Doyle looked over at Ed Maddox and studied him for a moment, apparently trying to decide just how much trust was warranted. He made a decision.

"Byrd's an asshole," Doyle said. "Several a those boys are jealous of my connection to Royce, but it bothers Byrd the most. It eats at him."

Ward nodded. "I've seen how he tries to undercut you."

"More often than you know," Doyle said. "But it won't work. Royce trusts me. I'm kin. He values my advice, trusts my judgment. He knows he can rely on me."

"Of course, he does," Ward agreed. "There's nobody you can trust like kin."

"That's right," Doyle agreed. He stopped, put the truck in park, and then turned to Maddox.

"You need to keep an eye on Byrd," Doyle warned. "Jim doesn't like you, and that means he'll try to stir up trouble."

"Why is that, do you suppose?" Ward asked.

"It's part jealousy," Doyle explained. "Byrd can see that Royce values your input. He can't stand the thought that a newcomer would have *any* influence." Doyle chuckled. "As if Royce Lundgren wouldn't know what's worth listening to and what isn't."

"Exactly," Ward said, doing his best to appear sincere.

"But the fact that you and I are friends, just by itself, is enough to set Byrd off," Doyle explained.

Ward shook his head. "The man's got problems."

"He does," Doyle agreed. "But be aware," he added, his tone now ominous, "the man is clever...and dangerous."

Ward had no doubt about that.

Doyle slipped the transmission into drive. The truck moved forward.

After they had gone a ways, Doyle spoke. "Ed, big things are comin' down the pike. I can't tell you about it...not just yet. But mark my words, The Nation is gonna change the world."

Ward could feel it. This was the moment that came at some point in every successful undercover operation, the moment when you knew...you were in. But for Ward the sense of accomplishment was fleeting. Doyle's comments unnerved him. Now his mission would include finding out how The Nation planned to change the world, and then stopping it before it happened. Standing in the way would be Jim Byrd.

CHAPTER 57

12:40 p.m., Wednesday, July 22nd, Ankeny Community College, Ankeny, Iowa.

Meade walked out of the cafeteria. It was a quick lunch following Professor Goldman's history class. Today's lecture was one of only a handful he had attended since the break-up. And once again, Erin wasn't there. He had stared at her empty chair, aching to see her, to somehow make things right. Meade assumed that she'd dropped the class. He understood why and regretted that he hadn't done so first.

As much as he longed to talk to her, Meade knew that going to Erin's apartment was out of the question. She would not respond well to an appearance on her doorstep. How could he blame her? No, it would have to be a chance encounter, or at least appear that way.

Meade wandered the halls of the college. It was a sad, meandering ramble, not knowing where he was headed, physically or emotionally. Part of him didn't want to admit that he was looking for her, but he was. It made no sense. He knew that. What would he say if he found her? What could he say?

The smiling students surrounding Meade annoyed him. They joked with their friends, laughed. Why were they entitled to any happiness? He wanted everyone to suffer the way he was suffering. Damn them. Their joyous sounds made his head hurt. He had to get out of there.

As Meade made his way toward the exit, one faint, lilting laugh in a sea of noise caught his ear. A jolt of hope and paralyzing fear went through his heart. He paused, listened...and heard nothing. Meade sighed. Maybe he was just hearing what he so badly wanted to hear. He stepped forward, toward the door. Then, it wafted past him again. He was sure of it this time. It was a magical sound, the laugh that had charmed him, the laugh that still sparkled in his heart.

Meade spun around, expecting to see her nearby. He searched the throng of students. She wasn't there. Maybe he was hearing things after all. Or maybe he was so attuned to the sound of her that she could be heard over everything else. He backtracked, slowly, cautiously, not wanting to be seen. As he rounded the corner into an intersecting hallway he saw her.

Some guy was attempting to entertain Erin and another female student. Meade recognized the female as one of Erin's friends, Stephanie. He didn't know the male. But he did know that he didn't like what he was seeing. The two young women seemed to be enthralled. Every comment the guy made caused both of the young women to laugh with delight. Meade was burning, knowing that some other man had brought forth *that* laugh. It wasn't right. That magical sound was supposed to be for him... only him.

Suddenly Meade realized that he was standing in the middle of the hallway, motionless, staring, other students jostling him as they went by. The realization came too late. Erin was turned so that her back was toward him. But it wasn't she who noticed him, it was Stephanie.

Meade watched as Stephanie nudged Erin and nodded in his direction. Erin turned toward him. The smile that had been on her face evaporated. It was replaced by a look that held annoyance and anger, but also some sadness. Meade attempted a smile. It wasn't returned. Erin excused herself from her friends, and then walked toward the man she had known as Carl Ramsey.

"Hello, Jacob," she said.

Before he could answer, Erin's expression changed to one of curiosity coupled with concern.

"It is Jacob...right?" she inquired. It was a gratuitous gesture, but she was still angry...and hurt.

"I suppose I deserve that," Meade said. He looked around to see if anyone had noticed the use of his real name.

"Yeah, I suppose you do," she fired back.

Meade hung his head. He had desperately hoped that it wouldn't go like this, even though no reasonable person could have expected anything else.

"What do you want?" Erin asked.

"I don't know. I guess that I just..."

"Yes?"

"I guess that I just wanted to tell you how sorry I am, how much I miss you." Meade struggled to keep from choking up. This wasn't like him. He was embarrassed.

Meade looked over to where Stephanie and the guy had been standing to see if they were watching. The guy had moved off. Stephanie, on the other hand, was pretending to look for something in her backpack, obviously waiting to quiz Erin about the encounter. Meade desperately wanted to ask Erin about the guy but held back. He did not want to appear as pathetic as he actually was.

"Is that it?" Erin asked. "And just how is that supposed to make me feel? Is everything supposed to be okay now?"

"No, of course not," he said.

There was an awkward silence.

"I do want you to know that I'm trying to make things right," Meade continued, "make things right for some of the mistakes I've made in my life."

There was no response. For Erin, the fact that she was still listening was enough, more than he deserved.

Meade told her of his travel to Victoria, the testimony against Pierce and Simmons, the threat from Willie Hammond. He told her how the experience had restored a portion of the self-esteem that he thought he'd lost forever. As Meade recounted these events, he saw signs of a slight softening in Erin's attitude. But, while the anger appeared lessened, it was still light years to any reconciliation.

He wished he knew what she was thinking. Erin looked down at her feet. She struggled for the words. "Look, I'm sorry, Jacob," she finally said. "I wish things had worked out differently between us."

It was a gift, meant to alleviate some of his suffering, but also meant to send a message.

Meade thought he understood. "Me, too," he replied. It was all he could say.

Meade took a deep, almost sobbing breath, the kind a person takes to keep from completely losing control. Then, he turned and walked away.

Erin found a quiet corner in the library. She sat for a moment before opening her laptop. It was difficult to get the image of Jacob Meade, or Carl Ramsey, out of her head. His pained expression tugged at that part of her heart that still held some feeling for him. At times, while listening to his story, she had wanted to slap his face for the way in which he had deceived her. But there were also moments when she fought an urge to embrace him, comfort him, and, just maybe, be comforted herself.

An English paper was due by the end of the day. Erin needed to put some finishing touches on it before handing it in. She flipped open her laptop and powered up, preparing to get to work. But Jacob's tale of his trip to Texas, the trial, the threat, it piqued her curiosity. She wondered if there was anything about him that could be trusted, if her judgment had really been that bad. So much of what he'd said to her in their short time together had seemed so genuine. Could she really be that much of a dupe?

It was probably a need to confirm what he'd said more than

anything else. Erin logged onto the Internet. It took her only a few minutes to find several newspaper accounts of the trial of Troy Pierce and Willard Simmons, members of a radical anti-immigrant group known as The Nation. One of the stories recounted the dramatic testimony of Jacob Meade, a former member of the organization who had been placed in the Witness Protection Program. Erin felt a strange sense of relief as she read the article. What Jacob had told her was true. Her assessment of him hadn't been *all* wrong. There was some integrity there, and, it appeared, some guts.

CHAPTER 58

6:25 p.m., Wednesday, July 22nd, the residence of Charlie Kirklin, Yoakum, Texas.

Ward pulled in at Charlie Kirklin's place. The house was a plantation style on the outer edge of Yoakum. It sat back maybe eighty yards off the road on what Ward estimated to be about ten acres. A good-sized metal barn was off to the right of the house, just ahead of a gate that led into some pasture. A half-dozen or so cattle grazed there. Ward assumed that Kirklin had cattle for the same tax reasons that Doyle had described. He had to admit, it made sense.

Kirklin had insisted that he come to dinner, intent on giving some of the others a better chance to get acquainted with Ed Maddox. Ward was more than happy to oblige. This was exactly the type of get-together he needed to attend to secure his place in the organization. He couldn't simply rely on Doyle's goodwill. People like this could be fickle, especially the insecure ones like Doyle.

There were several vehicles parked in front of the house. In addition to Kirklin's pickup, there was another truck, and a Lincoln with Arizona plates. Ward pulled up behind the Lincoln and hopped out. His feet had no sooner hit the ground than Kirklin was out the front door, two beers in hand.

"Ed, glad you could make it," Kirklin hollered from the front porch.

The diminutive accountant bounded down the front steps, holding a bottle out toward Ed Maddox.

"Here you go, pardner," Kirklin said, shoving the beer at Maddox.

"Thanks, Charlie," Ward said. He took a swig and looked around. "Nice place...really nice."

Kirklin beamed with pride. "We like it," he said. "I'll show you around later. I've got some people I'd like you to meet."

"Lead the way."

They marched up the front steps and across the covered porch. Once inside, they made their way through the living room and into an expansive and well-equipped kitchen.

"My wife loves to cook," Kirklin said in explanation, patting his belly for emphasis.

Given the aroma emanating from the oven, Ward believed it, and believed that she was good at it.

Just then, a smiling, somewhat roundish woman entered the kitchen.

"Ed, this here's my wife, Carol," Kirklin said. "Honey, this here's Ed Maddox."

"Oh, Ed. Charlie's told me a lot of good things about you," she said with a pronounced Texas drawl. "We're sure pleased you could join us."

"My pleasure," Ward replied.

"Let's head out to the back porch, Ed," Kirklin offered. "The other fellas are out there already."

"That sounds good," Ward agreed.

As soon as they were away from the kitchen, Kirklin leaned in. "I don't like to discuss business in front of the missus," he whispered. "If you know what I mean."

"I got ya," Ward assured him.

Kirklin opened a door that led out onto a large screened-in back porch. Two men were seated there. They both stood. Ward recognized one of them as Eric Brandt, the training coordinator he'd met at the group's Fourth of July festivities. Brandt had wanted to question him about his Special Forces background. Ward planned to provide enough fictitious details to really whet the man's interest, and at the same time learn as much as he could about the organization's rumored vigilante operations. The other man was a tall, blond, hawk-nosed individual with riveting blue eyes. The eyes seemed cold, ruthless, almost sociopathic. Combined with a powerful build, they gave the man a threatening aura. Ward briefly wondered if he'd been found out, and if this was the man sent in to do the job.

"Ed, you remember Eric Brandt," Kirklin said.

"I sure do. Good to see you again," Ward said as he extended his hand.

"Same here," Brandt replied.

"And this is Bruno Alt," Kirklin said, introducing the other man. "Bruno is in from Arizona. He represents an organization that shares some of our…philosophies. Just the sort of organization that you, in fact, suggested we link up with. We're very pleased that they're interested in that prospect."

"Nice to meet you," Ward said warily.

"Good to meet you, sir," Alt said, his voice almost monotone. As they shook hands, Alt sized-up Ed Maddox, making no attempt to hide the fact that he was doing so.

"Let's sit," Kirklin suggested.

The four of them settled in.

"Looks like rain," Kirklin noted, looking out at the dark blue-black horizon. "We could use it."

"Amen to that," Brandt agreed. "Keeps up the way it's been, and I'll have to go out and buy hay for the cattle."

Kirklin nodded. Just then, a rumble of thunder could be heard in the distance.

"Music to my ears," Brandt said with a smile.

As the men talked, the rain moved in. It was a cool, wind-whipped rain. The breeze provided relief from what had been an oppressive July heat. With the rain came talk of more serious business.

"The Aryan Tribe is prepared to offer logistical support to your mission," Alt said, the comment being directed at Kirklin. "I have discussed this with Mr. Brandt. As you know, we share certain goals. We feel that our armies in Arizona and Southern California could do much to further your important work."

"Outstanding," Kirklin said. "Mr. Lundgren will be pleased."

"We'll start to work out the details tomorrow," Brandt announced. "Tonight, we should celebrate this powerful alliance."

"I agree," Kirklin said. He looked around. "Anybody else need a drink?"

"I'm ready," Brandt said.

Ward looked at his bottle. It was still half-full. "Sure, why not," he said.

Alt waved off the offer. "Nothing for me, thank you."

Ward noticed that Alt had consumed very little of the beer in his hand. Clearly, he was a man who believed in keeping himself under control.

Kirklin rose to fetch the drinks. When he was gone, Brandt turned to Ed Maddox.

"Ed, you promised to tell me about your Special Forces background," Brandt reminded him. "I understand that you did a tour in Afghanistan."

"Two, actually," Ward lied.

"I suspect that you have some skills that could be quite useful to us."

"I suspect you're right," Ward said with a sly smile. His expression masked a deep concern over why these men saw usefulness in Ed Maddox's special ops training. He needed to find out.

Brandt chuckled. Even Alt allowed himself an expression of slight amusement.

At that moment, Kirklin returned with beers for Brandt and Maddox.

"We were just discussing Ed's background," Brandt told Kirklin.

"He's an interesting man," Kirklin said, smiling at Maddox.

"That he is," Brandt agreed.

Brandt was silent for a moment. He appeared to be contemplating something. Finally, he spoke. "The government is never gonna get a handle on the situation at the border," Brandt said. He eyed Maddox closely, appearing to gauge his reaction. "They lack the will, all of 'em too busy tryin' to get the Hispanic vote." Brandt shook his head in disgust. "The only way we're gonna take our country back is to deal with these *wetbacks* ourselves."

"Amen," Kirklin proclaimed.

"I couldn't agree with you more," Ward announced. He felt a knot form in his stomach, then a fleeting nausea. As often as his job required him to declare allegiance to one repugnant philosophy or another, some things were just involuntary.

"You know," Brandt said, "we have our own...special forces."

"Is that so?" Ward asked. "I guess it has come to that, hasn't it?" Now they were getting somewhere, he thought.

Brandt smiled. "Maybe you could assist us with our...training," he suggested.

"Maybe I could," Ward replied. "Maybe I could."

As soon as dinner was over, and he was on the road, Ward called Richter and started to fill him in on the details.

"I expect that I'll have a pretty good idea what exactly Brandt's up to sometime soon," Ward said.

"I can't wait to hear."

"Sounds like I might get some good stuff on The Aryan Tribe as well. I've wanted to get into those bastards my whole career."

As concerned as he was for Ward's safety, Richter was excited. This stuff was world-class.

"Just be fuckin' careful, man," Richter said.

"Hey, *careful* is my middle name, brother."

"Yeah...right."

"You know what I'm really concerned about?" Ward asked.

"What's that?"

"If I do get some useful intelligence on these supposed vigilante raids, how do I share it with the Border Patrol without them blowing my cover?" It was a serious concern. Ward knew damn well how tough it was to keep the source a secret in any case, much less one like this. He would be the obvious suspect if it didn't play out just right.

"You sayin' Homeland Security can't keep a secret?" Richter asked facetiously.

Ward snorted at Richter's rhetorical question. "No, I'm sayin' I don't wanna get smoked because some idiot can't make it look like it was good police work versus a tip."

"Yeah, I'd have to say that seems like a reasonable concern," Richter agreed. It wasn't a particularly comforting response, but it was the truth, one that both of them knew only too well.

CHAPTER 59

12:35 a.m., Thursday, July 23rd, Meade's apartment, Ankeny, Iowa.

Meade stared at the ceiling, unable to sleep. At work he'd been off his game all day, his thoughts constantly wandering to the encounter with Erin. When his absentmindedness caused a badly flawed weld, he asked his foreman for the rest of the day off. Randy Kroeger had been surprisingly happy to oblige. Meade wondered about that. What did he know?

His mind was still fixed on the conversation with Erin. Her words haunted him: *I wish things had worked out differently between us.* Meade replayed the phrase over and over again in his head. Was it crazy to see some glimmer of hope there? He remembered her reaction when he told her about the trial, his testimony, how it made him feel. He could see that it changed something in her attitude. He wanted so badly to win her back. What would it take? Would something heroic do it? If so, he was prepared to go there, the costs be damned.

Meade thought back on what he'd told the agents in the debriefings that followed his arrest, the things that really seemed to catch their interest. There were the rumors about illegals being killed at the border, and drugs being taken off of those who were mules. He knew all of that could be bullshit, but there were certainly people in the organization who were capable of doing it. Willie Hammond, the bloodthirsty thug who had threatened him at the trial, was one. There were others.

The other thing that really caught their attention, Meade recalled, was when he mentioned overhearing two of the members talk about a killing, something big, a sniper. He remembered the look the agents exchanged. They immediately left the interview room. When they returned they asked him to take a lie detector test. It was after the polygraph that they decided to give him a pass and put him in the Witness Protection Program. It was that information that had really hit home.

Meade resolved to do something. He didn't know what, but something. If it failed, even if the worst happened, at least he would have made the attempt. It was the only way to win back Erin, and that was why he had to act.

There was one name from the past that stuck out. Joe Collins was a good friend, a member his own age who often seemed less than enthusiastic about The Nation's goals. Meade knew why. Like himself, Collins had dated a beautiful young woman who was part Hispanic. When his family found out about it, they forced him to end the relationship. Collins had once talked to Meade about leaving the group, but he never followed through. His family was too involved. Both parents were members, and his uncle, Warren Graves, was the organization's chief mouthpiece, the man behind much of the propaganda.

Despite the situation with the ex-girlfriend, Collins was still connected, he knew things. His parents had written off the episode with the Hispanic girl as a youthful indiscretion, one fueled by hormones. Meade knew that it was much more than that. He thought that he could get to Collins, take advantage of his ambivalence, and convince him to help bring down The Nation.

A squad car sped by on the street just north of the apartment building. The wail of the siren reminded Meade of his handler, Deputy Willis. He knew that Willis would be righteously furious if he found out about this planned breach of Witness Protection protocol. It was a major violation of the rules to contact anyone from your former life, a violation that could, in fact, get you booted from the program. Willis had repeatedly warned him about it. Meade knew that he would have to be careful, very careful.

The anxiety and despair of a dark night launch some of life's more ill-advised adventures. That truth lived deep in the recesses of Meade's mind, never quite coming to the fore to sober his thoughts. There was only a vague sense of unease. But it was overwhelmed by more powerful emotions. He had made his choice.

CHAPTER 60

9:35 a.m., Thursday, July 23rd, the White House, Washington, D.C.

President Samuel T. Buckley paced back and forth behind his Oval Office desk. He thought better on his feet, always had. Seated to his immediate right, calm and collected as always, was Attorney General William Bradford. They were awaiting the arrival of several cabinet members and the press secretary.

"So, you're in agreement on this?" Buckley asked his attorney general.

"Yes, sir. I think it's a bold move, one sure to put the ball in Congress's court."

Buckley nodded. "And you're okay with El Paso as the location?"

"To be honest, I'm a little less okay with that," Bradford said. "Juarez is just across the border. It's one of the most violent, lawless cities in Mexico. In fact, right now, it's one of the most dangerous places on Earth."

"I thought you agreed with the idea of a border town. It's an immigration speech, Bill. Makes perfect sense to me."

"I was thinking of something more along the lines of San Diego," Bradford replied. "El Paso? I don't know."

"People will take the message more seriously if I deliver it in a town like El Paso," Buckley said. "That area is a major entry point for illegal immigrants and a major route for the drug traffickers."

"So is the San Diego/Tijuana area."

"San Diego looks too much like a vacation," the President said. "It's El Paso."

Bradford knew better than to push the point any further.

There was a knock at the door.

"Come in," Buckley called.

Chief of Staff Michael Cooper entered the Oval Office.

"Mr. President, they're all here."

"Send them in, Mike. And stick around. I want you to hear this."

"Will do."

As usual, the first through the door was Secretary of Homeland Security Donald Page. He was followed by his sometimes nemesis, National Security Advisor Brent Dixon. Secretary of Commerce Amanda Peterson, and Secretary of Labor Frank Butler were close behind. Bringing up the rear was Press Secretary Ellie Drake. As soon as the group entered, Cooper shut the door. The President motioned for everyone to take a seat.

"I wanted you all to come in today so that I could tell you that I plan to give a major address on immigration policy," the President began.

Looks were exchanged around the room.

"I've already discussed this with Bill and Ellie, but, obviously, I want to get input from the rest of you."

"I don't suppose this address would include anything about a guest worker program?" Commerce Secretary Peterson asked.

The President smiled at her perseverance. "No, Amanda, it will not," he said.

"How about an amnesty plan?" Cooper asked. He couldn't resist.

The President shot his chief of staff a look.

"Just asking," Cooper joked.

There was a chuckle around the room.

"I intend to put some pressure on Congress to be more...

helpful on matters of enforcement and border security," Buckley continued. "Everyone on the Hill just wants to complain about what we're doing. They lack the political courage to float their own ideas. We're going to help provide some incentive, and hopefully loosen the purse strings in the process."

"I like the sounds of that," Page said. The Secretary of Homeland Security was always looking for more funding in this area. "Mr. President, I hope that you plan to note some of our accomplishments, technological enforcement, for example."

Buckley stole a glance at Bradford, and then returned his attention to Page.

"I don't know that that helps us, Don."

"But Mr. President, I think that we've made great..."

Buckley held up his hand, cutting off his Homeland Security chief.

"One of the objectives here is to get more funding from Congress. I'll make reference to a few high-tech tools, pilotless drones, thermal imaging, but, frankly, I don't want to put much emphasis on an area in which we've had...*limited* success. It invites a negative response. We can deal with that issue in direct negotiations with committee members."

Page looked down at the floor and nodded his head.

"Ellie, why don't you pass around the draft we've put together," the President said, gesturing to his press secretary. "I've had the speechwriters working on this for a few weeks. I'd like each of you to look it over and get back to me with any comments. You're all familiar with my thoughts in this area. I don't think you'll find many surprises."

"When do you plan to deliver this?" Cooper asked.

"Sometime in the next two weeks," Buckley replied. "I've selected El Paso, Texas, as the site for the address."

There was a collective gasp. Brent Dixon's head jerked up from the draft he was reading.

"You can't do that, Mr. President," Dixon insisted. "Security will be a nightmare. Hell, Ciudad Juarez is just across the border.

It's one of the major burial grounds for those targeted by the drug lords, and a totally lawless town."

"The speech isn't in Juarez, Brent," the President reminded him. "It's in El Paso."

"It doesn't matter. We won't be able to..."

"I've made up my mind," Buckley said firmly, cutting off Dixon.

"Oh my God," Dixon muttered, putting his head in his hands.

The President turned toward Page. "Don, I trust you'll notify the Secret Service immediately. They'll need some time to prepare for this one."

"I'll say," Page replied.

Buckley began to pace, his hands clasped behind his back.

"Look, I understand the problem," he said. "But I think it's important to deliver this speech in a location that suffers with these issues every day. If I go to El Paso, that says I'm serious about this, damned serious. Besides, there are unique security considerations with any location. I'm confident that our people can handle it. I've been to more dangerous places than El Paso, Texas, you know."

No one spoke. It was obvious that the President would not be dissuaded.

Buckley stopped pacing and turned toward the group. He focused on Cooper.

"Mike, I want to notify some of the friendlier members of Congress from the Border States, maybe give them an idea what's coming. Start making the calls today."

Cooper chortled. "I take it you weren't planning to keep it a secret, then?"

Buckley smiled. "Just stirrin' the pot, Mike. Just stirrin' the pot."

Mike Cooper listened to Congressman Wesley Lindell babble on about his support for the President's immigration proposals. It was Cooper's third call of the morning to Border State members, and it was by far the most painful. The truth was he despised Lindell. The Congressman from Arizona had run on a strident anti-illegal immigration platform that bordered on racism. Cooper considered Lindell to be a dangerous bigot and it galled him to know that Lindell considered the President to be an ally in his cause. Nothing could be further from the truth. Buckley's approach, even though Cooper personally disagreed with it, simply mirrored what the President believed was wanted by the majority of the American people. Lindell's rhetoric, on the other hand, was close to that of a white supremacist. Finally, Cooper had heard enough.

"As I said, Congressman," Cooper interrupted, "the President simply wanted to give you a heads-up on the speech. We know how much these issues impact your district."

"Well, you tell the President that I appreciate it," Lindell said. "And tell him that the folks in my district like what he's tryin' to do."

"I'll do that," Cooper replied, looking for a way to end the call.

"I just wish we could get a few more people up here on the Hill to see it *our* way. You know what I mean?"

Cooper sighed. *Our* way? This guy had to be kidding. It was times like this when he truly hated his job.

"Couldn't have said it any better myself, Congressman," Cooper lied, fighting off the urge to throw up. "You take care now. I'll tell the President we had a good chat."

"Do that. And you let him know if ol' Wes Lindell can be of any help to just give a call."

Cooper groaned. Now Lindell was referring to himself in the third person. Most members of Congress were capable of it, but it was singularly annoying coming from this asshole.

"I'll be sure to tell him," Cooper said, having no intention of doing so. "You take care now," he repeated, hoping that Lindell would take the hint. The next step was to simply start banging the phone on his desk.

"You, too," Lindell said.

And with that, mercifully, it was over. Cooper hung up the phone, reminiscing about his days in the private sector.

Wes Lindell sat back in his chair, a smile on his face. He could picture that smug jackass Cooper satisfied with himself for having played another congressman. Most of the attention-seeking dolts he worked with were overly flattered to get a call from the White House. It made him sick. In his opinion, Sam Buckley was nothing special. Lindell didn't give a rat's ass about getting a call from the President's chief of staff, or Buckley himself, for that matter. Using the President and his people was simply a means to an end. They were pawns in a greater struggle, a much greater struggle.

Lindell slipped open the lower left-hand desk drawer. It was there, tucked back in a corner, that he kept the cell phone used for such calls. The number came back to a fictitious name and address. Plausible deniability was, after all, the key to any successful career in politics.

The number was committed to memory. It couldn't be listed in the cell phone's directory, too dangerous. Lindell punched in the digits and hit send. It rang once, twice. The answer came before the third ring.

"Hello, Congressman."

"Jim, I've got some news that I think you're gonna like." Lindell explained what he'd just learned from the chief of staff.

"That's good to know."

"I thought you'd be pleased."

"And when will he be delivering this speech?"

"Sometime in the next two weeks. I was told they would get back to me with that in a few days."

"I'll alert those who need to know."

"You do that." Lindell paused. When he spoke, his tone was

solemn. "This could be our chance."

"Yes, it could."

Congressman Lindell clicked off the phone, certain that Jim Byrd would take care of things.

CHAPTER 61

11:45 a.m., Thursday, July 23rd, Office of the Registrar, University of Georgia, Athens, Georgia.

Flagg walked into the Office of the Registrar expecting little trouble in securing a copy of Maddox's college transcripts. The ruse of being Sylvester Harding from the U.S. Office of Personnel Management conducting a federal background check had worked well at Columbia East High School. Flagg had little reason to believe it wouldn't work just as well here.

In his long career, Flagg had never failed to get the transcripts. They were always a rich source of information and leads. He hoped that this would not be the exception. Edward Michael Maddox was proving to be a real mystery. There were too many unanswered questions.

Flagg walked up to the counter. A small, slender woman, prim in appearance, noticed him and approached.

"May I help you, sir?" she asked.

Flagg smiled his most charming smile. "Yes, thank you. Name's Sylvester Harding, with the U.S. Office of Personnel Management," Flagg lied. He laid his bogus credentials on the counter.

"What can I do for you, Mr. Harding?"

"Well, I'm conducting a background check on an Edward Michael Maddox. His questionnaire says he's a University of Georgia graduate."

"A background check?" the woman asked.

"He applied for a position with the federal government," Flagg explained, "one that requires a security clearance."

"I see."

"I can't really say more than that," Flagg whispered. "I'm sure you understand."

The woman said nothing. It was Flagg's first hint that there might be a problem.

"Anyway," Flagg continued, "I'd like to get a copy of his transcripts."

"We don't just give those out," the woman replied. "I'm sure *you* understand, what with the rise in identity theft and all."

"Oh, I do, I do," Flagg assured her. "That's why we have the applicants sign a waiver allowing us access to their records." Flagg produced the form with the neatly forged signature of Edward M. Maddox.

The woman examined the form. "I'm sure that you're who you say you are, Mr. Harding, but this waiver form would be rather easy to forge. And why wouldn't Mr. Maddox simply supply you with a copy of the transcripts himself?"

Listen, you officious bitch, Flagg wanted to say, but didn't. He took a deep breath and remained calm. A professional was prepared for these situations.

"We prefer to get the transcripts directly from the school," Flagg said. "It's sad to say, but students do doctor their transcripts these days."

The woman nodded. It made sense. "Given the grade inflation I've seen over the last twenty years," she said, sounding disgusted, "I'm surprised they would have to."

"True enough," Flagg agreed. "It's a disgrace." Now, he was sure that he had her in his pocket.

"Maybe our office could call Mr. Maddox," the woman suggested, "have him send in a written request."

You've gotta be fucking kidding me, Flagg thought. His mind raced.

"There's no need for that," Flagg said. "I'll contact OPM and have them get in touch with Mr. Maddox about producing the transcripts. You're not the first registrar's office that has refused to provide us with a copy. As you say, identity theft is on the rise." Flagg smiled pleasantly, hiding his aggravation.

"I appreciate your understanding," the woman said.

Flagg thought for a moment. "Could you just confirm something for me?" he asked hopefully. Leaving empty-handed would result in an unpleasant phone call to Jim Byrd, one Flagg didn't want to make. "Maddox is a geologist," he said. "I assume he was a geology major. I believe that's what his application indicated. If you could verify that, then at least I could conduct some interviews with members of that department. The trip wouldn't be a total loss."

The woman tapped her fingers on the counter, considering the request.

"Well, I guess I could do that," she finally said. "What was his full name?"

"Edward Michael Maddox."

"Give me a minute. I'll go check."

A few minutes later, she returned.

"He did major in geology," she said. "The Geology Building is at 210 Field Street. Do you need directions?"

"Yes, that would be helpful," Flagg said, "and a phone number." So, he thought, the transcripts actually exist.

Flagg walked into the Geology Building and made his way to the third floor. He had called ahead, explained his situation, and arranged to meet with the head of the department, Professor Bryson Cook.

Flagg knocked on the door to Room 329. A tall, bearded man answered the door. His hair was graying, and he had the look of a scholar, but there was also an air of adventure about the man that Flagg picked up on immediately.

"Mr. Harding, I presume?" Professor Cook asked.

"At your service, Professor. Thank you for agreeing to see me on such short notice." Flagg smiled and held out his hand.

"Please, come in."

As he looked about the small office, Flagg could see that he'd been right about the good professor. There were numerous photos of Cook conquering this or that mountain peak.

"If I may say," Flagg offered, "you appear to be quite an adventurer."

"It's nothing, really," Cook said modestly. "A hobby. It's not as if I'd climbed Everest."

"Still," Flagg said.

"So, Mr. Maddox has applied for some sort of federal position?" Cook asked.

"That's right. One that requires a background check, I'm afraid."

The professor stroked his beard. "Can't say that I remember much about him. I do recall that he was a solid student, mostly A's and B's. I don't know if that helps much."

Not really, Flagg thought. It appeared that the professor actually recalled Maddox. He was hoping for something more along the lines of, *never heard of the guy.*

"Yes, that's helpful," Flagg lied, masking his disappointment. "What else can you tell me about him?"

"Not much really. It's been some time ago. There are so many students. I'm sure you understand."

"I do," Flagg said. He thought for a moment. "You mentioned that he was a good student. *Solid*, I believe you said. Do you have a record of his grades? Those received in geology courses would be fine, if that's all you have."

"I'm afraid you would have to get something like that from the registrar's office. It's university policy."

"As it should be," Flagg said, not surprised by the answer. He wouldn't press the issue. It would draw too much attention. He rose to leave.

"Professor, thank you for your time."

"Sorry I couldn't be of more assistance," Cook apologized.

They shook hands and parted company.

Once back in the hallway, Flagg considered his next move. There was little left but to visit Odessa Oil's Alaska operations. "Oh well," he muttered to himself, "I've always wanted to go to Alaska."

Flagg pulled out his cell and punched in the number for Byrd. This was a conversation he was not going to enjoy.

As soon as Harding left, Professor Cook phoned the number that had been provided.

"Hello, Professor," a voice answered.

"Hello."

"I take it you have news?"

"You were right. He was just here."

"What did you tell him?"

"No more than we discussed."

"Very good. We appreciate your assistance."

CHAPTER 62

8:25 p.m., Thursday, July 23rd, Royce Lundgren's residence, Compound One.

It was the monthly meeting of what could be called The Nation's leadership council. Tonight, it just happened to coincide with receipt of possibly the most important bit of intelligence the group had ever received. Byrd, not known as one to show much emotion, displayed his excitement as he described his conversation with Congressman Lindell. Lundgren had instructed him to share the information with these men, and them only. Byrd's only concern was the presence of Doyle. He had never trusted Lundgren's cousin and doubted that he ever would. It wasn't a matter of Doyle's loyalty so much as it was his lack of capacity... that, and an admitted jealousy concerning Doyle's influence. Byrd often wondered to what degree Lundgren was aware of his cousin's limitations.

"Do we have time to get our assets in place?" Graves asked.

"Steps are being taken even as we speak," Byrd assured him. "The key is to move quickly, before the Secret Service begins its preparations."

"That's right," Brandt agreed. "They're on-site well before any event. We need to have people on the ground as soon as possible."

"The Congressman promised to alert me as soon as he hears the date," Byrd told the group.

"What's in it for him?" Kirklin asked. "I know we've been funneling money to his campaign war chest for years. He definitely owes us, but not this much."

So far, Royce Lundgren had remained quiet. He sat, listening to the others, elbows on the table, his hands pressed together as if in prayer.

"Congressman Lindell shares our beliefs," Lundgren began, staring straight ahead as he spoke. "The man is an exemplary public servant." He turned to Kirklin. "The Congressman also believes that the anti-illegal immigrant backlash from this...*incident* will sweep him into higher office. I agree. That's what's in it for him."

Kirklin nodded. He felt foolish for asking the question.

"You know, a guy like that Ed Maddox could be helpful with this type of operation," Brandt suggested. "He's got the right background. I mean, if you think he's ready, Royce."

"Absolutely not!" Byrd objected. "I'm still not sure this guy's legitimate. There are a lot of unanswered questions with Ed Maddox. Ron Flagg has run into a series of dead ends."

"By *series of dead ends* I take it you mean you have no evidence of any kind of problem with the guy," Doyle threw in. "Why don't you just admit it, Jim. You just don't like him. I think you're jealous of his expertise...that and the fact he probably knows more about your job than you do."

Byrd's face turned red. He'd had enough of Doyle and didn't care who knew it.

"You're an idiot," Byrd shot back, "and beyond naïve."

"That's enough," Lundgren said firmly. "If you have some evidence, Jim, share it with us."

Byrd pondered how to reply. To respond with what Flagg had been unable to find would sound feeble at this point.

"I think it's way too early to trust Maddox with this information," Byrd said. "He hasn't earned it."

"Well, I agree with Harold," Kirklin interjected, nodding toward Doyle. "Ed could be very useful on this."

The atmosphere was tense. Brandt spoke up. "I have an idea," he said. "I've already asked Maddox to help with training our special forces. Any training he provides…"

Byrd went rigid. "Nobody told me about this."

"Royce already cleared it," Brandt said. He turned to Lundgren. "Sorry, I thought everybody knew."

Byrd shook his head. "This is a mistake, Royce. I need more time to check this guy's background."

"Continue, Eric," Lundgren said to Brandt. He then leveled a stern look on Byrd that told him to be quiet.

"I'm not sharing any mission specifics with him," Brandt assured Byrd. "Maddox will be helpful in areas like desert tracking, ambush, sniper techniques. With his experience, there's a lot he can teach us."

"And you don't think he'll ask questions?" Byrd asked, unable to stay silent.

"He might. I'll just tell him that we're preparing for the revolution, for when the border completely breaks down, somethin' like that. He doesn't need to know anything about our interdiction efforts, not yet." Brandt turned back to Lundgren. "Anyway, my point was simply that any training Maddox provides to my men will also be useful in our new mission. He'll be making a contribution. He just won't know it."

Brandt turned to Doyle, then Kirklin, trying to gauge whether the idea seemed to mollify them.

Byrd started to speak. Lundgren cut him off.

"For now, we'll proceed with Eric's proposal," Lundgren announced, acknowledging Brandt with a single nod of the head. "I'll make the decision as to whether Mr. Maddox is to be brought further into the fold."

Lundgren turned to Byrd and smiled. It was the kind of smile that could mean many things, the kind of smile that could be read as a warning.

"You will continue your background investigation of Mr. Maddox," Lundgren said to Byrd.

Byrd should have felt some relief at the comment. Instead, he felt vaguely uneasy.

"But I'll expect you to wrap it up in short order," Lundgren continued. "If something's there...find it. If not, let's move on."

CHAPTER 63

8:20 a.m., Saturday, July 25th, Harold Doyle's ranch, just out-side Yoakum, Texas.

Ward threw out his first cast of the morning. The line whistled as the lure sailed out over the pond and plunked into the water. It was a perfect shot, landing two feet from a patch of weeds and close to an old tree stump.

"Nice cast!" Doyle hollered from nearby. "That's a good spot. Pulled a couple of eight-pounders from right in there."

"That'd be all right," Ward shot back.

"Bet you did some good fishin' up there in Alaska, huh?" Doyle asked.

"Not as much as I would've liked," Ward replied. "But when we did go, it was good."

"What'd you catch up there?"

Ward thought fast, cussing himself for inviting this line of questioning.

"Oh, you know...salmon, halibut. Sometimes we'd get rain-bow or steelhead trout." Ward prayed that Doyle would ask no more questions. He couldn't fake it for long on this subject.

"That sounds fun," Doyle said.

Just then, Ward felt a tug on his line. "I think I got one!" he yelled as he set the hook. Ward was as thankful for the bite as he was for the opportunity to change the subject. The fish put up a good fight. When he got it to the bank, Ward lifted the hefty largemouth bass out of the water by its lower jaw. He estimated the weight at six or seven pounds.

"Damn, that's a nice one," Doyle announced as he walked over to Ward's spot.

"I'll say." Ward removed the hook and admired the lunker. He turned to Doyle. "Catch and release?" he asked.

"Up to you, pardner. If you wanna clean him, you can take him with."

"I'll just let him go," Ward said, "keep the population up."

"Suits me," Doyle said with a shrug. He started back to his spot. After he had gone a few feet, he turned back. "Hey, I brought some coffee. You want some?"

"Yeah, that sounds good."

Doyle walked over to his truck and returned with the thermos and two mugs. He handed one of the mugs to Ward and then filled it. After pouring his own, Doyle reached into his pocket and pulled out a small flask.

"I like to give mine a little...*flavor*," Doyle said, pouring a shot into his coffee. He offered the flask to Ward.

"No, thanks," Ward laughed, waving it off. "It's still a little early for me."

"Suit yerself," Doyle said. He took a swig. "Whew, that hits the spot." He made one final offer to Ward.

Ward held up his hand. "Maybe later," he said.

Doyle shrugged and slipped the booze back into his pocket. He walked about twenty yards down the bank and tossed in his line. Soon he had his own bite. Minutes later, a five-pounder was hoisted out of the water.

"How 'bout that?" Doyle asked, proudly displaying the fish.

"You got a helluva spot here, Harold," Ward proclaimed.

"It's nice, ain't it?"

"It sure is."

They fished in silence for a few minutes. Then, Doyle spoke.

"You know, Ed, you got some real allies in the organization."

"I'm glad to hear that."

"Me, Charlie, even Eric Brandt. He's an admirer."

"That's good to know," Ward said. It *was* good to know. Still, he had the sense something was left unsaid.

"But?" Ward asked.

"Well, we've already discussed Jim Byrd," Doyle offered.

"Still got it out for me?"

"Just watch your back. That's all I can say."

"I appreciate the heads-up, Harold," Ward said with sincerity, though not for reasons that Doyle would suspect.

"Don't mention it. We're friends. Friends look out for each other."

"That's right," Ward agreed. He hated to admit it, but the exchange gave him just the slightest pang of guilt.

"The important thing is, Royce likes you," Doyle said. "Nothin' else really matters."

"I'm sure you're right."

Ward felt a tug on his line. "Son of a bitch if I don't have another one," he announced. He set the hook and began to reel.

"Hell, I got one, too!" Doyle hollered. "I think she's a big one."

They fought the fish for the next couple of minutes, Ward landing his first, then Doyle. Ward's bass was in the five-pound range. Doyle's was closer to seven.

"You got the touch, Harold," Ward said, tossing his own fish back. "That's a nice one."

Doyle beamed, happy to land a good catch in front of his accomplished friend.

"I've had a lot of practice," Doyle said. "Besides, I've got home-field advantage."

Ward noted the false modesty, aware that it was born of insecurity. He watched with interest as Doyle celebrated the catch by adding another splash from the flask to his increasingly potent mug of coffee. It was clear that Harold Doyle had even more of a drinking problem than had already been suspected. That was fine with Ward. The drinkers were always the best sources.

"Royce wants you to come to dinner tonight," Doyle said, "if you can make it. It would just be the three of us, a chance to talk. He'd like to get to know you better."

Ward struggled to hide his excitement. This could be his chance for a real breakthrough to the inner circle.

"I'd like that," Ward replied.

"Good. Come on out around seven. Royce wants to give you a tour of his ranch before we eat."

"That'd be nice. I'd like to see the place."

Doyle walked over to where Ward was standing. "Ed, he doesn't do this for just anybody. You've impressed him, and it takes a lot to impress Royce Lundgren."

"Well, that's flattering," Ward said. "Royce is a visionary, a true leader. I'm honored that he feels that way." If there were an Oscar for undercover work, he thought.

"You should be," Doyle said. "By the way, I understand that you'll be helpin' Brandt train his men."

"We've discussed it," Ward acknowledged.

"Well, from what I hear, it's gonna happen. I'm glad. You'll be real helpful."

"I hope so."

"I know so," Doyle said. He paused. "Like I told you before, big things are comin'. You'll play an important part, Ed."

Ward nodded solemnly.

"People don't know it," Doyle continued, "but The Nation has friends in high places, friends who want to see us succeed. They tell us things."

Ward's brow furrowed as he pondered just what these bastards were up to.

CHAPTER 64

10:05 a.m., Saturday, July 25th, Meade's apartment, Ankeny, Iowa.

It had been easy enough to open a cell phone account under a fictitious name...another fictitious name, that is, Meade reminded himself. He'd thought it necessary, just in case the Marshals Service was listening. What he was about to do was a massive breach of Witness Protection Program protocol.

Meade looked at the phone, then at the scrap of paper lying on the counter. On it was written the number for Joe Collins, the one man who Meade believed might be willing to help him. He took a deep breath, then another, before slowly punching in the numbers. This was the course he had chosen. There was no turning back. He hit send.

"Hello?"

"Joe?"

"Yeah. Who's this?"

"It's Jacob Meade."

Nothing was said on the other end. Meade could almost hear Collins' mind at work.

"I guess I'm not exactly who you expected to hear from," Meade said.

"You could say that," Collins replied. "A lot of people are wonderin' what happened with you, Jake." Collins was aware of Meade's testimony in the trial of Pierce and Simmons, and of the desire of many of the members to see him dead.

"I'm sure they are," Meade acknowledged

"Where are you?"

The question, so early in the conversation, gave Meade a chill. Maybe he had miscalculated…badly.

"I'd rather not say," Meade answered.

"Fair enough," Collins said. "I certainly understand that. You don't know who you can trust."

"I called you, Joe. I'm hoping I can trust you."

"We've always been friends, Jake. Nothing's changed that."

Meade felt relieved. This sounded like the Joe he remembered.

"So, why the call?" Collins asked. "Just lonely for the voice of an old friend?"

Even though the reason wasn't loneliness, Meade had to admit, it felt good to hear Joe's voice.

"No, it's more than that," Meade answered, "much more."

"I'm listening."

Leaving out any details that could be used to identify his whereabouts, Meade described his experiences since arriving at his new location. He told Collins about Erin, how her love had opened his eyes. He spoke passionately about his change of heart concerning The Nation and Royce Lundgren. It was a compelling performance, one that Meade felt sure would strike a chord with Collins. But it was also less than totally honest. What Meade didn't say was that, in truth, the ideology hadn't completely left him. Despite his feelings about the organization, much of what Royce Lundgren said still rang true. The man still owned a piece of him. But right now, for Collins' ears, there would only be the message of conversion to a new way of thinking.

"I always thought that, at least at one point, you felt the same way," Meade said. He knew that he didn't need to elaborate.

"Yeah, I guess that's true," Collins said.

"If you still feel that way, maybe you'll help me," Meade said.

"Me?" Collins asked. "What can I do?"

"I need information. You know things."

"Not as much as you think. Some people aren't inclined to share things with me, you know…because of the past."

Meade suspected that was at least partially true. Still, Collins' uncle was Warren Graves, and the two of them had always been close.

"Anyway, what kind of information?" Collins asked.

Meade explained what he was looking for.

"I don't know anything about that stuff," Collins said. "If I did, and I told you, they'd probably kill me, regardless of who I'm related to. Hell, I shouldn't even be having this conversation with you."

Meade understood Collins' concern, but pressed on.

"It's important, Joe. These people need to be stopped. I know you agree with me."

"Well…"

"Please, Joe. Nobody will know that it came from you. I promise you that." Meade hesitated. "If you don't want to discuss it over the phone…I'm willing to come to you."

"You'd do that? It's that important to you?"

"It is."

"Well, *if* I can even get any useful information, and it's a big if, I suppose we could meet halfway, halfway between me and wherever the hell you are."

"Thanks, Joe."

"Don't thank me yet," Collins said. "I'll be in touch." He hung up the phone.

Meade stared at the cell after the call ended, praying that he'd done the right thing.

Joe Collins made the call within minutes of ending his conversation with Meade.

"Uncle Warren?"

"Joe! How's my favorite nephew?"

"I'm good. I've got some interesting news." Collins described his talk with Meade, and how he'd played it.

"You handled it perfectly," Graves said. "I would have expected nothing less."

Collins beamed. It made him happy to please Uncle Warren. The man was a second father to him, and the person who had shown him the error of his earlier ways.

"You've performed a great service for The Nation," Graves continued. "Mr. Lundgren will be quite pleased."

"What should I do next?" Collins asked.

"For the moment, nothing," Graves said. "I'll contact Jim Byrd. We'll coordinate a plan on how best to proceed. Then I'll call you with the details for your meeting with Mr. Meade, date, location, etcetera. I'm sure he'll agree to whatever you suggest, as long as he thinks the information makes it worthwhile. You'll tell him just enough over the phone to assure his appearance at the designated meeting place."

"Understood. I'll wait for further instruction."

"I'm proud of you, Joe...very proud."

"Thanks, Uncle Warren."

As he hung up the phone, Collins flashed back to a time when he and Jacob Meade had been the best of friends. He was sorry that Jake had lost his way. But the betrayal was simply too great. There could be no mercy. Jacob Meade would have to pay for his treasonous behavior and pay dearly.

Byrd called Willie Hammond as soon as he got off the phone with Graves. Hammond was a devoted follower, and an enforcer of utter ruthlessness. His talents had proved useful many times in the past. Byrd knew that Hammond would love to have the opportunity to deal with Jacob Meade and send a message to all those who would betray The Nation. He would have his chance.

"Guess who's been in touch," Byrd said, anticipating Hammond's delight.

"Who?"

"Jacob Meade."

"No shit!"

"Called Joe Collins, Graves' nephew," Byrd said. "They were friends. Apparently, Meade asked Joe for help in gettin' information on us. He wants Joe to help him bring down the organization."

"What?" Hammond asked. "Why would Collins help him? What the hell would even make Meade think that?"

"That's what I asked Warren," Byrd replied. "I guess Joe was screwin' some *spic* a few years back, thought he was in love. He even thought about leaving The Nation. Warren straightened him out. The kid musta confided in Meade back then, making Meade think he could be approached."

"Big mistake," Hammond said with a chuckle. There was a note of something like glee in his voice.

"It gets better," Byrd continued. "Joe told him that he'd try to help, but that they wouldn't be able to discuss anything over the phone."

"Beautiful," Hammond said. "I take it he asked Meade to meet him someplace?"

"Didn't have to...Meade offered."

"Whew, boy! Please tell me that I'm gonna get a shot at this punk."

"Why do you think I called? I just can't have you kill him right off," Byrd cautioned. "I need to get some information out of him first, find out what he's already told the Feds, see if he knows anything about any informants, undercover agents, stuff like that."

"I hear ya," Hammond said knowingly. "Make it slow, painful. I got no problem with that."

"I'm sure you don't," Byrd said. Sometimes, Hammond even made him a little nervous.

"So, what's the plan?" Hammond asked. "When's this gonna happen?"

"Don't know yet. We'll get Joe a date and location, along with a little teaser info, enough to make sure that Meade shows."

"Damn!" Hammond exclaimed. "That son of a bitch is gonna regret the day he snitched on us."

"Yes, he is," Byrd agreed. "When we're done with him, it'll be a long time before anyone else dares to betray The Nation."

CHAPTER 65

7:20 p.m., Saturday, July 25th, Compound One.

The tour was about to begin. Ward watched as Lundgren pulled out of the metal barn in a four-wheel drive utility vehicle.

"Gentlemen, hop aboard," Lundgren said.

Ward and Doyle moved toward the vehicle.

"Ed, why don't you sit up front with me," Lundgren offered, patting the seat next to his. "It'll give us a better chance to talk."

Ward looked at Doyle. The only other seat was in a cargo box, similar to the bed of a pickup truck, only much smaller.

"No problem," Doyle said with a wave of his hand. "I'll jump in back."

"You sure?" Ward asked.

Doyle gave him a wink. "I want you two to get better acquainted."

The men climbed in, Doyle carrying a beer for the ride. Within minutes they had passed over a cattle guard and were traveling along a well-worn track through the small, fenced-in pasture behind the main structures. Cattle grazed contentedly. A few turned to look at the vehicle and its passengers, then quickly lost interest and looked away, knowing there was no threat. It was a pleasant evening, cool for late July. Ward would have found the ride enjoyable if it weren't for the company. Nonetheless, by all outward appearances, he was delighted to be there.

"How long has your family owned this land?" Ward asked

Lundgren, eager to generate conversation.

"Oh, it's been close to ninety years," Lundgren said. "My great-grandfather bought the place. We've added different parcels over the years."

Ward nodded.

"Almost lost it during the Depression," Lundgren continued. "It was a struggle to hold on."

Crossing another cattle guard, they left the pasture and followed the dirt track as it ran between two wooded areas and along a creek. Ward looked down at the rippling water to his right. He could see a small beaver damn. Several trees bore their tooth marks. It was a project still under construction. Lundgren noticed Ward's observation.

"The beavers are becoming a problem," Lundgren noted. "They're taking out a lot of trees. I've had to knock out that dam four or five times already. I need to start shootin' the bastards."

"Sounds like you've got yer own wetback problem right here," Doyle joked, clearly pleased with himself.

Ward forced a laugh. He looked at Lundgren, who displayed only a smirk.

Up ahead, Ward could see where Lundgren, or someone, had damned the creek, creating a respectable pond.

"You stock your pond, too?" Ward asked Lundgren. "I had pretty good luck out at Harold's this morning."

"I do," Lundgren replied. "In the evenings I come out here and toss in a line. It's a good place to think things through, ponder the big questions. I've solved a lot of problems out here."

Something about the last comment made Ward uneasy. He glanced back at Doyle, who smiled.

The dirt road ran along the bank. At the far end of the pond it turned into a raised gravel drive that crossed the damn and a spillway where the creek was allowed to flow through. Lundgren stopped the vehicle when they were halfway across. He turned to the man he knew as Ed Maddox.

"Tell us, Ed, why do you want to join our struggle? What

brings you to The Nation?"

Ward felt his heart race. Had he miscalculated? Was this a setup? He again looked back at Doyle. The man's expression was serious as death. Ward quickly glanced at his surroundings, assessing his avenues of escape. To his right was the creek. To his left was a steep twenty-foot drop onto a rock pile. Ahead and behind, the gravel drive ran thirty feet in either direction. The nearest woods were at least eighty yards off, with an open meadow between him and tree cover. If they were armed...he was in trouble. Ward looked for signs that either of them was carrying a weapon. Seeing none, he began to calm down, preparing to address Lundgren's question with a long-planned answer. As the two men stared at him expectantly, Ward readied himself for the performance of a lifetime.

"Well," Ward said, struggling to appear matter-of-fact, "I believe in your mission." He thought back to his words one night at Bubba's, and the effect they had on Sullivan and Kirklin. His words this evening would be similar but would also flatter Lundgren.

"Our government has failed its people," Ward began, now settling into his persona, "failed in one of its most basic missions...securing our country. It has lost control of the border, and has done nothing, so far as I can see, that shows the will, or even the intention, of fixing the problem. As I told Charlie Kirklin one night, I've been in my share of countries where they've lost control, where the border is totally open. Afghanistan and Pakistan are good examples, but there are many, many others. A breakdown in border security will eventually lead to economic chaos, political instability. It opens the door to terrorism. Ultimately, the country will fail. It has to. There is no other result. It has happened throughout history. If the politicians in Washington can't get the job done, which they've already proven, then we need to do it ourselves. We need to take our country back. Our founders would have expected nothing less. They knew the value of revolution. This is not a problem that can be ignored. We must act now."

Lundgen nodded solemnly.

"You understand that, Royce," Ward said, looking him in the eye. "You see what needs to be done. I admire you for that, and for having the strength to tell the truth." He looked away, as if into his own past. "But I also have personal reasons for joining your battle." Ward lowered his head, holding a hand over his eyes. He appeared to choke up. "I've seen what happens when politicians abandon the fight simply because the polls have changed. I've seen their cowardly self-preservation result in withdrawing support, sometimes going so far as to cut funds in the middle of battle, leaving our brave soldiers effectively abandoned in theater, inadequately supplied, unable to complete their mission. At the same time, they cynically profess to support our troops. It makes me sick. Their actions have caused real casualties, real deaths, some of them my friends." He paused, taking a long breath. "Gentlemen," Ward said, mustering every bit of indignation that he could produce, "I love my country, the country that once was. But be assured, I owe this government no allegiance whatsoever. If *this* nation is ever to be strong again, it's up to people like us...members of The Nation."

Lundgren put a hand on Ward's shoulder. Ward could see in Lundgren's face that he'd actually pulled it off. He was being welcomed into the fold. Damn, he deserved an Oscar.

CHAPTER 66

10:15 a.m., Monday, July 27th, the White House, Washington, D.C.

Chief of Staff Michael Cooper closed the door behind him as he followed the others into the Oval Office. Present in the room, along with President Buckley, were Secretary of Homeland Security Donald Page, White House Press Secretary Ellie Drake and Special Agent Jesse Carlson, head of the Presidential Protective Detail.

"Take a seat, everyone," the President said, gesturing toward two sofas in the middle of the room. He remained standing.

"I've been working with Mike and Ellie on a list of possible sites in El Paso for the immigration speech," Buckley announced.

Page spoke up. "Mr. President, does this really need to be in El Paso? I really think we should consider other…"

"Already decided, Don," Buckley said. "It's going to be in El Paso."

Page looked over at Jesse Carlson, who was shaking his head. Most people didn't realize that as Secretary of Homeland Security, Page was responsible for the oversight of the Secret Service. If this went to shit, it would be on him.

"Mike," the President continued, "Why don't you brief us on the three possible locations, some of their pros and cons."

Cooper pulled out some notes and large satellite images of the three potential locations.

"The first site is Sun Bowl Stadium," Cooper said. "Obviously, here we're talking about an outdoor speech and the accompanying heat."

"May I say something?" Carlson asked.

"Go ahead, Jesse," the President replied.

"Stadiums are always a problem, sir. I don't know who you intend to open this up to, but with that many people there are always a lot of security issues. Besides, to be blunt, there are just too many vantage points from which to fire a shot. If you're out in the middle of a football field, Mr. President, it poses some unique challenges."

"We've done it before, Jesse," the President said.

"True," Carlson agree, "but never across the border from Juarez, Mexico."

"I don't like it anyway," Cooper said. "Aside from the security problems, it's just too big. If the place is half empty when you're giving the speech, Mr. President, it makes it look like there wasn't much interest. And that brings me to the second possibility, the El Paso Convention and Performing Arts Center, a nice air-conditioned facility."

"It'd be easier to secure," Page said, looking at Carlson, who nodded his agreement. "And I'm sure that the Secret Service detail would greatly appreciate an indoor facility. After all, we are talking El Paso, in the middle of the summer no less. By the way, what date are we looking at?"

"A week from today," Cooper said. "We're planning on Monday, August 3rd."

Page and Carlson exchanged worried glances. A little more notice would have been nice for such a challenging locale, Page thought. But with an indoor facility, they could probably handle it.

"I don't like it," the President interjected. "I can give a speech in a convention center anywhere. What's the point? It lessens the impact. I want impact. I want a dramatic backdrop. Ellie, tell us about the third site."

"Yes, sir, Mr. President," Drake said. "The third spot is the Chamizal National Memorial," she began. "It's a park that commemorates the peaceful settlement of a border dispute with Mexico that lasted for more than a hundred years."

"What dispute is that?" Page asked.

"The Chamizal Dispute resulted after the Rio Grande changed course. The park is located on that portion of the disputed land that went to the United States as part of the resolution reached in the Chamizal Treaty of 1963."

"I like the symbolism," Buckley said. "Besides, there's an international bridge that can be seen from that location. Isn't that right, Ellie?"

"That's correct, Mr. President. There's a port of entry adjacent to it, the Bridge of the Americas. The park also has a small amphitheater, although we may want to construct our own speaking platform."

Page and Carlson studied the satellite image. Both appeared mortified.

"Mr. President," Carlson pleaded, shaking his head, "from this image, it looks like the Mexican border is less than a thousand feet away."

"More like four to five hundred," Cooper said, glancing at his boss.

Page caught the look. It was obvious that the Chief of Staff and the President had already discussed the issue. The President had clearly come into the meeting knowing full well what he wanted to do. Page let out a sigh, knowing that he couldn't win this one. It was well known that when Sam Buckley made up his mind on something, that was the end of it.

"Jesse, can you secure this site?" Page asked.

"Hey, I'm a can-do sort of guy," Carlson said.

Page wanted to believe him.

CHAPTER 67

4:20 p.m., Monday, July 27th, a rest area off Interstate 35 in southern Oklahoma.

Meade hit his turn signal. The exit for the rest stop was just ahead. This was the one, seventy miles south of Oklahoma City, just north of mile marker 55. There was a rest area on both sides of the interstate, but Collins had specified the southbound facility. It seemed an odd choice for a place to meet, and Meade was slightly annoyed that he had to drive more than halfway. Still, he had no way to complain and was simply happy that Collins had agreed to help. The small amount of information that had already been shared over the phone told Meade that the trip would be worthwhile.

Meade pulled into a parking spot and looked around. Collins had been specific about the vehicle he would be driving, a blue Ford F-150 pickup with a matching topper. Meade didn't see the truck. He must have arrived first. It made sense. Last he checked in, thirty miles back, Collins was just crossing the Texas/Oklahoma border. It would probably be another twenty minutes before he arrived.

The door creaked open as Meade slid off the driver's seat. It had been a long haul, first through southern Iowa, then half of Missouri. After that he'd covered a good chunk of Kansas, and then, finally, three quarters of Oklahoma. The trip required an early departure, damned early, and he was physically exhausted. But, at the same time, he was excited, pleased with what he was about to do. Having asked for a day off, Meade was now thankful that his foreman, Kroeger, had insisted that he take two. It was a pleasant surprise, what with it being on short notice and all. He would need the extra time to recover after the drive back. Meade checked his watch. He would take a short walk and stretch his legs, killing time until Collins arrived.

Fifteen minutes went by with no Joe Collins. Meade went in to use the restroom. When he came out he still didn't see Collins' truck anywhere. Frustrated, Meade walked back to his Impala and climbed in, failing to notice the man who had concealed himself in the back seat. When he did, it was too late.

"Hello, Jake," said a familiar voice.

Meade's hair stood on end. He looked in the rearview. Staring back at him was the devilish face of Willie Hammond, a sadistic gleam in his eyes. Meade's blood ran cold. He realized that Collins had set him up. A gun suddenly appeared and pressed into the back of his skull. The passenger door opened. Another man slid in beside him. It was Jim Byrd.

"Good to see you, Jacob," Byrd said ominously.

"Please don't kill me," Meade begged. It sounded pathetic, obvious, but he could think of nothing else.

Hammond snorted.

Meade's heart thudded in his chest. His mind raced, trying to think of a way out. He could feel a clammy sweat start to ooze from his pores. Nausea hit him as he realized there was no escape. Hammond would pull the trigger...and enjoy doing it.

"Drive, you piece of shit," Hammond spat. "And don't try anything stupid. We've got an escort." Hammond jerked his head toward a white panel van parked two spots down.

Meade's hands shook as he started the car and kicked it in reverse. Against his better judgment, he stole a glance in the rearview. As their eyes locked, an evil grin spread across Hammond's face. It told Meade everything he needed to know. This would be his final homecoming.

As he put the car in drive, Meade could hear Hammond begin to hum *The Yellow Rose of Texas*. It made him want to cry.

CHAPTER 68

7:45 p.m., Monday, July 27th, just northeast of Yorktown, Texas.

It was the same shooting range that Ward had been to more than a month earlier, northeast of Yorktown, almost a mile off Texas Highway 72. This time, however, the men present were much more formidable than those on that earlier trip. These were Brandt's men, The Nation's special forces. And while they were a little rough around the edges, from what Ward could see the group functioned as a reasonably well-organized paramilitary force. He wondered what they had done, what they planned to do. It seemed odd that Brandt insisted on getting them together after work, on a Monday evening, no less. Wouldn't the weekend make more sense? Was some sort of mission imminent? Ward wanted to ask questions but couldn't risk appearing too inquisitive. Hopefully, Brandt would start to talk.

The weapons were mainly AR-15s and AK-47s, lots of them, along with an assortment of handguns, mostly higher calibers. More importantly, there were also several sawed-off shotguns and two machine guns. Possession of either type of weapon was grounds for arrest. But that would come later, accompanied by more serious charges. Ward had infiltrated many heavily-armed organizations over the years. For him, seeing a large collection of weapons was nothing new. But this was an impressive arsenal, even by his standards. And it was probably just the tip of the iceberg. On the plus side, it was all great evidence against the organization, and evidence that would scare the hell out of a jury.

Most of the questions put to him so far had concerned things like desert tracking, ambush, sniper techniques. It was enough to confirm that rumors of vigilante raids along the border were true. There were also questions about the range of sniper fire, what weapons to use. Those really gave him pause. Were they related to the border raids...or something else? All of it made Ward want to bring the bastards to heel sooner rather than later. But there was still work to be done.

As Ward examined one of the AK-47s, Brandt approached.

"The men really appreciate the techniques you shared with 'em," Brandt said.

"Glad to help," Ward lied.

"I'm plannin' to call Bruno Alt later tonight," Brandt continued. "He suggested some joint training exercises between us and The Aryan Tribe's militia. You willin' to help?"

"Sure. Happy to."

"Great. You've been a big help so far, Ed. And I'll make sure Royce knows it."

"I appreciate that," Ward said. He studied Brandt, considering how best to draw him out.

"Quite a force you've got here," Ward noted. "What are there, forty, fifty men? You've done a great job with them."

Brandt was pleased by the compliment from a professional. "This isn't all of 'em," he said. "I've got twice this many scattered around this part of Texas." He hesitated, as if deciding how much to say. Finally, apparently concluding that Ward was trustworthy, he added, "We also have a presence in the other Border States. Each group has its own leader. I oversee all of our special forces, and personally command this contingent."

Ward nodded. "I take it your training is related to border raids," he said, deciding to throw it out there, see where it went.

"I guess that's pretty obvious, isn't it?" Brandt asked with a laugh.

"It's like we discussed, like I told Royce, we're gonna have to deal with the problem ourselves," Ward said. "The government's sure as hell not gonna do it."

"You got that right."

"Looks to me like you've already taken the first step," Ward pointed out. "I admire your guts."

Brandt gave Ed a pat on the back, leaving his hand on his new colleague's shoulder. "We've done a lot more than take the first step, Ed."

"I assumed that," Ward said. A sense of dread came over him. "Are you takin' out decent numbers, makin' a good impact?" he asked, afraid to hear the answer.

"You bet," Brandt replied, giving Maddox a wink.

"You've got that kind of manpower, huh?" Ward wondered how many people these bastards had already killed.

"Oh, we've got the manpower," Brandt replied, matter-of-factly. "Hell, Ed, we've got more volunteers than we can train. Some of 'em just can't handle any kind of military discipline. Ya know what I mean?"

"I do."

"We just get those folks workin' in some other area," Brandt said, "doin' somethin' where they can make a contribution to the cause."

"Sure."

"Besides, the guys out here, we've checked 'em all out. We can't have just anybody involved in this part of it."

"Of course not," Ward agreed. He wondered just how thoroughly he'd been checked out. He assumed that Jim Byrd had put in some extra effort on him, and probably still was.

"Who pays for all this?" Ward asked. "I mean, this has to get awful expensive. Hell, just the guns." Brandt was talking now, feeling more at ease. Ward decided to see how far he could take it.

"We have friends," Brandt replied, "friends with deep pockets." He looked around, more as a show that he was letting Maddox in on something than any fear that someone might be listening. "We also take dope off some of the, uh, *casualties* who were mulin' it up here," Brandt chuckled. "No point in lettin' it go to waste, right? That dope's bought us a whole lotta weapons, including some of 'em you see here."

Bingo, Ward thought. An adrenaline rush hit him. Brandt was now making the government's case stronger by the minute. Ward struggled to suppress his excitement and stay in character. Right now, he needed to keep this guy talking.

"They're sendin' that dope up here to enslave *our* people," Ward said. "Why not use it against them. Hell, it's a great idea."

"I'm glad you agree," Brandt said. "Not everybody's in favor of usin' the dope like that."

"We're at war," Ward said. "We need to use every tool at our disposal."

Brandt smiled. It was the smile of a man with a secret he was dying to share.

"But how do you know when the illegals are comin' through?" Ward asked. He was going for broke now, sensing that he'd made a real connection with Brandt. "Just sittin' out in the desert waitin' for a sighting isn't very efficient."

"No, it wouldn't be," Brandt said, the left side of his mouth twisting into a wry smile. "Let's just say...we get some pretty good intelligence."

A quizzical look appeared on Ward's face. "Oh?" he asked.

Brandt leaned in. "Even some of these guys don't know the full extent of it," he said, jerking his head toward his troops.

Ward waited.

"We've got people in the Border Patrol," Brandt said. He watched Maddox for his reaction.

Ward went rigid. "How the hell did you manage that?" he asked, now deeply concerned. He had to remind himself...appear impressed.

"They've lowered their hiring standards over the last few years," Brandt assured him. "It wasn't too tough to get a handful of sympathetic deputy sheriffs hired in."

Ward envisioned the world-class fallout that would happen when this hit the fan. Heads would roll...big-time. Problem was, if the right people didn't cooperate post-arrest, identifying the dirty agents would be damn near impossible. He would have to try to find out as much as he could before coming in. Suddenly, he remembered his audience.

"Damn, you guys are good," Ward said. "I'm impressed." He forced himself to give Brandt a smile.

As soon as he was back in his own vehicle, and certain that no one was following him, Ward dug out the cell phone that he now used to contact Richter. Earlier, he'd decided to hide one in the lining of the vehicle's passenger seat...just in case. As he started to punch in the number, Ward became so excited to share his information that it took three tries to get it right. When he did, Special Agent Jason Richter answered immediately.

"Richter."

"Have I got a story for you," Ward said. "Get a notepad."

Ward laid out everything he'd learned from Brandt, pausing only when Richter interrupted with the occasional *Wow*.

"Notify Olin would ya?" Ward asked, after he'd finished.

"You bet," Richter said. "And I'll start workin' on a preliminary draft of an affidavit, so it's ready to go when we're set to bring 'em down."

"Good idea," Ward agreed.

"I'd like to hear that pissant Winborn complain about our investigation now," Richter added.

"No shit," Ward laughed.

"Good job, partner," Richter said. "Damn good work tonight."

"Thanks."

As he drove toward Cuero, Special Agent David Ward could begin to taste it...the beginning of the fall of The Nation.

CHAPTER 69

10:35 a.m., Tuesday, July 28th, outside Erin Larson's apartment building, Des Moines, Iowa.

Deputy U.S. Marshal Pete Willis was growing concerned. Something wasn't right. Meade had failed to return his calls after several messages were left for him yesterday and again that morning. A search of Meade's apartment, courtesy of the building manager, showed signs that he might have packed for a trip. Toiletries were missing that normally would be present. His foreman, Kroeger, said he'd asked for a day off. Kroeger gave him two. Meade didn't mention going anywhere.

As he parked in front of Erin Larson's apartment building, Willis wondered if he was making too much of this. Maybe the kid just went on a short road trip, turned off his cell phone. By now he had to be aching to get out of town, see something different. After all, he'd been there for two months and hadn't done much of anything other than work and go to school. Well, that wasn't exactly true. There'd been the girl, and that was why he was here. It was a couple of weeks ago that Meade mentioned the breakup. Willis wanted to know if they'd talked since, what he might have told her.

Willis climbed the steps to Erin's apartment. He'd called ahead, catching her on the way out. She promised to wait. Willis didn't want to question her over the phone. He needed to observe her reactions.

Willis rapped on the apartment door. Almost immediately it opened. The girl that answered was a dark-haired beauty. Despite the reason for the visit, she gave him a smile, one that was naturally, effortlessly enchanting. Willis smiled back and awkwardly fumbled for his credentials, now more fully appreciating why Meade had seemed so smitten. Finding them, he held up the ID for Erin's inspection, feeling somewhat foolish for doing so.

"Hello, Ms. Larson," Willis said. "Deputy Pete Willis, U.S. Marshals Service."

"I see that," Erin replied, nodding at the credentials. "Please, come inside."

Willis entered. He surveyed the apartment. It was tastefully decorated, not the typical student decor.

"Nice place," Willis noted.

"Thanks."

Reminding himself why he was there, Willis got down to business. "As I mentioned on the phone, I need to ask you a few questions about Carl." Willis pulled out a notepad and pen.

Erin's smile faded. "He's not in some sort of trouble, is he?"

Her tone told Willis that she still had some feelings for Meade, despite what had happened between them.

"It's more a question of whether he might be in any kind of danger," Willis said. "He's been out of touch."

A concerned look swept over Erin's face.

"When's the last time you saw him?" Willis asked.

"About a week ago, at school."

Willis was surprised by the answer. "What did you discuss?"

"You know, us, how sorry he was. Stuff like that. He told me that he was trying to make up for some of the mistakes he'd made in life."

"What do you mean?" Willis asked. His furrowed brow said that he didn't like the answer.

"He told me about testifying at that trial in Texas," Erin replied, "how it made him feel, to do the right thing and all. He said it gave him back some self-esteem."

Willis felt a knot in his stomach. This was going to be bad.

"Did he mention any plans, any specific action he intended to take, you know, to make up for his past mistakes?"

Erin shook her head. "No, I don't recall anything like that."

Willis looked her in the eye. "You need to tell me *everything* that Carl's told you about himself," he insisted. "And I mean *everything.*"

She told Willis everything she could remember, what Jacob had told her about his childhood in Houston, how he came to join The Nation, and how he entered the Witness Protection Program.

Willis shook his head, scribbling furiously in the notepad. Clearly Meade had ignored his warnings about the girl. Willis wondered what else Meade had ignored. He had a sinking feeling that the dumb bastard was bent on doing something heroic, thinking it would redeem him, thinking it would win her back.

"You cannot tell a soul about any of this," Willis cautioned her. "It could get him killed." As he said it, Willis was wondering if that ship had already sailed.

"I understand," Erin said. "I won't tell anyone."

When he was satisfied that he'd learned all she knew, Willis thanked Erin and headed toward the door. As he reached for the knob, she called after him.

"Deputy Willis?"

Willis stopped and turned to face her. "Yes?"

Erin took a breath. "I have to ask." She paused. "Jacob is he a good man?"

Willis looked at the floor and thought for a moment. There was much about Jacob Meade that he hated. On the other hand, he had to give the guy some credit. Willis looked up at Erin. Her expression begged for something, some morsel to tell her that the man she had let herself love wasn't all bad.

"I'll say this, what he did…it took guts." With that, Willis let himself out.

* * *

Once back in his vehicle Willis started the job of finding his wayward charge. He called the main office and had them start the process of notifying all U.S. Marshals Service facilities along the various routes to Texas. That had to be where Meade was headed. Cell tower information might show his path. Phone records and credit card charges could help. Willis planned to check with the cell phone company, see if Meade's phone was equipped with a GPS device. After that, he would interview co-workers, neighbors, anyone Meade might have talked to about travel plans. Willis cursed himself. He should have seen this coming.

The next call Willis made was to his ATF contact. Knowing how the news would be received, he cringed when he heard Special Agent Ian Brewster answer the phone.

"It's Pete Willis. I've got some bad news."

"Shoot," Brewster said, businesslike.

"Jacob Meade's flown the coop."

There was a brief silence on the other end of the line before Brewster erupted. "Please tell me that you are *fucking* kidding me," he said. "God *damn* it, Pete! How the hell did this happen?"

Willis did his best to explain.

"Son...of...a...*bitch*!" Brewster growled.

"How much does Meade know?" Willis asked.

"He doesn't know everything, but he knows enough to cause problems, serious fucking problems."

"I was afraid of that," Willis said, dejected.

"Look, Pete, it's not your fault," Brewster offered. "Meade made his choice. He knew the rules."

"Maybe, but that doesn't solve our problem, does it?"

"No, it doesn't," Brewster agreed. "Keep me informed. Right now, I need to call the case agent and prepare for damage control."

CHAPTER 70

10:35 a.m., Tuesday, July 28th, an abandoned warehouse, San Antonio, Texas.

Meade had no idea where he was. He only knew that it was hot, stifling hot...and that he was going to die. Thinking back over the night before, he searched for a clue to his whereabouts. After abducting him, Byrd and Hammond had ordered that he drive to a deserted ranch south of Waco. There, his Impala was torched and abandoned. He was forced into the white van that had been following them, blindfolded, his hands and feet bound. They drove for what he guessed to be about two hours until arriving at the hell where he now found himself. After being dragged to this room and thrown inside, he was left for the night, no food, no water, no toilet...nothing. Meade could still hear Hammond's chilling words as he left: *Sweet dreams, Jake. We'll see you in the morning.* With that, the door had slammed shut, what sounded like a padlock securing it.

Meade was hungry and desperately thirsty. The humidity of the place, combined with the stench of his own urine, was making him ill. He had no idea what time it was, why it hadn't already started. He wished they would just get it over with. The wait itself was torture. He was sure that they meant it to be just that.

Still bound and blindfolded, Meade managed to struggle to his knees. He lowered his head and began a silent prayer. It wasn't a miracle that he asked for, but the strength to do the right thing.

Someone jostled the lock. Meade uttered his *amen* and scooted back against the wall. He heard the door as it was yanked open. Several people entered the room.

"It's time for us to have a little chat, Jacob."

Meade recognized the voice. It was Byrd.

"Take off his blindfold."

The covering was yanked from Meade's head. He squinted as his eyes adjusted to the light. Before him stood Byrd, Hammond and two large, angry-looking men, neither of whom he'd ever seen before. One of them held the blindfold.

"Lift him," Byrd ordered.

The two men jerked Meade to his feet, almost separating his shoulders in the process.

Byrd turned to Hammond. "Bring in the chair," he said.

Hammond quickly returned with it, a basic metal office chair with armrests. He slid it behind Meade, jamming it into his legs, almost knocking him off balance.

"Sit," Byrd ordered.

Meade lowered himself into the chair, perched forward because his hands were still tied behind his back. He stole a quick look around the room. There were no windows. He could hear no sound outside. A scream for help would be futile, he was sure of that. But Meade knew that he would scream...for other, unimaginable reasons.

"Secure him," Byrd said.

The two men untied Meade's hands and feet and strapped them to the arms and legs of the chair. When he was bound, Byrd stepped forward, slipping on a pair of leather gloves as he moved toward Meade.

The first blow crushed Meade's eye socket. The leather tore his flesh. A searing pain shot through his head like a lightning bolt as stars flashed in his eyes. Meade groaned. His head drooped forward, drool coming from his mouth, blood dripping onto his lap.

"That one was just for me," Byrd said with a smile. The others laughed. He began to circle Meade, like an animal coming in to finish off wounded prey.

As the fog in his head began to lift, Meade regained enough composure to speak. "You don't have to do this," he muttered.

"Of course, we do, Jacob," Byrd said matter-of-factly. "You're an example to anyone who might betray us. The Nation deals with its traitors."

"So, you plan to kill me," Meade said. It wasn't a question.

"We have some questions," Byrd replied.

Meade wondered if there was any way they would let him live. It seemed unlikely. What was the incentive?

"What did you tell them, Jacob?" Byrd asked.

"Tell who?" Meade replied.

It was the wrong answer. Byrd nodded to Hammond. A mischievous, sadistic smile appeared on the enforcer's face as he pulled on his gloves.

Meade began to whimper softly. He tried to keep his eyes on Hammond as he circled, working his closed fist into the palm of his other hand.

Hammond wound up. There was a horrible crunch as his knuckles smashed into Meade's nose. Blood gushed. Snot spewed. Tears began to flow. Meade shook his head. He began to choke on the fluids that drained into the back of his throat.

"Once again, what...did...you...tell...them?" Byrd repeated. He glared at Meade as he asked the question.

Hammond waited for a signal. Byrd held up his hand, indicating that he should hold off.

Meade decided it was time to tell them something.

"I told them about the drugs for guns trades, machine guns, all of that," Meade answered. He had no intention of telling Byrd what he'd passed along about the shooting, the reference to a sniper. No one in The Nation could possibly be aware that he had any knowledge of that.

"Jacob, Jacob, Jacob," Byrd repeated, shaking his head. "This is not a good start." He nodded at Hammond, who had picked up a piece of lead pipe. The pipe was roughly the length of a ball bat and at least an inch thick.

Hammond swung the pipe like a slugger trying to knock one over the fence. There was a sickening *crack* as it connected with Meade's kneecaps.

Meade howled in agony. The intensity of the pain made him wretch, the vomit covering his shirt, dribbling down his chin. He began to sob.

"Of course, you told them that!" Byrd yelled. He was all too familiar with Meade's testimony at the trial of Pierce and Simmons. "Do you think I'm a fool?"

Byrd walked toward Meade, grabbed his hair and violently yanked his head back.

"What else did you tell them?" Byrd growled.

Meade struggled to get his breath. "Said...I'd heard rumors... border raids...shooting illegals," he said between gasps.

Byrd smiled. "Now we're gettin' someplace. What else?"

"Stealin' dope off 'em...to buy guns." Meade let out a low anguished moan. His thoughts began to blur. He drifted off to another place, his brothers and sisters...Erin.

"Do they have any other informants?" Byrd asked.

Meade shook his head back and forth. "I don't know," he cried. "I don't know anything about that."

"Wrong answer, Jacob." Byrd gave Hammond the go-ahead.

There was a snapping sound as the pipe hit Meade's right shin.

"Ohhh God!" Meade shrieked. He thrashed back and forth the in the chair, almost toppling it over.

Byrd waited a few moments, and then asked again. "I'll ask you one more time, Jacob. Do they have other informants...an undercover cop on the inside?"

Meade began to shake. There was a warmth in his crotch as he peed himself. Should he lie...tell them what they want to hear? Was there any shame in that? Meade lowered his head and wept. Then, suddenly, his purpose returned. He remembered why he undertook this journey. He thought about Erin, and how he'd felt after testifying. Meade knew that he would die here anyway. He vowed to die with dignity. His head rose. He looked Byrd in the eye.

"I don't know *anything* about an informant or any undercover cop," Meade said stoically.

Byrd eyes narrowed. He turned to Hammond.

"Finish him."

Byrd turned and left the room, leaving the rest to Hammond and his helpers. As he walked away, he could hear the screams echo through the abandoned warehouse, each one more intense than the one before.

Byrd reached the main entrance. As he stepped through the door, he heard one more cry, this time like the guttural howl of a mortally wounded animal. And then, he heard nothing.

CHAPTER 71

11:45 p.m., Tuesday, July 28th, Erin Larson's apartment building, Des Moines, Iowa.

I'll say this, what he did...it took guts. The words of Deputy Willis echoed in Erin's head. She looked at her watch, eleven forty-five. He would be home from work by now. That is, if he ever showed up for work. She studied the phone, pondering what she might say, or what message she might leave.

Erin thought back on their last meeting. She remembered the pride in Jacob's voice as he described how he'd risked his life to testify, how it made him feel. She realized that there was a lot of good in him, and that the bad, much of it, was the outgrowth of a horrible childhood. She wondered what he might have become with any kind of guidance. He was intelligent and, despite the mistakes he'd made, kind-hearted. If nothing else, she wanted to help him heal. Maybe she wanted something more. For now, at least, she had to know that he was okay.

Erin picked up the phone and punched in his number. She wasn't surprised to get voicemail. Part of her was relieved, another part disappointed.

Howdy, this is Carl. Leave a message and I'll get right back to ya.

Erin smiled at the Texas drawl that had been part of his charm. Suddenly she missed him terribly.

"Jacob...I," Erin began, "I just wanted to make sure you're

okay. A Deputy Willis stopped by today. He said he couldn't reach you, couldn't find you." Erin paused, her mind awhirl with memories of him, the good ones. Her eyes began to well up. Then, she remembered the recording. "Anyway," she continued, starting to choke up, "*please* call me when you get home. I'd like to talk."

Erin hung up, wondering if she'd ever see him again.

CHAPTER 72

10:05 a.m., Wednesday, July 29th, the offices of Odessa Oil, Alaska Operations, Anchorage, Alaska.

As he approached the entrance to the Alaska offices of Odessa Oil, Flagg wondered if he'd ever been on a longer journey as part of a case. He certainly couldn't think of one. The flight had seemed eternal. Still, it had given him time to think, plan his approach. The ruse of Sylvester Harding and a federal background check clearly wouldn't work here. If this job was legit, or people at Odessa thought it was legit, and Maddox was looking for other employment, word would get back. If the job was just a cover, then the people at Odessa, at least some of them, would know damn well that Maddox hadn't applied for any federal job. Weighing the pros and cons of several options during the long flight, Flagg had settled on a method that was tried and true, the old Army buddy. Given Maddox's supposed military background and its secrecy, it was the perfect fit.

It had been a lengthy investigation already and there was little to show for it. Other avenues of inquiry following the Georgia trip had produced nothing. Flagg consoled himself with thoughts of the large fee he was earning. In fact, he had to chuckle. It didn't occur to him the night before when he landed at Ted Stevens Anchorage International Airport, but maybe this was his *bridge to nowhere*. The thought amused him. Whether it was or not, there was one thing he knew for sure—he planned to run down every imaginable lead. A guy like Jim Byrd, and a group like The Nation, would keep paying until there was nowhere else to go.

Flagg started to get in character. He squared his shoulders, straightened his posture, adopting the manner in which a former Green Beret might carry himself. The name he'd come up with, Scott Thompson, didn't matter much. There would be no way for anyone to check the identity, and he planned to make his inquiry so casual that no one would think to alert Maddox. Besides, by now the guy had almost certainly figured out that The Nation was checking his bona fides.

The offices of Odessa Oil were bustling. Flagg knew it was a fairly large operation, but he was surprised to see this much activity in the Alaska offices of a mid-sized Texas oil company. He approached a large counter staffed by two receptionists. Flagg assessed which of them appeared most friendly, and then made his move.

"Hi there," Flagg said to the pretty brunette. She looked young, maybe twenty-one, twenty-two at most.

"Hello," the receptionist replied, all smiles. "Welcome to Odessa Oil. May I help you?"

Flagg glanced at her nametag. "Well, I hope so...Melissa." She was perky, eager to please. Perfect, Flagg thought.

"This is kind of a long shot," Flagg continued, "but I was in town on business and remembered that an old Army buddy worked for you folks up here, at least I think he's still up here. I haven't talked to him for a good, oh, eight or nine months."

"What's his name?" Melissa asked.

"Ed Maddox," Flagg replied, "Edward Maddox, to be precise. I think his middle name is Michael, if I remember right."

Melissa tapped away at her computer. After a moment, she stopped, studying the screen. Her brow furrowed slightly.

"Hmmm," she said. "Edward Maddox, right?"

"That's right," Flagg answered, wondering what the problem was.

"Let me go get someone," Melissa said. "Can you wait a moment?" she asked.

"Sure."

"I'm sorry. What's your name, sir?"

"Scott Thompson," Flagg lied. "My friends call me Scotty," he added, giving her a friendly grin.

"I'll be right back, Mr. Thompson."

A few minutes later, Melissa returned, accompanied by a man in a suit. Flagg did a quick appraisal. His smile was outwardly pleasant, though businesslike. His body language seemed reasonably relaxed. But Flagg sensed something, maybe it was in the man's eyes, something that said this guy anticipated a problem.

"Mr. Thompson?" the man asked.

"Yes," Flagg said, smiling pleasantly.

"I'm Stuart Purcell, Odessa Oil's Director of Human Resources for our Alaska operations." He extended his hand. "Melissa tells me you're looking for an old friend," he said cheerfully.

"That's right, Ed Maddox. Eddy and I were in the Army together."

"I see," Purcell replied.

"Afghanistan," Flagg added, assuming it would help.

Purcell nodded solemnly.

"Anyway," Flagg continued, "I just thought I'd stop in and say hi, catch up. You know."

"Sure."

Purcell hesitated for a moment, deciding what to do.

"I'll tell you what," Purcell said. "We don't usually give out any information on our employees. But under the circumstances, you two having been in the war together and all...let's make it happen."

"That'd be great," Flagg said. "Thanks."

Purcell walked behind the counter and logged on to Melissa's computer. After a few seconds he stopped to read, then frowned.

"I'm sorry, Mr. Thompson," Purcell said. "It looks as if Mr. Maddox transferred to Texas a couple months back."

"I see," Flagg said, feigning disappointment. "That's too bad. I was looking forward to seeing him."

"Sorry about that," Purcell said. "Anything else we can do for you?"

"No, not that I can think of," Flagg replied. "I appreciate your help. Thank you." He turned to leave, and then paused. "There is one thing, I guess."

"What's that?"

"In case I ever get back down to Texas, where's your office down there?"

Purcell thought for a second. Flagg had the impression that he wasn't sure what he was supposed to do.

"I guess that wouldn't hurt anything," Purcell said, smiling nervously. "We have several locations in Texas. He's at our Victoria facility."

"Victoria," Flagg said, "got it."

Purcell punched in the number that he'd been provided, surprised that he had to use it at all. He didn't know the contact's name. It was just a number.

"Hello," a voice answered.

"It's Stuart Purcell."

"You've got something?"

"A man was here, asking about Ed Maddox." Purcell provided the details.

"Thanks for your help," the voice said, gruff.

The line went dead.

CHAPTER 73

11:55 a.m., Wednesday, July 29th, United States Marshals Service, District Headquarters, Des Moines, Iowa.

Deputy U.S. Marshal Pete Willis settled in at his desk. He opened the Styrofoam container that held his lunch and navigated the computer to the ESPN website. It was time to check the day's baseball headlines. As he took the first bite of his sandwich, his cell phone went off. Never fails, Willis thought, as he reached for the device.

"Deputy Willis," he mumbled through a mouthful of pastrami on rye.

"Pete? It's Ian Brewster."

Willis instinctively knew that the call from his ATF contact would not be good news. His appetite already starting to wane, he dropped the sandwich on his desk.

"What's up?" Willis asked, not really wanting to hear the answer.

"It's not good. They found Meade. Well, not so much found him as he was delivered."

Willis lowered his head. "Tell me."

"The body was dumped in front of the U.S. Courthouse in Victoria," Brewster said. He hesitated. "It wasn't pretty."

Willis felt like he was sinking. "You mean the one where they had the trial, where he testified?"

"Right," Brewster replied. "Looks like they wanted to send a message."

They sent one, Willis thought. "What did the surveillance cameras show?"

"A white van, nondescript, plates blacked out. Body was shoved out the sliding door."

"Pretty ballsy."

"Yeah."

"No identifiable faces, I suppose."

"Correct."

Nobody spoke for a moment.

"What are you gonna do?" Brewster finally asked.

"Fuck if I know. Maybe look for another job."

"Wasn't your fault, man."

"I own this one, brother. It's on me."

"Let me know if there's anything I can do to help," Brewster said.

"Yeah, man. Thanks." Willis ended the call. He thought for a moment. There was one thing he needed to do. He grabbed his keys and headed out the door to see Erin Larson.

CHAPTER 74

8:15 a.m., Thursday, July 30th, the streets of Juarez, Mexico.

Anything could be bought on the streets of Juarez. Thad Kolb had always heard that. Now he knew it to be true. He opened the case and admired his purchase, a Barrett M82 .50 Caliber NATO sniper rifle. Also known as the M107, it was a weapon with which the former Army sniper had some experience. Its range was well over fifteen hundred meters, and Kolb had seen shots much longer than that. Given that the weapon was also used by the Mexican Army, it was readily available to the buyer on the street...for the right price.

Kolb examined the rifle. Everything appeared to be in order. He handed over the rest of the payment and watched as the seller disappeared down the street. He quickly loaded the weapon into the vehicle that he'd rented the night before. Once the gun was secure, Kolb jumped in and took off.

The sniper allowed himself a smile. The day of glory approached. There had been many months of training in preparation for a situation like this one, one in which they left an opening, provided a long-awaited opportunity. It was foolish to select a location like El Paso. But they were fools, weren't they? That's why he was here. That's why he'd joined The Nation.

Many of his former Army colleagues had seen the need. Recruitment efforts were strong. It wasn't just The Nation, there were other groups, some even more active. His best friend, Kevin, had entered The Aryan Tribe, a common choice. The believers were still a small percentage of the active duty military, but Kolb knew that their numbers would grow, their influence spread, until it was time to take action. Then, they would do what needed to be done. He only hoped that his action would hasten the day of reckoning. It had to. That's why he'd left the Army.

Ever since learning of the location, a select few had moved quickly, studying the site and everything around it. Their friends in the Border Patrol had been of great assistance, be it providing useful connections, or simply looking the other way. A plan had already been formulated. The trucking facility was directly across the border, approximately a thousand feet from the amphitheater where the President would likely give his speech. The only problem was that the back of the amphitheater faced Mexico. That meant that a shot might have to occur at some point during his arrival or departure. Hopefully, like the politician that he was, Buckley would work the crowd. That would allow plenty of time to put him in the crosshairs.

Kolb had little doubt that he could hit his target. The trucking company had several buildings. His shot would come from the roof of the tallest of those to assure that it would clear border fencing and other obstacles. He would fire from inside a structure that would appear to be part of the normal air-conditioning system. Of course, the facility would be closed. No employees would be present. A truck would be idling below him, backed up to a loading dock. After the shot, he would rappel down the side of the building and jump into the semi-trailer. The truck would then escape onto the Mexican highway system. Payments would be made to speed that process, with the recipients told only that they were assisting a certain shipment. That was all that need be said in Juarez.

Kolb wondered why the owners of the trucking company would so readily cooperate. Presumably they were all *spics*. On this question, few details had been shared with him. That was fine by Kolb. The less he knew the better. He assumed their silence had somehow been assured. It had been suggested to him by someone who should know, that the company's leadership might be sympathetic to the immediate goal—the termination of President Buckley. It made sense. Buckley's views were unpopular with many Mexicans. That was the point, wasn't it? Kolb assumed that the politics of the group that was *actually* behind the assassination had not been shared.

The way Kolb understood it, the plan was for a Mexican organization to take credit. There would be calls to the media, claims that it was in retaliation for Buckley's hardline immigration policies. All Kolb knew was that the backlash would start the clock ticking, and that the revolution would come that much sooner. His heart filled with pride at his role in bringing about a glorious new beginning for America. He would take a place in history next to those great figures of the American Revolution, men he was sure were smiling down on him even now.

Kolb felt no qualms about taking out his former Commander-in-Chief. He was just another politician, part of the problem, part of the gutless cast of characters in Washington who cared only about themselves. They would never solve a thing, let alone a problem as serious as illegal immigration. They would let the country be overrun by fucking *spics*, ruined beyond recognition. No, Royce Lundgren was his leader now. Lundgren was a man of vision, a man who understood what needed to be done.

Kolb looked at the brown faces walking the streets around him, driving the cars next to him. They made him sick. These people will not take over *my* country, he vowed.

CHAPTER 75

11:05 a.m., Friday, July 31st, Gate C3, South Terminal, Ted Stevens Anchorage International Airport, Anchorage, Alaska.

Flagg looked at his watch. It was five after eleven. He had already been in the airport for almost two hours. The Alaska Airlines flight to Seattle would begin boarding soon. From Seattle, it was on to Denver, and then back to Houston.

The trip had been a complete bust. Flagg couldn't even get the Alaska Division of Motor Vehicles to release any records on Maddox, not even the basic data from his driver's license. Their privacy rules were strict, and the woman who waited on him would not bend. She kept babbling something about needing to be a duly appointed agent. All talk of background checks and waivers had failed. Finally, he gave up. Flagg cursed himself for not anticipating the problem. He usually didn't have much trouble getting DMV information, but identity theft concerns were making things a lot more difficult in his line of work. Unfortunately, that's where he'd planned to get Maddox's old address. No address meant no way to interview his former neighbors. He had checked the other usual sources, property records, court records. Nothing else had panned out. Flagg had even gone so far as to check old phone books. There was no listing for Ed or Edward Maddox going back five years. It didn't make sense. If Maddox had been here, then someone somewhere would have an address for him.

Flagg planned to call Byrd when he got back. He didn't feel like dealing with him right now. The man never reacted well. This time would certainly be no exception. Even if Odessa Oil confirmed Maddox as an employee, Byrd would want some additional information. Flagg could only point out that the lack of anything in Alaska was an indicator in its own right. It smelled of a cover.

Flagg took a sip from his coffee and ate the last of a blueberry muffin. As he was finishing up, two men dropped heavily into the seats that backed up to his.

"Yeah, Odessa's sending me to Texas again," Flagg heard one of them say. He turned his head enough so that he could see them out of the corner of his eye. One of the men was clearly older. He was heavy, balding, bifocals perched on his nose. Flagg guessed him to be in his late fifties. The other man was athletic with longish hair. He appeared to be in his mid to late thirties.

"What for this time?" the younger man asked.

"Gotta brief the main office on what the geologists have been doing up here," the older one said. "You know how it goes. They're unhappy because we haven't found the next Prudhoe Bay, blah, blah, blah."

The younger man laughed.

Flagg couldn't believe his luck. He looked at his watch. The flight would start boarding within minutes. He had to act fast.

"Did I hear you fellas say that you worked for Odessa?" Flagg asked, leaning back toward the two men.

"Yeah, that's right," the older of the two replied.

"I was in the Army with a guy who worked for you folks up here. He's a geologist," Flagg lied. "Happened to be in town on business, so I stopped in at your offices the other day to see if I could find him, catch up. Turns out he transferred down to Texas, Victoria I think they said."

"Yeah, we've got a facility there," the older one said. "What's your friend's name?"

"Ed Maddox," Flagg answered.

A puzzled look came over the older man's face. "You say he was a geologist up here?"

"Yeah, that's right," Flagg replied. He started to get that tingle, the one he got when he was on to something.

"I've never heard of him," the older man said, "and I'm pretty sure I've met just about every geologist that's been up here in the last twenty-odd years."

Flagg suppressed a smile.

"You ever heard of him?" the older man asked his colleague.

"No, can't say that I have," the younger man replied.

"Well, maybe I've got the geologist part wrong," Flagg said, looking for a way to end the conversation. He had what he needed. "It's been a long time since I talked to him," he added.

The two men appeared satisfied with that explanation. Just then the boarding call came for the flight to Seattle.

"You two gentlemen have a good trip," Flagg said. He gathered his carry-on and headed toward the gate.

CHAPTER 76

5:35 p.m., Saturday, August 1st, Harold Doyle's ranch, just outside Yoakum, Texas.

Ward threw out a cast and watched the lure *plunk* into the water. It was a warm, muggy afternoon. He used his shirtsleeve to mop the sweat from his brow.

"Hey, toss me another cold one, would ya?" Ward yelled over to Doyle.

"You got it, pardner." Doyle fished around in the cooler and pulled one from the bottom. "Here ya go." He lofted the can into the air.

"Thanks," Ward said as he caught the beer. He held the fishing pole under his arm as he popped the tab and took a drink.

"Whew! That hits the spot," Ward said. He rubbed the can across his forehead.

"You got that right." Doyle finished the one he was working on and tossed it to the side. "I believe I'll have another."

Ward looked over to see that Doyle had, in fact, done just that, and was now sucking that can dry with roughly the same speed you could pour one down an open drain. It was impressive, in a way, particularly given that after two hours of fishing he had already gone through half a case. It was also useful. The talk had again become loose.

"By the way," Doyle said, "Royce is havin' a little get-together Monday evening, kind of a celebration. Why don't you stop on over?" He hadn't been told to invite Ed but was sure Royce wouldn't mind.

"Celebrate what?" Ward asked.

"You'll see when you get there."

Ward was intrigued. He was certain to be in attendance. "Is Byrd gonna be there?"

Doyle snorted. "Yeah, he'll be there...unfortunately." Doyle thought for a second. "Ya know, you really need to watch out for him, Ed. He's gettin' downright paranoid about you."

"Paranoid how?"

"I don't know what that sumbitch's problem is," Doyle said. "Must think you're some kinda undercover agent or somethin'."

Ward felt a jolt of fear. It wasn't like he didn't know that Byrd suspected something, but to hear it like that.

"Undercover agent?" Ward laughed, nonchalant. "He's off his rocker."

As he pulled away from Doyle's ranch, Ward punched in the number for Richter.

"What's up?" Richter answered.

"A couple of things." Ward filled him in on the details of his conversation with Doyle.

"Watch your ass, bud," Richter said. "Byrd's dangerous." There was a note of deep concern in his voice.

"Yeah."

"You carryin' your piece?" Richter asked.

"Not always. Been leavin' it in the truck most of the time."

"What the fuck, man? These guys wouldn't freak if they did catch you packin'. Hell, you're former Special Forces, remember? They'd probably expect it. Besides, it's Texas. Carryin' a gun is a birthright."

"I suppose."

"Just promise me," Richter insisted.

"Yeah, yeah," Ward assured him. He knew Richter was

right. From now on he'd carry all the time, probably an ankle holster.

"What do you make of this little get-together on Monday?" Richter asked.

"Don't know," Ward said, "but have that affidavit ready to go, just in case. These bastards are up to somethin'."

CHAPTER 77

4:25 p.m., Sunday, August 2nd, the streets of Juarez, Mexico.

Kolb stood in the background as the payment was made. His associate handed over the suitcase. He tapped his fingers nervously as the Mexican transportation official opened it and examined the contents. Satisfied, the official nodded and spoke.

"It will be taken care of," he said.

With that, the man rose and exited the room, knowing only that he was to take certain steps to expedite a truck's departure, a truck he believed to contain a certain shipment. He didn't think to ask, or didn't want to know, why that shipment was headed further into Mexico instead of over the nearby border.

It was the last bribe of many. Kolb was sickened by the need to do business with these people. They were corrupt, lacking any sense of honor. Of course, the Mexicans knew nothing of the ultimate objective. But would it even matter to them? He doubted it. For men like the one who had just departed, only money mattered. They would sell their mothers. Kolb, contemptuous of them all, spit on the ground. He reminded himself that this was for a glorious cause, one that would save his country.

CHAPTER 78

9:25 a.m., Monday, August 3rd, the offices of Ron Flagg, Private Investigator, Houston, Texas.

Flagg had been thinking about it on the drive in. The high school, it didn't make sense. There were too many unanswered questions, too many dead ends. The lack of transfer records, the home address conveniently located in transient military housing, the history teacher who couldn't recall Maddox...it wasn't right. If this was a cover, no question they had put in a good effort in the areas where you might expect it...the current employer, military records, college. Maybe they'd thought it wouldn't get any farther than that, no one would dig deeper. In truth, it probably was enough of a story, under most circumstances. After all, a couple of dead ends at the high school level, especially for a military brat who moved around a lot, what's the big deal? There was enough corroboration everywhere else, right? It shouldn't be a problem. Even Flagg had to admit, absent a client with the paranoia of a Jim Byrd, this one probably would have been over a long time ago. But a paranoid client with a large budget allowed a man to be thorough.

Flagg took a sip from his coffee. He pulled out the number for Columbia East High School. What was the name of that woman he'd dealt with? Maybe he'd jotted it down. Yeah, there it was...Betty. Flagg punched in the number. Hopefully, the very helpful Ms. Betty would be there.

"Columbia East. May I help you?"

"Hello, yes. May I speak with Betty in the principal's office please?"

"Just a moment, I'll see if she's available."

Flagg prepared himself, slipping into character.

"This is Betty."

Flagg recognized the voice, heavy with southern drawl.

"Betty, I don't know if you'll remember me," Flagg said, friendly. "This is Sylvester Harding, from the Office of Personnel Management? I was in there the other day, doing a background check on an Edward Maddox."

"Oh, sure, I remember. Did you find everything you needed, hon?"

"For the most part," Flagg said. "And I want to thank you again. You were very helpful."

"I was pleased to help."

"There is one more thing, though," Flagg said.

"That's no problem. You just name it."

"Mr. Maddox, could you get your hands on a copy of the yearbook for his graduating class?" Flagg asked. "I mean, if it wouldn't be too much trouble."

"Well, I guess I could do that," Betty replied, some hesitancy in her voice. "It'll take me a minute."

"Take all the time you need."

Flagg was put on hold. He drank the last of his coffee as he waited. After several minutes, Betty returned.

"I've got it right here," Betty said. "What would you like to know?"

"Is Mr. Maddox pictured with the graduating class?"

Flagg could hear the pages rustle as Betty checked.

"Hmmm," she said. "No, in fact he's not. Of course, might just be he transferred in too late to have his picture taken."

"Could be," Flagg acknowledged. "Tell me this, is he listed as one of those not pictured?"

Flagg waited for the response, which took too long.

"That's odd," Betty finally answered. "No, he's not."

There was an almost imperceptible snort of satisfaction on Flagg's part.

"Thank you, Betty," Flagg said. "Again, you've been *very* helpful."

Flagg ended the call. He stared at the phone for a few seconds, and then punched in the number for Jim Byrd.

CHAPTER 79

4:50 p.m., Monday, August 3rd, Compound One.

Ward parked his SUV in the small lot that sat behind Lundgren's residence. According to Doyle, Lundgren had insisted that everyone arrive before five o'clock. No reason was given. Ward found it odd. Most of the group's meetings started much later, well after normal working hours. Something was up, and he needed to find out what.

Of the four vehicles parked nearby, Ward recognized those belonging to Doyle, Kirklin and Byrd. It was clear that this was a gathering of the organization's top leadership, and Ward was sure that Byrd would not be happy to see him there. Byrd's investigator had been working overtime, trying to expose any weakness in his cover story. The guy was thorough. Ward had to give it to him. No one suspected that this Flagg character would make the effort to travel to Alaska. Fortunately, the people there had handled the situation properly. Still, it could be a tense encounter with Byrd. Ultimately, though, there was little reason to be concerned, not with Doyle, Kirklin, and now Lundgren, in his corner.

Ward stepped out of the SUV. As his feet hit the ground, he felt the weight of the pistol strapped to his ankle. It gave him comfort. Just before he shut the door, he had a thought. Reaching back in, he retrieved the cell phone hidden in the passenger seat lining.

***

Royce Lundgren looked around the room. The men present, Charlie Kirklin, Warren Graves, Jim Byrd, even his cousin, Harold, they had all been with him for a long time. They had given much to support the struggle. It was only appropriate they would be here to share in this glorious achievement.

Lundgren looked at his watch. It was almost five o'clock. The speech had been scheduled for late in the day, five-thirty, presumably to avoid the mid-day heat of El Paso. He had been sorely tempted to be there when it happened, to bask in the chaos that would ensue. But it was too risky. Brandt had insisted he stay home, enjoy the media coverage, and savor the first breathless reports of a Mexican organization claiming responsibility for the assassination of President Buckley.

Lundgren quivered with anticipation. Everything had worked toward this moment. The country, when it absorbed what had happened, would react violently against *them*. It would be open season on the infestation that was already here. The borders would be slammed shut. Men who understood the threat would sweep to power, men like Congressman Lindell...men like himself. He would finally be seen as the hero he already was, recognized as a visionary on par with the Founders. His destiny was about to be fulfilled.

Lundgren's thoughts were interrupted by a knock at the door. Annoyed at the intrusion, he wondered who it could possibly be at a time like this. All those invited were present. He turned to Doyle, who was already headed toward the door.

"Ed, glad you could make it," Doyle announced as he waved Maddox inside.

Ward walked in. The others stared at him. Then, in unison, they turned to Lundgren. Ward immediately got the sense that his presence was totally unanticipated, and possibly unwanted.

"What the hell is he doin' here?" Byrd asked angrily.

"I invited him," Doyle answered. He turned to Lundgren for support. "Royce, I didn't think you'd mind."

"You idiot!" Byrd exclaimed.

Lundgren whirled on him. "Ed is welcome here." His eyes narrowed.

"Is he?" Byrd shot back.

"As I've told you before," Lundgren said ominously, "If you've got something, share it. Otherwise, be silent."

"Oh, I've got something," Byrd said. He marched toward Maddox until he was inches from the man's face.

Ward could feel the man's anger like heat from a raging fire. He struggled to maintain his cool. What was it that Byrd thought he had? What had his investigator uncovered?

"There are a few holes in your story, Mr. *Maddox*," Byrd said through gritted teeth.

Ward remained outwardly impassive.

"Columbia East High School wasn't that it?" Byrd asked.

"Yes," Ward answered, expressionless.

"We talked to one of your history teachers, a Mr. Bagley."

Ward shifted his weight.

"He has no recollection of you," Byrd announced.

"You gotta be kiddin' me," Doyle interrupted. "We've all got teachers that wouldn't remember us." Doyle looked to his cousin to put a stop to this nonsense. "Royce, haven't we heard enough of this?"

Lundgren studied Byrd and Maddox for a moment. "Go ahead, Jim," he said.

Byrd inched closer. "Your photo doesn't appear in the yearbook, and you're not listed as one of those not pictured."

"I think I transferred in too late in the year," Ward said with a shrug.

"You heard him," Doyle said. "Back off, Jim."

Byrd stared at Doyle, his look a warning that violence was likely if he heard one more word. Doyle backed up a step.

"It really got interesting when we got to Anchorage," Byrd continued. "There was no home address for you listed anywhere, no trace that you ever lived there."

Ward's brow furrowed, ever so slightly. He knew that the people at Odessa had done what they were supposed to do. Obviously, Flagg hadn't left it at that.

"Any response?" Byrd asked.

Ward could hear the murmurings from Kirklin and Graves, a bad sign. Even Doyle was waiting for an answer.

Ward thought quickly. "Did you ask our Anchorage office for my old address?" he fired back defiantly. "Did you check with the DMV?" He knew that if such personal information had been requested, both would have refused to supply it, citing privacy grounds.

"The state won't release that information," Byrd said, "as I expect you know. But you see, the problem is, you weren't listed in any database, government records, old phone books... nothing."

Ward felt the sweat start to form on his upper lip. Did anyone notice? He looked at the other men. No one said a word. They were waiting. He had nothing.

"And here's the best one," Byrd announced, a smug look on his face. "We ran into some of your fellow geologists."

Ward started to feel something approaching panic. This was not good.

"And not *one* of them," Byrd said, drawing the .40 caliber from behind his back, "has ever heard of anybody by the name of Ed Maddox."

Ward knew then that his cover was blown.

An unearthly growl emanated from somewhere deep inside Royce Lundgren. *He* did *not* misjudge men, and this one had played him for a fool.

Byrd glanced at Lundgren. "Let me finish him, Royce."

Lundgren shook his head. "Not yet. Have a seat, Mr. *Maddox*," Lundgren ordered. "You'll enjoy the event with us."

Ward's instinct was to go for his gun. But he was sure that Byrd would pump a bullet into his head if given any excuse. Better to wait, hope that Byrd became distracted. Besides, if he drew attention to the gun, and failed to get his hands on it, that option would be gone...forever. He prayed that they didn't frisk him.

Lundgren glanced at his watch. It was ten after. "Turn on the television, Warren. It's almost time."

Ward looked at Lundgren. The gleam of madness in the man's eyes was intense. What the hell were these people up to? The television flickered on. Graves turned the channel to one of the news networks. The broadcast was live from El Paso, Texas. Ward could read the caption at the bottom of the screen, *BUCKLEY ABOUT TO SPEAK ON IMMIGRATION POLICY*. That's when it hit him.

Lundgren noticed the reaction. The laugh that followed was crazed, excited...mad.

"That's right, Mr. *Maddox*," Lundgren said. "You are about to witness the assassination of President Samuel T. Buckley."

Ward's breathing grew rapid, his heart pounded furiously. He had to get out of there, get word to the Secret Service...now. He quickly assessed the situation. Byrd stood ready to shoot, smiling down at him, the barrel of the gun less than two feet from his head. The others were fixated on the screen. Ward tried to appear cool. It was a struggle, but he could not give any sign that he was about to move. Surely Byrd would eventually turn toward the television screen.

"Why Buckley?" Ward asked calmly. "It doesn't make sense. He's an immigration hardliner." Ward wanted them to believe he was resigned to sit there and watch. Maybe Byrd's attention would drift away from him and toward the coverage in El Paso.

"Buckley is a politician," Lundgren said with disgust. "Like all politicians, he will say anything he deems expedient. Buckley is a useful tool, a necessary casualty in our struggle."

"I still don't get it," Ward said, although an idea was beginning to form.

"Shortly after the assassination," Lundgren continued, a satisfied smile forming on his face, "a Mexican organization will claim responsibility. They will announce that their act is in retaliation for Buckley's intolerant views on immigration. The reaction will be swift, fierce. This country will be forced to open its eyes to the threat from south of the border. There will be no denying the true nature of the brown horde that continues to contaminate our land. *Real* immigration reform will follow, with all necessary eradication methods sanctioned by the people."

Ward was nauseous. "Ingenious," he lied, still attempting to deflect attention from himself.

Lundgren studied him, and then turned back to the screen. The news anchor was announcing the President's arrival, noting that the speech was set to begin in approximately fifteen minutes.

Byrd turned his head toward the television, watching as the Presidential motorcade came to a halt within the grounds of the Chamizal National Memorial. It was the opportunity Ward had been waiting for. He deftly slipped his hand down toward the ankle holster. By the time Byrd turned back, Ward's gun was already aimed at Byrd's head.

"Drop it!" Ward said, nodding at Byrd's weapon.

There was a brief moment when it looked as if Byrd might do something stupid, then it passed. He dropped the gun to the floor.

"It's too late," Byrd said. There was a smug grin on his face. "The plan is already in motion."

"We'll see about that," Ward replied. "Back away from the gun."

Byrd did as ordered. Ward bent to pick up the weapon, glancing quickly at the others in the room. "Nobody moves," he ordered.

Ward fished the cell phone out of his pocket and punched in the number.

"Hey, man," Richter answered. "I've been wonderin' where the hell you've…"

"We need Secret Service on the phone…NOW!" Ward yelled over him. He quickly briefed Richter, all the while keeping his gun trained on the group, slowly moving it from one man to the next.

"I'm on it!" Richter fired back. "And I'll get backup out there right away!"

Ward looked down briefly as he terminated the call. When he looked up, Lundgren had backed up against a nearby bookcase. His hand slipped inside a small metal box.

"Don't do anything stupid," Ward told him.

Lundgren smiled as he lifted a small pistol from the box. It was a Walther PPK, the kind Hitler had use in his bunker just before the Russians arrived. Ward saw the flames of madness flickering in the man's eyes, burning more brightly than ever. He had seen that look before. Nothing he could say would matter, but he said it anyway.

"Don't do it, Royce. It doesn't have to end this way."

"It won't end," Lundgren said. "You can't stop us. My people will prevail. It begins today." He nodded toward the television screen. "It begins now."

Ward slowly moved forward, his weapon aimed at Lundgren's chest.

"Hand me the gun, Royce," Ward said as he inched closer. He scanned side to side, making sure none of the others were about to make a move.

Lundgren held the gun out to his side, at arm's length.

No one in the group uttered a word. They were frozen in place, petrified by what might happen.

"C'mon, Royce," Ward said calmly. "Hand it over. You don't want to do this."

Lundgren slowly brought the gun up to his head. A look of contentment swept over him.

"Royce, no!" Doyle wailed.

A shot exploded. Lundgren slumped to the ground.

Ward shook his head. A false martyr was not the result he wanted. He tried to console himself with the thought that the taxpayers had been saved the expense of a trial.

Minutes later, an ATF backup team stormed through the doors. Within seconds, all present were facedown on the floor, hands cuffed behind them.

Ward slipped his gun back into the ankle holster. As he did, he heard Doyle call out to him.

"Man, I thought we was friends," Doyle grunted.

"Not even sort of," Ward replied.

CHAPTER 80

5:25 p.m., Monday, August 3rd, Chamizal National Memorial, El Paso, Texas.

As head of the Presidential Protective Detail, Special Agent Jesse Carlson had encountered many difficult scenarios, but this one offered some unique challenges. He cast a wary eye toward the border as he opened the door to The Beast, the heavily armored Presidential Limousine. Despite assurances of complete cooperation from the authorities in Juarez, and the outward appearance that they had done everything possible to assist his men, Carlson felt uneasy. Things in Juarez were never quite what they seemed.

President Buckley stepped out of the limousine. POTUS, as the Secret Service referred to him, was in his shirtsleeves, the heat too intense for a jacket and tie. Buckley nodded to his security contingent. He surveyed the crowd, smiled and waved. There would be a few handshakes on the way to the podium, but most of the glad-handing would wait until after the speech.

It was a short walk, less than a hundred feet, to the speaking platform. It had been built specially for the occasion. The stage sat eight feet high. Carlson would have preferred that the President stay at ground level. As usual, however, factors other than security won out. Carlson signaled his men. A phalanx of agents surrounded the President. They were ready to move, eyes on the crowd.

"Ready, Mr. President?" Carlson asked.

"Ready, Jesse," Buckley replied.

CHAPTER 81

5:25 p.m., Monday, August 3rd, Juarez, Mexico.

Despite the installation of large vents and a small fan, the heat in the mock air-conditioning unit was stifling. The assassin, Kolb, had anticipated the worst, bringing several bottles of water so that he could stay hydrated. Heavy-duty shooter's earmuffs would protect him from the explosive report of the .50 caliber M82. Without them the damage to his hearing would be tremendous in such a small, enclosed space.

The truck was waiting in the loading bay as promised, engine idling, ready to haul its cargo into the bowels of Mexico. Everything was in place as the Presidential motorcade came to a halt on the other side of the border.

Kolb sighted in the rifle. Buckley was out of his limousine and moving toward the speaking platform. He flicked in and out of the crosshairs as the Secret Service agents moved around him, ushering him forward. Kolb silently thanked whoever had insisted on the raised stage. It provided a better shot than he could have ever anticipated.

As Kolb watched, Buckley shook hands with several dignitaries on the platform. One of them moved to the podium, presumably to do the introduction. Now, it would be only a matter of seconds and the world would be changed forever.

CHAPTER 82

5:30 p.m., Monday, August 3rd, Chamizal National Memorial, El Paso, Texas.

President Buckley took the podium, thanked the mayor for his kind remarks, and prepared to begin. Carlson stood at the far-left end of the stage. He and three other agents were on the platform, ready to move at a moment's notice.

As the President started his speech, Carlson felt his cell phone start to vibrate. Annoyed, he slipped a hand inside his jacket and retrieved the device. As soon as he saw the caller ID, he knew that he had to take the call.

"Carlson," he whispered into the phone.

The message was brief, the reaction quick. Carlson barked orders to his men. They rushed toward POTUS. Special Agent Joshua Parr was the first to reach the President. He placed himself in front of Buckley as the other agents moved to help sweep him offstage. But less than a second after Parr became the President's human shield, the first round thudded into his body, exploding his shoulder into a spray of muscle, bone and blood. Parr slumped to the ground. Two more agents took their place in front of POTUS as others rushed to the stage to assist. A second shot grazed Special Agent Anthony Giordano's arm as he pushed the President's head down and shoved him forward.

Two more shots followed. The mayor, in shock, frozen in place by the spectacle before him, was mortally wounded. The president was hustled back to The Beast. Only then did anybody realize that the bullet that had critically wounded Special Agent Parr had passed through him and into the President's chest.

CHAPTER 83

5:33 p.m., Monday, August 3rd, Juarez, Mexico.

Kolb hit the ground running. He sprinted toward the waiting semi-trailer. As soon as he was inside, the doors slammed shut. He heard them latched and padlocked into place. Mere seconds went by before the truck started to move. Within minutes, they were at what felt to him like full speed.

Kolb held his head in his hands, despondent over his sloppy performance. Had Buckley even been hit? Something, or someone, had tipped them off. Still, the thought that he had personally failed The Nation, failed in his attempt to change his country's destiny, made him physically ill. He dropped to his knees and retched.

CHAPTER 84

6:10 p.m., Monday, August 3rd, R. E. Thomason General Hospital, El Paso, Texas.

At ten after six, White House Press Secretary Ellie Drake stepped to the microphone in the hospital's hastily arranged pressroom. The look of obvious relief on her face gave away the news. The buzz of the press corps dropped off as they strained to hear.

"I've just spoken with several of the outstanding doctors who are attending to the President," she began. "I am pleased... pleased and relieved...to report that President Buckley's injuries are not life-threatening. He is expected to make a full and complete recovery."

Drake's tone then turned more somber. "Sadly," she continued, "the same cannot be said for one of the brave Secret Service agents who sprang to the President's defense. Special Agent Joshua Parr gave his life today to protect the President of the United States."

CHAPTER 85

8:15 p.m., Monday, August 3rd, Compound One.

The search warrants had been finalized and signed within an hour-and-a-half of Ward's phone call. By seven-thirty in the evening, ATF tactical teams were hitting multiple sites throughout the Southwest, including several in and around Yoakum, Texas.

Richter's team, consisting of fifteen agents, entered Lundgren's residence at a quarter after seven. The site had been secured by the agents who had arrived earlier to assist Ward. Six of Richter's men began to systematically scour every inch of the place, while the remaining nine covered the rest of the property.

The Nation kept good records. Richter was ecstatic to find several documents that referenced the group's organizational structure. They would be invaluable in proving up RICO charges. He was also sure that the computers seized from the residence, after thorough forensic examination, would only add to the case. He could hardly wait to get a look at the e-mails and any Internet chat records. Very few criminals were savvy enough to completely erase their electronic trail. This bunch would likely be no different.

Initial reports from some of the other search teams were encouraging. The financial records found at the Kirklin residence would be devastating evidence against the group. It was clear to Richter that The Nation, as an organization, would soon cease to exist. He could only imagine the list of state and federal charges that faced its leadership.

Richter sifted through some papers in a drawer in Lundgren's dresser. They were mostly personal items, nothing having any bearing on the case. He shut the drawer and turned away, only to see Bill Lehman approaching, a broad grin on his face. Lehman was waving some sort of notebook.

"Wait 'til you see this," Lehman said gleefully. He laid the notebook on top of the dresser and flipped it open.

It was some sort of ledger. Dozens of names appeared. Dollar amounts were written next to each of them. Richter's brow furrowed. He thought he recognized some of the entries.

"Is this what I think it is?" Richter asked.

"Yes, it is," Lehman replied. "It's some sort of political contribution list. From what I've been able to find out so far, these appear to be state and local politicians, mostly from Southwest Border States."

Richter let out a low whistle. Some of the contributions were sizeable. He began to flip through the pages, and then abruptly stopped.

"Not all state and local politicians," Richter noted, placing his finger on one of the entries. In the middle of the page was the name that caught his eye.

"Wesley Lindell?" Lehman asked, clearly not recognizing the name.

"That would be Congressman Wesley Lindell," Richter replied.

CHAPTER 86

8:05 a.m., Wednesday, August 19th, just off Highway 152, one mile west of Hillsboro, New Mexico.

It was rural New Mexico, as out of the way as you could get, exactly the kind of place where Richter thought they might find him. The ATF warrant team prepared for entry. Twenty men were in place surrounding the small mobile home. Richter nervously fingered his walkie-talkie, waiting to give the command. Most of the leadership had already been arrested. Only a few remained on the lamb, including Eric Brandt. Today, they were set to arrest the assassin, a disgruntled former Army sniper by the name of Thad Kolb. He had stupidly returned from Mexico. It was a bad move, one that was hard to understand. Kolb had to have known that his day would come, even if it took a month, a year, or a lifetime. He had killed a federal agent. They would have hunted him to the ends of the earth.

Some of them had kept their mouths shut. Byrd, for one, was hardcore. But most had already talked, the magnitude of the charges they faced and the desire to secure a better deal dissolving any code of silence. That was the way it always went. Members of The Nation, it turned out, were no exception. Richter chuckled at how fast Kirklin and Graves had spilled their guts. Doyle, surprisingly, had taken a bit longer to break, some remaining misguided loyalty to his dead cousin clouding his judgment. But eventually he came around as well. It was his information that eventually led them here to the home of Clyde and Wanda Nelson. According to cooperators, they were the truest of true believers. They were also heavily armed, possessing an arsenal worthy of a small country. That, along with the fact that the highly sought Kolb was a well-trained, unusually dangerous fugitive, had been ample cause for United States Magistrate Judge T. Ward Blumenthal to sign off on a no-knock warrant.

His men in place, Richter gave the command. "Go, go, go!" he yelled into the walkie-talkie. Flash-bang stun grenades announced their arrival. Entry took mere seconds as a wave of masked men in black S.W.A.T. gear appeared through the smoke. Clyde Nelson was pouring himself some coffee when the explosions occurred. In shock, his cup crashed to the floor as he fell back against the kitchen table. "On the ground!" several of the men yelled in unison. One of them pushed Nelson to the floor and cuffed him. "Where's Kolb?" he asked fiercely, pressing his knee into Nelson's back. Deafened by the grenades, Nelson didn't immediately respond. "Where's Kolb?" the agent repeated loudly. Nelson jerked his head toward the front of the trailer. Four men quickly crashed into the front bedroom. Kolb was sitting up in bed, reaching for a pistol. He didn't make it.

Richter entered as Kolb was being introduced to the ground. When he was securely immobilized, Richter began the familiar procedure, reading from a card that he always carried in his pocket.

"You have the right to remain silent," he said. "If you give up that right, anything you say can, and will, be used against you in a court of law. You have the right to an attorney, and to have an attorney present during any questioning. If you cannot afford an attorney, one will be appointed for you."

Smiling, Richter slipped the card back into his pocket. It was unlikely that he had ever enjoyed Mirandizing someone as much. "Do you understand these rights?" he asked.

Kolb scoffed. "You've forgotten what those rights mean," he announced.

Richter smirked. "I'll take that as a yes," he said.

EPILOGUE

*3:14 a.m., Wednesday, November 4th, along the southern bor-
der, southwest of Las Cruces, New Mexico.*

It had been three months now. Brandt, along with a handful of
his men, had spent the time in hiding, shuffling from the home
of one sympathizer to another. He was one of the few senior
officials who had escaped arrest. Graves, Kirklin, Doyle, they
had all pled guilty. He spat on the ground when he thought of
them. They were cooperators, traitors. Others, like Byrd, still
faced trial, willing to have a jury of their peers decide their fate.
Then there was Lundgren. Brandt still mourned him. Lundgren
had always vowed that he would never be taken into custody by
a government that had betrayed its people. He had kept his word.

The men had grown restless, eager to resume the fight. Despite
the risk, Brandt had readily agreed. He missed the thrill, the
terror in their eyes when he welcomed them to America, the
anguished howls as he exterminated one *cockroach*, then another.
More importantly, he knew this was a fight that had to go on, a
cause bigger than one man. Now he would take up the mantle,
he would resurrect The Nation. Brandt was sure that Lundgren
would have wanted it that way and would have deemed him a
worthy successor.

"Here they come," Brandt announced as he peered through
the light-gathering binoculars. "I count nine of 'em." He turned
to his sniper. "You know the drill. The coyote goes first."

336

The shot was off within seconds. The smuggler dropped to the ground. Brandt watched as the others froze in terror, unsure what to do. Finally, one of them, a young man, made a run for it.

"Hit him," Brandt ordered.

The sniper took aim. One muffled shot dropped the target in his tracks.

"Nice shot," Brandt said, as one might to a fellow hunter who had downed a deer. "That should keep 'em from scattering." He lowered the binoculars. "Let's go."

As the group moved forward, Brandt pulled down his ski mask and drew his pistol. His heart pounded at the thought of taking out one or two of these *spics* himself. It had been a long time since he'd gotten in a good kill.

Border Patrol Agent Mark Payne perked up. "Did you hear that?" he asked his partner, Carlos Lorza. "It sounded almost like a muffled rifle shot."

"I did," Lorza replied. "I think it came from that direction." He pointed west.

On horseback, the two men had been looking for a small group of illegals in the area when they heard the sound. They galloped toward a rise in the terrain, unprepared for the sight that awaited them.

"Shit," Payne said as they crested the ridge. Below them, a group of heavily armed men, dressed in black, ski masks covering their faces, had surrounded a small band of immigrants.

"Vigilantes," Lorza said immediately. He unslung his rifle and peered through the night vision scope to get a better look. The illegals were lined up, side-by-side. One of the masked men was marching back and forth in front of them, occasionally stopping to wave his pistol in the face of one of the terrified detainees. Nearby, another of the immigrants lay dead.

"Call for support," Lorza commanded.

* * *

Brandt turned toward the sound of hoofbeats. Even in the darkness, he knew immediately that it was the Border Patrol, and that these would be agents unfriendly to their cause. He could make out two of them galloping in their direction. If no more than that, his men, eight strong, had them badly outnumbered. It would be an easy fight. Just then, Brandt heard the whir of chopper blades.

The AStar helicopter roared up on them and slowed to hover. Its spotlight blinded the group below as the rotors kicked up a swirl of dirt and debris.

"Drop your weapons!" a voice commanded over the speaker system.

Brandt's men did not wait for guidance. Their weapons were tossed aside, arms raised in the air.

Brandt hesitated, but not to consider surrender. That was not an option. His choice was simple, follow Lundgren's example and cheat them of their capture, or kill one last Mexican. He chose the latter.

Brandt turned toward the immigrant, raising his pistol as his finger tightened on the trigger. The sight came to a rest on the on the man's forehead as Brandt began to squeeze.

Death was instantaneous as the shot entered the skull. Brandt slumped to the ground, his weapon unfired.

Carlos Lorza lowered his rifle, the hint of a satisfied smile on his face.

7:30 p.m., Friday, November 6th, Lolo, Montana.

Ward stood on the deck, forearms resting on the railing. He breathed in the cool fall air as he stared out over the Bitterroot River. As always, its peaceful flow was soothing. The vacation in Belize had helped him depressurize, but Montana is where he

338

would return to normal, at least his normal. For now, though, images from the past summer kept coming back to him. Brandt's recent death made them more vivid. It would take a while to get this one out of his head. And there was still Byrd's trial.

Ward had called in the band. Stafford and McNeal were happy to oblige. Their get-together, as always in these situations, was an unspoken celebration of his safe return. When they arrived, the two old cops asked no questions. Ward decided that on this one, however, he might have to share a few more details than usual...just not tonight. Tonight they would play, relax...unwind. He needed it, as much as he ever had.

"Hey, Dave!" Stafford yelled from the sliding door. "We gonna play or what?"

"Be right in," Ward promised. "Beer's in the fridge," he added as an afterthought. "Help yourself."

"I'll do that," Stafford assured him.

A few minutes later Ward came in off the deck. As usual he locked the sliding door behind him, checked it twice, and slid the wooden dowel into the track to block it from opening. Even with two armed ex-cops in the house, he felt the need. It wasn't paranoia, it was well-founded caution.

Ward started toward the basement. As he walked down the steps, he heard his cohorts getting their instruments in tune. It was a comforting sound.

"You guys about ready or what?" Ward asked as he entered the room.

"What the hell?" Stafford asked, feigning annoyance. "It's about time. I'm tellin' ya, man, if you didn't supply the house, the beer, the food *and* the groupies, you'd be out." He shook his head. "No commitment to the band. No commitment *what*soever."

McNeal perked up. "We have groupies?" he asked.

Ward smiled at the familiar refrain. It was good to be home.

ACKNOWLEDGMENTS

Writing this book was an education, one that gave me a much greater appreciation for those peace officers and special agents who work in an undercover capacity. They possess courage beyond that of mere mortals and make this world a safer place by putting their lives on the line every day.

I gratefully acknowledge the many friends in law enforcement who contributed to this work. A few warrants special mention: Sean O'Neal, Linda Glenn, Cliff Cronk, and, Don Allegro. Their assistance gave this story a realism that I could not have achieved on my own. Any errors that remain are solely my responsibility.

A special thanks to my agent, Claire Gerus, who saw some well-hidden potential in me and took a risk; to my wife, Karen, who encouraged this effort and provided valuable support in so many ways; and to my editor, Mark Terry, who took my draft and made it vastly more readable; and, finally, to Eric Campbell, Lance Wright, and all the folks at Down & Out Books who gave me a second chance.

JOEL BARROWS is an Iowa district court judge who regularly oversees both criminal and civil trials. Prior to his appointment to the bench he was a practicing attorney for nearly twenty-three years; the last eighteen of those spent as a state, and then federal, prosecutor. As an attorney, Joel regularly argued before the United States Court of Appeals. His cases have been as diverse as white collar crime, environmental crime, cyber-crime, child exploitation, narcotics and firearms offenses, immigration crimes, bank robbery, health care fraud, public corruption, civil rights offenses and threats against the President, and have included many high profile prosecutions. He has traveled extensively in Central America. He lives with his family in eastern Iowa along the banks of the Mississippi.

BOOKS

On the following pages are a few
more great titles from the
Down & Out Books publishing family.

For a complete list of books and to
sign up for our newsletter,
go to DownAndOutBooks.com.

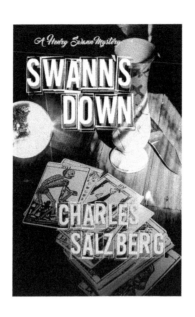

Swann's Down
A Henry Swann Mystery
Charles Salzberg

Down & Out Books
May 2019
978-1-64396-011-1

At skip-tracer Henry Swann's weekly business meeting with Goldblatt at a local diner, his inscrutable partner drops a bomb. He wants to hire Swann to help out his ex-wife, Rachael, who's been swindled out of a small fortune by a mysterious fortune-teller, who has convinced the gullible young woman that she's made contact with her recently deceased boyfriend.

At the same time, Swann receives a call from an old friend and occasional employer, lawyer Paul Rudder, who has taken on a particularly sticky case...

WARREN C. EMBREE
THE ORNERY GENE

The Ornery Gene
Warren C. Embree

Down & Out Books
April 2019
978-1-64396-012-8

When itinerant ranch hand Buck Ellison took a job with Sarah Watkins at her ranch in the Sandhills of Nebraska, he thought he had found the place where he could park his pickup, leave the past behind, and never move again.

On a rainy July night, a dead man found at the south end of Sarah's ranch forces him to become a reluctant detective, delving into the business of cattle breeding for rodeos and digging up events from his past that are linked to the circumstances surrounding the murder of Sam Danielson.

Countdown
Matt Phillips

All Due Respect, an imprint of
Down & Out Books
April 2019
978-1-948235-84-6

LaDon and Jessie—two hustlers who make selling primo weed a regular gig—hire a private security detail to move and hold their money. Ex-soldiers Glanson and Echo target the cash—they start a ripoff business. It's the wild, wild west. Except this time, everybody's high.

With their guns and guts, Glanson and Echo don't expect much trouble from a mean son-of-a-gun like LaDon Charles. But that's exactly what they get. In this industry, no matter how much money there is for the taking—and no matter who gets it—there's always somebody counting backwards...to zero.

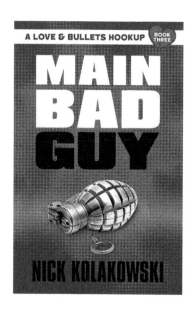

Main Bad Guy
A Love & Bullets Hookup
Nick Kolakowski

Shotgun Honey, an imprint of
Down & Out Books
978-1-948235-70-9

Bill and Fiona, the lovable anti-heroes of the "Love & Bullets" trilogy, find themselves in the toughest of tough spots: badly wounded, hunted by cops and goons, and desperately in need of a drink (or five).

After a round-the-world tour of spectacular criminality, they're back in New York. Locked in a panic room on the top floor of a skyscraper, surrounded by pretty much everyone in three zip codes who wants to kill them, they'll need to figure out how to stay upright and breathing...and maybe deal out a little payback in the process.